There was a time such scrutiny would have brought some response from her—pleasure, feminine insecurity, discomfort, maybe even arousal. Now she didn't give a damn what he saw, what he thought, or what he might like.

As the silence drew out, she took her own measure.

At last he spoke in a voice that was shaded with derision. "Didn't your mama teach you that it's impolite to stare?"

Kate's smile was equally derisive. "You're Tucker Caldwell."

He waited a beat. "Whatever you want, I'm not interested."

Stiffening, pretending that Caldwell hadn't just turned her down without even hearing her out, she went on. "It's about a job."

With a backward jerk of his head, he directed her attention to the construction behind him. "I've got a job."

"I'm talking about one that pays." He was waiting for more, but she found the words harder than she'd expected. She had thought them so often, had whispered them in her nightly prayers, had comforted herself with them. They had become her good-luck charm.

"I want you to kill Jason Trask."

PRAISE FOR THE NOVELS OF MARILYN PAPPANO

ALSO BY MARILYN PAPPANO

In Sinful Harmony
Passion

PUBLISHED BY
WARNER BOOKS

MARILYN PAPPANO

Suspicion

WARNER BOOKS

A Time Warner Company

WARNER BOOKS EDITION

Cover design by Diane Luger
Cover photo by Wendy Schneider

Warner Books, Inc.
1271 Avenue of the Americas
New York, NY 10020

Visit our Web site at
http://pathfinder.com/twep

W A Time Warner Company

Printed in the United States of America

First Printing: March, 1997

10 9 8 7 6 5 4 3 2 1

Prologue

After giving the kitchen counter one last swipe with a
damp cloth, Kate Edwards stepped back to survey the results
of a long afternoon's work. Redecorating the kitchen had
been her sister's idea, and although Kate had resisted, it had
been a good one. The fresh coat of paint on the walls and
woodwork brightened the entire room, and the new curtains
over the windows met both Kate's need for privacy and
Kerry's desire for a brighter, softer touch than the ancient
venetian blinds that had hung there.

A brighter, softer touch. Kate needed that not just in her
kitchen but in her life in general. She got it in Kerry. Nothing
could cheer a dreary day quicker than a visit from her baby
sister. No one else could even begin to make her think that
someday things would be all right, but Kerry did.

Brightening Kate's life, giving her hope, loving her—
heavy burdens for a nineteen-year-old girl. Kerry's biggest
concern right now should be college, what she was going to
do with her life, and nineteen-year-old boys, not a big sister
whose downhill slide was finally starting to slow.

With a sigh, Kate switched off the kitchen lights and went
down the hall to the living room. It was a chilly evening, and
the last thing Kerry had done on her way out was build a fire.
Sit there, she had advised. Enjoy a cup of hot cocoa and the

crackle of the flames. Relax. Kate hadn't made any cocoa, but she sank into her favorite chair, tucked her feet beneath her, and gave another forlorn sigh.

Then the phone rang. The shrillness shattered the stillness of the house and made her stiffen. On the third ring, the answering machine came on, playing the outgoing message, switching tapes for the incoming.

There was a moment of silence—of faint breathing—then, after seven seconds without conversation, the tape automatically stopped. In the last few months, she had listened to thousands of seconds of silence . . . and thousands more of obscenities. Of curses, threats, and vulgar promises.

Get an unlisted number, Travis McMaster—friend and chief of police—had advised, and she had done just that. She had done it three times, in fact, until she could barely remember it herself, but somehow they always found out. They were determined and resourceful for such a small group— only three of Jason Trask's friends—and they took a great pleasure in tormenting a woman who couldn't stop them.

And she *couldn't* stop them. Short of running away and never coming back, she couldn't make them quit harassing her, couldn't make them stop their lewd offers or leave her in peace. They were punishing her for daring to speak out against Jason, for daring to believe that she had a right to decide who would do what to her and when. They were treating her like the tramp Jason and his lawyers had branded her. They were arrogant, ignorant, chauvinistic men who had little respect for the women they used and none at all for a woman who dared to fight back.

Even when that woman had already lost the fight. The jury had acquitted Jason of all charges. They, along with everyone else in town who had voiced an opinion, had believed him over her. Oh, there were people on her side—people besides Travis, the district attorney, and Kerry—but most of them were afraid to speak up. The Trask family had thrown its considerable support to their son, had used its considerable influence to paint her as the villain, the liar, the sick one.

They had found her guilty, and Jason's friends were now meting out her punishment, as he had promised—keeping her on edge, terrorizing her. She consoled herself with the hope that someday they would grow tired of their game, that someday soon they would leave her alone, but it seemed as if someday would never arrive. They were never going to let her life return to some semblance of normalcy.

The second call came only moments after the first. Kate expected it, but still it made her flinch. Three rings, then silence. Three more rings.

On the next call, she picked up the receiver, but didn't speak. She never spoke, never gave any indication that she was hearing whatever obscenities they were spouting. She never gave them the satisfaction of knowing that their words were reaching their target, that they were indeed scaring her. She just waited and listened.

"Kate." The voice was low, intimate, definitely male. It made her go utterly still, made her blood turn cold and her chest tighten until she could barely breathe.

It was Jason. Heaven help her, it was never him, always his friends but *never, ever* him. He'd done his threatening before the trial, had made his terrifying promises then, but nothing since—hadn't tried to see her, hadn't called her, hadn't harassed her.

Hang up the phone, Kate. Don't listen to him. Don't let him do this to you.

But she couldn't move. She couldn't manage the simple

straightening of her arm, the uncurving of her fingers, that would return the receiver to its cradle.

"I've kept my promise, Kate. I've done what I said I would do. Just remember: it's your fault. You could have prevented it. You could have stopped it from happening, but you refused. It's all your fault, Kate."

"What—" Her voice had no sound, only choked air. Swallowing hard, forcing breath into her lungs, she tried again. "What are you talking about?"

"It's your fault," he repeated softly. "Just like before. Everyone's going to blame you. Everyone's going to hate you—even Kerry. Poor Kerry will hate you most of all."

Terror spreading through her, she managed only a strangled whisper. "What have you done?"

He laughed, a frighteningly ominous chuckle. "Do you know where your sister is? Do you know if she's safe?"

"Damn you—"

"Where is Kerry, Kate?"

Chapter One

Tucker Caldwell came out of the hardware store, glanced toward the gravel lot to see if the lumber he'd just paid for was being loaded into his truck, then turned toward the end of the slatted wood porch and the old man who waited there.

Ben James had been sitting in exactly the same place, in the creaky cane rocker with a walking stick clasped between two gnarled hands, the first time Tucker had ever seen him. That had been about twenty-five years ago, in the middle of one of Arkansas's hot summers, when he'd been dumped on the uncle who lived ten miles outside Fall River. Old Ben had been at least 190 then, his shoulders stooped from a lifetime of hard work and as fragile as spun glass. He'd worn neatly pressed overalls, a denim shirt, and work boots that had lost their leather one scuff at a time, and a soft, faded cap had protected his bald head from too much sun. The same cap—or, at least, one very similar—protected it today from autumn's chill wind.

As he approached the old man, Tucker took note of his clothes: a plaid woolen coat, a brown scarf around his neck, a pair of worn brown gloves, and the loose-fitting legs of those old overalls. An old man felt the cold more deeply, Ben had once told Tucker, who was comfortable this morning in jeans, a T-shirt, and a denim jacket. Ben surely was old. One of these days, Tucker fully expected to stop by for supplies and find the rocker empty, to walk inside and hear that the only friend he had in town—hell, in the whole damned world—was gone. One of these days . . . but not too soon. He wasn't ready to let go yet.

Taking a position against the railing, he offered two sticks of hard candy. The old man chose the peppermint, as Tucker had known he would, reaching for it with a hand that trembled. "What are you going to do when winter sets in, old man? Bundle up like a snowman?"

Ben laughed, showing a row of healthy white teeth that gleamed in the ebony darkness of his face. "I'll do what I've done the last thirty winters. I'll carry my chair inside and cozy up to that potbellied stove. You've never been in town for one of our winters, have you?"

"Nope. But it can't be too different from winter in Fayette." His hometown was only forty miles south of Fall River, not far enough in these Ozark Mountains to make much, if any, difference in the weather.

"I see you're buying supplies. You planning to build something?"

Tucker broke off a chunk of the yellow-and-green candy stick with his teeth, then bit it into tiny pieces. "A house."

The old man nodded wisely. "Your uncle's place isn't fit for man or animal."

"How would you know? You told me you'd never been out there."

Ben continued to nod. "But I knew your uncle. He was not a man who believed in hard work, cleanliness, godliness, or any other virtues that I can think of."

In other words, a typical Caldwell. Poor white trash. That was all they'd ever been, all they ever would be. Except him. He had another distinction in addition to the label of trash that made him even worse than the typical Caldwell. Jesus, whoever would have thought there could be anything worse?

"You building this house alone?"

Exaggerating his actions, Tucker took a long look around. "You see anyone here to help?"

"Where did you learn to build a house all by yourself?"

Losing his taste for sugary sweets, Tucker pulled the cellophane wrapper around the remaining candy, then tossed it into the trash can near the door. "Where do you think, old man?"

Ben looked past him, his eyes slightly distorted and out of focus behind the thick lenses of his glasses. "You need to make yourself some friends, Tucker. It's not good for a man to live alone." Looking at him once again, he grinned slyly. "It's not good to live without a woman."

Tucker crouched down, bracing his back against the spindles that supported the rail. "What do I want friends for? You talk my ear off every time I come into town, trying to run my life. As for a woman, don't you know that all the virtuous women in Rutherford County are afraid of me?"

"Not all of them. I know a woman . . ."

"No." Standing up, Tucker shoved his hands in his pockets. "No fix-ups. I wouldn't trust a crazy old coot like you to set me up with a woman. If I want one, I know where to find one." Namely, Little Rock. Sure, it was a few hours away, but it was easy. Nolie was oh so easy. She didn't care that she was married, didn't care that, in the two months Tucker had spent in the city, she had spent more time in his bed than in her husband's. It had taken a while, but he'd gotten over the reluctance and the guilt. Besides, given his rather limited experience with women, guilt over taking from another man was nothing compared to his aversion to meeting a new woman.

"No fix-up." Bracing both hands on his walking stick, Ben pushed himself out of the chair, rising slowly to his full five-and-a-half-foot height. He tilted his head back to look Tucker in the eye, and his cap slid an inch or two. "I'm sending her out to talk to you. I'm counting on you to help her, Tucker."

The old man was more serious than Tucker had ever seen him, and it sent a shiver of uneasiness down his spine. He had never seen that look before, had never heard those words addressed to him before. Hell, he was Tucker Caldwell. No one counted on him for anything but trouble. "Help with what?"

"That's for her to tell you."

"Who?"

Ben looked away, opened his mouth as if to answer, then pursed his lips and blew out a soft, whistling breath. "You'll know her when she comes. It's not like you get many lady visitors out there. Just listen to her. Consider what she wants you to do. Help her, Tucker. As a favor to me."

It took him a moment to find his voice, to force it past the unaccustomed tightness in his throat. "I don't do favors, old man." His words were tinged with a regret that he told himself he didn't really feel.

"Do this one for me, and I'll never ask again."

"Never," he repeated, mildly scoffing. "How long is 'never'? You're one hundred and five—"

"A hundred and one."

Jesus. He was only a year short of living out three of Tucker's entire lives.

"But I intend to see my hundred and fifth birthday," he continued with a grin before turning serious again. "Talk to her, Tucker, and help her. For me." Reaching out, he patted Tucker on the arm, then, as if the effort tired him, slowly sank back down into the rocker. Signaling that the conversation was over, he closed his eyes and began humming softly. "Swing Low, Sweet Chariot." Tucker's granny had also been fond of using spirituals to bring conversations to an end. For her the occasion had always been his mother's talk of putting the old woman into a nursing home, and the song had always been "Precious Memories." It had worked, too, at least for the eighteen years he'd lived with them.

Putting the memory out of his mind, Tucker watched the old man for a moment, looking for a way to say no that Ben would accept, until a voice called his name from the parking lot. He turned to see the owner of the hardware store and adjoining lumberyard standing beside his truck.

"Caldwell, you need to get this truck out of here."

Slowly he walked down the steps. His order had been loaded and ready to go for a while now, but it wasn't as if business had suddenly picked up and the spot was needed. There was enough empty space for a half dozen customers to park on either side of his truck.

Mortenson just wanted him gone. But that wasn't anything new. Just about everyone in Rutherford County wanted to be rid of him. He'd be happy to oblige them . . . if he had anyplace else to go.

When he reached the truck, he stopped to check the order. He knew it wasn't necessary, knew Mortenson wasn't stupid enough to short him on something. He did it to get on the narrow-minded bastard's nerves. He counted the sheets of plywood, examined the stacks of two-by-fours, and checked the tools, giving it all the same overdone perusal to which Mortenson always subjected *him*. Finally he gave the guy a cheery grin as he climbed behind the wheel. "It's been a pleasure doing business with you."

"Yeah, right," Mortenson spit out, as Tucker slammed the door.

He drove through town, noticing for the hundredth time what a nice little place it was. Everything was old, but neatly maintained. There weren't any vacancies in the blocks that made up the downtown business district. The schools, located together in one large complex, looked the way schools should look, with lots of windows, plenty of jungle gyms, swings, and one crooked merry-go-round. Fall River was the sort of place people wanted to raise their kids.

It *wasn't* the sort of place that welcomed ex-cons.

He had spent the better part of a half dozen summers growing up here, and they'd been the best part of his life. Maybe food had been a little scarce, but that had been nothing new, and the rest had made up for it. He'd had the sort of freedom other kids only dreamed about. He had hiked the mountains, swum in the frigid creeks, fished and hunted, stayed out all day and late into the night. His uncle might have been lazy, self-absorbed, and disinterested in the various kids he'd gotten saddled with every summer. He might have been a lousy provider, might have offered no concern or affection at all, but he hadn't been much for discipline, either. He had never gotten angry, had never raised his hand— or his fist—to Tucker or his brother Jimmy or any of their cousins. The weeks Tucker had spent in Rutherford County had been the only times in his life he had escaped the violence that was an everyday part of his life at home.

Even so, he had never intended to return to Fall River. But after two months in Little Rock, searching for work and never finding any, living with Jimmy and his wife, sleeping with another man's wife, he'd felt the almost desperate need to go *somewhere*, and this place had won by default. Although his uncle was dead, the land was still in the Caldwell family, belonging now to Tucker's mother. He hadn't asked her permission before he'd moved in. He hadn't felt the need, but even if he had, he hadn't known where to find her. He'd lost touch with her sixteen years ago, and Jimmy hadn't heard from her in almost as long. Tucker didn't even know if she was still alive. He wasn't sure he cared.

He drove west out of town. The two-lane road seemed to go on forever, deteriorating with each mile, switching from blacktop to gravel, then dirt, growing increasingly bumpy. There was little enough money for road maintenance, and no one who lived out here was important enough to warrant special consideration. All the folks with money lived in town, including the Trasks, Fall River's most prominent family. They had a big fancy place built of native stone on the east side of town. Made Tucker happy he lived out west. The less contact he had with them, the better.

The truck scraped and bounced over a particularly deep rut, then abruptly the lane branched into the grass to skirt a ditch that had swallowed up the road. Tucker had hauled in truckloads of dirt and rock in an attempt to fill it, but after yet another rainfall had washed it away, he'd given up, as he'd done in so many areas of his life, and chosen the bypass instead.

The house appeared out of the trees, unexpected and unsightly. It wasn't merely a poor place, Tucker acknowledged, but *ugly*. Old Ben was right. It wasn't fit for habitation. When he'd moved in over a month ago, he had made an effort at livability, at cleaning and fixing up, but, like the rut in the driveway, that had been futile, too. Some things were beyond help, and this house was one of them. There was junk everywhere—rusted-out vehicles, cannibalized appliances, heaps of rotting tires. The yard was dirt, the steps leading to the house broken, the house itself crooked and tilted on the concrete blocks that supported it. Most of the glass in the front windows was broken, replaced by squares of cardboard taped in place. The only thing the shack was fit for was burning. Once he finished the place out back, that was exactly what he would do—build himself a bonfire.

He drove past the house, then parked next to the new place. He had already laid the foundation and was working on the framing. It wasn't going to be anything fancy—just one big room with a bathroom. Because of the lay of the land, he could get running water with a simple gravity-line system, but he would have to do without electricity. Like his uncle and the Caldwells before him, he would have to rely on a woodstove for heat and cooking and on oil lamps for light.

He wouldn't be staying long enough to mind the inconvenience. Sooner or later, his money would run out. No matter how self-sufficient he was—cutting his own firewood, hunting and fishing for his food, growing whatever vegetables would grow in the thin, rocky soil next summer—he was going to need an income at some future time, and there was no way he was going to find a job in Rutherford County. Hell, he hadn't even been able to find a job in Little Rock, the biggest city in the state. No matter how slim the pickings of job applicants, there was always someone better than an ex-con.

Climbing out of the truck, he tossed his jean jacket on the front seat. It was a cool day, but sawing the lumber by hand would work up a sweat in no time. He'd often wished for a power saw, but it was an extravagance he couldn't afford.

Jesus, so many things that were an everyday part of most people's lives were out of his reach. Simple conveniences like electricity. Simple obligations like a job. Simple comforts like a family. Friends. A woman.

Muttering a curse at the direction of his thoughts, he headed for the house for a tape measure, the penciled drawing that served as his blueprint, and the saw. He had no time to waste thinking, wishing, or wanting. He had work to do.

Glancing in the mirror at the road behind her, Kate Edwards wondered if she'd missed her destination, if one of those wide, semicleared places along the side of the road had been a seldom-used driveway, if the thick undergrowth that lined the road had obscured the house.

No. The old man's directions had been simple: follow the old Hatfield road until it ended. Surely that would be soon. The road was now little more than two tracks separated by tall grass that brushed the bottom of her car. Soon she would find the place, the house—the man—she was looking for.

Soon she would take a step in her plan from which she could never turn back.

As the car scraped bottom, she moved her foot to the brake, slowing to five miles an hour. For nearly ten miles the road had wound deeper and higher into the hills, had taken her places she'd never been even though she'd lived her entire thirty years in the county. It was like her life. For twenty-nine years and a few months, it had been dull, routine, and straightforward. She had been perfectly normal Kate Edwards, living a perfectly normal life. She had worked, dated, spent time with her family, and gone to church. She had expected that someday, like most women, she would get married, would have a perfectly average family of three kids, a dog, and a station wagon, would be a perfectly ordinary wife and mother.

But six months ago, her life had taken an unexpected turn, and the ride, like this one, had been bumpy ever since. She wasn't perfectly normal anymore, and she never would be again. She no longer dated, spent time with her family, or went to church. She didn't want to get married, didn't want to have children. She wanted only one thing, had only one goal.

She wanted to see Jason Trask punished.

Her fingers clenching around the steering wheel, she took a deep breath. Not *punished*. From the moment she'd made this decision, she had been adamant about facing it squarely. There would be no sugarcoating, no less damning or nobler words such as punishment, justice, or vengeance. She wanted to know that Jason Trask could never hurt anyone else the way he'd hurt her, the way he'd hurt Kerry. She wanted to know that *she* was responsible for stopping him, that *she* had succeeded when no one else could.

She wanted him dead.

Dead. Lately the concept that had once frightened her had become comfortingly, intimately close. In the last six months she'd thought about death a lot—about her own, about Kerry's and Jason's. Thought of Jason's death—images of him lifeless—brought her tremendous satisfaction. It was something she had learned to want, something she had come to need.

It was the only thing that would ever bring her peace again.

After one last bend, the road ended in a clearing, dominated by a sadly shabby little house. She brought the car to a stop in front of it, wondering if it was as depressing inside as out, wondering what kind of person could be satisfied living in such a place. Someone who'd never known any better. Someone to whom squalor, poverty, and deprivation were the norm. Someone who had lived half his life in places this bleak and the other half in a place even bleaker.

Someone like Tucker Caldwell.

Shutting off the engine, she forced her hands from the steering wheel, sliding her right hand inside her purse, reaching straight to the bottom and the pistol there. It was a Beretta .22, semiautomatic, seven shots. It looked like a toy, but a well-placed shot could kill a man as easily as a shotgun. She had become damned skilled at well-placed shots. It was fully loaded, with one round chambered, and had been ever since she'd bought it. An unloaded gun was of no value to anyone, and, if necessary, she intended this gun to be of very great value.

If necessary. If her trip out here failed. If Tucker Caldwell wasn't as willing to accept her offer as Mr. James had believed he would be.

She got out of the car and for a moment just stood there. Six months ago she would have been afraid to face a man like Caldwell alone. Now the only thing she was afraid of was Jason. There was nothing Tucker Caldwell could do to her that could possibly be worse than what Jason had already done.

She was taking a step away from the security of the car when she became aware of a distant, rhythmic tap. It was a hammer, and it was coming from somewhere around back. Picking her way carefully, she circled the old house. The back view was no less depressing than the front—garbage, weeds, junk, and, a few hundred yards away, a green pickup. The tailgate was down, the bed loaded with building supplies. On the other side of the truck, his bare back to her, wielding the hammer with sure, powerful blows, was the man she had come to see.

She wrapped her fingers around the textured grips of the Beretta. She was distrustful enough to view every man as an enemy. After all, Tucker Caldwell had already shown a propensity for violence. He had beaten a man to death with no weapon other than his fists, for no reason other than his anger.

She approached him slowly, quietly, warily, not stopping until only the truck was between them. Oblivious to her presence, he continued to work, nailing two-by-fours together, framing what appeared to be a rectangular building.

She knew little about him—that he'd been raised down in Fayette, that this place had belonged to some relative of his, that he'd been barely eighteen when he'd killed that man. Although Mr. James had known more, had offered more, she hadn't wanted to hear it. She didn't want to think of Caldwell as a person. She needed to know only one thing about him: that he was capable of killing.

Gradually he became aware of her. He didn't look over his shoulder or turn around, but his work slowed, the muscles in his back tensed, and his grip on the hammer grew tighter. He finished securing the plank he was working with, then slowly turned around, still clutching the hammer.

The look he gave her was long and hard. There was a time such scrutiny would have brought some response from her— pleasure, feminine insecurity, discomfort, maybe even arousal. Now she felt nothing. She simply stood there and let him look. She didn't wonder if he found her attractive. She didn't give a damn what he saw, what he thought, or what he might like.

As the silence drew out, she took her own measure. He wasn't tall, maybe an inch under six feet, or heavy. His hair, eyes, and skin were varying shades of brown. His mouth was thin, his jaw square, his expression empty.

At last he spoke in a voice that was shaded with derision. "Didn't your mama teach you that it's impolite to stare?"

Kate's smile was equally derisive. Bea Edwards had insisted on impeccable manners in her girls. Right after *Mama* and *Daddy*, their first words had been *ma'am, please,* and *thank you*. But politeness was overrated. She had said *please* to Jason—*Please don't do this, please don't hit me, please don't hurt me*—and what had it gotten her? A beating more vicious, she suspected, than if she hadn't begged.

Lately, her mother hadn't been interested in teaching her anything. Bea worked at putting back together the pieces of her life, lavished her attention on her other daughters, and ignored Kate. She blamed Kate for everything that had happened, just as Jason had promised in his late-evening phone call nearly a month ago.

That was one more reason he had to die.

Caldwell approached the truck, stopping across from her, resting his arms on the sidewall and letting the hammer drop into the bed with a clang. He looked at her but didn't speak. He didn't ask what had brought her all this distance from town because he didn't care. She could turn around and leave now without saying a word, and he might feel a moment's curiosity, but nothing more. Before she reached the rock-filled hole in the road out front, he would have already forgotten her.

But what she'd come here to say would probably ensure that he would never forget her. Especially if he agreed.

"You're Tucker Caldwell."

"And you're old Ben's friend."

Her nerves quivered a little. "He told you about me?"

"Only that he was sending you out." He waited a beat. "I told him not to bother. Whatever you want, I'm not interested."

The quivering intensified, bringing to life a dull ache in the pit of her stomach. Her ulcer-in-the-making was another of Jason's legacies. Stiffening, pretending that Caldwell hadn't just turned her down without even hearing her out, she went on. "It's about a job."

With a backward jerk of his head, he directed her attention to the construction behind him. "I've got a job."

"I'm talking about one that pays." Surely he could use the money. The truck was twenty years old and looked older. The T-shirt draped over the tailgate and his jeans were worn beyond comfort, and his tennis shoes, she had noticed before he'd come too close, were broken down and out.

He picked up the shirt, shook it, then pulled it over his head. "What kind of job? And how much does it pay?"

She looked away, her gaze sliding over a stack of firewood that stretched from the corner of the house to the tree line, curving this way and that. The half farthest from the house was green, recently cut. They wouldn't be ready to burn for at least a year. Odd. She'd never thought Caldwell might stay around Fall River for a whole year.

He was waiting for answers, but she found the words harder than she'd expected. She had thought them so often, had whispered them in her nightly prayers, had comforted herself with them. They had become her good-luck charm. But now they remained locked inside.

Instead she reached deep into her pocket, her fingers gliding across the smooth steel of the Beretta before closing around the envelope underneath it. She drew it out, thinking as she did about the step from which she couldn't turn back. Without hesitation, she took that step, tossing the envelope into the bed of the truck, meeting Caldwell's gaze straight on.

He looked from her to the envelope, then back again. "What's that?"

"A down payment."

"For what?"

She drew a breath, cool air smelling of rust, metal, and sawn wood, then let it seep out again. "I want you to kill Jason Trask."

For a moment, it seemed, everything went still—the birds in the trees, the babble of water running nearby, and, most especially, the man across from her. He didn't move, didn't blink, didn't even seem to breathe. Then he suddenly, noisily inhaled. "Who are you?"

"My name is Kate Edwards. Mr. James suggested I come to you."

"Why me?"

She shrugged. "You've been in prison."

"Lots of people have. So why me?"

Her expression turned a degree harder. "Because you were there for murder. You know what it's like to kill a man. You know you're capable. Hopefully, you've learned something about not getting caught this time."

The last part was unnecessary. She knew he hadn't gotten caught *last* time. When she had first conceived of her plan, she had asked Travis about the county's new ex-con. She remembered nothing about the incident. She'd been not quite fourteen, and the killing had taken place forty miles away in Fayette. But there had been two local connections: the nineteen-year-old victim was a Trask on his mother's side, first cousin to Jason, and the killer—the worthless, white-trash, cold-blooded murderer—had spent summers in Rutherford County with his worthless, white-trash uncle.

Travis hadn't filled her in on the details. He remembered little enough about it himself, and she hadn't wanted to rouse suspicion by pressing for more. He *had* told her, though, that Caldwell had turned himself in to the local authorities hours after the killing. Of course, it would have been only a matter of time before they went looking for him. There was bad blood between him and the Henderson boy; Caldwell had threatened Henderson in front of a dozen witnesses; his own mother had been convinced of his guilt; and his girlfriend had become the state's best witness against him. Turning himself in had been the only thing to do.

"Yeah," he agreed sarcastically. "I learned something about not getting caught. I learned to stay out of trouble and keep my hands clean, and maybe, just maybe, the cops will leave me alone." He started to turn away, then swung back around. "You're crazy, lady. You don't just walk up to a stranger out of the blue and offer him money to kill somebody. I don't know you from Adam. For all I know, you could be a cop, trying to trap me in something so you can revoke my parole and send me back to prison."

"I'm not a cop. I'm a teacher—" Breaking off, she bit her lower lip. Three months had passed since she had changed jobs—since she had been forced to change jobs—but it still filled her with anger, and the most overwhelming helplessness she'd ever known. "I'm an administrator with the school board."

What she really was was an embarrassment, a problem to be hidden away in a back-closet job until frustration left her no choice but to quit.

Well, she was tired of paying the price for Jason's crimes. She was tired of watching him go about his life as if nothing had changed, as if the entire episode with her—and with Kerry—had never happened, while *her* life, *their* lives, would never be the same again.

"Mr. James never would have sent me here if I were a cop."

He acknowledged that with a grudging nod.

"And he never would have sent me if he hadn't believed that you could help. That you *would* help." Clasping her hands tightly together, she forced all the tension she was feeling into them and out of her face and her voice. "So, Mr. Caldwell, what is your answer? Will you kill Jason Trask for me?"

I'm counting on you to help her, Tucker. Just listen to her. Consider what she wants you to do. Help her . . . as a favor to me.

Exactly what was it the old man wanted him to do for Kate Edwards? Tucker wondered as he stared at her across the pickup bed. Kill for her? No way. As surely as he breathed, Tucker knew that Ben wouldn't approve of murder, not for any reason. His friend was a good man, honest, possessing decency and integrity in full measures. He would never help anyone take someone else's life, not even by merely directing her to the person most likely to do it for her.

Maybe he was supposed to change her mind, to make her see that she really didn't want Trask dead. Maybe he was supposed to tell her exactly how it felt to kill someone, to describe for her the shock and the horror, to make her feel just a fraction of the guilt, the sorrow, and the awful sickness that would haunt her for as long as she lived. Maybe he was supposed to frighten her with tales of prison life, with glimpses of the despair and the hopelessness, of the fear and the self-loathing and the ugly certainty that no matter how much time you served, no matter how much of your life you gave up, you would never finish paying. You would never be free of the guilt, the sorrow.

He would *never* be free of that awful sickness.

"What do you have against Jason Trask?"

Her eyes turned colder. "Do you know him?"

"I know of him." It was impossible to live within fifty miles of Fall River and not have passing familiarity with the

Trasks. Their name was on the bank, the insurance office, the only department store, the elementary school, and the street that ran by the courthouse. They even had a park named after them.

Then, of course, there was the matter of Jeffrey Henderson. His relationship to the Trasks helped explain how Tucker had been arrested on the charge of manslaughter and wound up convicted of murder. Nobody screwed with the Trasks and walked away from it. Maybe *that* was what Ben wanted him to teach her.

"If you know anything at all about Jason, then you know why this is necessary. He has to die." With her next words, her control slipped. "I *need* him to die."

He gave her another long, studying look. So revenge was her motive, but for what? Maybe she was Trask's ex-wife, an old girlfriend, a jilted lover . . . but, if Trask was anything like his cousin Jeffrey had been—and sixteen years ago they had been exactly alike—she didn't seem the type to attract a man like him. There was nothing flashy about her. She wasn't unattractive, but she wasn't pretty, either. What he could see of her clothing was conservative—an oxford shirt, open at the collar, and a tweed jacket, tailored and neat, in colors that didn't flatter her. Her blond hair was carelessly combed, her makeup inadequate, her only jewelry a plain brown-banded wristwatch. She looked as if she never smiled, never relaxed, never traded that steely expression and hard-set jaw for anything softer or warmer. No, she definitely was not a woman to attract a man like Trask.

So what was the source? Whatever the cause, he didn't care. He wasn't about to involve himself in her problems, even if the old man had asked him to. He had enough troubles of his own to live with.

Apparently sensing that he was about to send her away,

she spoke, her tone taut and cool again. "There's twenty-five hundred dollars there. I'll pay you another seventy-five hundred when it's done."

Ten thousand bucks. Damn, the things he could do with ten thousand dollars. The places he could go. He had always thought South America sounded nice. His Spanish, learned from a Mexican inmate, was passable, and Brazil or Argentina was far enough from Arkansas to be appealing. With her money, he could make a new life for himself, a brand-new start where nobody knew who or what he was and nobody cared. He could forget the one detail that had brought this woman—and her money—to him: he could forget what it was like to kill a man.

And all he had to do to forget was kill another man.

Even ten thousand dollars wasn't worth going back to prison. It wasn't worth risking execution. It wasn't worth throwing away the rest of his life, sorry as it was.

He walked to the back of the truck, pulled on the work gloves he'd left there, and began unloading the sheets of plywood. Pulling them to the edge brought the manila envelope and the money it held to him, and he picked it up, holding the thick packet for a moment before slapping it down on the sidewall of the truck. "Go home, Ms. Edwards, and take your money with you. Put it back in the Trasks' bank, spend it in their store, or, better yet, take it to Little Rock and find a good shrink. Forget about killing anything but time, because, lady, you aren't prepared to deal with the consequences."

Something—his words, his refusal, his condescending tone of voice—angered her. Her face paled, and her bearing grew more taut. "Don't patronize me, Mr. Caldwell. I'm an intelligent woman, and I know what I want. I want to see Jason Trask dead. I've considered the consequences, and I've determined that being responsible for that man's death will be much easier to deal with than knowing that he's alive and well and walking around free."

He dropped the first heavy sheet of wood, then returned for another before facing her again. "What did Trask do to you?"

Her shoulders went back, and her head came up regally high. "That's none of your business."

"You *made* it my business when you came waltzing in here with your money and your offer. What did he do?"

She stared at him, hatred the only emotion in her eyes. No, not the only. Underlying it was shame. Sorrow. Hopelessness.

Although he didn't expect an answer to his question, she gave one. "He hurt someone I love. Now he has to pay for it."

"Who?"

"My sister." As if the admission had drained her, she drew a deep breath, then fixed that cool gaze on him again. "Will you do it, Mr. Caldwell?"

He glanced at the envelope with the twenty-five hundred dollars in it. Thought again of the ten thousand.

But it couldn't make him kill again.

What the hell *did* that old bastard want him to do?

Give her time to cool off, maybe. She was convinced that whatever Trask had done to her sister could be made right by his death, but she was wrong. Killing him would only ensure that nothing would ever be right again. Killing him would destroy her and probably, if she found out, her sister, too. She needed time to consider what she was asking, time to calm down and see how desperately wrong she was. *He* could give her that time.

All he had to do was accept the money and lie to her. Tell her that he would take care of Trask. Send her home thinking she had hired herself a killer. Maybe he would even keep the twenty-five hundred bucks. After all, he would be doing her a big favor—saving her from committing a crime that would devastate her. Protecting her from consequences that, no matter how she protested, she hadn't thought through. That was worth *some* reward.

He reached for the envelope and opened it, thumbing through the stacks of bills, mostly fifties with a few hundreds on the bottom. She had withdrawn them from the Trask bank so she could hire someone to kill the Trask son. He appreciated the irony.

Closing the flap again, he glanced at her and caught the desperation that flashed across her face, then disappeared behind cool, unimpassioned emptiness. She was afraid he was going to turn her down, and she didn't know what to do next. She didn't know where else to find a potential murderer. She would be left with no choice but to admit failure or try to take Trask out herself . . . unless she came to her senses first.

He wondered if that would happen. Hearing again in his mind the deeply buried anguish in her voice when she'd said, *I need him to die*, he didn't think so.

He leaned across the tailgate, opened the battered toolbox, and crammed the envelope inside. When he turned to her again, she was wearing a look of such relief that he almost felt guilty for deceiving her.

"When will you do it?"

"You'll hear about it."

"I want to be there."

"No way." He hauled the next sheet of plywood out and let it fall to the pile with a crash.

"I want him to know why—"

"I'll be sure and tell him."

"Will it be soon?"

"No. It'll take some time." Long enough for her to come to her senses.

"Mr. Caldwell . . ."

Her hesitation made it sound as if a thank-you were sure to follow. He spoke quickly, before she could get it out. "Come by Saturday. I'll need some information from you." With any luck, all she would have to say by Saturday would be something along the lines of, I've changed my mind.

She nodded solemnly, started to speak again, then turned and walked away. Once more Tucker stopped working and watched her go. A moment later she disappeared around the old house, and a moment after that he heard the revving of an engine. Another moment or two and even that faded.

He looked at the toolbox, and the twenty-five hundred dollars inside, and muttered a curse. "Christ, Ben, what have you gotten me into?"

Chapter Two

Kate stood in front of the bathroom mirror that night, staring at her reflection. She didn't look any different after her meeting with Tucker Caldwell than she had before. She didn't look as if the weight of the world had been lifted from her shoulders or as if a bit, just a little, of the guilt she'd been carrying had disappeared.

She didn't look like a woman who had just solicited a man to commit murder.

Slowly she smiled. She might look the same, but she felt ten years younger and a thousand pounds lighter. For the first time in six months, she felt in control.

Through the open door came the sound of the phone ringing downstairs. She didn't tense, didn't feel the customary shiver of fear dancing up her spine. Jason's buddies could say all the vile, nasty things they wanted, but soon he would be dead.

"Hey, Katie." The voice floated through her answering machine and up the stairs. It belonged to Tim Carter, Jason's best friend since kindergarten and the most persistent of her tormentors. "I've been thinking about you, sweetheart. I like a woman who fights, you know. I like it rough, *real* rough. Invite me over, darlin', and I'll show you what I can do." His voice, first soft and coaxing, turned harsh. "Jason will seem like a Sunday in the park compared to what I'll do to you, bitch. I'll tie you to the bed and—"

Kate pushed the door shut, then turned on the water in the sink. Tim's calls had gotten a little tame. The first few weeks after the trial, she had cowered by the phone and listened to his hateful, perverted threats, had listened to him describe acts that she had never even imagined, and then she had seen him out shopping with his wife, taking his kid to a Little League game, or singing in the church choir. He had always looked so *normal*. No one would have believed her if she'd told them the awful, sick things he was saying to her, and back then he'd had the sense not to say them on the answering machine, where the tape would make a record that could be used against him. Since she'd never taken legal action, he had gotten brave and started recording his filth. They all had. They all believed they had her too cowed to do anything. They were all wrong.

Dead wrong.

Turning off the water, she opened the door and stepped into the hall, listening for a moment. Tim had hung up. Maybe that call would be the only one tonight.

She was still standing there when a knock sounded at the front door. The fear that had been missing with the phone call rushed in now. No one but Travis ever came to her house, and he never came after dark without calling first.

Another knock echoed through the house as she approached the landing at the top of the stairs. There was no reason to panic. The alarm was turned on. If her unexpected guest tried to force his way in, the system would automatically alert the police station, and help would arrive in minutes. Still, her fingers were clenching tightly around the banister, and her feet refused to obey her brain's command to take that first step down.

"Kate?" came a shout. "It's Travis."

Breathing a sigh of relief, she let go of the polished wood rail and hurried down the stairs. She didn't pause to look out the peephole before she deactivated the alarm and unfastened the three sturdy locks that secured the door and opened it.

She'd known Travis McMaster all her life. His family had lived across the street from her own. Kate had been best of friends with his little brother Bobby, and Travis had dated her sister Kristin. After high school he had gone away to play college football for the Razorbacks, then had tried his hand at big-city police work in Little Rock. There had been a marriage, then a divorce, and, after ten years, he had returned home to take the job as Fall River chief of police. Kate and Travis had gone out a time or two, had even gone to bed a time or two, but the intimacy had been uncomfortable. They'd never forgotten that he was Bobby's big brother, that she was Kristin's little sister. They had decided to be friends instead. Right now he was the only friend she had.

"I tried to call before I came over, but your line was busy." He glanced at the answering machine and saw the flashing light. "Who was it this time?"

"Tim Carter."

"Son of a bitch. Are you okay, Kate?"

Closing the door and relocking it, she nodded. "Take off your jacket and sit down."

He obeyed her, tossing the uniform jacket across the chair before settling on the sofa. "Want to play the tape for me?"

"It's just more of the same." As she passed the machine, she hit the rewind button.

He scowled at her disapprovingly. "You should be saving those tapes, Kate. We could use them to get the entire bunch of them."

"Oh, really? And how would we do that, Travis?" she asked sarcastically as she settled at the opposite end of the sofa. "Would you take me to District Attorney Marquette's office so I could sign a complaint against them? Then would you arrest and charge them so they could go to trial? So we could appear before Judge Hampton and accuse them of making obscene phone calls? So Judge Hampton could tell me—*again*—that I deserve what I get because of my shameful behavior?" She shook her head in disgust. "I've had it with the legal system, Travis. I depended on the court to help me the last time, but Hampton let Jason's lawyers make me out to be the sick one. I'm not dealing with them again."

"There are other ways. I could talk to them. Hell, I could talk to their wives. You think Nancy Carter, Renee Tyler, and Susan Hogan wouldn't be interested in hearing how their husbands amuse themselves?"

"Brilliant idea. Why would their wives believe any accusation I made? They'd probably convince themselves I faked the tapes somehow."

"So what are you going to do? Spend the rest of your life barricaded behind triple-locked doors? Never again set foot outside after the sun goes down? Never answer your phone without letting the machine pick it up first to see if it's someone you can bear to talk to?"

"I plan to live my life my way."

Travis gave her a chastening look. "This isn't living, Kate. It's cowering. It's hiding. It's surrendering to Jason Trask and his friends."

Her responding smile felt smugly satisfying. "It's surviving, Travis, and it's enough." For now. But she intended to start living again. The day that Jason Trask died. "What brings you out tonight?"

"I went by your office this afternoon, but you weren't there. Irene said you'd had an appointment."

Kate knew he wouldn't ask what kind of meeting or with whom. He knew too well what her appointment book had looked like in recent months: interviews with Travis himself, depositions with Jason's lawyers, examinations by doctors, sessions with psychiatrists, consultations with her own lawyer when Jason had threatened to sue her for false, slanderous claims. She had gotten through the worst of it when, nearly a month ago, it had started again, only this time it had been Kerry's doctors, Kerry's psychiatrists, and this time there'd been no lawyers or cops involved. Her parents had refused, and even if Kerry had wanted to cooperate with Travis's aborted investigation, she'd been in no condition to do so.

"How's Kerry?"

"I talked to her doctor this morning. Nothing's changed."

Nothing's changed. The sweet, innocent, trusting girl everyone had adored was gone. The Kerry who'd done volunteer work at the local hospital now needed twenty-four-hour caretakers of her own. The girl who had breezed through high school couldn't find her way out of the distant place to which she'd retreated long enough to put two coherent thoughts together. The young woman who had dreamed of mothering a half dozen babies all of her own could no longer dress or feed herself. *Nothing's changed.* Just her entire life.

Travis slid down on the cushions and stared morosely at the fireplace, watching the flames flicker. After a long, heavy silence, he asked, "Is she ever going to get out of that place?"

"Sure. They're planning to move her to a residential facility in Little Rock any day now," she replied flippantly. Then, feeling once again the burden Tucker Caldwell had temporarily lifted, she slid down, too. "They don't know if she'll ever be all right again. She was always so fragile, so sweet and innocent. She couldn't even begin to comprehend what Jason had done to me. There's no way she can deal with what he did to her."

"If there was some way to make him pay . . ." Clenching his fist tightly, Travis brought it down on the sofa arm with enough force to vibrate the cushions. "Damn, this *isn't* why I became a cop, Kate. I thought I could do good. I thought I could make the world safer for people like Kerry, for people like you."

"Not as long as there are people like the Trasks." She stared at the fire, too, feeling little of its heat. It was like her life: bright with warm promise but delivering only cold. "You know what I don't understand, Travis? I see Eleanor Trask occasionally. She *knows* what he did. She *knows* in her heart that Jason is guilty as sin, and yet she doesn't care. She lies to protect him. She spends the family money to clean up after him and to keep him out of trouble, but she doesn't spend a penny to get help for him. She doesn't use her influence to try to stop him."

"He's her son. He's the most important thing in the world to her. On the rare occasions he does wrong, it's not his fault. Someone made him do it. Someone seduced him into it. *You* seduced him, Kate."

She grinned. "The only time in my life I've ever been considered seductive, and it has to be an insult." Certainly, this afternoon, Tucker Caldwell had found neither her nor her offer very seductive. If not for his disdainful use of the word *lady* in addressing her, she wouldn't have been certain that Tucker Caldwell had even noticed her gender. No desire or lust had been competing with the discussion of Jason's death for his attention . . . which was a sad comment on her womanly charms, considering where Caldwell had spent the last sixteen years.

It suited her fine, though. No man without an MD attached to his name had touched her in the last six months, one week, and five days. If she never had sex again as long as she lived, she would be perfectly satisfied.

"I'd better be going," Travis said with a yawn as he pushed himself to his feet. "The next time you see Kerry, give her my best."

"I will," Kate agreed, but she wouldn't. Men didn't come up in her visits with her sister. Kerry had no male doctors or nurses, and she regarded even their father with suspicion and distrust. Jason's attack on her had robbed her of all reason and had left her with nothing, not one single emotion, stronger than her fear of men. *All* men. Someday, her psychiatrist hoped, she would learn to trust the opposite sex again, but Kate wasn't holding her breath. She didn't believe that *she* would ever again trust any man but Travis, and she had come through her experience with Jason stronger both physically and mentally than Kerry could ever hope to.

At the door, Travis shrugged into his jacket, then reached out but didn't touch her. He always remembered before he made contact. Still, she stiffened a little, even as his hand dropped, unoffered, to his side. "I'll see you later," he said, regret shadowing his eyes. "Be sure you lock up behind me."

"I will." It was an unneeded reminder. "Take care."

As soon as the door closed, she secured the three locks and reactivated the alarm, then leaned against the door for a moment, missing him. When Travis had returned to Fall River and they'd renewed their acquaintance, she had thought that she'd finally found her future. Then they had made love, and, while the sex had been fine, the awkwardness afterward had been unbearable. It had felt shameful. Wrong. They had agreed that they wanted more in a romance—breathless passion, reckless thrills—and so they had settled for platonic friendship.

Too bad their timing had been off. Now she would be more than happy to settle for friendship, respect, and passionless love. Now the idea of satisfying sex seemed foreign. Now the entire act—the intimacy, the closeness, the joining—seemed perverted. Sick.

One more thing she could thank Jason for. Her list of grievances against him kept growing. He had beaten her. Raped her. Viciously attacked her sister. He had destroyed her reputation, cost her the job she loved, and alienated her from her father, who blamed her for what had happened to her, and from her mother, who blamed her for all that had happened. He had made a normal life impossible. He had degraded her body and destroyed her soul. She would have no husband, no children, no lover, no future.

But Tucker Caldwell—*She* and Tucker Caldwell were going to make him pay. Finally. Dearly.

With his life.

Saturday was a perfect day. Tucker had lived for days like this when he was a kid. He and Jimmy used to cut school and head off into the hills around Fayette, going nowhere, doing nothing. They had waded in creeks, climbed trees, and explored old caves. They had lain in the sun, telling jokes and lies and talking about the things they were going to do someday. Even back then, he had known none of his dreams and fine plans would happen. Nobody in their family had ever amounted to anything, and it wasn't likely that either he or his brother would be the first. It had all been empty talk.

He hoped he could say the same about Kate Edwards. According to the clock beside his bed, it was after two o'clock now, and there'd been no sign of her all day. Maybe she had changed her mind. At least, that was what he was hoping.

But his hopes faded before they were even fully formed when he heard the sound of a car out front. Crossing the uneven floor, he stopped at the window beside the door and watched as she maneuvered the red compact over the bumps and ruts that his truck easily cleared. She didn't park out front this time, but instead drove around the house. By the time he'd crossed to the open back door, she had pulled in beside his truck, shut off the engine, and climbed out.

Tucker picked up the beer he'd come inside for and took a long drink as he watched her. She had to know that he was probably inside the house—there sure as hell wasn't anyplace out there where he could be hiding—but she didn't look in that direction. Instead, hands shoved deep into the pockets of the jacket she wore but didn't need, she seemed to be studying the new house. In the three days since her last visit, he had sawed all the boards for the walls, completing the framing this morning. He'd taken a break to eat a sandwich on the tailgate of the truck and to try to figure out how he was going to raise the walls and secure them in place by himself. Now that Kate was here, maybe he could put her to work. She looked sturdy enough to be of use. Emotionally, though, she was pretty fragile.

He scowled fiercely. He didn't give a damn about her

emotional makeup. Beyond his obligation to old Ben, he didn't give a damn about Kate Edwards at all.

Finally, she directed her gaze to the house, right to him, as if she'd known all along that he was standing there. She didn't smile, didn't acknowledge him in any way beyond that long, steady look.

Tilting his head back, he drained the last of the beer in one deep swallow. Just to be perverse, he ignored the wastebasket next to the door and instead sent the bottle soaring over the woodpile and into the overgrown grass there. It hit a rock and broke with a crack that exploded like gunfire. He moved down the steps formed by wobbly rows of concrete blocks and approached her slowly, feeling the reluctance and the wariness increase with each step.

She was the one who should be uncomfortable and afraid. After all, she was a woman miles from town, all alone with an ex-con who'd done time for murder.

But she seemed neither uncomfortable nor afraid, while he was both.

When he got close enough, she offered a greeting. "Mr. Caldwell."

The last person to call him mister had been the court-appointed attorney who had defended him at his trial sixteen years ago. It sounded strange. "I wasn't sure you were coming."

"If you had wanted me to come at a specific time, you should have said so."

"I don't suppose you've changed your mind."

She shook her head. "I suppose *you* have."

He shook his head, too. He *hadn't* changed his mind. He had lied to her Tuesday, and he was lying to her again. There was no way in hell he was going to kill Jason Trask for her.

"Where do you want to talk?"

He shrugged. "Your only choices are inside or out here."

She looked at the house, subjecting it to the same judging look she'd given him. After a moment or two, she turned back to him. "Out here will be fine."

He felt the heat creeping up his neck. Why had he even offered? The house was old and ugly. Why in hell would someone like her want to set foot inside a place like that?

Walking over to the truck, he sat down on the tailgate. He waited until she moved, too, coming to a point in front of him, close enough to carry on a conversation but distant enough to be out of his reach.

"What is it you want to know?" she asked him.

"What did Trask do to your sister?"

A harsh, pinched look came across her face. "What does that matter?"

"You expect me to kill the man. I have a right to know the reason."

"I've offered you ten thousand reasons, Mr. Caldwell. You don't need one more."

"*I* think I do."

She considered his answer for a moment. Tension made her eyes dark and her jaw taut. "My sister is nineteen years old. Do you remember how young that is? You have your whole life ahead of you—all the chances, all the risks, all the successes, all the dreams."

Feeling as stiff as she looked, he said stonily, "When I was nineteen, I was in prison. I didn't have anything ahead of me but twenty-four more years of hard time."

For a moment, she simply looked at him. Then she nodded slightly, acknowledging the differences before continuing. "Kerry has—Kerry *had* a future. She was bright and well liked. She was the sweetest kid you could ever hope to meet."

"Until she met up with Jason Trask."

Another small nod.

"What did he do?"

She took a minute or two to prepare, then launched into her answer in the flattest, dullest voice he'd ever heard. "One cold Saturday night, four weeks ago today, Jason Trask kidnapped my sister. He took her someplace outside of town, beat her into submission, and brutally raped her. When he was finished, he dumped her on the side of the road, with her clothes torn and her shoes missing. He tossed her coat out of the car a quarter mile away. Then he went home, called me, and told me what he'd done. It took the police and the sheriff's department over two hours to find her. When they did, she was incoherent and in shock. Since then she's been in a hospital in Little Rock, receiving both medical and psychiatric treatment. Monday she's being transferred to Tubman Hospital. That's a state hospital for the mentally ill. Her doctors don't know how long she'll be there. Maybe a few months. Maybe the rest of her life."

Tucker stared at the thin soil, leached of whatever nutrients it had once possessed, unable to look at her.

"Is that reason enough for you, Mr. Caldwell?" she asked softly.

"Why haven't the police arrested Trask?"

"They have no evidence."

He looked at her. "But he confessed. You said he told you—"

Her smile was thin and painful to see. "There's something you should understand about me. I'm no longer particularly well respected in Fall River. If I said the sky was blue, people would walk outside to see for themselves before believing me. My reputation is that of a malevolent and malicious liar, a bitter, vindictive woman, and a poor loser—" She broke off, then drily added, "Among other things. No one would believe any claim or accusation I might make against Jason Trask. There must have been evidence to connect him—fingerprints, fibers, skin scraped from beneath her nails—but without the victim's cooperation, the police couldn't get a warrant to gather it. Kerry couldn't cooperate, and our parents wouldn't. They thought it best to put it all behind them, to avoid the trauma of an investigation. They refused to let anyone question her, to do anything to punish Jason for doing this to her. My sister very well might spend the rest of her life in a mental hospital, and he's walking around free."

She turned away, moving to the sawhorses a few yards away. She was focusing her attention on the lumber stacked there, her back to him, when he finally spoke again. "Why did he call you?"

"He had to tell me. He had to gloat."

"Why?"

A shudder rippled through her, making her seem suddenly small and insubstantial. "That was the whole point. He did it because of me." She faced him again, looked at him again, and the sorrow he'd seen Tuesday was in her face again. "Do you understand, Mr. Caldwell?" she asked, her voice quavering and sending a chill down his spine. "It was *my* fault. Jason Trask beat and raped my baby sister because of me."

Silence followed her admission. Tucker knew he couldn't deny her words, and he couldn't offer absolution. And so he said nothing.

After a moment, she turned away and walked to one end

of the house. "How are you going to set the framing in place?"

Though the walls weren't particularly tall or long, they were big enough to make maneuvering them all alone difficult. The foundation varied on the sloping lot from about two and a half to three feet high. He had to get the walls onto the foundation and keep each section upright and squared until it was secured. Two people could probably manage easily enough, but he hadn't yet decided how to do it alone.

"Don't know yet. I'll think of something." He moved away from the truck and passed behind her, stepping up onto the foundation. "It's only going to be one room, with a bathroom over there."

She moved closer, raising one foot onto the foundation. It was a tall step up, and clearly she needed assistance. Surprising her, surprising himself, he offered it.

She drew back an inch or two before she could stop herself. She stared at his hand for a moment, then clumsily climbed up, carefully avoiding him.

He turned away with a scowl. Women like her—educated, smart, from the right part of town—didn't take kindly to physical contact with men like him. He had learned that lesson the first time someone had called him trash.

"Mr. Caldwell—"

"My name is Tucker."

She swallowed once. There was a certain intimacy to the use of first names that she obviously would prefer to avoid. She didn't want to think of him as a person, as a man. She wanted him to remain *Mr.* Caldwell, the man who was going to take care of her biggest problem. Suddenly angry, *he* wanted the intimacy of Tucker.

"You said you wanted information about Jason." It didn't escape his notice that she chose to avoid the issue by avoiding use of his name. "What do you need to know?"

He stood for a moment in the corner, drawing the toe of his boot back and forth across a chalk line on the sheathing that marked the bathroom. Another chalk line marked a rectangle on the back wall—the location of the wood-burning stove he'd already found.

After a time, he faced her, his expression flat. "What has Trask got against you?"

"I took him to court."

"And he lost?"

"No. He won."

"But he didn't like being inconvenienced."

She smiled tightly. "No, he didn't like it at all."

"And so, to get back at you, he brutally assaulted your little sister." He approached her slowly, giving her plenty of time to back away, but she held her ground. She stood, still and barely breathing, looking at him as he looked at her, and waited for his next move. He offered it in a low voice, pleasant enough on the surface, suspicious and disbelieving just underneath. "It sounds to me a lot more personal than a little annoyance over a court case which he won. I happen to be personally acquainted with a number of rapists and other men who get off on hurting women. Your story doesn't quite fit."

Kate stared at him but said nothing.

"I'd say it's something a *hell* of a lot more personal. You weren't married to Trask, by any chance?"

"*No.*"

"Did you have an affair with him?"

Her face grew hot. "Yes."

"And he dumped you for someone else."

"No."

"I don't believe you."

She pulled her jacket tighter and took a step back. "I don't give a damn what you believe, Mr. Caldwell. All I want to know is that you'll do the job you were hired for. I want to know that you'll earn the money I've already paid you and the fee yet to be paid. If you can't do that without more questions and answers, fine. Give the money back, and I'll leave. I'll find someone else to do it for me, or I'll do it myself. I think that would be by far the more satisfying option, anyway."

"And how many people have you killed, Ms. Edwards?" he asked, the softness of his voice serving to emphasize the subtle mocking.

"Only one less than you have, Mr. Caldwell—unless you were a busy boy in prison."

"And how would you kill Trask?"

"I would shoot him. Right between his lying, deceitful, scheming blue eyes."

"You think it's that easy? You think you can walk right up to him, look him in the eye, and blow him away?" He shook his head. "If you could do it, you never would have asked the old man to find you a killer. You never would have come to me. *If* you could do it, you would have done it by now."

Her smile was chilling. "No, Mr. Caldwell, you're wrong. I have no doubt that I can kill Jason Trask. I just don't know if I can do it without getting caught. If I don't have an airtight alibi when he dies, I'll be the prime suspect. I don't want to spend the rest of my life in prison because of that bastard. *That's* why I came to you. Because you've done it before. Because you can use the money.

And because I don't think *you* want to spend the rest of your life in prison, either."

"No," he agreed. "Sixteen years was enough for me. So . . . you tell me the truth about what's between you and Trask, then we'll get down to business."

Kate stared at him a moment longer, then put the width of the house between them. "I told you the truth."

"Trask raped your little sister."

"Yes."

"I don't believe you."

"As I told you earlier, most people around Fall River don't believe anything I say. I don't care whether you do or not."

"You'd better care, lady, because until I'm sure that you've been honest with me, I'm not doing a damned thing for you. *My* life is on the line here. If I do what you're asking and get caught, with my record—a two-time loser on murder—they're going to want to execute me. My life may not mean much to you, but it's all I've got, and I'd like to hang on to it for a while. Humor me. Tell me what I want to know . . ." He broke off, looked away from her to the woods in back, then continued in a grimmer voice. "And I'll do what you want me to do."

Tucker waited and stared at the trees, at the myriad shades of gold and red that colored them. He couldn't imagine a place more beautiful than the Ozarks in October . . . not that he'd ever seen any other place in the world. He was thirty-four years old, and only once had he set foot outside the state of Arkansas. He'd been sixteen then, and his mother and her boyfriend had taken him and Jimmy to New Orleans for Mardi Gras and left them there.

Here's some money, the boyfriend had said. Go out and have some fun. Tucker and Jimmy had divided the hundred bucks evenly, and they'd found their fun in two pretty little girls in the French Quarter. When they had made their way back to the motel a day later, their mother and her friend were gone. With what was left of their money and another fifty bucks Jimmy had stolen from a drunk tourist, they had walked and hitched all the way back to Fayette.

He still remembered the disinterest in their mother's expression when they had finally gotten home. "There you are," she had said, as if they'd been late coming back from the corner store, not a neighboring state. She had never offered a reason for leaving them, and neither he nor Jimmy had expected one. They hadn't even really cared. After all, they'd had a great time. They had seen New Orleans, experienced the world's greatest party, and Tucker, at least, had gotten laid for the first time. Being abandoned without a ride home had seemed a small enough price to pay.

He wondered about Kerry Edwards's first time. Did teenage girls stay virgins beyond the age of eighteen these days? Had Jason Trask been her first, or did she have some other, less terrifying experience to compare it to? If Trask was guilty of the things Kate claimed, then she was right: he *did* deserve to die. But *was* he truly guilty?

Tucker had no doubt that the woman was lying about something. Maybe Trask really did assault her sister, and maybe he really had done it to punish Kate for something she'd done . . . but Tucker wasn't convinced. Her story just didn't add up.

But *something* had happened, something so significant that Kate Edwards was willing to kill Trask, or have him killed. If she were crazy, it could be something so simple as a lost court case or a broken affair . . . but she didn't strike him as crazy. She seemed to be a woman haunted by shame and guilt. A woman who was no longer well respected in town . . . *no longer*, meaning that, at one time, she had been. A woman who had lost her reputation, who was emotionally fragile, a woman who was cold, withdrawn inside herself, but impassioned enough to actively seek the death of the man she held responsible for whatever had gone wrong.

A woman who had herself been Jason Trask's victim?

Abruptly, he shifted his gaze to her. She was standing utterly still, her face empty of all emotion. Her eyes weren't empty, though. She was struggling with the silence she wanted to keep, the secrets she needed to protect, and the demand he'd made. *Tell me what I want to know . . . and I'll do what you want me to do.* He felt a moment's guilt, because she so obviously didn't want to obey him and because even if she did, even if she offered him her deepest, darkest secrets, there was still no way in hell he was going to live up to his end of the bargain. Because he was accusing her of being dishonest when he had lied to her practically from the beginning. Because he had given her hope that—like him—was never going to amount to anything.

"Do you *have* a sister, Ms. Edwards?"

She tried to appear composed. "I have two. Kristin is older, and Kerry is the baby."

"But Trask didn't do anything to Kerry, did he?"

Spots of color appeared bright in the paleness of her face. "He kidnapped her. He beat and raped her. He ruined her life."

"Her life? Or yours?"

She opened her mouth, closed it again, and said nothing.

"What did he do to you?" he asked. "That's why you want him dead, isn't it? Because of what he did to *you*."

"What happened to me doesn't matter. He has to be punished for what he did to Kerry. That's all that counts."

Tucker wanted to turn and walk away without hearing anything else, but even more, he wanted to know. "What happened to you?"

There was pure hatred in her eyes. "I don't have to answer to you. I don't have to explain anything to you. We made a deal: you would kill Jason, and I would give you ten thousand dollars. That's *all* you get. You don't get to ask questions. You don't get to make demands." She sucked in a deep breath before continuing. "Do your job, Mr. Caldwell, and do it quickly. Then take your money and get the hell out of my life."

She started to leave, but he blocked her way, catching her arm to hold her. Before he had a chance to even blink, the barrel of a small pistol was pressing hard under his chin, forcing his head back and up, allowing his eyes to connect with hers. She hadn't lied about one thing, he realized grimly. She *was* capable of killing.

He didn't twitch so much as a muscle, didn't even breathe. He stood absolutely motionless and waited for her next move.

"Let go of me," she whispered, and he did so immediately. For a long time, she simply stared at him. Then, with deliberate slowness, she lowered the gun, backed away, and circled around him, heading for the edge of the foundation, for the safety of the driveway and her car.

Tucker let her jump to the ground and go about ten feet before he turned and spoke. "He raped *you*, didn't he?"

She stopped, hesitated, then slowly faced him. "No," she denied, and he knew she was lying. "He was just an innocent man, doing what men do with women like me. I *seduced* him. I *made* him tear my clothes and hit me and hurt me. I wanted it rough, you see. I like it that way. It's the only way I can get off."

The empty way she told the lies, parroting what others had said about her, made him feel queasy inside. He knew how it felt to be damned by labels. He knew how it felt to be scorned and put down for nothing you did, for nothing more than other people's prejudices.

Jesus, the last thing he needed was to empathize with Kate Edwards. He was leading her along, scamming her, for old Ben. *Only* for old Ben.

Still, he asked the next question, and he asked it for himself, not Ben. For his own simmering anger. "How rough?"

"He broke my jaw and my nose. He blackened both eyes. He choked me. I had bruises on my face, throat, arms, and legs. When he threw me to the floor, I hit my head, resulting in a concussion. And there was extensive vaginal tearing."

She didn't flinch during the recitation, but Tucker did. He had known men that vicious, but they were in prison where they belonged. Jason Trask was a free man. He had made himself into the injured party and painted his victim as the guilty one. He had convinced a town full of people who knew her that he had given her only what she'd asked for and that she had been warped enough to enjoy it. He had destroyed her life. No wonder she wanted to destroy his.

Still emotionless, she gestured with her left hand toward the framing at her feet. "I can help with this," she offered flatly, "but not today. Tomorrow." She waited a moment, but when he didn't say anything, she walked away.

As she drove out of sight, Tucker sat down at the edge of the sheathing, letting his feet dangle above the bare dirt. She was right. Trask did deserve to die . . . but *he* couldn't be the one to kill him. Thanks to the old man, he couldn't let her be the one, either. Killing the bastard would be the easy part. Living with it would be more than she could bear.

What was he supposed to do, damn it?

Chapter Three

In the office of her Little Rock condo, Colleen Robbins was spending her Saturday night catching up on work. She'd had offers for the evening—a movie with her neighbor, a party at the home of one of the lawyers in her firm, even a real, honest-to-God date—but, as usual, she was working.

The stack of newspapers scattered around her had been accumulating for three months. She usually put off dealing with them as long as she could, then jumped in with both feet, spending endless hours combing through them, clipping articles, immersing herself in a past that was long ago and best forgotten.

But she couldn't forget. She would never forget.

With a sigh, she unfolded the latest issue of the *Fall River Journal*, the last in the stack, and scanned the front page. How quickly life in the northern Arkansas town had returned to normal. Only a few months ago the most sensational trial in county history had been played out with every detail noted and documented on these pages. Having represented several rape victims in lawsuits before she'd traded civil law for criminal, Colleen had followed the story with interest. Now, only a few short months later, it was as if the trial had never happened. Fall River had judged their favorite son, found him innocent, and moved on.

She doubted that Kate Edwards had moved on. The woman might never move on. She might pick up the pieces of her life. She might continue working and seeing family and friends. She might pretend that everything was all right, but inside she was probably going quietly mad. She would probably never get beyond the trauma of what Jason Trask had done to her.

God knew, Colleen hadn't.

Tossing the stack of *Journal*s into the recycling basket, she turned to the *Fayette Observer*. It was a smaller pile, a once-a-week publication of never more than six pages. There was rarely anything of interest in its pages, but she continued the subscription, as she'd done for twenty years, out of habit.

The paper on top proved to be one of the rare ones. The story wasn't much—a few inches in the bottom corner. "Murderer Paroled," declared the headline. The few lines underneath filled in the details.

Tucker Caldwell, formerly of Fayette, was granted parole from the Arkansas State Penitentiary after serving sixteen years of a twenty-five-year sentence.

Caldwell, 34, was convicted of murder in the death of Jeffrey Henderson, 19, son of Mr. and Mrs. Philip Henderson of Fayette.

When contacted regarding Caldwell's parole, the Hendersons offered no comment.

Colleen checked the newspaper's date—July 16—and noted it in the margin before clipping the article. She slid it between the pages of a cheap scrapbook, behind all the clippings already mounted.

So Tucker Caldwell was finally out of prison. She was

surprised by the satisfaction she felt. If *she* had been his lawyer, he would have gone to prison, but he wouldn't have rotted away half of his life there. But she hadn't even been a lawyer at the time of his trial. She had been twenty-two, a first-year law student, filled with idealism, convinced she could save the world. She had learned some hard lessons since then. She knew now that the world couldn't be saved. Thanks to people like Jason Trask, it was going to hell in a handbasket.

Thanks to Jason Trask, a number of people were already living in hell.

Kate Edwards. Tucker Caldwell. Colleen herself. She could name three with her limited knowledge of the man. How many others were out there?

She scanned the remaining newspapers with no luck, then opened the scrapbook on the table in front of her. There was a picture of Caldwell on the first page, a mug shot taken following his arrest and printed on the *Observer*'s front page. He had been so young, turned eighteen a few weeks earlier. Young, hot-tempered, foolish, and trusting. He had believed the justice system would protect him—the system and the attorney appointed to defend him. The Hendersons had protested the appointment, claiming that worthless trash like Caldwell didn't deserve the services of the best attorney in town.

Colleen's smile was bitter. Her father had been the *only* attorney in town, but, yes, he had been good. Harry Baker had won many an unwinnable case. He had saved people worse than Tucker Caldwell from long prison terms, but he hadn't saved Caldwell. He had, in fact, played a vital role in the boy's conviction.

If Tucker Caldwell had come from money, if he hadn't grown up on the wrong side of town, his trial would have turned out differently. He could have hired his own attorney, could have bought a lawyer's allegiance.

If . . . She'd spent much of the last sixteen years lamenting the *ifs* in her life. If she had been older, if she had magically finished law school a few years early, if Caldwell had killed anyone but the Henderson boy, if the Trasks hadn't been brought into the case . . . So many things would have been different. Her entire life would have been different. She still would have become a lawyer, and a good one, but she wouldn't be here in Little Rock. She wouldn't be working for the oldest, most prestigious firm in the state. She wouldn't be using her skill, talent, and knowledge of the law to free people who she knew beyond a shadow of doubt were guilty.

If the Caldwell trial had never taken place, she would be home in Fayette, earning one-tenth her current salary but making up for it in satisfaction in a job well-done. She would be carrying on the family tradition of helping those in need. She would even, more than likely, still be living in the family home, in that great old white house with the big porch and the leaded glass windows—raising a family, maybe, and having breakfast every morning with her father before heading off to the office together.

If Jason Trask hadn't destroyed her father. If he hadn't, in less noticeable ways, destroyed her.

She turned the page and scanned the articles taped there. They were yellow with age, the print difficult to read in places, the paper crumbling in others, but that was all right. She knew the details in the stories by heart—how Tucker Caldwell had discovered that his girlfriend was secretly involved with Jeffrey Henderson, how he had publicly threatened Henderson if he ever came near her again, how the very next night he had begun a fight with the older boy and had viciously beaten him to death. She also knew the truth about the incidents. Amy Wilkins had never been Henderson's secret sweetheart but rather the target of his unwelcome advances. Just like his cousin Jason, Jeffrey Henderson had felt a grand sense of entitlement. From the cradle, they'd been taught that they deserved whatever they'd wanted, like all Trasks, regardless of anyone else. Amy hadn't had the right to turn Jeffrey down, just as Jason had denied Kate Edwards the right to say no.

In truth, all Tucker Caldwell had been guilty of was trying to protect his girlfriend. Yes, he had started the fight, but for most men in Fayette, resolving disagreements with their fists was a time-honored tradition. Unfortunately for Tucker, one of his blows had sent Henderson tumbling from a four-foot retaining wall. He had landed awkwardly, and he had died.

Bad luck and trouble. They had dogged Tucker most of his life, and the rest of it wasn't likely to be much different. Surely sixteen years in prison had changed him. He'd been a scared kid when they'd sent him away. He had grown up there, surrounded by men ten times tougher and meaner than he'd ever been. He might have spent his time constructively, might have earned his GED or even a college degree, but when the job market was tight, who wanted to hire an ex-con—a convicted murderer, no less? He was out now and finding that life was even harder than it had been sixteen years ago, and it had been plenty tough then. How easy would it be for him to become a career criminal? How hard would it be for him to survive at anything else?

She flipped through the scrapbook pages, reading nothing, skimming over the photos. There was Jeffrey Henderson's senior picture, showing a young man whose good looks were spoiled by the arrogance and smug superiority in his eyes. There was another photograph of Tucker, seated in the courtroom beside his lawyer. He had remained handcuffed throughout the trial, impressing upon the jury that he was a dangerous criminal. Harry had protested in the beginning, but after a visit from Jason Trask, he had let the issue slide. He had told Colleen that it was no big deal, that it wouldn't influence the outcome of the trial, and, in the end, maybe it hadn't. What *had* influenced the jury had been the lies offered on the witness stand, the rehearsed testimony painting a picture of a vicious, brutal man, and the fact that his own lawyer had obviously believed he was too guilty to deserve a defense. Harry Baker had done as much to convict his client as the district attorney had.

Three months later he paid for it. Sixteen years later Colleen was still paying for it.

Closing the scrapbook before reaching the photographs of Kate Edwards and Jason Trask, she pushed it away from her, gathered the copies of the *Observer*, and rose from the chair. She was about to toss the papers in the basket when a name in a corner article of the *Journal* on top caught her eye. Pulling the paper loose, she sank into the chair again and read the story. The column was full of harmless gossip and down-home flavor. The Isaacs boy was planning to show his new bull at the upcoming Rutherford County fair, where Miss Opal would likely add another slew of blue ribbons for pickles and apple butter to her extensive collection. Randy Hawkins was finally out of the hospital and recuperating back home after his unfortunate accident at work the middle of last month. Miss Eleanor had been waiting at his home upon his arrival with a basket of goodies and a *generous* check from the administrators at the plant. How fortunate the Hawkins family was to have such support.

Colleen leaned back in the chair. Miss Eleanor had to be Eleanor Trask, mother of Jason, wife of the ruthless old bastard himself, Rupert. Colleen could well imagine the woman who had helped give life to a man such as Jason— cold, with the same regal bearing, the same smug superiority, the same sense of entitlement. She had, after all, stood proudly by her son through his trial and had loudly, scornfully, and savagely maligned Kate Edwards to anyone who would listen. She doubted that Eleanor Trask felt any remorse or regret for her son's actions, other than possibly wishing that he'd chosen some quiet little mouse who wouldn't have had the nerve to fight back.

So Randy Hawkins worked for the Trasks and had suffered an unfortunate accident on the job that had required nearly a month's hospitalization. He was home to recuperate, which meant he wasn't yet returning to work. After an injury requiring a month in the hospital, he might never return to work. He could be permanently disabled, maybe through his own carelessness . . . or maybe through no fault of his own.

The Trasks were so big on entitlement. Well, Randy Hawkins might be entitled to a hell of a lot more than a basket of goodies and a generous check. He *might* be entitled to payment for actual damages and, more importantly, for pain and suffering—payment that a determined attorney could secure for him. An attorney who'd handled more than her share of disability cases and had come away with little to no respect for management. An attorney who couldn't imagine a company she would like more to take to court than Jason Trask's. An attorney like *her*.

Laying the paper aside, she pulled the basket closer and retrieved the last month's *Journal*s. Maybe it was time for a visit to Fall River. Even if Randy Hawkins's story amounted to nothing, it wouldn't be a wasted trip. It was pretty in the mountains this time of year. She would find a quaint little place to stay, would enjoy the scenery and being away from the city for a while.

And if Randy Hawkins's unfortunate accident held promise? So much the better.

Tucker stepped out of the tub, shivering and blue, and reached for the towel on the bed. His uncle had told him once that the water in the Ozarks remained a constant fifty-eight degrees year-round, which was fine in the middle of a hot July day. It wasn't so comfortable on a chilly October evening.

He rubbed the towel over his skin, chasing away the chill. He could have taken the time to build a fire and heat a couple of kettles of water to warm his bath, but he hadn't wanted to bother. After sixteen years in prison, he'd gotten used to minor physical discomforts.

Someday he would like a chance to grow used to a few physical luxuries—a decent house. A comfortable bed. Central heat and air. A long, leisurely shower with hot water on demand. The easy, lazy pleasure of a woman.

He'd never had it lazy. The little girl down in the French Quarter had been eager. Amy, in the few times they'd done the deed, had endured it only to please him. That left only Nolie down in Little Rock, who had been easy but never lazy. She had preferred it fast and hard, and when it was over, she'd wanted it again, faster and harder. She'd had no use for taking it slow.

Kate Edwards moved like a woman who would like it slow.

Thought of her made the muscles in his jaw tighten. He wished she hadn't shown up this afternoon, wished she had never set foot out here. Long after she'd left, he had kept seeing her eyes and the rage that darkened them. He kept hearing the utter lifelessness of her voice when she'd repeated Trasks' version of her assault. *I made him tear my clothes and hit me and hurt me. I wanted it rough, you see.*

And Trask had given her *rough*. Why had the bastard done it? Had it made him feel powerful to use his greater strength against someone as slender and powerless as Kate?

Too bad she hadn't had her little gun then. With her injuries, surely no jury would have convicted her for blowing Trask away, even if her victim *was* a hotshot, all-important Trask. She could have saved herself and her sister a lot of heartache and Tucker a lot of trouble.

He got dressed in clean jeans and a T-shirt, then ran a comb through his hair. He was going into town to talk to Ben. The old man had to explain exactly what it was he wanted, or Tucker was going to wash his hands of the whole mess. He didn't need this kind of hassle in his life, and he sure as hell didn't need Kate Edwards.

Grabbing a jacket from the hook beside the door, he went outside to the truck. His headlights picking out the way in the deepening night, he began the long drive into town. Some people would consider plenty of places along the road downright spooky. For a person who was the slightest bit skittish, it was easy to imagine that evil lurked in the shadows. Kate was skittish. Had she been uneasy the first time she'd driven the road, or had it seemed fitting, under the circumstances, that her destination wasn't a pleasant drive away?

Probably the latter. Since Trask had gotten his hands on her, Tucker doubted that she'd found much pleasure in anything.

Reaching the town limits, he slowed the truck and turned

onto the first road on the right. Like his own road, it was dirt with an occasional sprinkling of gravel. Unlike his own, it lay entirely within Fall River town limits. Since no one important lived along its three-mile length—only the town's poor and most of its black residents—the powers that be saw no reason to expend the time or money to pave it.

The truck bumped over an abandoned railroad track, then Tucker passed a shut-down general store bearing a faded advertisement for chewing tobacco. His destination was the third house on the left past the store. He had never been there before, but old Ben had given him the directions, just in case he someday needed them.

Would the old man be surprised that someday had arrived?

The house sat fifteen feet off the road, a neat little box with a front porch, a picket fence in need of paint, a small yard, and plentiful flower beds. It was probably the best-kept house on the block, in good repair because old Ben wouldn't have it any other way.

Tucker pulled into the narrow driveway that ran right up to the side of the porch and shut off the motor. He didn't want to get out. He just wanted to go back home, to go back to his life the way it was a week ago, when everyone had kept their distance and he had kept to himself.

Reluctantly he climbed out of the truck, opened the low gate that allowed entry into the yard, and went up to the glass-paned front door. He stood there a moment, then knocked twice on the wooden jamb.

There was a response from inside, a distant call of indistinct words. He waited a long time before the porch light came on, accompanied by the sound of the lock being twisted. When the door swung open, his friend greeted him as if he'd been expecting him. "Come in, Tucker, come in. Have a seat."

Ducking his head to clear the door, he stepped inside and found himself in the living room. The ceiling was low, only an inch or so higher than he was tall, which helped contribute to the uncomfortable warmth. Heat rising from the gas stove in the corner didn't have far to go before it was turned back to the floor.

Tucker removed his jacket before taking a seat in the nearest armchair. The sofa and matching chair were beige, the glider wood. The tables were lacquered, and the lamps were fringed. There was lace everywhere—inexpensive panels over white roll-up shades at the windows, doilies on the backs and arms of the sofa and chairs, and runners on the tables, across the console television, and hanging over the edges of the shelves.

Leaning his cane against the wall, Ben settled himself into the glider and reached for the glasses sitting on a TV tray alongside the chair. He fitted the curved pieces over his ears, adjusted the bridge across his nose, then gave Tucker a broad smile. "What brings you out on a Saturday evening?"

"Like you don't know, old man."

Ben nodded, an action that set the entire upper portion of his body in motion. "You met Kate. Well?"

"Why did you send her to me?"

"I believed you could help her."

"Help her how?"

"She told you want she wants?"

"She wants me to kill a man for her."

Ben shook his head. "She wants peace."

"She's not going to find it in Trask's death."

"Are you sure about that?" Ignoring Tucker's surprised

stare, the old man continued. "When someone has harmed you the way Jason Trask has harmed Kate, I imagine you could find a great deal of peace knowing that he was dead."

Tucker shifted uncomfortably. "You know what he did to her?"

"Everyone in the county knows what he did to her and in great detail. There surely has to be a place in hell for a man like that."

Tucker glanced at the TV tray and the Bible lying there. Its leather cover was worn from frequent handling, and the stamping that read Holy Bible, King James Version, had lost most of its gold. "So you want me to help send him there. You want me to kill him for her."

Ben pointed to the Bible with a bony finger that trembled. "The Word says 'Thou shalt not kill.'"

"I don't care what the Bible says. What do *you* say?"

"I want you to help her."

Frustration made Tucker's voice taut when he responded. "By killing the guy? By not killing him? By stopping her from killing him? What is it you want from me, old man?"

Ben leaned his head back, and his eyes drifted shut. "I want you to do what's right. You have to decide for yourself what that is."

"What if I decide that 'right' is taking her money and leaving her high and dry?" he asked derisively.

Ben gave him a long, level look. "You're not a thief, Tucker. You never have been. If you choose not to help her, if you choose not to do this for me, that's your right. But I know you. You won't rob her blind while she's counting on you."

Because deep inside Tucker knew he was right, his scowl was tinged with resentment. "No one counts on me for nothing, old man," he disagreed, but Ben immediately disputed that.

"I do. Now Kate does." Abruptly his friend laughed. "It's not entirely comfortable, is it—having two people depending on you to do what's right?"

Not comfortable at all. Aloud, though, Tucker chastised Ben. "You should know better at your age than to trust someone like me."

"Why is that? Because you grew up poor? Because you never knew who your daddy was? Because your mama was never much of a mama? Because you never had any of the advantages but all of the disadvantages?"

"Because I'm an ex-con. I spent damned near half my life in prison for killing a man."

"Jason Trask has everything you never had—money, a mother who adored him, a father who kept him out of trouble. Nobody ever called him trash, nobody ever looked down on him, and look how he turned out. He likes to hurt women, and if they don't take it quietly, he makes their lives pure misery. You think a little thing like a trial stopped him?" He gave a shake of his head. "Ask Kate about the phone calls. Ask her about the threats."

Threats. Was that why she found it necessary to keep a gun within reach at all times?

Tucker's scowl deepened as he rose from the chair. He didn't want to ask Kate about anything. Hell, he didn't even want to see her again . . . but he would. Damn the old man, he would see her, ask her, try to help her.

"Where are you going?" Ben asked as he headed for the door.

"Home." He hoped it was true, hoped that when he reached the highway, he wasn't tempted to turn right and go into town. He hoped he didn't stop at the first pay phone he came to and look in the telephone book to see if she was listed. As jittery as she was—and if Ben was right about her getting threatening phone calls—she probably wasn't. Maybe, for a single woman living alone, her number had always been unlisted . . . but maybe not. Maybe this mess had started after the last phone book had been published. Maybe her number was newly changed, but her address was the same.

He opened the door, then looked back. Ben was using the cane to pull himself slowly to his feet. "Come back sometime when you're not in such a hurry. Maybe I'll cook for you."

Tucker's only response was a tight nod.

"She lives on Elm Street between Washington and Jefferson. It's a yellow house."

Where she lived wasn't important, Tucker reminded himself as he pulled his jacket on. He wasn't going over there. He wasn't going to ask her any more questions, wasn't going to spend one more moment tonight even thinking about her.

He started to walk out, then looked back once more. "The next time you want a favor from someone, forget that you know me."

As he closed the door behind him, he heard the quiet sound of Ben's laughter.

Getting into his truck, he headed back toward the highway. If he went straight home, he could eat a sandwich and be in bed by nine o'clock. Or he could drive through Fall River and have dinner at the café on the other side of town.

What he would really like to do, he decided as he approached the stop sign, was go to the bar over on McKinley Street. Dim lights, smoke in the air, loud music on the jukebox, and all the ice-cold beer he could handle. Sounded like a winner . . . except for the small fact that frequenting an establishment where alcohol was sold would be a violation of his parole. Besides, he had beer at home. He didn't need to waste his time or money drinking in a bar.

He brought the truck to a complete stop at the intersection and looked left, then right. To the left the road curved out of sight almost immediately, winding its way up into the hills. To the right it became Main Street. Down that way was traffic, life, people going out to dinner or a movie, to one of the bars or a friend's house.

Down that way was Kate Edwards.

Muttering a curse, he turned left, his tires spinning in the soft dirt before finding traction on the pavement. The rear tires squealed as he accelerated to a speed just above safe, then squealed again as he slowed down, made a tight U-turn, and headed back toward town. It wasn't the smartest idea he'd ever had, but, hey, no one had ever accused a Caldwell of being smart. No, if he were smart he would never have been in prison, he wouldn't be here in Fall River, living like some sort of outcast, and he wouldn't be eternally frustrated from trying to deal with the old man. He wouldn't know Kate Edwards from the man in the moon, wouldn't have any interest in her life or Jason Trask's, and, most importantly, he wouldn't be about to get himself into a mess that he just might not be able to get out of.

If he were smart.

There had been a time when Travis McMaster had relished working Saturday nights. He'd been younger then, more gung-ho, fresh out of college and the academy and eager for action. Saturday nights were busy nights. A cop could see just about anything.

Then he'd gotten married, and Cherie had put an end to

those regular Saturday nights. She had found going out to dinner, to a party or a club, much more enjoyable than sitting home alone. For the four years they'd been married, he had tried to adjust his schedule to hers, but there toward the end, he'd gone back to his Saturday night shifts while she'd gone out on her Saturday night dates with other men.

Now he worked weekends again, never scheduling himself but coming in to the office or going out on patrol when he wanted. It had been a Saturday evening more than six months ago when Kate had called him, nearly hysterical and barely able to talk, thanks to the broken jaw. It had been another Saturday, exactly four weeks ago, that she had called again, hysterical again, panicked by Jason's call and terrified by her inability to locate her sister.

Travis leaned back in his chair and gazed at the wanted posters on the bulletin board. Four weeks. Kerry was still hospitalized and might never recover. Kate might never recover, either. Dealing with the trauma of her own rape had been nothing compared to the guilt she'd suffered over Kerry's. Jason, damn his soul, felt no guilt. He hadn't let the incidents of the last six months affect his life in any way. He had done nothing more than what he'd always done—taken what he wanted—so why should he feel guilty?

With a glance at the clock on the wall, he got to his feet, took his jacket from the coat tree, and went out to the dispatcher's desk. "I'm going home, Wally. If anything comes up, you can reach me there."

The dispatcher acknowledged him with a nod. Travis didn't bother to tell him that he wasn't going straight home. Everyone in the department knew that he went by Kate's house a dozen times a day and always the last thing at night. He didn't usually go in, especially if it was late, but he always checked to make sure that everything appeared okay.

He was about to pull out of the parking lot when two figures on the sidewalk alongside the bank caught his attention. The woman's back was to him, so he couldn't identify her, but the man's face was clearly lit by the nearby streetlamp. Jason Trask was smiling as if he didn't have a care in the world, gazing down at her as if she were the perfect princess to his Prince Charming.

He'd made his ex-wife feel that way. Kate had felt it, too, for a while, until she'd made the wrong choice, and he had punished her for it. It would happen again. Trask's temper would explode, and some unfortunate women would pay—with pain, like his ex. With her reputation, like Kate. Maybe with her sanity, like Kerry. It might be this woman, maybe the next, but it *would* happen. He would give ten years off his life to be able to bring Jason down before anyone else got hurt.

Travis was still watching when Jason raised his head, saw him, and smiled. It was a chilling, soulless gesture that made Travis sick. With a curse, he pulled out of the parking lot, drove down Lincoln, then turned onto Elm.

Slowing to a bare crawl, Travis studied the green pickup parked one house down from Kate's. He hadn't seen it often, but, like any good cop, he had a tendency to remember vehicles . . . especially ones that belonged to local excons.

What the hell was Tucker Caldwell doing in this neighborhood? Whatever he was up to, it was no good. He was standing underneath a tall, fat oak whose branches spread wide before dipping low over the ground, standing there as if accustomed to the shadows, motionless and intent, staring at Kate's house.

With a surge of anger, Travis brought the Explorer to a stop, left the motor running and the door open, and crossed the pavement to the curb. Caldwell was so absorbed that he didn't hear Travis's approach, didn't have a clue that he was no longer alone until he felt the cool tap of the baton between his shoulder blades. "Do me a favor," Travis said, his voice quiet, his tone steely. "Get your hands up, arms away from your body."

Caldwell obeyed with just the right degree of speed—no sudden moves, but not slow enough to antagonize an impatient cop. Sixteen years in prison and a lifetime of trouble before that had taught him well.

"Take two steps back. Step off the curb, then walk backwards until you reach my truck."

Caldwell did so.

"Face the truck, put your hands on the hood, then take two steps back with your feet apart." When that was accomplished, Travis patted him down, finding nothing but a set of car keys and a ten-dollar bill folded in half. He laid both items on the hood, securing the bill under the keys, then moved to the side of the truck so he could face him. "What are you doing here?"

For a moment Caldwell's expression wavered between belligerence and pure misery before he wiped it clean and fixed his gaze on the keys on the hood. He remained silent for a long time, his muscles taut as if he were thinking about fleeing. Then, just as Travis was about to reach for the handcuffs tucked into his waistband in back, Caldwell exhaled and grudgingly answered, "I came to see Kate."

"You know Kate?" he asked skeptically. In the last six months, Kate had avoided contact with every man in town except him. She was afraid of every man in town, and that would go double for a man like Caldwell.

"We've met."

"How? Where? When?"

Caldwell stared harder at the hood and didn't respond.

"You don't want to answer, fine. I'll ask Kate." He started to move around the open door, but paused just a moment. "Don't try to leave, Caldwell. If you do, I'll have to shoot you, and I'm a damned good shot."

After reaching for the microphone, Travis called the dispatcher and asked him to call Kate at home. "Tell her I'm out front. Tell her to come out and talk to me." It wouldn't take Wally but a minute to make the call, wouldn't take Kate more than a minute or two to come out here and verify what Travis already knew, that there was no reason in hell for Caldwell to be here. Then, instead of going home, Travis would have to return to the police department with a prisoner in tow, where he would have to try to find out why the bastard was hanging around here. Had he heard the talk about Kate and figured she was just his type? Had he thought he could do whatever he wanted with her and, thanks to Trask, no one would care? If so, he'd guessed wrong.

Across the yard, the front door of Kate's house opened and she stepped outside. Travis watched Caldwell. His prisoner heard the door close—the muscles in his jaw tightened and the fingers of his right hand curled under on the hood—but he refused to look in her direction. He didn't watch her approach with the relief of an innocent man. Instead, he merely stared more intently at the keys as if he'd never seen such a thing before.

Just before she reached the sidewalk, Kate's steps slowed until she was barely moving. She looked from Travis to Caldwell, then back again, her expression bewildered and surprised. Then, with a deep breath and a sudden shudder, she picked up the pace, coming to stand on the opposite side of the truck from Travis. "Gee," she began, her voice soft, her tone wry, "is this why I never have guests anymore? You put them all through a search and the third degree before they make it to the door?"

"This guy was standing out here in the shadows watching your house. He says he was coming to see you. Do you know him?"

She looked at Caldwell, and some expression too faint to identify—guilt? shame? embarrassment?—came into her eyes. "Yes, I do," she said at last.

Travis stared at her, words failing him. There were a dozen questions he wanted to ask. How could she have met Caldwell when she went nowhere and did nothing, when she spent her days at work and her evenings locked up safely inside her house? Why would she want anything to do with him when she knew he was a murderer, nothing but trouble from the start? What could they possibly have in common . . . besides the fact he'd lived his entire life with the derision, the contempt, and the scorn that Kate had found herself enduring lately? Jeez, was that it? People treated her like trash, so she might as well shoot to hell whatever was left of her reputation and prove them right . . . and what better way to do that than taking up with Tucker Caldwell?

"Are you crazy, Kate?" he asked once the words would come. "This guy . . . He's an *ex-con*, Kate."

"And what was it you said to me when he moved here? Something about having served his time. Having paid his debt." She shivered, and he realized that she'd come out without a jacket. "It's too cold to stand out here for a debate. Are you arresting him?"

"No." But he offered the response reluctantly.

"Thanks for checking up on me. I'll talk to you later." Kate moved away from the truck, going to stand on the curb. After a moment's hesitation, Caldwell took his money and keys and he, too, moved to the curb, standing a healthy six or seven feet from her.

Travis remained where he was, until Kate spoke again, her tone final. "Good night, Travis."

Muttering a curse, he climbed into the truck, slammed the door, and slowly drove away. When he looked in his rearview mirror at the end of the block, they were still standing exactly where he'd left them. He glanced at the lighted numerals on the Explorer's clock. It wasn't even eight-thirty yet—too early to go home. There was plenty of evening left for a leisurely patrol. Plenty of evening for making sure everything was exactly the way it should be.

Hugging herself to retain some small measure of body heat, Kate let her gaze settle on her house while her attention locked in on everything else around her. The street was quiet. Though there were lights on in every house, hers included, there was no activity, no one out and about. For all the life around her now, it could as easily be three in the morning as eight-something in the evening.

From the corner of her eye, she saw Tucker shift. Travis's message, passed on by Wally Haynes, had been enough to stir her curiosity, but to walk outside and find Tucker Caldwell with him . . . Her first impulse had been to ask immediately why he was there. Curiosity, though, had quickly given way to embarrassment. Tucker had looked so unsettled leaning there on the hood of the truck—angered, frustrated, ashamed, and resentful, all at once. And why shouldn't he have been? He'd done nothing wrong, and yet Travis—the most fair-minded man she'd ever known—had automatically suspected that he had. He had immediately assumed that Tucker couldn't possibly have a legitimate reason for being in this neighborhood.

It was because of his concern for *her*. Although he'd never said anything, Travis was afraid that some quiet night, Jason's friends would discover that the satisfaction was gone from their phone calls, that simply harassing her from a distance wasn't enough anymore. He was afraid that they might come over to play out the game in person, face-to-face, tormentor to victim. That was why he'd recommended the alarm system, why he'd insisted that she arm herself, why he'd chosen the gun and taught her to use it. Truth be told, she shared the same fear. That was why she had *let* him teach her. That was why she practiced regularly.

But that didn't make her feel any better that Tucker had been harassed by the police chief simply for coming to her house.

Turning to face him, she brushed a strand of hair from her face. "I can't stay out here. Do you want to come in?"

He hesitated before offering a noncommittal shrug. He didn't want to be here. Even before Travis had come along, he had probably wished that he was anywhere but here. So why had he come?

Without looking to see whether he followed, she retraced her path across the yard, her shoes leaving shimmering trails in the dew. After opening the door, she finally glanced back as she turned to hold it open. He was coming up the steps, looking uncomfortable and ill at ease. Well, he couldn't possibly be any more uncomfortable with being inside her house than she was with having him there. No man but Travis had walked through this door in the last six months. If this tight feeling in her chest was anything to judge by, she might not be able to endure having Tucker there. She might feel too trapped, too panicked . . . but not unless she let herself. She could handle this. She could force herself to get through it, and then the next time wouldn't be so hard.

He entered the house, moving the few feet down the hall to the living room. Drawing a deep breath, Kate went inside, too, closing the door behind her—but not locking it. Clasping her hands together, she joined him in the living room, where he stood in the middle of the room, obviously at a loss.

"How did you find out where I lived?" she asked, taking up a place near the wide door, as if she always stood at the closest exit while entertaining guests.

"The old man told me."

"I wasn't aware that he knew."

"Old Ben makes it his business to know things," Tucker said, a sardonic twist to his mouth.

She nodded in vague response while searching for a polite way to ask why he had come here. Before she found it, though, he was speaking again.

"How do you know Ben?"

"He's lived in Fall River all my life. He used to work for my grandfather. When Grandpa's company went under, he and Mr. James remained friends. They went fishing together."

"How many other fishing buddies did your grandfather have?"

"I don't know. A half dozen."

"But old Ben was the only one you asked to find you a hired killer, wasn't he?"

Her fingertips were starting to ache from pressing them together. Deliberately she forced her hands apart, then slid them into the pockets of her jeans. It felt odd, standing in her house with a man, having her hands in her pockets with no gun. Shutting herself away the way she had was no good, Travis had often warned. Avoiding all men, blaming them all for the actions of a few, wasn't healthy, he'd insisted. But it certainly felt safer than this.

"Yes. Mr. James was the only one I asked."

"Why? Because he's black? Because black people are more likely to know about this sort of thing than white folks are?"

"Because my grandfather always said he was a man you could trust. Because he makes it his business to know things." She hesitated, then finished. "Because he knew *you*." When no response came, she gestured toward the furniture around him. "Have a seat."

He shook his head. Was he too uncomfortable to sit, or did he choose to stand because she was still standing? She would take a seat if she could, if she could bring herself to move more than ten feet from the safety of the front door.

"After what happened . . ." The hesitance in his voice told her exactly what he meant by "what" and made her gaze connect with his face. He was looking away, though, at anything besides her. "Do you ever see Trask? Do you ever talk to him?"

"I see him around town from time to time. Fall River is small. It's impossible to avoid someone completely." Not that it couldn't be done. Her friends had done a pretty thorough job of avoiding her after the trial. Her mother had managed, too. But she still ran into Jason, going about his easy, privileged life, satisfied, still smug as ever, and with virtually every single woman in town lined up for dates. "I haven't talked to him since the night he called to tell me what he'd done to Kerry."

"Has he threatened you?"

She gave him a sharp look, then, unable to stand still any longer, moved to the bay window at the front of the room. Framed with glass on three sides and thickly padded on the seat, it had long been one of her favorite places in the house. Now she could rarely bring herself to sit there. Even with heavy drapes, glass provided no protection. It could be broken so easily, allowing access to her house, to her.

Slowly she turned and lowered her weight to the bench. She sat on the edge, spine straight, testing to see if she could remain there. It wasn't comfortable. The window seat wasn't made for sitting rigidly but rather for snuggling in among the dozen or more pillows scattered around, but *she* couldn't snuggle. Not with thin panes of glass behind her and Tucker Caldwell in front.

At last she answered his question, her tone flat. "No. Jason hasn't threatened me since his trial."

"But?"

"His friends call me. They don't want me to forget what he did. They tell me what they would like to do, what they intend to do when the time is right."

"Why doesn't your cop friend do something about it?"

"He's tried. He wants me to take the tapes of the calls to a judge to ask for a restraining order."

"Why don't you?"

"I tried the legal route before. It didn't work. Jason's lawyers transformed him from the accused into the innocent victim. If I go back to court, Judge Hampton, an old and dear friend of the Trask family, will insist on hearing the case himself, just as he insisted on hearing the rape case. It will be worse than doing nothing, because he'll tell them that what they're doing is perfectly all right, that they're safe under the law. If that happens, if they have that bastard's blessing, God only knows what they'll do next."

Tucker started walking toward her, and the muscles in her legs clenched. Animals reacted in two ways to a threat: flight or fight. Run and hide, or stay and stand up to the danger. Whatever fighting instincts that hadn't been beaten out of her on Jason's kitchen floor had withered away in the Rutherford County Courthouse. All she'd done since then—all she wanted to do now—was run and hide, but she forced herself to remain utterly motionless. When he sat down on a hassock a half dozen feet away, she allowed herself one small sigh of relief.

"You think Trask is behind his buddies' calls."

She nodded.

"And you think killing him will stop them."

Another nod, answered almost immediately by the negative shake of his head. "Even if you have an alibi, Kate, they'll blame you. They'll want to make you pay, and they'll see it as justice."

Ben James had brought up the same point, but she had disagreed. If she had an airtight alibi, if she could prove that she couldn't possibly have killed Jason, no matter how much they hated such a conclusion, his family and friends would have to accept it. But what if they didn't? What if Tucker and Ben were right? What if killing Jason further inflamed his pals? What if they decided to destroy her?

"It won't happen," she insisted. "I've known these men all my life. They're bullies, no denying, but Jason's their leader. Without him to tell them what to do or how to do it, they're harmless. Jason is the evil one. He's the one who matters. He's the one who has to be destroyed."

Tucker stared at her for a moment, frustration with her stubbornness evident on his face. Then, abruptly, he got to his feet and started toward the door. "I've got to go," he muttered.

She watched until he passed through the doorway and disappeared. A moment later the front door opened and closed, and, through the glass, she heard the sound of his footsteps on the porch. Soon after, quiet settled once more over the house, even as unsettling shivers tickled down her spine. She stood up, moving quickly away from the window and the vulnerability it represented, going to the door to secure the locks and reset the alarm. When the bell chimed just as she reached the door, she gave a startled cry, then forced herself to breathe deeply.

Travis had installed a new peephole in the door months ago, one with an oversize lens that didn't require her to go closer than five feet to see who stood on her porch. Forcing her gaze from the unsecured locks to the lens, she sighed with relief when she recognized her visitor, then with frustration because she knew the purpose of his visit.

Opening the door, she invited Travis in with no more than the wave of a hand. She realized she didn't have to tell him that Tucker had just left when she saw the position he'd taken up down the street. His truck must have been the first thing Tucker had seen when he'd stepped out a moment ago, probably convincing him that he would never want to come back here again.

Maybe she was simply lonely after so many months with no one's friendship but Travis's, but some foolish part of her thought that no more visits from Tucker might be a thing to regret.

"I'm not here to tell you that Tucker Caldwell has been nothing but trouble from the day he was born," Travis said in place of a greeting. "I'm not going to remind you that he killed a man, that he spent nearly half his life in prison for it. I know you know that."

"Everyone who lives in Rutherford County knows it."

"Why was he here, Kate?"

"He came to see me."

"You don't *see* men, Kate, and you've *never* seen men like him. What did he want?"

"It was just a visit, Travis. No need to make such a big deal over it."

He ran his fingers through his hair. "Just a visit. Right. You haven't had 'just a visit' with anyone for six months, and now suddenly you've taken up with an ex-con like Caldwell. How the hell did you manage to even meet him?"

"Through Mr. James."

"Ben James? Your granddad's old friend set you up with a convicted murderer? *Why?*"

Kate knew what Travis most likely suspected—that she'd been treated so badly by so many people that she found it easier to relate to someone equally despised and scorned. It wouldn't take much, though, to turn his thoughts in another direction, to lead him to a connection between her hatred of Jason Trask and Tucker's prison sentence for murder. There was a time when Travis never would have believed that she was capable of taking a life, but now she doubted that he would have much trouble. If she allowed such a thought now, when Tucker did the job, together they would be Travis's first suspects. He would make a case against them, and when he made a case, it usually stuck— Jason being the notable exception, of course. He could ruin all her lovely plans . . . unless she steered him in another direction.

She offered him a cool smile. "Do you know how many places I can go in this town without running into someone who believes everything the Trasks have said about me? They believed them at school. They believed them at church. Travis, my own father believed it all. He *believed* that his little girl had grown into some sort of warped, twisted slut."

"And hanging out with Caldwell will just convince those people that they're right, that you're no good."

"Maybe they *are* right. Maybe I *am* trash." Her smile wavered, then disappeared. "Tucker has enough problems of his own. He doesn't care about mine. He doesn't look at me the way everyone else looks at me."

"Not everyone. There are plenty of people who believe you told the truth, people who have known all along that you were the victim in this whole mess."

"Yes, people who are afraid to say so because they're afraid of the Trasks, because they're afraid to take a stand. I get derision and disgust from three-fourths of the town, and silent pity from the rest." She drew a calming breath. "Tucker doesn't look at me and see Jason's vile accuser, the Edwards slut who gets off on pain, or poor Kate, another of the Trasks' victims. None of that means anything to him." Truthfully, she wasn't sure Tucker saw her as anything other than an annoyance, and a source of some seriously needed income.

"If it's acceptance you're looking for—"

She interrupted, her voice weary. "I'm not looking for anything. Mr. James introduced us, we talked, end of story."

He gave her a long troubled look, and when he finally spoke, his voice was also heavy with weariness. "Don't do anything that you'll live to regret, Kate."

"I won't."

With a grim nod as his only farewell, Travis left. She

locked up, shut off the lights and climbed the stairs to her bedroom. Her last words to Travis had been God's honest truth. She would never regret being responsible for Jason's death. He had committed a great many wrongs, a great many unforgivable sins, and the only thing that was *right* was that he be punished for them. No, she had been entirely truthful with Travis. She would never regret being the one to stop Jason. She would never regret being responsible for his death.

Chapter Four

Rain was falling in Tulsa, a chilly winter-was-on-the-way sort of rain. Mariana Trask stood in her darkened living room, gazing out the glass doors that led to the balcony, a knitted throw around her shoulders and a glass of bourbon in one hand. Somewhere out there in the darkness lay the Arkansas River. During the day she could see it, brown, sluggish, as much sand as water until the floods came. Tonight through rain-stained glass, it was indistinguishable.

Behind her the stereo was on, a CD filling the air with heartsick, homesick, crying-in-your-beer music. It was corny sometimes, depressing always. She listened to it when she'd had more of this city than she could stand, when the need to go home tugged strongly enough to hurt.

She had been living in this cramped apartment in this strange place for five months, and not a day had gone by that she hadn't wished she was back in Fall River again. For the last four months she had called home daily, just to hear her mother's voice and see how she was feeling. On Patricia Wilson's good days, the calls were a source of comfort to Mariana. On her bad days, they simply added to Mariana's despair—and the bad days had been coming more frequently, it seemed.

In the beginning, she hadn't called home at all. She had

wanted to, had wanted it so badly that she was sick with it, but she hadn't been able to face her mother's inevitable confusion and disappointment. Eventually, though, she had faced Patricia's questions. *Why did you run away? Why didn't you testify at Jason's trial? Why didn't you tell the court what you'd seen? Why didn't you fight him? Why did you let him win yet again? Why didn't you help that sweet Kate Edwards?*

She'd had only one answer to the questions: fear. She had run because she was afraid. She had failed to appear at Jason's trial because he had threatened her. She hadn't fought him because, for the entire ten years of their marriage, they had fought and he had always, *always* beaten her. She had let him win yet again because he had offered her two options: testify and be destroyed, or disappear and take a nice little bit of Trask money with her. She was no fool.

As for helping Kate Edwards . . . She had tried to do that weeks before the rape. As soon as she'd heard that Kate was dating Jason, that his car had been parked overnight in Kate's driveway, she had gone to the other woman's house. She had warned Kate about Jason's temper, about his anger at being told no, about his penchant for hitting and hurting people weaker than he was. But Kate hadn't believed her. She had looked at her with such condescension, Jason's newest love pitying his old rejected wife. She had attributed Mariana's accusations to the divorce settlement so heavily weighted in Jason's favor, had actually suggested that Mariana forget about trying to get back at her ex-husband and get on with her own life.

After that, Mariana hadn't been much interested in helping Kate, especially when it meant putting herself on the line. Still, she regretted leaving. She regretted helping free

Jason so he could continue ruining everyone's lives. Until the day she died, she would regret what he'd done to Kerry Edwards.

Finishing the last of the bourbon, she turned to survey the apartment. While it was nice enough—certainly a step up from her mother's little frame house where she'd lived after the divorce—it was nothing compared to the twelve-room showplace she had shared with Jason. She had never known such luxury, paid for with such terror. A bath towel on the floor had been deserving of a slap. Wearing red when he wanted her in black had been worth getting punched. The mistaken impression that she was flirting with another man had earned her exactly what Kate had gotten that night on the kitchen floor.

At least in this pretty little apartment, no one threatened her. No one had ever hurt her. But no one cared about her, either. She was lonely and unhappy, and all she wanted was to go home, even though she had promised Jason she wouldn't. He would be angry and full of threats, but, as she'd said, she was no fool. She was going back with protection in the form of cassette tapes, those nifty miniature ones that fit into recorders small enough to slip into a handbag or a pocket. Those unobtrusive little jobs that no one ever noticed, that made such fine, clear recordings. She didn't have many of them, only five, and not one of them ran more than twenty minutes, but that was enough. Twenty minutes had been long enough for Jason to threaten a witness in his upcoming rape trial. It had been long enough for him to bribe that witness with more money than she'd ever seen before. It had been long enough for him to admit that he'd raped Kate, just as he had often raped Mariana.

It would be more than enough to interest the district attorney, to make possible a new trial, to make right the things that had gone so terribly wrong.

Feeling a weight lift from her shoulders, she slowly smiled. Yes, she would go home. Tomorrow she would start packing, and first thing Monday morning she would give notice on the apartment. She would lose the money she'd paid as a security deposit, but it was Jason's money. It was fitting that it should be lost in an effort to make his life miserable.

Feeling more alive than she had in five long, dark months, she refilled her glass and made a silent toast. To herself, to her mother, and to Jason damn-his-black-heart Trask. Might he rot in hell.

Sunday morning found Tucker still in bed, staring up at the ceiling. He should have been up and working hours ago, but he hadn't yet solved the problem of raising the framing by himself. After the night he'd just had, he hadn't given it much thought beyond wondering whether he should even bother.

He had come straight home from Kate's house, watching his rearview mirror for the first couple of miles for the flash of the cop's lights. When he'd rounded the curve past the turn for old Ben's house, he had relaxed a little, but the tension hadn't completely disappeared until he'd reached the ditch that had swallowed up the road. Finally, back home on his uncle's place, he'd felt safe.

It had happened before—getting harassed by the cops, being questioned for no reason other than who he was, because he didn't belong in their safe little neighborhoods. When he was a kid, he'd gotten rousted on a regular basis, but he hadn't really much cared. It had been a game to him then.

It wasn't a game anymore. He'd lived his life locked up,

and he'd sworn on every one of the six thousand or so nights that, once he was out, he was never going back. He'd sworn it on the only thing left him: his life.

If he wasn't careful, Kate Edwards was going to make a liar of him, and that was something he couldn't risk, not even for old Ben. He was out of prison on parole. A suspicious cop wouldn't have to look far to find some excuse for sending him back, and if he went back on a parole violation, he would have to serve out the rest of his sentence day for day. Nine long years. It might as well be a death sentence.

From outside the sound of an engine filtered into his consciousness. He slid from the bed and moved close enough to the front window to see but not be seen. Maybe it was the cop, out here to offer a friendly warning backed up with a badge and a gun. But it was Kate, he realized, as her car came into sight. He would almost prefer the cop. Returning to the bed, he pulled on the jeans he'd discarded the previous night. He shoved his feet into his sneakers, then tugged a T-shirt over his head.

Although she had said that she would help with the framing this morning, he hadn't really thought she would show up. But there she was, getting out of the car, dressed in jeans, a T-shirt underneath an open flannel shirt, and sturdy hiking boots. Her hair was pulled back in a ponytail, and dark glasses protected her eyes until she pulled them off and turned her gaze toward the house.

He opened the back door and stepped out onto the steps. "Good morning."

Returning her greeting with no more than a nod, he moved down the steps. When he was on the ground and halfway between the house and her, he finally spoke. "You didn't have to come."

"I said I would."

"People say they'll do things all the time but never do."

She smiled tightly. "Not me."

If that was true, she was a rarity in his world. Then he smiled sardonically. His world right now included only two people: Kate and old Ben. She was, indeed, a rarity.

She came a few feet closer, then stopped. "About last night . . . Travis is a little overprotective of me," she said, her tone tentative, her words unsure, as if she were feeling her way through the explanation. "He had no way of knowing that I knew you. All he saw was someone in the shadows watching my house. His reaction was understandable."

He couldn't argue the point with her. If he'd been the cop, he probably wouldn't have shown as much restraint. He shouldn't have been there, and he sure as hell shouldn't have been standing beside that tree trying to convince himself to either walk up to her door or go home. But he'd still been embarrassed and resentful.

"It doesn't matter. I'm used to it."

She started to speak, then decided against it. Had she been about to point out that he hadn't acted as if he were used to it? Had she seen his discomfort, his uneasiness, his sick dread of what might happen next?

"He was parked outside when I left," he said, circling around her and walking to the truck, where he fastened a tool belt around his waist.

"I know. He came to the house."

"To warn you about me?"

She answered with a noncommittal shrug that, of course, meant yes. He would bet Jason Trask never got harassed for being in a neighborhood other than his own. The bastard had beaten and raped two women, one of them barely more than a kid, and yet he could go wherever he wanted and no one said a word to him, while Tucker, who had never hurt a woman in his life, got hassled the first time he ventured into the residential side of Fall River. What was wrong with this picture?

"Want some gloves?" he asked, reaching into the bed of the truck for two pairs, both cheap leather, both sized to fit his large hands. Her hands were much smaller, delicate, her fingers long. They didn't look as if they'd ever done any hard work. Lacking strength and bearing short, rounded nails, they probably hadn't been much help at all in fending off Trask. At least with fingernails, she could have clawed his damned eyes out.

Now she wanted to put a bullet right between those eyes.

He offered one pair of gloves, but she didn't take them. She was looking at him, edgy and afraid. Was it simply *his* touch she found repulsive, or had Trask left her afraid of all men?

Laying the gloves on the tailgate, he pulled his own on, then went to the foundation. Ideally, the framing would have been handled one wall at a time—assembled on the flat work surface of the subflooring, then lifted upright, slid into place, and nailed down before work was started on the next. But conditions here were far from ideal. He had put together the sections on the ground, each only a few feet from its destination. Setting them up would require effort. He hoped Kate was up to it.

When she joined him, she was sliding her hands into the oversize gloves and—he was surprised to see it—finding their fit cause for a smile. Her fingertips barely reached the middle of the long fingers, and she could have easily fitted both hands into one glove. They wouldn't be much help to her while working, but at least they would protect from splinters.

Working from opposite corners, they lifted the first wall at the top, tilted it upward until it was on end, then lifted it to the sill plate. He plumbed it, hammered in the first few nails so he could release his end, then secured the length of it and nailed a brace at his end. When he moved toward Kate to fasten a brace there, she moved away. The action grated on his nerves, but he said nothing. He simply finished, then joined her at one of the shorter end walls.

"How long are you planning to stay here?" she asked, her voice strained as they lifted the wall nearly three feet to the sill plate.

"I don't know. A year. Maybe two. Until my money runs out."

"Why build a house? Why not just rent a place in town?"

"Because then my money would run out a hell of a lot quicker. Besides, I don't want to live in town, and I doubt that anyone wants me there." He repeated the process—plumbing, nailing, bracing—then moved to her end. Even knowing what he was doing, she still retreated. He still found it frustrating. As soon as the brace was in place, he faced her from a safe distance away. "Why are you afraid of me?"

She didn't try to deny it, didn't offer excuses. Instead, she smiled breezily. "Sometimes I think I've already lived through the worst times in my life. Surely nothing that might happen to me in the future could be as bad or as frightening as what's already happened. Other times . . ." She shrugged. "I'm afraid of everyone."

"I've never hurt anyone."

She shrugged again and didn't point out that he had certainly done some damage to Jeffrey Henderson. "I don't claim that my fears are rational. Last night was the first time in six months that I've sat on that window seat in my living room. Telephone calls terrify me. I can't go out after dark. I meet people who used to be my friends with hostility. For weeks after it happened, I couldn't even cook dinner for myself."

"Why not?"

"Because it happened in the kitchen. In Jason's kitchen. I was trying to reach the back door, but he caught me and threw me to the floor. I tried to catch myself by grabbing the baker's rack, and it fell over. There were pots and pans and utensils all around me, all just a little bit out of my reach." Her smile was faint, unnatural. "There wasn't a knife in the bunch. If there had been, I would have cut his heart out right then and there."

It seemed a reasonable response to him. "A kitchen is full of weapons. You couldn't find anything?"

A flash of disappointment colored her eyes, then disappeared. "The floor in his kitchen is brick," she said flatly. "When he shoved me, I hit my head. I had a concussion. Before I could move again, he was on top of me, hitting me, tearing my clothes, forcing himself inside me. *No*, I couldn't find a weapon."

"I didn't mean—"

She turned away, cutting him off, leaving him feeling like a bastard. He hadn't meant to imply that somehow she'd been at fault, that, in a room like a kitchen, if she hadn't found something with which to defend herself, she hadn't been trying. But, obviously, she'd heard it before. Kitchens were well stocked. There were knives for stabbing, skillets for bashing skulls, stoves for burning, cleaning supplies for blinding. How frustrating had that been to Kate to know that help was just a drawer or a cabinet away, only a few feet out of her reach? How much more had that heightened Trask's enjoyment?

He moved around her, careful not to get too close, to secure the corner posts, then gestured for her to follow him to the opposite end. "Why do you stay in Fall River?" he asked, crouching to get a grip in the middle of the framing so he would bear most of its weight.

She mimicked his position, wrapping her hands in those ridiculously big gloves tightly around the wood. "It's my home."

"You have friends here?"

"Not anymore."

"You close to your family?"

Her mouth thinned, and her jaw tightened. "Not anymore."

"What happened with your job?"

She started lifting, and he followed suit, walking toward the house as the framing tilted onto the sole plate. Once it was upright, she asked, "What do you mean?"

"When you came here the other day, you said you were a teacher. Then you immediately changed that and said you were an administrator with the school board. Were you a teacher when it happened?"

"Yes. I taught first grade." She stared off into the distance for a moment before directing her gaze his way. "After the trial, the school board decided I wasn't fit to be around impressionable young children. They didn't fire me outright for fear I would sue, but they removed me from the classroom and stuck me in a little back office where they could keep an eye on me. They're hoping to make me miserable enough to quit, but I don't intend to give them that satisfaction." After a moment, she tapped the wood beneath her hands. "Are you ready?"

They finished that wall, then, before moving on, Tucker repeated his question. "So why do you stay here? Why don't you save yourself a lot of grief and get the hell out?"

"This is my home. I have as much right to live here as Jason Trask does."

He didn't understand it. If everything she'd said was true, the town didn't want her around almost as much as they didn't want *him*. The only reason he was in Fall River was because living at his uncle's place didn't cost him anything he didn't want to spend. With his parole officer's permission, he could move anywhere in the state, but he would have expenses—rent and utilities—and, as he'd learned in Little Rock, legitimate job opportunities for ex-cons like him were few and far between.

But Kate was different. She was bright. She had a college degree. She had potential. She *didn't* have a murder conviction in her past. She could go anywhere in the country and start over. She could live in any of a hundred thousand places where the Trask name meant nothing, where she would find the same acceptance and respect that she'd once known. She had no reason to stay in Fall River . . . except a burning desire for revenge.

A desire that she expected Tucker to satisfy for her. Considering everything he'd learned in the last few days, he almost regretted that he couldn't do it. He couldn't even pretend any longer. As soon as they were finished here, he had to tell her. He had to give her money back.

As they moved to the final wall, the breeze picked up from the west, bringing with it the scent of fall—crackling leaves, cleaner air, colder weather—and rain. The sky to the west had grown a hazy gray that streaked all the way to the ground in patches. With any luck, they would have the last wall in place before the rain came. The shower wouldn't last long, and once it was over, he could get started on the roof. Maybe he could hold off on telling Kate that he wasn't going to kill Trask until the trusses were in place, he thought with a humorless smile.

They had the last wall upright and more than two feet off the ground when she broke the silence between them. "How did it feel to kill that man?"

For a moment he froze, unable to move, then his muscles, trembling from the strain, demanded action. He slowly lifted his end six inches higher, settled it on the sill, then turned toward her. "It was the worst moment of my entire life."

"But you hated him." Her words were simple, her tone challenging.

Had he hated Jeffrey Henderson? Probably. The Hendersons had played the same role in Fayette that the Trasks still played in Fall River. They'd been the richest family, the most powerful. Jeffrey had been a hotshot jock, popular with the girls, the undisputed prince of Fayette. Like his cousin Jason, whatever Jeffrey wanted, he took, and no one told him no.

Except Amy. Like Tucker, she had grown up on the wrong side of town. Her mother had cleaned house for some of the more affluent families, while her father had tended their gardens. Amy had worked, too, as a waitress at the Dairy Barn, the most popular place in town for teenagers with nothing else to do. That was where she'd caught Jeffrey's attention. That was when Tucker had started hating him. "I didn't mean to kill him."

"But you did. You beat him to death." There was an odd hopefulness in her voice, asking for confirmation that he was as violent and brutal as rumor claimed.

He shook his head slowly. "I hit him, and he fell off a

ledge. I went down after him, waiting for him to get up so we could finish, but he didn't. His head was bent at an odd angle, and his eyes were open, but . . ." He remembered leaning over Henderson, sweat and blood in his own eyes, blurring his vision, and seeing such emptiness. He'd known the kid was dead, had felt it in the despair and the sick fear that filled his soul. He had known in that moment that he would never be the same again. He would never forget that look, that fear, that guilt. He would never be free of the memories or the sorrow.

With a shrug, he went on. "There was nothing there. They said later that the fall broke his neck. I panicked and ran."

"You left him there, knowing that he could still be alive, knowing that he could die before anyone found him." That faint hopefulness again. She wanted to believe that she'd hired herself a cold-blooded killer who could easily kill again. He wasn't sorry to disappoint her.

"There were other people around—my girlfriend, a couple of Jeffrey's buddies. They got help for him, but he was dead before the sheriff arrived." He hesitated. "There are people who have no regard at all for the lives of others. Trask is probably one of them. But you're not, and I'm not. Trust me, Kate. It's far easier to live with the knowledge that Jason is alive and unpunished than with the guilt of being responsible for his death."

Her expression was one of such disappointment that he felt like a bastard for putting it there. "You're not going to do it, are you?"

Grimly he shook his head. "I can't. I can't go back to prison, and I can't live with any more guilt. I have no doubt that Trask deserves to die, but I can't be the one to kill him."

She stood motionless, her gaze distant and bleak.

"You think you'll find peace with him dead, but it's not going to happen. If you go through with it, Kate, it'll destroy you."

For a long time he waited for some response from her, for argument or acceptance. When she simply continued to stare, he picked up his hammer, took out a handful of nails, and began hammering the frame to the sill. Once that was done and the braces wedged into place, she released her grip on the wood, ducked under the brace, and went to the opening for the door. It was a high step for her, more than two feet, but she managed it and walked inside, her footsteps hollow on the subflooring.

Tucker climbed up, too, standing in the doorway until he realized after one of her wary looks that he was blocking the easiest exit. Shoving his hands into his pockets, he moved farther into the room and watched as she made a slow circuit, stopping at each window, studying the scene outside. At the window on the opposite side of the doorway, she rested her hands on the sill and stared out. A glance out his own side showed what she saw: the ramshackle house, the woodpile weaving across the yard, the scarlet-and-gold forest, and the rain-darkened sky. The clouds were closer now, only a few miles, a few minutes, away.

"Maybe you're right." Her voice was quiet, subdued. "Maybe wanting to kill Jason has served its purpose. It got me through the trial, through Kerry's ordeal. Maybe it's time to give it up and put that energy to better use."

He wanted to believe that she meant it, but he had his doubts. For six months she had wanted only one thing: Trask's death. The last month, since her sister's ordeal, as she called it, could only have intensified the desire. Now, just like that, she could say that she'd changed her mind? He didn't think so.

If he was right, what would she do next? Look for someone to take his place? He seriously doubted that she would find another killer for hire in Fall River or all of Rutherford County. The city would be her best bet, but she wouldn't have the first idea how to find someone there. At best she would come back empty-handed. At worst, she could lose her money or, given her inexperience and naïveté, would solicit somebody with enough of a conscience to set her up with the cops.

Or she could decide to eliminate the risk of future disappointment and take care of Trask herself. She had proved yesterday that she was capable of the job. For a moment then, feeling the fury that had darkened her eyes, Tucker had believed that she might kill *him*. She would find it easy to kill Trask.

But living with it afterward . . . That was the hard part.

"Do you have the materials for the roof?" She was still staring out the window, still oddly subdued.

"Yeah."

"Do you want to get started on it after the rain passes?"

He was surprised she hadn't tried to change his mind, hadn't offered more money, or demanded her twenty-five hundred bucks back and gone away. He was surprised that she would stay around and help now that she owed him nothing, when she would get nothing from him in return. But she'd told him earlier that she wasn't one of those people who said they would do something, then didn't.

No doubt, she was thinking now that *he* was.

"Sure," he agreed. Then hesitantly, awkwardly, he added, "I would appreciate the help."

*   *   *

The rain was just on the other side of the house, the air rich with the scent, when Tucker put down his hammer and offered a reluctant invitation. "Do you want to go in the house?"

Kate didn't. She wanted to remain exactly where she was. She wanted to let the freshening breeze cool her face, let the raindrops wash away any tears that might come. She wanted to let them wash *her* away. But getting soaked to the skin wouldn't accomplish anything besides making her cold and uncomfortable. She'd been both those things for a long time now.

As the clouds drifted overhead and the raindrops began peppering the yard, she responded to his question with a gesture. Jumping to the ground, he started across the clearing, and she followed a half dozen feet behind, only a little damp when she stepped through the back door into shelter.

For a moment she stood there, feeling that panicky tightness in her chest once more. She forced herself to breathe deeply, reminded herself that she could handle this. She'd spent enough time alone with Tucker. He wasn't going to turn on her suddenly. He wasn't like Jason. She was safe.

Breathing a little easier, though still edgy, still just the slightest bit afraid, she forced herself one step at a time into the house, calmed herself by looking around, by making note of windows and doors. The place was gloomy, with too few windows admitting too little light. Like the new house out back, it was only one large room, with a cramped bathroom tucked into one corner. The floor sagged precariously by the front door, and wind whistled through cracks in the walls. All color and pattern had faded from the linoleum, leaving an ugly floor that was worn black in places and showed bare wood in others.

"Have a seat," he invited.

She shook her head and went instead to stand in front of the cold fireplace. Keeping the stone at her back, she watched as Tucker crossed to the unmade bed. It was iron, with fat curved rails stretching from side to side at both the head and foot, supporting narrow, ornately decorated spindles. It had recently been scraped down and painted white and was made up with white sheets, a blue blanket, and an old string quilt. "Mine was a crazy patch."

He gave her a baffled look. "What?"

Clasping her hands to opposite elbows, she walked a few feet closer. "When I lived at home with my parents, my bed was just like this, without the frills." Letting go for a moment, she brushed her fingertips over the cool metal of one spindle. "My sheets were white, and my blanket was blue, but my quilt was a crazy patch that my grandmother had made. Did your mother or grandmother make this?"

"No. When I left Little Rock, Nolie— A woman I know there gave it to me." His face flushed, he made a half-hearted effort to straighten the covers, bringing some little bit of order to the bed.

Nolie. For a woman who'd lived an entire life with a good, sturdy, no-nonsense name like Kate, Nolie seemed a particularly fine name. It was a name that couldn't possibly belong to a good, sturdy, no-nonsense sort of woman. It was a name that could make Tucker Caldwell—lifelong troublemaker, bad boy, and convicted murderer—blush. "Let me guess. She gave you the quilt to remember the time spent under it with her."

The flush deepened to a rich crimson. Talk about sex had once embarrassed her, but no longer. Once you'd gotten up on the witness stand in front of every soul in the community and described in step-by-step detail the act of rape—the struggling, the grabbing, the punching, the bruising, the penetration, the ejaculation—there was very little embarrassment to be found in the normal, consensual act of sex. Of course, there was little chance that normal, consensual sex would ever be a part of her life again.

Crouching on the opposite side of the bed, he thrust his hand between the mattress and springs. The envelope crackled as he drew it out. "Here's your money."

Kate stared at it. It was supposed to have meant a new life for her and an end to the old one—an end to Jason's life, period. From the moment Tucker had accepted it last Tuesday, she had felt the first peace in more than half a year. Instead, it had turned into another loss for her, another victory for Jason.

When she didn't extend her hand, he came around the bed and started to reach for it. At the same time, they both drew back, and instead he laid it on the quilt. "I'm sorry."

"I shouldn't have asked. I should have known . . ." That she couldn't count on someone else to handle her problems for her. That destroying Jason wouldn't be easy. That she couldn't accomplish his death with the simple paying out of her life's savings. If she wanted to get rid of him, she would have to do it herself. She would have to devise a plan, put it in motion, and carry it to its logical conclusion by herself.

It was only fair. Killing a man was a serious thing. She wanted Jason dead, so she should be the one to do it. She should have the satisfaction—along with the risk and whatever guilt accompanied it—herself.

"What will you do now?"

She glanced at the envelope, then at Tucker. He hadn't

wanted to get involved with her. He had listened to her, had agreed to her proposal and accepted her money only because Ben James had asked him to help. Now that he'd rejected the proposal and returned the money, he was out of it. He didn't need to know anything about her plans. That way, when Jason was dead and Travis went looking for a killer, Tucker wouldn't know. He would only have suspicions.

Leaning across the iron railing, she picked up the envelope and drew the money out. "I guess I'll take your advice. I'll put the money back in the bank."

"And then what?"

"I don't know. Get on with my life. Maybe take a vacation."

"What about Trask?"

With a heavy sigh, she walked to the window beside the bed and watched the rain. "I've hated him for so long. He dominates my life—which, I'm sure, gives him tremendous satisfaction. I would like for him to be no more important to me than a stranger I pass on the street. I would like to remove his power and his presence from my life."

"Can you do that with him walking around free?"

"Maybe. With the help of a good therapist." But she could undoubtedly do it with Jason in his grave.

After a moment, she turned to face him, listening to the steady plop of runoff puddling beneath the window. "Does your family still live in Fayette?"

"No. After the trial, they had to move away."

She smiled thinly. The Trasks would have liked that, if they could have forced her to move after Jason's trial. It would still give them great pleasure to see a For Sale sign in front of her house, to hear that a resignation had crossed the board members' desks. "The Hendersons didn't think sending you to prison for twenty-five years was punishment enough?"

"No. They bought the house we had lived in all my life and threw them out—my mother, my grandmother, and my brother."

"Where did they go?"

"My grandmother wound up in a nursing home. She died a few years later. Jimmy's living in Little Rock. We don't know where our mother is."

"What about your father?"

He moved around to sit on the bed, settling in with a squeaking of springs, leaning back against the footboard. "Never knew who he was. My mother liked men—lots of men. The only thing she knew for sure was that Jimmy and I didn't have the same father."

Of course. When everything else was going against you, when you were born into a poor family, when the so-called decent folks in town considered you and every generation that had preceded you trash, when your mother liked *lots* of men, it just wasn't possible to get by without the added stigma of illegitimacy. That way, when people called you a dirty little bastard, they had the righteous comfort of knowing that they were right, that in the truest definition of the word, you *were* a bastard.

"Fathers are overrated," she said simply. "I had one. He didn't do me much good when I needed him."

"He believed Trask?"

"He believed I deserved what happened. He believed that if I hadn't slept with Jason before, if I hadn't been so willing the other times, Jason wouldn't have expected it then. He blamed me for getting raped, for going to the police, for going to court, for dragging the fine Edwards name through the mud." Tears welled unexpectedly, filling her eyes before she could get them under control. "He blamed me for what happened to Kerry."

"What about your mother?"

"She would never think a woman deserved to be raped. However, she did believe dignity and pride were far more important than justice. She wanted me to keep my mouth shut, never to tell anyone what had happened. It was supposed to be my dirty little secret, my own private shame." She stared off into the distance, her gaze focused on the front door, but the images she was seeing were a month distant. Kerry, pretty, laughing, having a great time slapping paint on Kate's kitchen walls, making her laugh. Then, eight hours later, cowering, terrified, barely recognizable, and barely functioning.

"The night Kerry was raped, I went to the hospital with her, and Mom and Dad came as quickly as Travis could get them there. Mom went into the room where Kerry was being examined, and when she came out again, she walked up to me and said, 'See what you've done. Look at what you've done to my baby.'" The venom in Bea's voice had stunned Kate. Granted, her relationship with her mother had already been strained by Kate's insistence on taking Jason to trial, but that night had shocked her. It had destroyed whatever was left between them. It had broken Kate's heart and had very nearly broken her spirit. Abruptly bringing her attention back to the room, she blew her breath out heavily. "I haven't spoken to either of my parents since then. I don't think I ever will again."

Tucker's head was down, his gaze locked on the pattern he was tracing on the old quilt. Right about now, she would bet, he would be a hell of a lot more comfortable talking about his Nolie and the wicked things they had done underneath that quilt.

Did he miss her? Had it been hard to leave her? Or had she simply been a convenience, a willing woman in the right place at the right time? Silently Kate mocked her own question. After sixteen years in prison—years in which he'd grown from a boy into a man without any female contact at all—Nolie had probably been far more vital than convenient. Kate was surprised he'd found his way out of Nolie's bed as quickly as he had.

"You'll have to overlook me," she said, striving to sound more cheerful than she felt. "According to my mother, I have no shame. I'll tell anyone anything."

At last he looked up. "It's better than suffering in dignified silence." Rising to his feet, he gestured out the window behind her. "Looks like the rain has stopped. Does the offer to help with the roof still stand?"

What did she have to go home to? In Fall River, Sundays were family days, but her family had shut her out weeks ago. Sundays were also church days, but her church had closed its doors on her. The minister hadn't actually asked her not to come back, but it had been implied. Apparently, a church filled with God-fearing people was no place for a harlot like her. A true man of God would have thought it was exactly the place for a woman like her, but not the good reverend. He *had* offered to pray with her. He had suggested that she ask God's forgiveness for her sins, that she ask for God's strength in dealing with her carnal and immoral nature. She had suggested that the good reverend stay the hell away from her. Since then her relationship with God had been strictly personal, without the benefit of pastoral guidance.

Now that Tucker had turned her down, it seemed she was living her entire life without guidance. But that was all right. She would get by. She would do what had to be done, and she would live with the consequences.

She offered him a tight smile. "Sure. I've got nothing else to do."

Chapter Five

The highway leading into Fall River was narrow and full of hairpin curves, winding its way up one side of the mountain and twisting down the other. Colleen held the Mustang's steering wheel tightly with one hand and used the other to shift gears as the road zigged, then zagged. The highway crews who'd built these mountain roads in the early part of the century, according to her father, had used a snake's trail as their guide, resulting in sinuous, tortuous lanes that tested the patience of cautious drivers and offered thrills and spills to the reckless.

At this time of the year, the mountains were decked out in reds, yellows, scarlets, and golds, offset here and there by the rich, dark green of the pines. The maples, planted in virtually every yard and dotting the cemeteries, were particularly breathtaking. They'd had a giant maple in the front yard of their house in Fayette, perfectly shaped and colored. It had signaled the arrival of fall with its blazing glory and the arrival of winter when its last crackly brown leaf had blown away. She wondered if it still stood, if the neighbors still made a point of driving past it every day of its peak color.

She could find out on this trip. Fayette was only forty miles from Fall River, much of it on roads like this. She could make the drive down there and back in two hours. She could make an event of it—see the house and the tree, Harry's office, the courthouse, the cemetery. Her father was buried there on the edge of town, sharing a granite headstone with the mother she couldn't remember. She paid a small sum every month to keep the graves mowed and weeded and to have flowers placed there the day before Memorial Day and removed the day after, but she had never gone there herself, not since the bleak, rainy day her father had been laid to rest. At first she had been too angry with the choices he'd made to find any peace in a visit to his grave. Later she had traded anger for obsession, and that, because of her certainty that Harry would disapprove, had also kept her away.

Soon the obsession would also be laid to rest. She would visit his grave to tell him so, but not before.

As the road crested a hill, a clearing on the left revealed the town below. The trees were sparser there, giving way to houses and shops. Like most Ozark towns, Fall River was built in a valley, its streets relatively flat and straight. The town had been founded nearly a hundred years ago, laid out in an orderly fashion, a planned community from the start, and it remained an old town. Surrounded on all sides by hills and steep bluffs, it offered little room for expansion. It had grown to the size the valley could support and no more. It was isolated, practically self-sustaining, a close-knit community with little violent crime, a clean environment, small-town values, and minimal interference from the outside world. It was probably a wonderful place to live . . . if your name was Trask. It wasn't so great for people like Kate Edwards. It probably wasn't feeling too great right now for Randy Hawkins, either.

Pushing away thoughts of business, Colleen followed the road as it wound down the side of the mountain, reducing her speed each time the posted limit dropped. By the time she reached the town limits, she was driving a safe twenty-five miles an hour past gas stations, two bars, and a number of small businesses. She had called ahead and reserved a room at the town's one and only motel, a cinder-block office with a half dozen log cabins set back in a stand of pines.

She drove past the Log Cabin Lodge and into the downtown business district. The Trasks' bank, built of massive stone blocks with marble steps, dominated the main intersection. Jason had an office there, she knew from sixteen years' worth of newspapers, but running the bank was his father's territory. Jason's was the plant on the north edge of town, along with a half dozen smaller enterprises.

Sharing the four corners with the bank were the police station, the courthouse, and the Presbyterian church. Law and order, money and God—the foundation of life for most of the good people of Fall River. How convenient for Jason, to have to go no farther than across the street when he was arrested, across another street to be tried and acquitted, and across yet another street to receive forgiveness. She wondered if Kate had ever forgiven him. Colleen never would, not even when she had destroyed him.

She drove to the edge of town, then returned to the motel. She was an hour early for the four o'clock check-in, but the clerk didn't seem to notice. She ran Colleen's credit card through the machine, got her signature on the imprint, then gave her the key to Cabin 6, at the end of the winding gravel lane.

The cabin had the typical motel smell, cheap furniture, cheaper carpet, and a fireplace with a supply of wood stacked on the hearth. Colleen laid her suitcase on the bed, hung the garment bag on the closet rod beside the sink, and began undressing. She'd had a busy morning, clearing her unexpected leave with the firm, turning her work over to other lawyers, and packing. The partners hadn't been happy to grant her time off with so little notice, but she had insisted. She hadn't failed to remind them how reliable she'd been in the years she had worked for them or, more importantly, how much higher her billable hours were than anyone else's. She brought in far too much money to be denied the first favor she'd asked, and they all knew it.

She had also made a call to Information, talking both a phone number and an address out of the disinterested operator. When she'd spoken to him, Randy Hawkins had insisted that he wasn't interested in talking to a lawyer, that the Trasks had been good to him. They were helping with his expenses and keeping his job open for him. Maybe all that was true. Maybe she had underestimated the almighty Trasks, and Jason was standing by his injured employee the way any decent human being would.

And maybe Mr. Hawkins needed a little enlightening.

She dressed in a pale gray suit that was both businesslike and feminine. The slim, straight skirt ended just above the knee, and the tailored jacket closely followed the curves of her body without clinging. The collarless neckline dipped modestly, revealing nothing more than the pendant she wore.

After locking the door behind her, she picked her way carefully in heels across the gravel drive. Her first task was to find the Hawkins house without asking for directions. Until she'd had a face-to-face meeting with Mr. Hawkins, she would prefer that her reason for coming to Fall River remain private. Jason Trask was a smart man. If he heard that a stranger from the city had come to visit one of his employees, he would be curious. A stranger wearing a suit and carrying a briefcase would make him downright suspicious.

A stop at the gas station down the road netted the news that, as far as the old man there knew, there were only two maps of Fall River in the entire town: one in the town offices, another at the police station. He seemed tickled by the idea that anyone could possibly need a map to find her way around town. "What exactly is it you're looking for?"

"Nothing in particular. I was just curious."

He clasped his hands together on his chest underneath the bib of his faded overalls. "Nope, there's no maps for sale, but it's easy enough to find your way around. Just remember that, for the most part, the streets running east and west are named after presidents and the ones going north and south are named for trees. Except, of course, up there in Ridge Crest where the fancy people live. They got streets like Magnolia Lane and Wisteria Drive."

Fancy people. Sounded like the perfect place for Jason Trask, Colleen thought, thanking the man for his help and climbing back into her car. After her meeting with Randy Hawkins, she would drive around until she located Ridge Crest. It never hurt to know where to find your enemy.

After a few wrong turns, she found the Hawkins place in the fourteen hundred block of Spruce. It was a world away from Ridge Crest and its fancy people. The yards were small, as were the houses. Every fourth house was exactly the same. There were no garages, just carports. The streets needed work, the houses needed repairs, and the area needed a general cleaning. Like the rest of the town, this, too, was a planned community—planned for the servants, the housekeepers, and plant workers. Use their labor, pay them a minimal salary, benefit from their services, and tuck them away out of sight. The philosophy of the ruling class was alive and in practice in Fall River.

The house at 1407 Spruce was a little shabbier than its neighbors. The screen door hung crooked. The yard was more dirt than grass. It needed painting, screens needed replacing, and the steps that led to a small concrete stoop wobbled unsteadily under her weight. She knocked on the door and felt it give more than it should. The lock that secured it was little more than decorative. A good shove would render it useless.

From inside came the sound of a baby's cry, then footsteps. The woman who answered the door was young, with frizzy red hair, shadows under her eyes, and a cranky infant cradled on one hip.

"Mrs. Hawkins?"

"Yes."

"I'm Colleen Robbins. I'm an attorney in Little Rock." She handed the woman a business card she had slipped from a stash in the car. "I'd like to speak to your husband."

The woman studied the card a long time. When she finally met Colleen's gaze again, her eyes were rounded and dark with worry. "He ain't here. His brother took him down to Springfield to see the doctor."

"When do you expect him back?"

"Not 'til later. Sometime before supper." She started to hand the business card back, but Colleen stopped her with a gesture.

"You keep that. Since your husband isn't here, Mrs. Hawkins, can I talk to you?"

"Is Randy in some sort of trouble?"

Colleen didn't ease her worries right away. "He may be. But if he is . . . *I* can get him out of it." After a brief pause, she went on. "May I come in, Mrs. Hawkins?"

The Rutherford County School Board was located in a brick-and-stone building on the edge of the school complex and shared a parking lot with the faculty. When Tucker slowed to a stop on the street out front late Monday afternoon, there were fewer than two dozen cars in the lot. School had been dismissed shortly after three, and most of the teachers had been gone by four. Only an occasional straggler, along with the administrative staff, remained.

Kate was part of that staff.

Her car was in the nearest corner of the lot, all by itself. He wondered if it was coincidence or a conscious choice made by Kate, who felt totally shunned, or by her coworkers, who believed she deserved to be shunned. He wondered again why she didn't leave Fall River, why she didn't find a place where she could live without the gossip and the pointing fingers.

He wondered what the hell he was doing there.

He had driven into town more than an hour ago, trying all the way to talk himself out of the trip. So he wouldn't feel like a complete idiot, he had stopped at the hardware store and bought a few inexpensive items, and he had spent a few unproductive minutes talking to Ben. It hadn't been easy telling the old man that he'd turned Kate down after all, that he'd returned her money and turned his back on her. Ben had looked disappointed and had had little to say.

Do what's right, the old man had counseled him Saturday night. *You have to decide for yourself what that is.* Right for him, he had decided, was not getting arrested. Not giving Kate's cop friend any reason to be watching him. Not risking a parole violation, real or trumped-up, that would send him back to prison. Not doing anything he couldn't live with. Right for him was not getting involved in Kate Edwards's troubles.

So why was he here, parked on the side of the street where she worked, watching her car, waiting to see her? Because he was a fool.

Shutting off the engine, he settled more comfortably in the

seat. He had argued the point with himself all day. He had work to do. He had no business going into town. It was none of his concern if Kate had gone to work today or if she'd taken the day off and driven down to Little Rock. If she tried to kill Trask herself, well, he had warned her against it, hadn't he? It would be unfortunate as hell if she got caught and locked up for it, but that was the way the justice system worked. If you did the crime, you had to do the time.

But Jason Trask wasn't doing any time. He had committed a number of vicious crimes, and he was a free man. More than likely, he hadn't spent even one night in jail. By the time the cops had fingerprinted and photographed him, no doubt his lawyer had been there with the cash to get him out. After all, he was a Trask, a fine, upstanding member of the community. He had ties to the town that made him a minimal flight risk—ties that also made conviction on criminal charges a minimal risk.

As the double glass doors of the administration building swung open, Tucker glanced at his watch. It was 4:45. The first people out were women—secretaries, he assumed, leaving in groups of two and three, walking to their cars together. Next came three men and a woman, all in business suits. Between them and the last bunch was Kate, walking by herself, her head ducked, her gaze on the ground. Through the open windows, Tucker heard the others calling good-byes, but no one spoke to Kate. No one acknowledged her at all.

She crossed the parking lot to her car, unlocked the door, then glanced up, unexpectedly making eye contact with him. Her expression was difficult to read. She was surprised to see him, no doubt, but what else was going through her head? Was she curious? Or was she embarrassed? he wondered as she glanced furtively over her shoulder at her coworkers.

The possibility made him feel foolish and ashamed. It

made his neck hot and sent an uncomfortable desire to squirm down his spine. Of course she wouldn't want to be seen in public with him. Wasn't it enough that Trask had destroyed the better part of her reputation? That people believed she was the twisted, warped masochist he had claimed? The last thing she needed, probably the last blow her character could sustain, was to be linked with him. The gossip would fly, and by morning, she would have sunk even lower in the estimation of the morally superior townsfolk than she'd thought possible.

Straightening in the seat, he turned the key and the engine caught immediately. He shifted into gear, then watched in the rearview mirror as her smugly condemning coworkers left the lot's back exit in a steady stream. The last car was just leaving when a voice made him go still.

"Hi."

Slowly he shifted his gaze from the mirror to the opposite window. Kate was standing on the curb there, her arms folded protectively across her chest. It was a posture she adopted a lot.

The last car from the parking lot drove slowly past, the driver giving them both a hard, suspicious look which Kate returned. When the man was gone from sight, she smiled tautly. "That's my boss. He tried his damnedest to fire me after the trial, but the school's lawyer wouldn't let him. He said there was too great a risk that I would sue for wrongful termination."

"Would you?"

She shrugged. "I don't know. They were wrong to take me out of the classroom. Even if I did like kinky sex, I was still a good teacher. I had never said or done anything the slightest bit inappropriate with the kids. What I do in private isn't supposed to affect my professional life."

He shut off the engine. "But by taking Trask to trial, you made it public."

"You know, if I hadn't insisted on bringing charges against Jason, I would have had everyone's sympathy. They all would have said, 'Oh, poor Kate, how awful that she suffered this terrible ordeal, we need to help her, we need to support her and get her through this.' I would still be teaching. I would still be welcome in church. I would still be part of my family. The identity of my assailant would be my secret—mine and Jason's."

My dirty little secret, my own private shame. But if she hadn't pointed a finger at Trask, she would probably be suffering far more than she was now. At least now she could blame him, but if she had stayed silent, all the blame and guilt would be directed inward on herself. It would eat at her and would, without help and some incredible strength, eventually destroy her.

"So what are you doing in town?"

He gestured toward the brown paper bag on the seat. "I had to pick up a few things."

"Did you get much work done today?"

"Some." Since they'd gotten the roof trusses in place yesterday, he had started on the sheathing. Though the plywood sheets weren't particularly heavy, their four-by-eight-foot size made them unwieldy. Still, he'd managed to finish three walls without help. Then he'd given in to the voice that had nagged him all day, cleaned up, and come to town.

"Are you going to work this evening?"

He glanced past her to the western sky. There was well over an hour of light remaining, but he was tired. Besides, if he finished the house too soon, what would he do with his days? Isolation was bearable as long as he kept busy, but once his hours were empty, he would go nuts or get into trouble—or both. "I don't think so."

"Do you want to get some dinner before you go home?"

He had thought on the drive into town that he would do that—go to the hardware store to legitimize the trip, check up on Kate, then get a hamburger. Now it didn't seem such a good idea—walking into a restaurant, the ex-con trash with the recently fallen schoolteacher. So why, instead of a polite refusal, did he find himself accepting her invitation? "Yeah, okay. There's a café on the other side of town—"

"I thought I could cook. I don't cook much anymore. It's just easier when I'm alone to fix a sandwich or a frozen dinner. But I used to be pretty good in—" Abruptly her words stopped and the color drained from her face. For a moment she stiffened, then forced herself, with only a slight tremble in her voice, to go on. "I used to be a pretty good cook."

Pretty good in the kitchen. It was an innocent phrase, harmless . . . unless the woman saying it had been brutally raped in a kitchen. No doubt, Trask had enjoyed raping her on the hard brick floor far more than seducing her in the comfort of his bed.

When he didn't say anything, she shifted uneasily. "I—I need to stop at the grocery store."

"All right."

Another uncertain little movement. "Do you want to go with me or meet me at the house?"

Go with her to the store, where other people were stopping on their way home from work. He shook his head. "I'll meet you."

With one last little smile, she returned to her car. Once she'd pulled from the lot and driven past, Tucker started the engine. She would make the shopping trip short, but he didn't want to spend any more time than necessary waiting outside her house. He didn't want to risk getting caught there by her cop friend, didn't want the neighbors getting suspicious and calling the police.

He drove to a gas station on the other side of town and filled up the tank, then turned aimlessly onto the first road he came to. Mimosa Street climbed to the upper limits of the valley, past neatly kept houses, a plant nursery with an impressive display of fall-blooming mums, and a riding stable. The street led to a relatively new housing addition, the entrance flanked on either side with elaborate brick columns, then ended in a circle of broken glass less than fifty feet beyond.

After turning around in the cul-de-sac, he slowed to look at the houses in Ridge Crest, as the brass plaque on one column proclaimed. The houses were built on a hill, each big and impressive, the moneyed class literally looking down on the average folks. If he even dared drive through that fancy gate, the residents would undoubtedly sic the cops on him.

In fact, a cop was coming down the drive toward the gate at that very moment. He felt no more than his usual uncomfortable twitch until he recognized the officer behind the wheel. Kate's friend—and he wasn't happy to see Tucker.

Easing the clutch out, he headed back down the hill, letting the truck coast while watching his rearview mirror. When the Explorer appeared behind him, his fingers tightened around the steering wheel. When the red lights started to flash, he muttered a curse, pulled to the side of the road, wiped his sweaty palms on his jeans, and waited.

"You know, Caldwell," the cop began when he reached the truck, "when you first came to town, I didn't much care. You'd served your time. You kept to yourself. You didn't bother the people in my town. Here lately, though, you've been making your presence known, first at Kate's, then out here. What business could you possibly have up here?"

Tucker glanced at the brass name plate on the uniform shirt. McMaster. *Chief* McMaster, according to the badge above the opposite pocket. Hell, how had Kate managed to overlook mentioning that her friend wasn't just another cop, but the chief of the whole damned department? "I was just driving around."

"Driving around? You mean like the kids do down on the main drag?" McMaster's voice turned mocking. "Aren't you a bit old for that?"

"I didn't know these houses were up here. I was waiting for Kate to get home, and I didn't want to sit outside her house." He let a little sarcasm creep into his voice. "I didn't want to upset the neighbors."

"And why are you waiting for Kate to get home?"

At last Tucker met his gaze. "Because she invited me for dinner."

He looked disbelieving. "Kate is cooking dinner for you. At her house. Just the two of you."

Tucker nodded.

Muttering a curse, McMaster turned away. Waiting for his next question—or warning—Tucker watched as a classic '67 Mustang slowed coming up the hill, passed, then turned into Ridge Crest. When he was a kid, he would have given anything for a car like that. Judging by the mint condition of this one, the brunette driving it had probably paid a pretty penny herself.

McMaster swung back around to face him. "I imagine you've heard the talk about Kate."

"Only from Kate." Then he added, "I keep to myself. I don't bother the folks in town."

"Between that bastard Trask and everyone else, this has

been a lousy year for Kate. Hanging out with you isn't going to make things any easier for her."

Tucker didn't respond. He couldn't offer an argument, not when he shared the cop's opinion.

"If you hurt her—"

"I won't."

"If you do . . ." McMaster didn't finish the threat. He didn't need to. After a moment's cold stare, he started to walk away. He took only a half dozen steps before backtracking. "Is that why you're up here? To see where Trask lives? Where it happened?"

Tucker forced his gaze to McMaster's face. "I told you, I didn't know these houses were here. I was just driving around."

"Right." The cop sounded as skeptical as he looked. "Be careful, Caldwell. It wouldn't be hard at all for a resourceful cop to get you sent back to prison . . . and I'm the most resourceful of them all."

Tucker watched in the mirror as McMaster walked away, then slowly shifted his gaze to the houses on the hill. One of them belonged to Trask. It wasn't a surprise. The bastard was too old to be living at home with his parents, and naturally he would want one of the newest, fanciest houses in town. Being able to look down on the town as if he owned it would please him—and, of course, in a very real sense, the Trasks did own Fall River.

Then the muscles in Tucker's jaw tightened, and his knuckles whitened around the steering wheel. It had happened up there in one of those big, expensive places. Kate had been raped by a man she'd trusted, beaten into submission by a man she had cared for. It had been an ideal location for Trask. In a house as substantial as those appeared, with a lawn as expansive as those were, there had been little chance of her escaping and reaching help before he caught her, little chance of anyone hearing her screams.

Aware that the cop was waiting for him to leave, he slowly drove away, through town to Elm Street. Kate's car was in the driveway. He pulled in behind it and simply sat there for a moment. If he had good sense, he would go home, and he would stay there.

Drawing a deep breath, he shut off the engine, climbed out, and went to the door. Even though he knew it was a bad idea, he wasn't surprised to find himself standing there ringing the doorbell. After all, when had Tucker Caldwell ever been accused of having good sense?

"I thought I'd been stood up," Kate remarked when she opened the door. She had wondered when she'd gotten home and Tucker wasn't there. She had given the possibility serious consideration when he hadn't soon arrived. Now, seeing the faint flush that crept into his face, she knew *he* had given it serious consideration, too. What did it say about her that even the county's least respected citizen would rather spend time anywhere but with her?

"I went to get gas." He offered the explanation with a hint of uneasiness.

"That truck must have a big tank."

"I ran into your friend. The chief of police."

Biting her lip, Kate closed the door and secured only one of the locks. "Did he hassle you?"

His shrug served as an answer, his following words as a reason. "Seems I wandered into the wrong part of town after leaving the gas station."

For a moment Kate was puzzled. She would bet that, in Travis's opinion, the wrong part of town for Tucker to be in was *this* part. Then she understood. "You must have discovered Ridge Crest."

"Nice houses."

"Jason's is the biggest and nicest of them all." When they had first started dating, she had indulged in little dreams of living in that big, beautiful house. She had been there for parties when he and Mariana were married, and he'd taken her there on their very first date. He had given her the grand tour, and she had fantasized about cooking in that fantastic kitchen, about spending quiet evenings in the cozy family room, curling up in the well-stocked library, throwing summer parties around the pool, and preparing for each day in the luxurious master bath.

She hadn't had to fantasize about spending nights in his elegantly decorated bedroom. That was where the tour ended. He had kissed her, and she . . .

Her face burned with the memory of how shamelessly she had behaved. Oh, God, her father had been right. If she hadn't been so easy, if she hadn't been so quick to strip down to nothing and crawl into bed with Jason, maybe he wouldn't have assumed a month later that she was his for the taking. Maybe he would have understood that *no* meant *no.*

"Kate?"

Slowly she focused her gaze on Tucker.

"The timer's beeping."

"Oh . . . yes . . . excuse me." She hurried down the hall into the kitchen.

A moment later he followed, coming only as far as the door. After a long look around, he commented, "Nice house."

"Thanks. It belonged to my grandparents."

"Did that dress belong to your grandmother?" As soon as

the comment was out, he grimaced. "Sorry. I know you dress that way deliberately."

She glanced down at her outfit. The dress was dark brown, plain, without style, the ivory jacket not much better. They *did* look like something her grandmother would have worn, except Gran's would have been made from double-knit polyester instead of a linen-look synthetic. "What makes you think it's deliberate?"

"To be able to pick clothes that look so bad, you have to know what looks good." He moved a couple steps closer to lean against the cabinet. "Downplaying your looks doesn't accomplish anything. Trask didn't do what he did because you were pretty, and looking frumpy wouldn't stop him from doing it again if he wanted to."

He was right. She did dress this way deliberately. She chose colors that were all wrong for her, used little makeup, let her hair hang straight and limp, and avoided jewelry. She hadn't wanted to appear the least bit attractive anymore, and obviously she had succeeded. Tucker Caldwell, a man who'd just spent sixteen years in prison, didn't find her attractive. He thought she was *frumpy.*

Someplace deep inside, that little insult mattered. Self-consciously she tucked a strand of hair behind her ear.

The microwave dinged, and she used a hot pad to transfer the potatoes from the glass plate inside to the hot oven. While waiting for Tucker, she'd made a salad and put the steaks into a plastic bag to marinate. When the potatoes were almost finished, she would turn on the range-top grill and cook the steaks. In twenty minutes, dinner would be ready.

"Would you like something to drink?"

"Sure."

She filled two glasses with ice and Coke and carried them to the breakfast table tucked into one corner. After sitting down, she glanced at Tucker, still standing across the room and looking uncomfortable. "You can come over and sit down."

He slid onto the opposite bench, his feet bumping hers as he settled. She drew hers back. "The next time Travis bothers you, let me know."

"He's doing his job. If you lived in Ridge Crest, would you want me hanging around?"

"I'd rather have ex-cons in the neighborhood than Jason."

He remained silent for a moment, then unexpectedly asked, "Didn't anyone believe you?"

She drew her index finger through the condensation that had formed on her glass, then wiped it dry on a napkin. "The district attorney. Travis. Kerry. Plenty of people believed me. Everyone who's ever found themselves on the wrong side of the Trasks believed me. But it's not that simple. They own the bank where everyone has to go for loans and the plant most of the lower-income families depend on for their livelihood. They own the majority of the rental property in town, both residential and commercial. They provide the majority of the credit. You want to shop, you shop at their stores. You want to do business, you do business with them. You want to work, you work for them. A number of people believed me, but they couldn't risk their jobs, their homes, or their families by saying so. But . . ." She sighed grimly. "Most people didn't. Jason's a charming man. He's very well liked and very much respected, and he plays innocent so very well. He fooled *me*. I thought he was wonderful."

"But you didn't know what kind of man he really was."

"Yes, I did." She turned to gaze out the window, but the view was obscured by the curtains. "Jason was married for ten years to Mariana Wilson. When they started dating, everyone thought he was just amusing himself with her. She was a local girl. Her mother worked in the Trask plant. Her father was worthless and didn't work at all. No one really believed Jason was serious about her. She just wasn't his 'kind.' But he married her, and he built that big house on the hill, and after ten years, he divorced her. He left her with nothing, no place to live, no money to live on. It was hard for her. One day she was Mrs. Jason Trask, with all the benefits, respect, and advantages that accompanied the name, and the next she was just plain Mariana, a nobody from the wrong side of town. When she heard that I was dating Jason, she came to see me. She told me that he had a violent temper, that he had beaten her, that on occasion he had raped her. She warned me to get out of the relationship while I could. She warned me that he could be ruthless if denied something he wanted."

Meeting his dark, somber gaze, she flatly continued. "I didn't believe her. I thought she was bitter that he'd divorced her, that she'd gotten such a bad deal. I thought she was lying to cause trouble for him. I advised her to get help. Three weeks later he raped me, and most people didn't believe me. They thought I was bitter because he'd broken up with me, that I was lying to cause trouble for him. They thought I was sick and advised me to get help. If I had listened to her . . ."

He didn't say anything, probably because he agreed. If she hadn't been so charmed by Jason, so flattered by his attention since she, like Mariana, wasn't quite on his social level, she could have saved herself such sorrow. She could have saved Kerry.

After a moment's silence, he asked, "Did you talk to her afterward?"

"I wanted to, but I didn't get the chance. She left town while I was still recuperating."

"Why?"

"Because Jason paid her. Because she was afraid. Because after finally freeing herself of him, she couldn't afford to get involved." She signaled her speculation with a shrug.

"Get involved. You wanted her to testify about what he'd done to her?"

"No. We wanted her to testify about what he did to me. She was there. She went to the house that night to get a few things she'd left behind, and she saw what happened. She stood in the hallway and watched through the open door." Kate drew a breath, clasped her hands tightly together, then moistened her lips. "She watched him rape me."

Removing his hat, Travis passed through the tiny glass foyer into the dining room of Ozark Annie's Family Restaurant and gave the room a quick sweep. There were some unfamiliar faces—people passing through, a tourist come to enjoy the fall color, a salesman or service rep doing business with someone locally. He paid them no attention, other than to note their presence, until he saw the woman. She looked vaguely familiar, but she was undoubtedly a stranger. He didn't often forget a woman's face, never a woman as pretty as this one. She sat alone at a booth along the north wall, totally unaware of her surroundings—but at the exact moment he thought that, she looked up, her gaze coming directly to him. She smiled distantly, then turned back to the newspaper in front of her.

He was a curious man by nature, and the badge on his shirt gave him the authority to satisfy that curiosity. Exchanging brief greetings with the diners he knew, he made his way to the booth and stood there, hat in hand, until the woman acknowledged him with a steady look.

"Are you the welcoming committee?" she asked, polite but not particularly friendly.

"To some individuals. Mind if I sit down?"

She folded the paper—a back issue of the *Fall River Journal*—then made a sweeping gesture toward the bench. He slid in, laid the hat on the corner of the table, then extended his hand. "I'm Travis McMaster."

"Colleen Robbins."

"Are you here on business or visiting someone?"

"Are you asking as the chief of police or as just one more friendly soul?"

He looked at her once more—dark brown hair in a sleek, short cut, porcelain skin, eyes dark as night, lips curved in a keep-your-distance smile—and found his answer. "Just a friendly soul."

"I came to see the foliage."

"Looking at trees is a lot more enjoyable in something other than a suit and heels."

"Actually, Chief—"

"Travis," he interrupted.

"Actually, my trip is both business and pleasure. I drove up from Little Rock to see a prospective client. It's just my good luck that it's such a beautiful time of year."

"What's your business?"

"I'm an attorney." She stated the fact pleasantly, with no apology, no acknowledgment that in many people's eyes, her profession was only one slippery step above the scum they so often represented.

He ran a mental check of the half dozen prisoners currently residing in his side of the Fall River–Rutherford County Jail. The ones waiting to appear in court already had lawyers, while the others were serving out their sentences. They had one bona fide ex-con in town these days, but Caldwell wasn't in need of a lawyer's services—yet. But if he didn't stay away from Kate . . .

If Caldwell didn't stay away from Kate, there was nothing Travis could do about it. She was a grown woman—emotionally fragile, guilt-ridden, and wounded, but an adult just the same, legally capable of making her own decisions. If getting involved with Tucker Caldwell was her choice, Travis couldn't stop her. He could impress on Caldwell that he'd do best to look elsewhere. He could appeal to Kate's good sense, but he couldn't protect her from her own choices.

Disliking the futility of his thoughts, he directed them back to Colleen Robbins. Maybe she wasn't a criminal defense lawyer. Maybe her specialty was divorce, estate, or corporate law. Just about the only people in town who could afford—or would go to the trouble—to hire a big-city lawyer were those who lived on the hill. No one up there was getting a divorce, and certainly no one had died, which meant that her business was probably business.

"What's your conclusion, Chie—Travis?"

"Excuse me?"

"You've mentally gone through all the cells at the local jail and couldn't come up with anyone I might be representing. You can't think of anyone who's divorcing, settling an estate, or having tax problems. What does that leave?"

"You tell me."

After a moment's silence, she replied, "I'm looking into a personal injury suit."

"You don't look like the sort of attorney who would handle personal injury cases."

His response made her laugh, a clear, easy sound that invited him to join in. "And how does a personal injury lawyer look? Predatory? Sleazy? Some of the richest and most successful attorneys I know got that way from PI cases. They wear thousand-dollar suits and drive hundred-thousand-dollar cars."

"So which one lives in my town? The one who's suing or the one who's being sued?"

"I really can't discuss this with you. Sorry."

Before he could say anything else, Annabelle came up, coffeepot and cup in hand. "Are you planning to eat here or at your usual table, Travis?"

He glanced at Colleen, who gave a barely perceptible shrug. As invitations went, it wasn't much, but, hell, he was a pushy sort of guy. He didn't need an invitation. "Here, Annabelle. I'll have the special with coffee."

"Good choice," the stout, gray-haired woman replied. "Your friend ordered the lite plate. Doesn't look like she needs the lite plate, does it?"

Colleen gave Annabelle a bright, charming smile in appreciation of the backhanded compliment, then leaned forward and folded her hands on the tabletop. They were nice hands, delicately shaped, slender fingers. Ringless fingers. "Tell me about your town."

"Fall River's a nice place. It's a good place for families."

"Have you always lived here?"

"Except for college and a few years in Little Rock."

"You like it better here?"

"Oh, yeah."

"What about the crime rate?"

"We have the usual stuff—occasional burglaries, vandalism when the kids get bored, shoplifting. We have a few domestic problems, and we're starting to see an increase in drug-related crimes, but who isn't?"

"What about violent crimes? Assaults, rapes, murders?"

Travis thought about Kate and sweet, naive Kerry, and the

muscles in his jaw clenched. "Yeah, we get our share of those from time to time."

"I read about a recent rape here." She gestured to the newspaper before moving it out of sight. "Sounds like the victim didn't get a fair trial."

"Didn't they teach you in law school that the victim isn't on trial?"

"Yeah," she agreed drily. "Right after they taught us that justice always prevails."

Justice. That was all Kate had been seeking, but she'd never stood a chance. Her mother had realized that from the beginning. So had everyone else. Don't bring charges, they had all advised, but Kate hadn't listened to them. She had listened to *him* and to the DA. She had listened to her own wounded, traumatized need for justice, and it had brought her nothing but more pain.

"No," he said quietly. "There was no justice in that case."

"Sounds as if you took it personally."

"I handled the case. The victim was a very good friend of mine. I advised her to bring charges against the bastard, to fight him in court."

"And instead she was raped again, only this time in public." Colleen sounded sympathetic, disapproving of how the system worked but resigned to it. "How is she doing now?"

"She's getting by." It was a major overstatement. Kate was living in fear. She couldn't bear any man's touch. Every relationship she'd had had suffered. She'd taken up with just about the only person in the county held in lower esteem. Life would never be the same for her again.

"And the defendant?"

"Oh, he's getting by, too. This entire incident was nothing more than a minor disruption in his life. It's business as usual for Trask."

"You must have had a strong case or the DA never would have brought charges. What went wrong?"

"What *didn't* go wrong? The judge was an old friend of the defendant's family. Our eyewitness disappeared. The defense lined up a half dozen witnesses of their own who told very convincing lies. Our victim was judged and condemned, and she wasn't even on trial."

"Justice in a small town," Colleen said softly.

"You say that as if you're familiar with the concept."

"I come from a town even smaller than Fall River. I know what it's like."

Seeking a lighter topic of conversation, he asked, "What took you from there to Little Rock?"

"I went away to college, then law school. By the time I graduated, my father had died, so there was no reason to go home. I wanted to make a new start and a name for myself, so I moved to Little Rock. I worked on my own a few years, then joined the firm of Handelman, Burkett, and Harris. I've been with them ever since."

His wince was only partly for effect. "There's a familiar name. I can't tell you the number of times airtight cases I'd made against your clients fell apart once your people got them into court. They're very good at twisting facts and skewing the jurors' perception."

She acknowledged his last statement with a nod and a faint smile. "You were a cop in Little Rock?"

"For ten years. To be with Handelman, Burkett, and Harris, you must be a damned good lawyer."

"I am," she agreed without conceit.

So what was she doing in Fall River? What was going on in his town that could interest a top-notch lawyer with one of the state's biggest and best firms, and how had it escaped his notice? He had thought that he knew everything happening in town, but apparently he'd been wrong.

"How did you wind up in Little Rock?"

Travis watched as Jake Scanlon's youngest daughter served their dinners, smiled shyly at Colleen's thanks, then scurried away, before he answered the question. "I moved there after college, too. I'd just gotten married, and her family lived there. It seemed like a nice alternative to Fall River at the time. I went to work for the police department, advanced through the ranks, and watched my marriage fall apart. After the divorce, I heard about the chief's position opening up here, applied, got hired, and came home."

"And haven't regretted it."

He considered the four years since he'd returned to Fall River. He had accomplished a lot with the department. He had renewed his ties to his family. He'd had a couple of good relationships, including a short but sweet affair with Kate. He'd made a home for himself. And tonight he'd met Colleen Robbins. Instinct told him that she just might turn out to be the sweetest affair of them all.

"No," he said with a brash grin. "I haven't regretted a moment of it."

Chapter Six

After being banished from the kitchen with a cup of coffee, Tucker found himself alone in Kate's living room while she did the dinner dishes in the kitchen. The meal had been good. The salad had been tossed with a creamy homemade dressing, the steak seasoned with a half dozen spices, the potato soft and buttery. He couldn't remember the last time he'd eaten so well . . . or with such company. Indeed, Kate was turning out to be very interesting company.

After he'd left her in the kitchen, she had turned on the radio to an oldies station. He remembered the song playing now. It had been one of Amy's favorites, playing on the radio the first time they'd had sex, a loud accompaniment to a less than satisfying experience. She had needed persuading, a tender touch that he, in his best moments, had barely been capable of—and that particular night hadn't been his best moment.

As the song segued into another, he glanced around the room. It was cozy, comfortable, exactly the style a woman like Kate would choose. The furniture was overstuffed, the fabrics coordinating. Nothing seemed remotely new, but it was all more than serviceable. There were personal touches everywhere—framed needlework samplers, signed in stitches with the initials KE. Shelves of often-read books. A stack of

CDs next to a compact stereo. A block from a quilt in progress, tucked into a basket with needle and thread. A collection of cornhusk dolls grouped on the mantel. Family photographs that, with one notable exception, seemed to be missing most of the family.

He picked up that photo, taken a number of years ago. They were posed casually in front of a little white church, parents and daughters gathered around an elderly, white-haired couple. Kate was easy to pick out. She hadn't changed much. She was a little older, a little prettier, a hell of a lot bleaker. Back then she'd had few cares. If she'd had even an inkling of the sorrows that were waiting to befall her and her sister, she never could have smiled so brightly, so charmingly.

He wondered if she would ever smile that way again.

Returning the frame to its place, he glanced at the other pictures. Though a few included Kate, most of them were of Kerry—standing in front of a Christmas tree, blowing out candles on a birthday cake, wearing a formal gown and standing arm in arm with a young man in a tuxedo. She was blond like Kate, had blue eyes like her, but she wasn't quite as pretty. She was too young, too innocent, too childlike.

At least, she had been.

Kate's voice came from behind him. "My parents tried for years after I was born to have another baby. They had finally accepted that Kristin and I were all they were getting when Kerry came along. I was eleven when she was born. Kristin was fifteen. We spoiled her terribly. We loved each other, but we loved Kerry more. She was special."

"Have you seen her since it happened?"

"I spent the first week in Little Rock with her. I've been back a number of times, but . . . I worry. She must know that it was my fault. On some level she must blame me. It must upset her to see me."

"It wasn't your fault." He turned to face her, standing halfway across the room, hands clasped tightly together, her expression a cross between misery and pure sorrow.

"If I had never gotten involved with him, if I had listened to Mariana when she warned me, if I had listened to Jason when he threatened me about dropping the charges, maybe—"

He interrupted. "Bottom line, Kate: Jason Trask is a violent, self-centered, arrogant bastard. That's why he raped you. That's why he raped Kerry. It wasn't *you*. You didn't *make* him do it. You aren't responsible for it."

"I wish I could believe that," she whispered. "For six months I've told everyone that it wasn't my fault, that I was the victim, that I wasn't to blame, but they didn't believe me, and, honestly, I don't fully believe it myself. I went to bed with him on the very first date. He didn't seduce me. I was way beyond willing. I was *eager*. I *wanted* to have sex with him that night and every other night." She shook her head sorrowfully. "I was so easy for him."

"Except the last night. It doesn't matter how many times you said yes, Kate. You still had the right to say no." He hesitated a moment, then continued. "Jason Trask didn't rape you because he wanted to have sex with you. He wanted to prove that he was stronger, that he was more powerful, that what he wanted was more important than what you wanted. It had nothing to do with sex or your being easy."

For a long time she simply looked at him, a faintly hopeful expression in her eyes. Then she shook her head as if to clear it, drew a deep breath, and gestured toward the sofa. "Want to sit down?"

Of course he didn't . . . and he did. He knew it would be

best all around if he thanked her for the dinner and went home. But what was best and what he wanted were a far cry apart. He *wanted* to sit down on her sofa, wanted to prop his feet on the coffee table, stuff a pillow behind his head, and listen to her talk about anything in the world besides Jason Trask. He wanted to pass a reasonably normal evening like any reasonably normal couple, and when it was over, he wanted her to walk him to the door, share a kiss good night, and—

Feeling as if he'd been sucker-punched, he sank down on the sofa. He didn't want to kiss Kate Edwards, didn't want to think of her in even the most remotely sexual way. She wasn't even close to his type. *His* type, he had learned in the first week out of prison, was Nolie—bold, brash, seductive. He'd never had to initiate anything with her. Even the very first time, she'd had him hard and horny before he'd even realized what was on her mind.

Seduction, tenderness, and gentleness—especially of the sort a woman like Kate, with all her fears, would require— were way outside the realm of his experience. He didn't know how to seduce any woman, not even one who was always ready, like Nolie. He sure as hell didn't know how to seduce a woman whose last sexual encounter had left her both physically and emotionally traumatized.

Kiss Kate? Not in this lifetime. Try to seduce her? Not in a dozen lifetimes.

She sat down in the armchair nearby and drew her feet onto the seat. "Where will you go when you leave here?"

It took him a moment to pull his thoughts back from the direction they'd taken. "I don't know. Maybe back to Little Rock."

"Your brother lives there, doesn't he?"

"Yes."

"And Nolie?"

He shifted uncomfortably. "Yeah, she's there."

"Do you miss her?"

"No." But that wasn't entirely true. He missed the ease with which he could be with her. He missed the sex. He missed not having to measure up to any expectations beyond whether his erection was hard enough and he could sustain it long enough. After sixteen years of enforced celibacy, getting hard and staying that way hadn't been a problem. Hell, much more thinking about sex, and he could get hard right here and now . . . and probably scare the hell out of Kate in the process.

Anxious for a change of subject, he cast his gaze around the room and came to rest on the answering machine on the table between them. The message light was blinking, and the number 1 appeared in the lighted window. "You have a message."

She didn't even glance at it. "It's nothing important."

"Have you listened to it?"

"I don't need to. Nobody important leaves messages for me."

"But Jason's friends do."

When she didn't respond, he reached across to push the Play button. Moving quickly, she pressed the Stop button, then hit Rewind.

"I want to hear it, Kate."

"I don't. When you gave back the money yesterday, you removed yourself from this. It's between me, Jason, and his friends. You're not involved. It's none of your business." Then she shrugged. "There's no point in listening to it. I know everything they have to say. I know their threats by heart. Why give them the satisfaction of hearing them yet again?"

"It could be someone else."

"No one else calls me."

He'd never seen such a stubborn look before. Obviously the calls upset her. She was a single woman living alone, a woman who had been victimized once before. It must be frightening to hear such threats—*They tell me what they would like to do, what they intend to do*—and be powerless to do anything about them. Maybe not listening was the only way she could deal with them . . . but it could be dangerous.

"Let me listen. Leave the room, and let me see what the bastard has to say."

Heat flooded her face crimson. "No," she answered flatly, closing the issue to further discussion.

She was embarrassed. The calls were undoubtedly explicit. They were bad enough for her to listen to when she was alone, but letting someone else hear them was more than she could handle. It was an understandable response. When he'd gotten rousted by her cop friend Saturday night, it had been bad enough from the start, but once she had come outside to witness it, discomfort had turned to bone-deep shame.

"You're right." His voice was quiet, as empty as hers had been. "It's none of my business." After all, he *had* given back the money. He had ended whatever sham of a business arrangement they'd shared.

So why did he feel obligated to look out for her? Why did he feel *damned* interested in what was going on and how to make it stop?

"Tell me about your brother."

He glanced at her. "Jimmy? There's not much to tell. He's a typical Caldwell."

"What is that?"

"Lazy. Worthless. He's never amounted to anything and he never will."

"That's a harsh assessment."

"I didn't make it. Generations of good, decent people in Fayette did." He'd heard it all his life. Based on no more than his parentage and the neighborhood in which he lived, he had been automatically labeled no-good, while a punk like Jeffrey Henderson could do no wrong, even when he was blatantly doing wrong and flaunting it in their faces. His harassment of Amy had been brushed off as unimportant, as harmless boys-will-be-boys behavior, while Tucker's defense of her had landed him in prison.

"What do you know about your brother that generations of good, decent people in Fayette don't?"

He gave it a moment's thought. "He's a nice guy. He's friendly, likes to party, doesn't care much for work. He would do anything for anyone. He has big dreams and big schemes. He's always believed he could make it the easy way."

"So he's an optimist."

"An optimist who's lost touch with reality," he said drily. "Someday his big break is going to come along, so, in the meantime, there's no reason why he should work hard. He quits jobs at the drop of a hat and sees no reason why he shouldn't treat his buddies to a night of drinking when the rent's due the next day and he's out of work again. The only thing that saves him is his wife. She keeps a pretty tight rein on him."

"Do they have kids?"

He shook his head. "I imagine Dawn thinks that raising Jimmy is tough enough. It would be hard to have kids when you never know from week to week whether you're going to have a place to live, whether you'll be able to make your bills, if your husband's going to gamble away this week's grocery money or bring his unemployed ex-con brother home to live with you."

"You stayed with them when you got out?"

"For two months. I thought I could find a job and get out on my own, but I was wrong."

"You could have stayed with Nolie."

"I probably could have, but her husband might have objected." He watched surprise darken her eyes, followed by a critical narrowing of her gaze, but she didn't say anything. She didn't need to. "I didn't go looking for a married woman," he said with a scowl. He had wanted sex, plain and simple—an end to sixteen years' abstinence. "I wasn't her first affair, and I damn well won't be her last. Hell, I didn't even know about the husband until a month into it because he was off with his own girlfriends."

"But, even knowing, you went back." Her voice was cool, subtly censuring, not so subtly condemning. She disapproved, no matter what the circumstances. Regardless of his reasons, what he'd done, in her eyes, was deserving of her scorn.

He stared at her for a moment, feeling the weight of her gaze and the need to somehow defend himself, to point out that he didn't approve of screwing around with another man's wife but, when she was so willing and he'd been so alone, he just hadn't found the strength to say no. But he didn't say any of that. He simply, sarcastically confirmed her last statement. "Yeah, I went back. Regularly. For another month."

She didn't say anything to his taunting response. She simply looked away, disapproval still heavy in her manner.

Rising to his feet, he circled the coffee table, then faced her. "Don't be so damned judgmental, Kate. You came to me in the first place because I was the only person disreputable

enough to do what you wanted. You thought I would kill a
man for money, yet you disapprove because I slept with another man's wife?" His laughter was harsh and derisive.
"Good, decent men with high morals don't kill for cash. Men
who do don't tend to be either good or decent, and they gen-
erally aren't troubled by insignificant little things like marriage vows. You went looking for trash, and you found it
when you found me. So what's wrong? You decide now that
you don't like the way it smells?" When she didn't respond,
he muttered a curse in disgust. Circling wide around her
chair, he crossed the room, turned into the hall, and jerked
the front door open. Reflexively he twisted the lock as he
passed through, then slammed the door behind him. It was
solid and closed with a satisfying thud, locking as it did.

The night air was cold, but it wasn't responsible for his
long, quick strides to the truck. He was angry—with Nolie
for seducing him, with himself for letting her, and with Kate
for judging him for it. So it had been wrong. Let her spend
damned near half her life locked up in a tiny cell, as far removed from the male population as was possible, and see
how she felt when she was finally freed. See if she gave a
damn whether the man responsible for making her feel
human again had a wife tucked away somewhere.

Then his scowl hardened as he backed out of her driveway. There was no cell, no bars to keep her safely secured,
but Kate *had* effectively locked herself up. She was in prison
as surely as he had been, even if it was one of her own making.

What did he care what she thought? It wasn't as if there
were anything between them. They weren't friends. Hell, if
he'd come back to Fall River before her trouble with Trask,
she would have been just like all the other contemptuous,
condescending folks in town.

But he hadn't come to Fall River before her fall from grace. In all their dealings in the past week, Kate had treated him better than he'd deserved, and he had come to expect it. He *hadn't* expected her to take that smugly superior attitude that he'd lived with his entire life.

It was just as well. This could be the end to their odd little relationship. What more could the old man want from him? Just yesterday she had stated that she wanted to take control back from Trask, to see a good therapist and get on with her life. Wasn't that enough? Couldn't he go home, forget his favor to Ben, forget Kate, and get on with *his* life?

Could he go home and forget that he hadn't believed her when she'd said that it was time to quit seeking Trask's death? Could he forget his gut feeling that she would find someone else for the job or would do it herself? Could he forget that damnable sense of obligation old Ben, curse his soul, had somehow instilled in him?

He would if he could. Hell, he was a Caldwell. His mother had never felt a moment's obligation to anyone but herself, and Jimmy wasn't overly burdened with it himself. He was just like them, wasn't he?

He was. He must be. He *needed* to be.

It was well after sunset when Mariana drove past the sign welcoming her to Fall River. Packing had taken longer than she'd expected. She'd had to dispose of the furniture she'd collected since moving to Tulsa. The manager of the apartment complex had been in and out of the office all day, and it had taken Mariana until midafternoon to catch her. She had loaded her car, taken care of a few last errands, then finally started the long drive—four hours, less if you ignored the speed limit. She hadn't.

But now she was home. For the first time in five months,

she was driving down Main Street, seeing old familiar places, feeling old familiar feelings. God, she had missed this place! All her life she had been content to stay in Fall River. She had never dreamed about living elsewhere. She had been born here, and she had intended to die here. Sometimes, when she'd been married to Jason, she had been sure she would. Sometimes, living in Tulsa, she had been afraid that she wouldn't.

Turning onto her mother's street, she drove less than a block before catching sight of the yellow porch light that pinpointed the Wilson house. For as long as Mariana could remember, her mother had turned the light on at dusk and left it on until morning. At first it had been a convenience for her father, who had come home late most nights, drunk more often than not. Marv Wilson hadn't come home at all one night the summer Mariana was fifteen. He'd had a few too many and had driven his car into a ravine five miles outside town. Although his body had been broken and battered, if it was any comfort, the doctor had told them at the hospital, he hadn't suffered. Of course not. In death as in life, his family had done the suffering for him.

Pulling into the driveway, Mariana shut off the engine and simply sat there. The house hadn't changed much in the sixteen years since Marv's death. It wasn't showy, not like Jason's place up on the hill, but it wasn't anything to be ashamed of, either. For a time, she had thought it was. When she'd begun dating Jason, she had been embarrassed for him to pick her up here, to see that the sidewalk was cracked and uneven where tree roots pushed against it, that the house needed painting, that the furniture was showing wear and tear and the carpet needed replacing. He had grown up in such luxury, and she had feared that seeing this plain little place would remind him that she wasn't good enough for him. That he should be marrying someone from a nicer part of town, a doctor's daughter, maybe, or a lawyer's—certainly not the daughter of a worker in his own plant.

She had been an idiot, she thought derisively as she opened the door and stepped out. No matter how high-and-mighty the Trasks thought they were, it would be impossible to find a woman in this county who wasn't too good for Jason. Surface charm aside, he was a mean, vicious son of a bitch who belonged in prison for what he'd done to her, to Kate Edwards, and to poor Kerry Edwards, and anyone else unfortunate enough to have earned his anger.

Thought of Kate made her uncomfortable. She had come home to make things right, and Kate was the person she had wronged. She wasn't eager to face the woman after letting her down twice. She wasn't anxious to search for words that could even come close to expressing how bad she felt. Her only comfort was that she *had* warned Kate. The fact that Kate had ignored the warning was on *her* conscience, not Mariana's.

Climbing the steps, she stood in a pool of yellow light and rang the doorbell. She probably should have called earlier. Because of her health, her mother had become a real homebody. She didn't go out at night, and, when sleep came easily, was in bed by nine. Visitors after dark, like middle-of-the-night phone calls, signified bad news to Patricia.

She was raising her finger to the bell once more when abruptly the lock clicked and the door swung open. Her mother stood there, robe belted around her waist, eyes wide behind thick glasses. Her graying blond hair stood on end, and there was an unhealthy pallor to her face that Mariana had never seen before.

"Mariana? Oh, my word, it *is* you! Oh, honey, it's been so

long, and I've missed you so much!" Patricia enfolded her into an embrace, patting her, rocking her, much the way she had that warm April evening when Mariana had returned, shaken and upset, from her last visit to Jason's house. It was a comforting place to be, but all too soon Patricia put her away. "What are you doing here? Why didn't you call and let me know that you were coming? When do you have to get back?"

Mariana drew a deep breath. "I'm not going back, Mom. I'm home to stay."

All the way from Tulsa, she had imagined her mother's re-action to her announcement—happiness, rejoicing, celebra-tion. She had expected her decision to bring smiles and tears and maybe even a little prayer of gratitude. Instead, Patricia pulled her inside, closed and locked the door, then drew her by the hand to the sofa before worriedly asking, "What about Jason?"

"It's a free country. I can live wherever I want. Jason can't stop me."

"You promised him you wouldn't come back."

"*He* promised to love and cherish me. The first dozen times he hit me, he promised it wouldn't happen again. The first time he raped me, he promised that would never happen again, either. He made a lot of promises, but he broke every one of them. It's hardly fair of him to complain because I broke only one." Not that the concept of fairness was a part of Jason's experience.

"He'll hurt you, Mariana."

She thought of the cassette tapes in her purse and shook her head. "Not this time. This time *I'll* hurt *him*."

"What do you mean?"

"I have proof, Mama—proof that he raped Kate Edwards, that it wasn't some sick game, that she didn't want him to do it. He admitted it on tape. He laughed about it, about how she begged him not to hurt her, about how he hurt her even more because of it."

In the silence that followed, Mariana could hear the ticking of a clock nearby and the distant sound of a television from the back of the house. Then her mother exhaled noisily and asked, "What are you going to do with this tape?"

It was plain from the weariness of her voice and the bleakness in her eyes what Patricia thought she was going to do: blackmail Jason. She thought her only child had come back to town to coerce Jason into paying for the evidence against him—and Mariana couldn't even blame her for it. She had accepted a bribe from him before. She had let him buy her silence—along with her pride, her dignity, and, apparently, her mother's respect. "I'm going to take the tapes to the DA," she said quietly. "Maybe they can get a new trial or file new charges against Jason for bribing a witness or something. Maybe they can provide a little justice for Kate and Kerry Edwards."

"I'm sorry. I shouldn't have . . ." Patricia reached out and clasped Mariana's hand. "I'm proud of you, honey. You're doing the right thing."

Mariana shrugged. "Even if it is a little late."

"Better late than never." Her mother smiled, and a little of the grayness left her face. "And who knows, sweetheart? Maybe this time *you* can get a little justice, too."

Kate sat at the desk in the cramped cubicle that served as her office and stared at the wall. She hated this place. For legal reasons, the school board had pretended that her move from the classroom to the administrative offices was a promotion. They had given her a title, an office, and a token raise in salary, along with a private warning that if she didn't accept their transfer quietly, she would be terminated. They would claim that she wasn't fit to work with young children. They would put her through a replay of the trial, and not only would she lose her job with the kids here, but they would see to it that no other school system would hire her.

So she had her title, her office, and her thousand-dollar-a-year raise, but the title was meaningless, the work make-work, something to occupy the troublemaker until she got so frustrated that she quit and left them in peace. The office was a renovated closet, with one small grimy window, damaged walls in need of paint, and a musty smell that all the air fresheners in the world couldn't overcome. The extra thousand dollars a year had come in handy, especially since she'd had a lot of extra medical and legal expenses this year. Still, every time she saw the additional money in her paycheck, she felt as if she'd sold out—and had sold herself cheap, no less. She should have fought the board, should have fought the parents who said she was too perverted to teach their children. She should have stood up for herself and made them show proof, back off, or pay dearly.

But she had been too tired to fight, too disillusioned to trust the justice system as it operated in Fall River. In all honesty, she had been too ashamed, and so she had taken their pretend promotion, their empty title, and their lousy thousand bucks, and she had slunk into this prison cell of an office to lick her wounds and brood.

Most of the day she had been brooding about Tucker.

At first she had tried to convince herself that he had been overly sensitive. They were entitled to differences of opinion. If marriage vows meant nothing to him, Nolie, or her husband, that was their business. They happened to be *very* important to her. Her parents and both sets of grandparents had taught her by example about the sanctity of marriage.

Try as she might, she couldn't imagine the circumstance, if she were married, even unhappily so, that could tempt her to violate her vows.

Finally, though, a bit of her conversation with Travis Saturday evening had forced its way into her thoughts. He had wanted to know why she was spending time with Tucker, when it could only do further harm to what was left of her reputation. Her reply had been meant to divert him from the real business between them, but it had also been true. Tucker didn't care about her problems, she'd told Travis. *He doesn't look at me the way everyone else in town looks at me.*

And that, she suspected, had been the source of Tucker's anger last night. It hadn't been about marriage vows and affairs. It had been *her* reaction to his affair—the way she had made her disapproval so clear. The way she had so easily judged him. It had been the way she had looked at him.

Who knew better than she how eloquent one look could be, how deeply one judgmental glance could wound? Every time she ran into her father, she suffered his long, damning stares—the ones that asked, *Where did we go wrong? How could our little girl turn out so sick? Why did you destroy our family?*—before he silently turned away. Her mother's looks were accusing, her sister's derisive. A few people treated her kindly, and others pretended not to see her at all, but most looked at her as if she were a corrupt, depraved degenerate whose mere existence defiled them.

Oh, yes, she knew how those looks could hurt, and she was ashamed to discover that she was as capable of using them as the people she'd scorned for the last six months. In another few minutes, she intended to do something about it. She had stayed in her office at lunch, wading her way through yet another tedious, time-consuming project intended only to keep her occupied. That extra hour, though, meant she could leave an hour early, and she fully intended to, as soon as the thin, gold second hand on her watch made one more revolution.

The instant it swept past the twelve, she left, locking up behind her. She reminded the disinterested secretary that she was authorized to leave early, then walked down the long hall and out the front doors to freedom. On a much grander scale, this must be how Tucker had felt the day he'd walked out of prison—as if a tremendous burden had lifted from his shoulders the moment he'd cleared the doors. He was luckier, though, because he would never have to return unless it was his choice. She did have to come back, tomorrow and tomorrow and tomorrow. To do otherwise would be to let them win, and she'd lost too much to let that happen.

She went straight home, taking the mail from the box next to the door, undoing various locks, resetting the alarm after she'd closed the door behind her. At the hall table, she scanned the mail, finding only junk and bills. For a time after the trial, she had gotten letters, some signed, most not. The signed ones had been filled with self-righteous condemnation from the parents of some of her students, from people she had known all her life, whose children she had taught year after uneventful year, demanding that she keep her distance from their young darlings or face legal consequences. How quickly they had all realized—the parents, the school board members, Jason's terrorizing pals—that she would rather do almost anything in the world, would rather endure almost anything, than go to court again.

She dropped the mail on the table and went upstairs. It took only a moment to slip out of the plain navy jacket, the matching skirt, and the dowdy white blouse that did nothing for her, only a moment longer to tug on her favorite pair of faded Levis. She was reaching for a T-shirt, also plain and white, when Tucker's comments from last night whispered from a dark corner of her mind. *Downplaying your looks doesn't accomplish anything. Trask didn't do what he did because you were pretty.*

He was right, of course. In her head, she'd always known it. She'd heard all the assertions over the years. Rape wasn't an act of sex; it was an act of violence. It was a display of power, a means of punishment, of establishing dominance over the weaker, inferior female. It was sick, it was demeaning, and it was demoralizing, but it *wasn't* about sex. Looking frumpy wouldn't protect her, and looking her best wouldn't put her at risk.

It had been a long time since she'd looked her best.

Closing the closet door, she padded across the hall to the guest room—not the yellow one where she'd spent so many nights when she was a kid, where some of Kerry's things were still scattered about, but the other one. After the rape, she had carried armloads of clothes in there, storing them in the closet and the antique armoire. Everything pretty, becoming in style, or bright in color had been relegated to this room and had been replaced in her closet with outfits that not even Gran, with her penchant for plain styles and serviceable fabrics, would have regarded with approval.

Opening the armoire, she removed a sweater from the top shelf. It was soft, of the finest knit, light in weight, and pale mint in color. The shade flattered her blond hair and fair skin, and the fit . . . Shaking it out, she pulled it over her head, catching the scent of the cedar that lined the armoire. The fit was perfect, she decided, facing her reflection in the dresser mirror.

For a moment she stared at herself. It had been so long since she had cared how she looked. Before Jason she had taken pride in her appearance. She'd had a dozen different styles for her shoulder-length hair, had shopped carefully for clothes that fitted properly and looked good, had put her cosmetics to their best use, had indulged in manicures and jewelry and a fondness for perfumes. After Jason, ugly clothes, a comb through her hair, a touch of lipstick, and she considered herself ready.

The power she had let him have over her was disgusting.

Back in her room, she brushed and braided her hair, slid her feet into a pair of loafers, then grabbed a jacket from the closet, folding it over her arm as she hurried downstairs.

It was a pretty afternoon for a drive in the country. A year ago she would have enjoyed it to the fullest, driving with her windows down, bringing her camera, pulling to the side of the road, and wandering off through fallen leaves to take a few pictures. This afternoon, the closer she got to Tucker's place, the less she noticed the scenery. Her fingers were tightening around the steering wheel, her nerves coiling in her stomach. She didn't know why she was so nervous. She was coming out here simply to offer an apology. She'd made so many of those recently that she knew the words by heart, knew how to break down in the middle of them and how to struggle through showing no emotion at all. It was no big deal.

But it was. Tucker would be perfectly within his rights to forget that he'd ever known her. Between her business proposition, her judgmental behavior last night, and Travis's harassment because of her, she'd been nothing but trouble from the beginning. It would be understandable if he didn't want to see her again . . . but if that was the case, she would be sorry. There were so few people in her life, and he was the only one who seemed to hold her totally blameless.

Even Travis couldn't help but think that she shared some responsibility for the things that had happened. He had never laid any blame, but she knew him, knew how his mind worked. A woman who took a wrong turn into a bad neighborhood didn't deserve to get killed in a carjacking, but she should have taken precautions to avoid getting lost in a bad neighborhood. *She* should have known better.

But Tucker didn't blame her. Maybe it was the way he'd grown up or spending half his life behind prison bars, but he thought *all* the blame belonged to Jason. It didn't matter that she'd had sex with him before or that the dress she'd worn to dinner that night had been deemed provocative. She had a feeling that it wouldn't matter to Tucker if she'd been stripped naked and aggressively seducing Jason when she'd changed her mind. No meant no, and saying yes a million times before didn't change it.

She needed someone who believed that in her life. She needed someone who could be one hundred percent on her side.

Reaching the rut, she drove around it and the house and parked beside his pickup. The sound of hammering came from the back side of the new house, competing feebly with the music that pounded from a boom box propped on the tailgate of the truck. Heavy-metal dissonance assaulted her ears and set the very air aquiver.

Leaving her car, she walked past the truck, convinced that the dusty green hood was vibrating with the music, giving off minuscule showers of dust. If she'd given any thought to the music he preferred, she would have guessed country or good, solid rock, but not this. She'd never known anyone who liked this.

Her steps slowed to a stop at the corner of the building. Tucker was working in the middle of the long wall, his back to her, supporting a sheet of plywood with his shoulder and one hand while using a hammer with the other to awkwardly

start a nail in place. In deference to the warm day, he was
working without a shirt, in jeans that fitted a little too snug
for comfort—her own, at least. *He* seemed quite comfortable.

Although her throat was dry, she forced herself to swallow. When was the last time she'd had a thought that was
even remotely sexual in nature? The last time she'd looked at
a man in tight jeans and noticed that they were tight? The
last time she had looked at a man's face and consciously acknowledged that he was handsome? The last time she'd felt
the little shiver of feminine awareness that should accompany such a thought?

Her smile was humorless. Before Jason.

So score one for her side, she thought flippantly, because
Tucker Caldwell was a handsome man who looked *damned*
good in tight jeans, and she had finally noticed.

Realizing that her palms were damp, she wiped them on
her jeans, then slowly approached him. He had finished the
nail in the first stud and was moving on to the second when
she reached out to brace the sheathing above his head. Startled, he turned abruptly, and she found herself closer to him
than she'd been to any man since Jason. He stared at her, and
she stared back, fighting the urge to back off just a little—
not to flee, not to run back to her car and all the way back to
town, but just a few feet. Just beyond the reach of his hard-
muscled arm. Just where she couldn't hear the tautly controlled tenor of his breathing or see the muscles tightening in
his jaw. Just where she could go back to thinking of him as a
person and not as a man.

She drew a deep breath and smelled him—sun, freshly
sawn lumber, and hard work. Jason had never done a day's
hard work in his life, and he always smelled of some ob-
scenely expensive cologne. She preferred honest sweat.

"What are you . . . ?" His voice was gruff, his scowl unwelcoming.

Feeling the plywood shift overhead, she offered an uneasy smile. "Put a few more nails in this, would you?"

Slowly he backed away, turning to the task, sinking each nail with a few powerful swings of the hammer. He had to pull the ladder into place to reach above his head. When he was finished, he came down, laid the hammer on the top step, and faced her again. "What are you doing here?"

She dusted her hands, clasped them together behind her back, then slid them into her pockets. This was ridiculous. She hadn't been this uneasy her first time out here, but her reason for coming here today just might be a little more important. Last week she'd been looking for a killer. Today she needed a friend.

"I—" At last she found her voice, looked him in the eye, and quietly, pleadingly, said, "I want to apologize for last night."

Chapter Seven

Tucker hadn't been on the receiving end of too many apologies in his life. He didn't even know how to accept them. Was he supposed to say, *Forget about it, it was nothing, don't worry about it?* If so, they were both out of luck, because he didn't *want* to forget it. He wanted to remind her that he had treated her more fairly than that. He had accepted her version of events with Trask as the gospel truth. He hadn't for a moment thought that she might have been at fault, that she might have deserved what the son of a bitch had done to her. He hadn't accepted everyone else's view of her as the sick one.

He also wanted to tell her that his affair with Nolie was none of her business, that he didn't care whether she disapproved. But if that were true, why had he made a point of telling her that Nolie was married? Her simple statement— *You could have stayed with Nolie*—hadn't required a response, and it certainly hadn't required an explanation.

But he had wanted her to know that he was the sort of man who slept with other men's wives. Maybe he had thought it would shock her. Maybe he had subconsciously wanted to see just how far her acceptance of him would go.

Now he knew: not very far. Last night he had acknowledged that if he'd come back to town before Trask got hold of her, she would have treated him just like everyone else. Some little bit of condescension that had survived Trask had now come to the surface. It was only natural. After all, unlike him, she hadn't been born trash.

"I guess I'm a little old-fashioned," she said, her gaze directed someplace over his left shoulder instead of at him. "I come from a long line of happy marriages. I believe that infidelity is wrong under any circumstances. But that's *my* belief. What other people do is none of my business. What you did with Nolie is none of my business."

But he had made it her business by telling her about Nolie.

He shrugged. "I come from a long line of miserable marriages and no marriages at all. My grandmother was married five times, and my mother never married. She's probably slept with as many men as these hills have trees. So maybe it comes as a surprise, but I don't believe in sleeping around, either. Like I told you, I didn't know in the beginning that Nolie was married. When I found out . . . Well, that's part of the reason I left Little Rock. I couldn't seem to stay away from her, and she wasn't offering to stay away from me."

"She must be special."

His first impulse was to deny it, but he checked it. "She's a nice woman. She has a healthy regard for sex. She's easy." He saw the shadows come into Kate's eyes, saw her flinch at his casual use of an insult that she had suffered herself. He didn't mean it in a sexual context, although it certainly applied. After he'd found out about Nolie's husband, he had tried to break it off with her, but it had been hard trying to tell her no, when she was making all the right moves in all the right places . . . and she had known every move, every place, every weakness a man had. She'd known *his* weaknesses better even than he had.

"I mean she was easy to be around," he explained. "She laughed a lot. She didn't take things too seriously. She didn't care that I'd grown up poor because she had, too. She didn't care that I'd been in prison. She didn't care about much at all besides having a good time." She hadn't cared that he was uncomfortable with people in general and women in particular. She hadn't cared that his social skills were minimally developed. She hadn't even cared that, for all his experience, he might as well have been a damned virgin. She had seduced him anyway. She had taught him.

But she hadn't taught him enough to deal with a woman like Kate.

"Actually, it doesn't come as such a surprise." Kate was looking at him now. When he raised one brow in silent question, she shrugged. "That you don't believe in sleeping around. A lot of kids follow the examples their parents set for them. A lot don't. The child of an alcoholic may drink because the parent did or may not for the same reason. A child who was abused by his father may abuse his own children because it's the only way he knows or he may never lay a hand on them because he remembers how it feels."

And the son of a promiscuous mother might become promiscuous himself or end up in a situation where he couldn't indulge at all, he thought. Prison had been just such a situation. Living here in Fall River was another. So was Kate.

"In my family," he said, deliberately distracting himself from unwelcome thoughts of Kate and indulgences, "the alcoholic and the abusive parent were both the mother. I do drink, but I don't get drunk, and I've never hit anyone who couldn't defend himself."

Turning, he picked up the final sheet of sheathing and lifted it into place. Once it was nailed, the four walls would be roughed in, and he could start on the roof. At the rate he was going, he might get moved in here before the harsh winter weather set in, after all. And then what would he do with his time?

As he did a visual check to make sure the opposite end was level, Kate came into his line of sight, reaching high above her head to help hold the board. The movement pulled her sweater up, revealing a thin strip of skin around her middle, pale and delicate. Skin like hers was easy to damage and formed particularly ugly bruises. Trask had probably taken particular pleasure in making that happen.

With a scowl, he hammered the first nail into the ply-wood, gaining satisfaction from each blow he struck with the hammer. He moved on to the second, then the third, before she broke the silence. "Your mother hit you and Jimmy?"

He sunk the nail he'd positioned before moving to the next stud, sixteen inches closer to her. "Yeah."

"What was she like?"

He worked for a time, considering her question. The closer he got to her end, the farther she edged away, until finally she released her hold on the relatively secure ply-wood and moved to sit on a boulder some six feet back. After hammering in the final nail, he faced her, leaning against the sun-warmed house. "When she was in a good mood, she was funny, generous, affectionate. When she wasn't . . ." He shrugged. That was when she'd gotten nasty. Her philosophy had always been that more was bet-ter. If one beer made her feel good, then two would make her feel twice as good. If slapping her kid once made him behave, then hitting him twice should make him a precious little angel. "She was always looking for someone to take care of her, to give her the sort of life she thought she deserved. She used every man who came into her life, but she usually wound up with nothing. She wanted so much, but all she ever got was disappointment."

"Was she pretty?"

"She was beautiful—barely five feet tall, delicate, dark hair, dark eyes, with a husky voice and a Southern drawl. Men were fascinated by her. She was brash and aggressive, feminine but not the least bit ladylike. She was a very sultry, very sexual woman. She had this smile, this walk, this manner, that promised things most men in Madison County couldn't even imagine."

"Did she deliver?"

"Enough to keep them coming back for a while. But she was greedy and selfish. Eventually she demanded too much, and they went back to their wives or on to somebody new. She never understood why. She was prettier than their wives. She was sexier than their girlfriends. She went through life ruining relationship after relationship, and she never had a clue."

"What was she like between relationships?"

"That was when she drank the most. She was nothing without a man." Living with her then—with the fights, the rages, the one-night stands with drunken strangers—had been almost unbearable. "The beginning of a new affair was always the best time for Jimmy and me," he said, able to summon up that incredible sense of relief even after all these years. "Every new guy held such potential. He was the one who would sweep her off her feet, the one who would take her away from the poverty and filth and the bleakness of life on Yancy Street. He was the one who would save her from being a Caldwell."

"But it never happened."

"Not to my knowledge."

Drawing her feet onto the boulder's sloping side, she wrapped her arms around her knees and exhaled softly. She looked grim, as if their conversation had depressed her. Hell, it had depressed *him*, and none of it was new to him. It was his life. It was all he'd ever known.

He slid down the wall until he reached the ground, sitting in a crouch, his back supported by the foundation. The position put him on her level, where he could see the somber set of her mouth and the shadows that troubled her blue eyes. She should be someplace else on a pretty October day like this—with friends or a boyfriend, taking a drive through the country or a walk through the woods in their autumn colors—away from the shabbiness of his uncle's old place and the plain, nothing-specialness of his own house.

But he wasn't her boyfriend, and she hadn't come out today to have a good time. She had come with an apology to ease her guilty conscience.

Some part of those last thoughts made him shift uncomfortably, unexpectedly annoyed, and he was pretty damned sure it wasn't the apology part. *But he wasn't her boyfriend.* It was a simple statement of fact, so why should it annoy him? He didn't want a relationship with her, didn't want to worry about her skittishness and his inexperience. He didn't want the trouble and grief of a relationship with anyone, especially Kate.

But last evening at her house he had thought about kissing her. Right now it wouldn't take more than a simple relaxing of his guard to think about a hell of a lot more. To notice that, for the first time, she'd taken some care with her appearance. To see that the sweater snugly followed the curves of her body, rounding over her breasts, gliding in at her waist. It wouldn't take any effort at all to think about removing the sweater, about pulling it over her head and seeing more of the creamy, soft skin underneath, or to consider removing the band from her hair and working the thick, blond strands free of the braid that restrained them.

No effort at all.

"I like your sweater." His voice sounded odd, strangled, as if giving compliments was foreign to him. In fact, it was. He couldn't remember the last time he'd said anything flattering to a woman.

She looked down at it for a moment before meeting his gaze. "You were right. Dressing the way I do doesn't accomplish anything. It doesn't protect me. It just makes me look mousy and afraid."

Of course she *was* afraid, he acknowledged without pointing it out. At the same time, though, she was also a hell of a strong woman. Considering the savagery of the attack and the total lack of support from people who were supposed to love her, her recovery had been nothing less than remarkable. She'd had the courage to face her tormentor in court and the strength to continue facing him and everyone who blamed her. No one would have been surprised if she had been destroyed by Trask's attack on her sister, as Kerry herself had been, but she had survived that, too. She was taking back her life, bit by bit. In her own way—planning her revenge, approaching Tucker, spending time with him, fixing her hair, and wearing a pretty green sweater that made her eyes brighter and warmed her face— she was still fighting back.

"Are you going to start on the roof?"

He shook his head. "Not this evening." He hesitated a moment. Then, so unexpectedly that the words surprised him, he asked, "Want to go for a walk?"

She hesitated, too, that familiar wariness crossing her face. He thought about reminding her that if he wanted to threaten her, he could do it as easily here as off deep in the woods. But she already knew that. As she'd pointed out before, her fears weren't always rational.

She got to her feet and dusted the seat of her jeans, her silent acceptance an acknowledgment that location wasn't particularly important. If he chose to overpower and harm her, he could do it anywhere, and there was little she could do to stop him. In some small way, in some scared little part of herself, she was trusting him not to do that. Trusting *him*. Tucker Caldwell.

"Do you want to get your gun?"

She watched him stand up. "Do I need it?"

"Do you think you do?"

"A part of me says yes."

So much for trust. "We've spent a lot of time together, and I've never done anything to make you feel threatened."

Her response was quiet, measured, and faintly apologetic. "I spent a lot of time with Jason. *He* never did anything to make me feel threatened."

With a nod of acknowledgment for the soundness of her reasoning, Tucker gestured toward her car. "Get it."

In the moment that she simply stood there, he found himself wishing that she wouldn't go, that she would shrug it off and take a chance. He was disappointed when she abruptly moved, walking away, crossing the ground with long strides.

His mother had wanted too much, he'd told Kate a few minutes ago, but all she'd ever gotten was disappointment. He had learned early not to want too much, to be satisfied with just the basics—a place to sleep, clothes to wear, enough food to keep a body going. Trust *wasn't* one of the basics. A woman's trust was foreign to him. The disappointment he felt now was almost as foreign.

Gathering his tools, he left them in the back of the truck, then shut off the music. He picked up his shirt from the tailgate, shook it out, and pulled it over his head while, ten feet away, Kate rummaged through her purse in the front seat of her car. After a moment, she climbed out, checked to make sure the door was locked, then joined him.

She walked alongside him, making no effort to avoid the piles of leaves that dotted the ground, crackling beneath her rubber-soled shoes. Her hands were in her pockets, and her head was bowed, her gaze on the rocky, uneven ground.

"You go to the falls often?" he asked, not the slightest bit interested in the falls but uncomfortable with the silence.

She skirted a boulder half-buried in leaves. "The Fall River Falls? I used to go there. All the teenagers in town have been at least a time or two. It's Fall River's version of Lovers' Lane. Have you been?"

"Only once. The summer I was ten or eleven, Jimmy and I were staying with Uncle Jed. He took us there one day when he was feeling a little more agreeable than usual to our presence. There were some kids there who dared us to swim across the pool under the falls."

"And you did."

"Yeah. I damn near froze—and damn near drowned when all that water came down on my head."

She smiled faintly. "I'm sure the kids didn't show it, but you earned their respect that day. No one ever swam across the falls. It was too risky." She fell behind him where the path narrowed, then came back alongside when there was room. "I don't remember your uncle. How long did he live here?"

"I don't know. Twenty years, maybe thirty." He gave her

a dry look. "It's not likely you two frequented the same places. He preferred bars, creek banks, cockfights, and comfortable beds."

"What did he do for a living?"

"As little as possible." Then he answered seriously. "He hunted and fished and earned his money selling moonshine. He had stills all over these hills."

Something about that last comment—so stereotypical, the uneducated, backwoods mountain man making 'shine—made her grin. It was a simple thing—just a curve of her mouth and a flash of even, white teeth—but its effect was intense. It lightened the sorrow that normally etched her face and made her look years younger, freer, more relaxed, while, at the same time, it made him feel stiffer, tenser, and needy. Too damn needy.

Slowing his steps, he stared at her until the grin faded and a faint tremor passed through her. Uneasiness, he told himself, and grimly forced his attention back to the trail they were following. She wasn't comfortable with any man, couldn't bring herself to endure even the most casual of touches. Hell, she had felt compelled to bring along a gun for protection on a simple walk through the woods. She couldn't be pleased to have him looking at her that way—not as hired killer to wanna-be employer or acquaintance to distant acquaintance, but man to woman.

Well, she couldn't be any less pleased than *he* was. Hell, he hadn't even thought she was attractive the first time they'd met. He had wanted never to see her again the second time. Now it seemed that every other thought had something to do with her. Kate and Trask. Kate and murder. Kate and prison.

Kate and intimacy. Kate and satisfaction. Kate and the best damned hours he might ever spend.

Maybe this sudden fixation was simply nature's way of telling him that it was time for a trip to Little Rock, time to forget his principles for one more long, hard night with Nolie. Two months of regular sex, no matter how good, wasn't enough to make up for a lifetime without. So, logically, it wasn't Kate herself he was wanting. It was the sex. Since she was the only female remotely in his life, it was only natural that his desire would center on her. It had nothing to do with her as a woman.

Something about the argument sounded shaky, but he didn't examine it too closely. He didn't want to think about the fact that, much as he had enjoyed his affair with Nolie, in the five weeks since he'd last seen her, he had given her damn little thought, while, since meeting Kate, he'd been able to think of little else. He didn't want to consider the reason a trip to Little Rock and a night with Nolie didn't particularly interest him at this moment, but watching Kate scramble up the slope after him did.

She moved gracefully. Even when her foot slipped on a patch of damp moss, she caught herself with the ease of someone who'd done it a thousand times. At the top, she stood near him and looked all around.

He gestured toward the trail that split and headed in opposite directions. "Which do you prefer—wildflowers or waterfalls?"

"Waterfalls."

"They're nothing like Fall River's."

She shrugged off his warning. "I've seen Fall River's. I played in the park, necked in the parking lot, and lost my virginity a few yards from the water's edge."

Such information offered so casually by any other woman would have embarrassed him. It was too intimate a detail to drop carelessly into conversation with someone you hardly knew. But it seemed perfectly normal coming from Kate. They'd been sharing intimate details from the beginning—of how it felt to kill a man, of his childhood and his affair with a married woman, her painful details of being raped, of being abandoned by her parents, of enduring her sister's ordeal. Maybe once you asked a total stranger to kill for you, the rules of propriety no longer applied.

"Did you enjoy it?" he asked drily, and she answered in an equally dry voice.

"I was seventeen, he was eighteen, and we were both inexperienced. It was an awful lot of fumbling and discomfort for very little pleasure."

"I was sixteen. She was fifteen and *very* experienced. She made me forget my own name."

"Your girlfriend in Fayette?"

He had mentioned Amy to her only briefly, when he'd given her the short version of how he had come to kill Jeffrey Henderson. He wondered what else she knew about her, wondered if old Ben had filled her in on Amy's role in his conviction. "No. This girl lived in New Orleans. My mother's boyfriend took her down there one February for Mardi Gras and let Jimmy and me tag along. It was one hell of a party."

Kate's expression turned wistful as she bent to pull a leaf from her shoe. "I wish someone could make me forget my name," she murmured, her voice barely audible. "I wish someone could make a whole new me."

Tucker looked away as she straightened, pretending he hadn't heard, wishing he hadn't. Woodenly he lifted a low-hanging branch and ducked under it, then started along the path to the east. "We'd better get going," he said flatly. "The falls are this way."

*   *   *

Colleen felt like a sneak as she made her way through the dimly lit bar to a booth in the back, but Randy Hawkins had been adamant on the phone. He didn't want her coming to his house or anyplace in town where people might see them. What he really didn't want, she knew, was for word of his business with her to get back to the Trasks. They were being accommodating at the moment, but that would undoubtedly change if they had any idea he was talking to a lawyer. She didn't mind the covert meeting. She could be very accommodating, too, and, frankly, she was no more eager than Hawkins for the Trasks to find out what she was up to. She wanted to take Jason by surprise when she served him with notice of the lawsuit, provided she could convince Hawkins to sue.

Laying her purse on the table, she sat down on the bench where she could see the door. Located more than four miles outside town, the Piney Green Lounge was a place for serious drinking. The decor was plain—unpadded benches in the booths, wood floor, a pool table, and a jukebox. The signs on the wall were for beer and tobacco. The stools at the bar were for the more gregarious customers. The rest, only three so far, sat alone in darkened booths.

A waitress with a perpetual tired look came to the table. Colleen ordered a beer and paid for it, then took a drink as the door opened for a customer, filling the room briefly with daylight. The plant in town closed at four-thirty. Around five, business probably started to pick up. It was nearly five now.

She had spent much of her day at the library combing through back issues of the newspaper. Randy Hawkins wasn't the only Trask employee to suffer serious injury at the plant. One man had slipped on a catwalk and fallen more than twenty feet to the concrete floor because there had been no railing in place. Yet another had been badly injured while operating equipment on which he'd never been trained. Malfunctioning machinery had caused a number of injuries, ranging from broken bones to one death.

It seemed the Trasks had a little safety problem on their hands, one that might extend all the way to the state capital. After all, the plant underwent regular inspections and, according to Hawkins, had never been cited for anything but the most minor violations. But there was nothing minor about the problems Hawkins had described and no way a knowledgeable inspector could miss them.

Unless he was being paid to. Bribing a state official sounded exactly like something Jason Trask would do.

The front door swung open once again, and she glanced that way. Because of the setting sun behind the newcomers, she could make out only silhouettes, but she knew one of them was Randy Hawkins from the way he moved. His accident at the plant was officially being considered a freak occurrence—he had been working in the warehouse when a section of ceiling and the second floor above had come crashing down on him—but everyone had known the structure was weak, he insisted. There had even been directives to move the inventory stored there to a safer location until engineers from Fayetteville could come in and make recommendations. The inventory hadn't been moved, though, and the engineers hadn't come until the day after the collapse.

Hawkins moved slowly, carefully. He'd suffered a half dozen broken ribs, a punctured lung, a broken arm that was still in a cast, and injuries to his back that had required surgery. Even after a month, he was still in pain and significantly disabled. The doctors figured the back injury would keep him on the disabled list. It was for sure that he couldn't go back to the plant, but what else could he do? He was a blue-collar worker who drove a forklift, loaded trucks, and did heavy work . . . and he could no longer do those things. He didn't have any other skills that could provide a living for his wife and four kids.

And that was why he was here. For his wife and four kids.

He greeted her with the faint grimace that passed for a smile these days, then awkwardly maneuvered onto the bench opposite her. His brother Bill, whom Colleen had met the night before, pulled a chair from the nearest table.

"Would you like a drink?" Colleen asked even as she signaled the waitress.

"Not me. I can't drink with the medication I'm taking," Randy replied.

When the waitress approached, Colleen ordered a Coke for him and beer for his brother. She waited until the woman was gone again before she spoke. "Have you considered my suggestion, Mr. Hawkins?" Last evening she had explained his rights under the law, had tried to appeal to his sense of justice and played on his concern for his family, but he had been unwilling to make a decision either way. She understood. When you lived in a town that was owned and operated by one family, it wasn't easy deciding to take that family to court.

"I have." He nodded his thanks to the waitress as she served their drinks, then glanced back at Colleen. "Why are you doing this? You do a good business down there with people who can obviously pay a lot for your services. Why are you willing to come all the way up here to take a case that doesn't mean anything to you?"

"Fair question," she replied with a smile before offering the answer she'd prepared earlier. "My father was a lawyer.

He did a good business with people who could pay, but he always believed in helping out people who couldn't, people who really needed his help." That was how he'd come to defend Tucker Caldwell. Officially, he'd been appointed by the court, but it had been at his request. He had heard about the killing, that the victim was a Henderson and the suspect a Caldwell, and he had known that Tucker would need the best defense money could buy. He had asked the judge to name him as Tucker's attorney, and he had proceeded to give his client the worst defense the victim's family could buy. Tucker had paid. Her father had paid. Soon Jason Trask would pay—and *that* was the real answer to Hawkins's question.

"I've tried to continue my father's practice," she went on, no hint of deceit creeping into her voice. And why should it? She was telling the truth—as far as it went. She did try to do a number of *pro bono* cases every year. She did occasionally see an injustice or a client in need of a good lawyer and, as often as her schedule would allow, volunteer her services. "I believe everyone has a right to justice—not just those who understand their rights and not just those who can afford to protect them in court, but *everyone*."

"What are the chances that you'd win?"

"I don't know. I can't predict that. I can tell you that I believe you have a strong case against the plant."

"But if it went to trial, it would be in Fall River, wouldn't it?" At her nod, he continued. "Do you have any idea what it's like here? The Trasks own everything. Bill works at the plant. So does my father. My sister's a secretary at their insurance agency. We shop in their stores. We bank at their bank. Hell, we live in one of their houses. And it's not just us, Ms. Robbins. Every family in town is like us. Do you honestly think you could find twelve people who *don't* depend on them in one way or another to hear this case?"

"I don't know, Mr. Hawkins."

"Well, we do," his brother spoke up. "They tried a couple of months ago, and it didn't work. The verdict was decided before the trial even started."

Colleen shifted her gaze to Bill Hawkins. "You're talking about Jason Trask's trial, when he was accused of rape."

"Oh, he did it. There's not a doubt in my mind. Anyone who's ever gotten on Jason's bad side knows he's capable of what he did to Kate Edwards and a hell of a lot more."

Colleen judged his age to be about thirty or thirty-two. According to the newspaper, Kate Edwards had been twenty-nine at the time of the rape. Bill Hawkins had probably gone to school with her, might even be friends with her. She hoped so. With an enemy like Jason Trask, Kate probably needed friends. "But the jury acquitted him."

"That's our point, Ms. Robbins," Randy said quietly. "There was an eyewitness to the rape, but she disappeared before the trial. Respectable people got up in the courtroom, swore on the Bible to tell the truth, and lied to protect that man. What he did to Kate Edwards was a whole lot worse than what he let happen to me, but the jury chose to believe him and his friends over her and the evidence. What makes you think it would be any different this time?"

"I can't promise that it would. But, Mr. Hawkins, nothing is going to change as long as no one is willing to stand up and speak out. The Trasks will continue to put profits ahead of workplace safety. They will continue to hurt others, to destroy families, to ruin lives." She finished the last of her beer, set the bottle aside, then leaned forward, her arms resting on the table. "Can you give me the names of everyone you know who's been injured due to conditions at the plant?"

The two brothers exchanged glances before the younger one answered. "I imagine I could."

"Do you think any of them might be willing to join in a class action suit?"

Again they looked at each other, then Bill spoke. "Gary Pritchard's going to have to file for bankruptcy to keep from losing his house. Carla Brownley swore at Dave's funeral that she was going to sue the Trasks for wrongful death, but her family talked her out of it. Tommy Leonard's still having a lot of problems with his hand."

"What's wrong with his hand?" Colleen asked.

He gave her a dry, bitter look. "One of those big mixers chewed it up and spit it out in pieces. He can't write, can't drive, can't go hunting anymore or play catch with his boy or do those carvings he used to do on the side to help make ends meet."

"What kind of reception would I get if I approached them directly?"

"Probably not a very friendly one," Randy answered. "You'd better let us talk to them first."

Colleen tamped down the elation that surged through her and solemnly asked, "Then we're agreed?"

Hawkins stared down at the table for a long time before finally meeting her gaze. "All right, Ms. Robbins," he said at last, with more than a hint of misgiving in his expression. "We're agreed."

As Tucker had warned, the waterfalls on his uncle's property weren't nearly the spectacle the Fall River Falls were, but Kate liked them anyway. She liked sitting on a slab of rusty-hued rock, her face tilted to catch the last rays of the setting sun, the crash of the falls blocking out all other sound. The relentless pounding of water on stone had worn a basin into the soft rock, which filled, then emptied in a fall of ten feet or so into yet another basin. It was a soothing sound. It made the muscles in her neck relax, easing the tension that she sometimes thought had taken up permanent residence.

There had been a time when she was always relaxed, easygoing. It seemed a hundred years ago, a totally different Kate, innocent and trusting. The innocence was gone forever, and for a time she had believed that the trust had disappeared with it, but maybe she'd been wrong. If she had no trust, what was she doing here deep in the woods with the one man logic insisted was completely untrustworthy? And why was her pistol still tucked inside her purse, locked inside her car, all the way back at his house?

She had wanted to bring it, almost as much as she had wanted not to. When Tucker had accepted her explanation without argument, when he had acknowledged that she had a valid concern and had sent her to get the gun, she had, for a moment, given in to the fear. She had let it carry her to the car, had let it guide her through a quick search of her purse, and then she had stopped. She had forced her fingers to uncurl from the grips and her hand to withdraw from the bag empty. In the last six months she had experienced a lifetime's worth of fear. Some of it she still couldn't control. She couldn't imagine letting a man touch her. She couldn't begin to comprehend the possibility of ever having a physical relationship again.

But she could be alone in a house with Tucker. She could work beside him. She could go for a walk in the woods with him. She could trust him. And if she could learn to trust a man like Tucker Caldwell, then maybe she could learn to do all those other things again. Maybe she could even have a love life again. *Maybe.*

"Do you like to fish?" she asked, lowering her head at last to watch the fish darting from one quiet corner of the pool to another.

"Not particularly, but I do it. I know some good places around here."

"What about hunting?"

He made a mocking snort. "Me and a gun—that's a scary proposition, isn't it?" Then he flatly went on. "I'm not allowed to have a gun. I'm a convicted felon. Possession of a firearm would send me back to prison."

"Even a hunting rifle?"

"It's a gun, isn't it? It can be used to threaten, intimidate, or kill. I figure if hunting becomes necessary, I'll overlook that little detail and have Jimmy pick one up for me anyway. But until then, I'm trying real hard not to violate parole."

And, for a time, she had been trying really hard to convince him to do just that. How arrogant she had been. Jason meant nothing to him. *She* meant nothing to him. All she'd had to offer was money, and she doubted there was enough money in the world to make him go back to prison—at least, not now. Maybe later, when his own money ran out, if he didn't find a job and a place where he could belong, but not right now.

"We'd better head back."

She wanted to protest, to stretch out right there in the little patch of sunlight that remained and let the sounds of the falls lull her away to a life more peaceful than the one she knew. But the sun was setting. The temperature was starting to drop, and the darkness would soon close in around them. The falls wouldn't be as enchanting a place in the night.

Standing up, she bent over in a long, slow stretch, the tip of her braid falling over her head to brush the rough surface of the rock. Her sweater pulled up a little, and she felt the oncoming chill along her stomach and across her back. When she straightened again, she found Tucker watching her, looking intently at her middle. Self-consciously she tugged the sweater down.

"Where's your gun?"

The only place she could possibly be carrying a weapon was in her waistband, and she had just shown him that it wasn't the case. "I left it in the car."

He looked up, his dark eyes meeting hers. "Why?"

"I didn't really need it, did I?"

"You thought you did."

"I was wrong."

Some emotion flickered across his face, then disappeared. She knew her fears were a burden to everyone else. The men at work knew better than to come into her office and close the door. The doctors she'd seen so much of in the weeks following the attack had hurried through every intimate exam. She'd seen Travis's frustration every time he reached out for an affectionate hug and watched her shrink away. She'd seen the tension that tightened Tucker's jaw and narrowed his eyes whenever she backed away from contact with him.

"One of these days," she said quietly, "I'm going to quit being afraid."

"When Trask is dead?"

She looked away, watching as a maple leaf drifted onto the water's surface. It floated lazily until the current picked it up and sent it tumbling toward the lip of the pool and the little fall that would send it crashing below. She would love to send Jason crashing over the Fall River Falls, would rejoice to see his broken and battered body floating lifeless in the basin at the bottom. While it wasn't likely that she could lure him to the top of the falls only to push him over, she *could* shoot him. She could run him off the road or, better yet, run him down in the street like a frightened animal. However she accomplished it, seeing him dead was still her primary goal. Soon she would plan the where, when, and how.

But Tucker didn't need to know that. For his own safety, he couldn't know.

She offered him a half smile. "They say that living well is the best revenge. Jason finds great satisfaction in everything he's done to me. If he knew that he was no longer controlling my life, that entire days passed without my thinking of him or being afraid because of him, it would take away his satisfaction."

"And how are you going to do that?"

Her smile tightened. "One step at a time."

For a long moment he studied her, then, accepting her answer, he turned to make his way across the boulders to the opposite side of the stream. She followed. "We can go back the way we came, or we can take a shortcut. It'll get us back before dark, but it gets kind of rough in places."

She didn't hesitate in her selection. "The shortcut." With all her bold talk about getting over her fears, she wasn't yet ready to spend time in these woods after dark.

He led the way, following the path the stream laid out for them. The terrain was rockier, the footing less sure, the leaves piled deep enough in places to reach her knees, but they reached the clearing just as dusk settled. She fished her keys from her jeans pocket and gave a moment's thought to the long drive home. It would be completely dark by the time she reached her house. In more than six months she had been outside after dark only twice—the night Kerry was raped and last weekend when Travis and Tucker had been out front.

So it was time, and it would be good practice. If Jason died sometime between dusk and dawn, people would suspect that she was somehow involved, but no one would be able to say she did it. After all, everyone knew she locked herself in before the sun set and didn't dare leave again. None of them, especially Jason's terrorizing friends, would believe she'd found the courage to slip out and confront him.

"Want me to follow you home?"

Her smile was too shaky to be convincing. "It isn't necessary," she replied, even though every frightened little part of her insisted it was.

He sounded impatient with her response. "I know it's not necessary, but would you feel more comfortable?"

She wanted to turn him down, wanted to do this on her own, but in the end, she simply nodded.

"Let me get my jacket."

She went to her car, sliding behind the wheel, locking the door after her. She started the engine, turned on the headlights and the radio, and felt a little safer, a little more foolish.

Tucker came out wearing a leather jacket over his T-shirt, looking disreputable, tough, and attractive—like exactly the sort of man who could stand up to the Jason Trasks of the world, the sort of man who would protect what was his. That single quality went a long way toward earning respect in her eyes. Of course, she already respected him. For all his disadvantages, he was twice the man Jason was. He had shown her more understanding and compassion than any of the so-called better men in town.

Once he was ready, she headed around the old house onto the road that would take them into town. The twin headlights of Tucker's old green truck stayed close behind, a comfort every time she glanced into her mirror. It made the long drive pass more quickly and eased the tension that tightened her fingers around the steering wheel.

At her house, she pulled into the driveway and shut off the engine. Would he simply wait until she went inside and then leave? she wondered, hoping the answer was no, hoping he would accompany her inside. When his lights went dark in the mirror and he opened the door to climb out, she gave a sigh of relief.

He walked to the door with her, waited while she unfastened the locks, then went as far as the foyer. "Do you want me to look around?"

She shook her head. She had to come home to an empty house every evening, and she couldn't afford to get into the habit of searching through every room every time. After all, she was trying to overcome her fears, not intensify them. "There aren't any cars out front. No one's tampered with the locks, and the alarm hasn't gone off. Everything's okay." She hesitated a moment, then asked. "Would you like to stay for dinner?"

He hesitated, too, then shook his head. "Not tonight. I'd better get back home." He was out the door and on the steps when she spoke again.

"Tucker? I really am sorry about last night."

He looked back at her, his expression solemn, his eyes too shadowy to read. For a long moment, he simply stood there, then, exhaling noisily, he said, "Forget about it. It was nothing." He moved to the sidewalk, then glanced back. "I'll see you."

"Okay," she whispered, watching until he was little more than a shadow in the dark night. When she heard the slam of his pickup door, she closed the door and locked it, then leaned against it. If he had accepted her apology and left it at that, she still would have felt bad, because she knew the incident *wasn't* "nothing." But those three little words—*I'll see you*—made a difference. They made her feel hopeful, at a time when hope was something she'd thought lost forever, along with innocence and trust.

But she had trusted Tucker this afternoon, and she trusted herself. She had complete faith that she could come up with a workable, foolproof plan to kill Jason. She had no doubt that she could look him in the eye and pull the trigger or spotlight him with the beams of her headlights before crushing his body beneath her wheels.

How desperately she had changed in six short months, she thought with a bitter smile. The old Kate hadn't been capable of hurting a fly. The old Kate had been a staunch believer in truth and justice, while the new Kate knew truth didn't matter and justice didn't exist. The new Kate was easily capable of cold-blooded murder. The new Kate—the woman Jason had created—was now going to destroy him.

The peal of the doorbell interrupted the quiet. Her first thought, forming with a pleasurable rush, was that Tucker had changed his mind about dinner. A look through the peephole, though, proved her wrong. Pleasure was replaced by surprise and hostility as she undid the locks and pulled the door open.

The woman standing there smiled uneasily, aware that her welcome was likely to be less than warm. "Hello, Kate."

Feeling tension race through every muscle in her body, Kate stared at her. Of all the people she least expected to find on her doorstep, this woman ranked right up there at the top. Kate had assumed that she was afraid to return to Fall River, too ashamed ever to see her again, but here she was, waiting for Kate's stony look and cool greeting. She gave it in her iciest tone. "Hello, Mariana."

Chapter Eight

Mariana waited for an invitation that, clearly, Kate didn't want to give. It would come, though. Kate would no more want to stand here with the door open, visible—vulnerable—to anyone who passed, than Mariana did.

Sure enough, after one long minute became two, Kate stepped back, waiting silently for Mariana to enter before closing the door. That was the extent of her hospitality, though. Taking up a position at the foot of the stairs, her mouth settled into a scowl, Kate waited for her to speak.

"Can we sit down?" Mariana gestured toward the living room. When the other woman offered no response at all, she accepted it as a yes and walked through the wide doorway into the next room. They'd had their last conversation in this room. Mariana's warning that night hadn't been well received. Kate had doubted her, brushed her off, and pitied her. Now she wished she had listened, Mariana thought with satisfaction. For that Kate owed her an apology . . . but what Mariana had done later was so much worse, so much more deserving of regrets.

She sat down on the sofa. After a moment, Kate followed her in, turning on more lights as she moved, finally settling in the big comfortable armchair.

"I hadn't heard you were back in town." Her voice was

colder than a harsh winter wind, her tone more cutting than a surgically sharp knife.

"I got in last night."

"Visiting?"

"No. I'm back to stay."

There was a flash of surprise in Kate's eyes at the news. "And what does Jason think of that?"

"He doesn't know yet." Mariana had spent the day at her mother's, not venturing out until most of the town's residents were sure to be otherwise occupied. She hadn't made a call to the district attorney or to Travis McMaster. She was simply luxuriating in being home again, she had told herself, but that wasn't necessarily the case. She had been watching her courage waver, had been witnessing her resolve to make things right weaken.

Her mother hadn't been of much help. On the one hand, she was ashamed of what Mariana had done and she *wanted* things put right. On the other, she knew better than anyone the hell Jason had put her daughter through and was against Mariana's doing anything that might bring him back into her life.

Mariana's instincts for self-preservation were against it, too. Months after the divorce, there were still times when she marveled at the fact that she had gotten out alive. Many were the times during her years with Jason that she had feared she would become a statistic, just one more woman killed by the man who claimed to love her.

She *had* escaped with her life, but she had lost her dignity, her honor, and her self-respect along the way. To get them back, she had to undo the wrongs she had done. She had to make Jason pay for the crimes he had committed, and she had to apologize to Kate.

"When are you planning to tell him?"

Mariana shrugged. "He'll learn soon enough. I came here to apologize, Kate. I could have stopped him—together *we* could have stopped him. But I was afraid. I let him buy me off. I let him scare me away. I've come back prepared to do what I should have done then."

"What do you mean?"

"I'm going to see Mr. Marquette tomorrow. I'm going to tell him everything."

Kate didn't look impressed. In fact, if Mariana didn't know better—if she hadn't been through what Jason had put Kate through—she would think the woman didn't care. She would believe Kate was as uninterested in justice as she'd been in Mariana's warnings last spring. "And what is 'everything'?"

"That I was in the house that night. That I saw what Jason did to you. I'm going to tell him about the threats he made, about the bribe he offered."

"The bribe you took."

The scorn in Kate's voice stung. "Yes, I did. I'm not proud of it, Kate. I was just so damned scared. He promised to destroy me if I testified against him. I knew he could do it. I knew he *would* do it."

"So instead you let him destroy me."

"I tried to warn you. I told you what kind of man he was."

"And I didn't believe you." Kate's smile was bitterly mocking. "One of my biggest regrets. So . . . what is it you think you can do now?"

"Maybe get a new trial."

"For me? I don't want one. I'm not going back to court, not ever."

"Don't you want justice?"

"There is no justice in this town against the Trasks. You were one of them. Haven't you learned that yet?"

"I was never 'one of them,'" Mariana heatedly denied. Once the violence had started, Jason had never let her forget that she wasn't good enough for him, that she was barely a step above the trash that lived on Fall River's west side. It had been part of his game, tearing down her self-confidence, destroying her ego. *You're ugly, you're stupid, you're worthless. You can't do anything right. All the fancy clothes and all the expensive jewels can't hide the fact that you're trash. No other man would want you. No other man would put up with you. You don't deserve better.* This *is what you deserve.*

This. Derision. Scorn. Hatred. Daily humiliation. Beatings and rapes. He had broken her spirit and her heart. He had made her hate herself even more than she had come to hate him. He had almost destroyed her . . . but not quite. You kick a dog often enough, and one day he'll bite. She had been kicked down as low as a person could go. She was ready to bite now.

"If you're coming forward on my behalf, don't bother," Kate said flatly. "I don't want your help. Besides, it wouldn't do any good. Jason and his lawyers would discredit you. They would say you were bitter about the divorce. They would call you a liar, and everyone would believe them."

"Not everyone." Mariana clutched her purse a little tighter. The tapes inside were her protection, her talisman that would keep Jason at a safe distance. As long as she held them, he wouldn't dare hurt her. "I have evidence, Kate."

For the first time there was a flicker of interest in the other woman's eyes. "What kind of evidence?"

"Tapes of Jason threatening me. Admitting that he raped you. Laughing about how you begged him to stop. Bragging about how he hurt you."

Kate's eyes grew a little brighter, and her jaw worked as if she were trying to find words but couldn't.

"I'm going to play them for the district attorney. Maybe it's not enough to get a new trial on the rape charges, but it's got to be enough to get Jason a trial for witness tampering. That's a crime, Kate. It's one he could go to prison for."

For a moment Kate looked hopeful, then the hope disappeared. "Not Jason. Not in Fall River." Scooting to the edge of the chair, she stood up and started toward the front door, signaling the end of their visit. Reluctantly Mariana followed her. There Kate faced her again. "Do whatever you have to to ease your conscience, but don't make yourself the target of Jason's anger because of me. I don't care anymore. I don't want a new trial. I don't want to be publicly humiliated again. I don't want to stir it all up again."

"If I don't do *something*, Kate, then he wins."

"He's already won. He raped you. He raped me and my baby sister. All the trials in the world can't change that. They're not going to convict him. They're not going to send him to prison. They're not going to stop him." Her smile made Mariana ache. "There's no justice in the court system for Jason Trask. If we want that, we're going to have to find it some other way."

"But—"

Kate opened the door and waited pointedly for her to leave.

She wanted to argue, wanted to refuse to go, but in the end, she walked through the door. She was barely outside when it closed behind her.

Jason *had* won, Mariana conceded, at least as far as Kate was concerned. She had fought him longer and harder than anyone else, and she had suffered more because of him than anyone else. She had finally admitted defeat. Just when Mariana had found her courage and conviction, Kate had lost *hers*.

So Mariana would do it alone. She would take her evidence to District Attorney Marquette by herself. She would take on Jason and would stop him by herself. Though some part of her had been counting on Kate's support, she liked the idea of going it alone. She liked the thought of bringing justice to the meanest bastard in Rutherford County, of single-handedly bringing down the golden son of the high-and-mighty Trasks, all by herself. She *loved* the idea of being the sole one to make Jason pay for every insult, every punch, every hurt he'd ever caused.

For once, when it came to Jason, *she* was going to be the winner. It would be the sweetest victory she'd ever known, and it would be all hers.

Travis drove through the parking lot of Ozark Annie's, looking for any unfamiliar cars, in particular one whose owner might have driven up from Little Rock. He wasn't disappointed, though, when he didn't find a single car that he hadn't seen a dozen times or more. The lady lawyer was staying at the Log Cabin Lodge across the street. If she'd decided to have dinner at Annie's a second time, it was entirely possible that she'd left her car and walked over.

It was also entirely possible that she was eating someplace else this evening—maybe with the prospective client she had come to see. He had given the identity of that client some thought today, and he had come up with one possibility. It was a remote one—he couldn't imagine this person filing a lawsuit in the first place, much less going though someone like Colleen Robbins to do it—but, hey, stranger things had happened.

He parked the Explorer close to the front door and went inside. Out of habit, he gave the dining room the once-over and, in a repeat of last night, his gaze stopped on a distant booth. Once again she sat alone, a newspaper going unread in front of her. Instead, she was watching the door—watching *him*. As if she'd been waiting for him.

He stood there a moment until she gave a little nod, inviting him to join her. "We've got to stop meeting like this," she said, as he slid into the booth.

Sounded good to him. He could certainly come up with some more private alternatives. "Fall River does have a number of restaurants besides Ozark Annie's."

"Yes, but I didn't know if the police chief frequented any of them. He seems to be a regular here."

So it wasn't convenience or coincidence that had brought her back. That sounded even better. "Have a busy day?"

"Hmm."

"See many leaves?"

"A few. How was your day?"

"Same old same old. You meet with your prospective client?"

"Any particular reason you're asking?"

"I was just wondering what the verdict is—how long you'll be in town."

"For a few more days, at least. I've still got work to do—" Abruptly she broke off, distracted by new arrivals gathering just inside the door. Travis looked their way, and his expression hardened into a scowl.

"The social elite of Fall River. Tim Carter, Brent Hogan, Jason Trask, Mark Tyler."

"Trask. Which one is he?"

"In the middle. With blond hair." He watched Colleen look at Trask. She seemed inordinately interested. Was six feet two, blond and blue her type? Was she simply admiring what women everywhere seemed to find irresistible, or was there a hint of professional interest in her curiosity?

Before he'd decided, Colleen drew back. Travis glanced across the room once more and found Trask looking his way. His smile was smug, an unnecessary reminder that he'd beaten Travis's system. He'd committed brutal acts on two helpless women—three, counting his ex-wife—and he had walked away without even a slap on the wrist.

Travis didn't need the reminder. He remembered every time he saw Kate, every time he drove down her street or past the school or through the neighborhood where Kerry had lived. He remembered every day. Hell, he would never forget.

Annabelle approached the men with menus and gestured to the private dining room on the other side. It was most often used for holiday parties, birthday or anniversary celebrations, and men's club meetings. That was exactly what Trask and his buddies had—a perverted little men's club.

As the others followed Annabelle, Trask came instead across the room. "McMaster. How's the police work?"

"We're not so busy now that you're not so busy."

The look in Trask's eyes turned ugly. "It's unfortunate that you don't spend as much time harassing the real criminals as you do the respectable people. Like that ex-con living outside town. The man's a cold-blooded murderer, and you do nothing to protect the decent citizens of this town from him."

It wasn't the first complaint a Trask had made about Tucker Caldwell. Neither Jason nor his parents had been happy to have him in their county, but—as Travis, the sheriff, and the DA had all explained—there was nothing they could do about it. They weren't too happy about that, either. "That ex-con served his sentence. He keeps to himself—" more or less "—and stays out of trouble, which is more than I can say for some of the so-called respectable people in town."

Trask called up one of his famously charming smiles—soulless smiles—as he turned to Colleen. "I don't believe we've had the pleasure. I'm Jason Trask."

"Colleen Robbins."

He offered his hand, and, after a brief hesitation, she took it. "Welcome to Fall River, Colleen. If you need anything while you're here, don't hesitate to give me a call. I have offices at the bank and Trask Industries, and I'm always eager to lend a hand to such a lovely guest."

Colleen pulled her hand free. "I'll keep that in mind."

The dry tone of her voice escaped Trask. He gave her a farewell smile, started to walk away, and then, as if on impulse, turned back. "How is Kate, McMaster? I don't see her around much these days. She seems to keep to herself."

Travis hated the son of a bitch. He deserved far worse than prison. Death—slow, painful death—seemed fitting. "She's fine."

Trask's smile was more than a little malicious. "That she is," he agreed in a chummy, two-men-who-have-shared-the-same-woman sort of way. "Kate is surely fine. Colleen, I'll see you again. McMaster—"

"You'll see me again, too."

Without responding, Trask turned and walked away. Once he had disappeared from sight, Colleen spoke. "He's the man who raped your friend, isn't he?"

"Yeah. He's the one."

"It's not your fault he got off."

"I know it's not, but . . . I should have talked her out of the trial. Everyone was against it. The only people who supported her decision to bring charges were her sister, the DA, and me."

"It was the right thing to do."

"Not in this town. Not against Jason Trask."

"She had a right to justice."

"But instead she got crucified. It would have been better for her if she had just dealt with it and gotten on with her life."

Colleen shook her head. "How do you just *deal* with being raped and beaten?"

"Better than you deal with being the reason for the same thing happening to your kid sister." He watched the shock darken her eyes before he explained. "Trask warned Kate the day before the trial that if she didn't drop the charges, he would make her sorry. The trial went on, he was acquitted, and just about a month ago, he kidnapped, raped, and beat her nineteen-year-old sister. After he dumped her on a road outside town, he went home and called Kate to gloat about it."

"And you didn't arrest him?"

"Kerry was just a kid. She was shy, naive. Hell, she was a damned virgin. She couldn't handle it. She couldn't tell us what happened or who did it. She's still in a psych ward down in Little Rock."

"But the physical evidence . . ."

He shrugged. "Her family was uncooperative. Trask was uncooperative. The Edwardses were in shock. They blamed Kate for taking Trask to court. They blamed me for encouraging her to do so. The last thing in the world they wanted was to cross the Trasks again."

"And so he got away with it." She shook her head in disgust. "I'm surprised someone hasn't killed him."

"I believe the idea has crossed a few minds." His own, for starters. Of course, he'd known he couldn't do it, no matter how badly he wanted to, no matter how badly Trask deserved it. He was a cop, for God's sake. He couldn't hand out his own brand of justice. "Maybe it'll happen yet. Maybe he'll assault the wrong woman, and she'll blow him away. Maybe someday the hatred that's eating at Kate's father will push him over the edge, and he'll get vengeance for his daughters. Maybe someone will just get damned tired of seeing the bastard destroying other people's lives and take him out."

"If that happens, you'll have to work as hard at putting his killer behind bars as you did to put *him* there."

He acknowledged her statement with a nod.

"If it happens, give your suspect my name. I'd be happy to defend him."

He nodded again, then rubbed his hands over his eyes. "Jeez, let's talk about something a little less grim, can we?"

"All right." She sat quietly for a moment, then smiled. It was thin and not too happy, but it was an effort. "I understand that Fall River gets its name from waterfalls."

"Only one's a real fall. The rest are more like water*drops*. But, yeah, there's a decent waterfall on the east side of town. There's a park—a few picnic tables, some playground equipment for the little kids, a place for teenagers to go parking. Nothing fancy."

"Would you like to show it to me tomorrow?"

His grin came slowly. "Yeah, I'd like that."

"Good. Why don't I pick up a picnic lunch and meet you at your office around noon?"

He repeated the same answer as the waitress approached. "I'd like that."

They talked through the meal and for a good while after, not about anything important, just getting-acquainted conversation. It had been a long time since he had taken part in such a conversation, a long time since he'd met anyone new.

It was a pleasant experience, sitting across from someone he hadn't known all his life, talking with someone whose entire family history wasn't as familiar to him as his own.

It helped, of course, that he was attracted to Colleen in a way he hadn't been in far too long. Not one of the women he'd dated since moving back to Fall River had appealed to him the way this woman did. The attraction had been immediate and intense. Maybe her invitation to lunch tomorrow meant that she felt it, too. He hoped so.

Folding her napkin in half, she laid it on the table and sighed. "I've got to go."

"Is your car here?"

"No, I walked over."

"I'll give you a ride."

She didn't hesitate but simply smiled.

Claiming both checks from the table, he followed her to the cash register. Annabelle rang up the bills, took his money, and handed him the change while giving her standard Thanks-a-lot-and-come-back-soon speech.

It was uncomfortably chilly outside. While the truck's heater warmed, Travis gazed through the restaurant's plate-glass windows into the private dining room where Trask and his pals were having a good time. In dress shirts with loosened ties and suit coats discarded on chair backs, they looked like thirtysomething businessmen in any city, unwinding after a hard day's work, telling jokes and swapping lies. In another half hour or so, Annabelle would chase them out so she could close up, and they would go home to their houses on the hill and, with the exception of Jason, the families that awaited them. Big nice houses, pretty little wives, adorably precocious kids . . . How much more wholesome could a picture get? But, more than likely, one of these wholesome family men would slip off into his study after greeting the wife and kissing the kids good night, and he would spend two, four, maybe as much as ten minutes making obscene phone calls to a woman who'd never done him a moment's harm. Wholesome family men with a sick twist.

Beside him Colleen spoke softly. "When I was growing up, whenever I got upset because something wasn't fair, my father would tell me that life *wasn't* fair—not much comfort to a ten-year-old who hadn't been invited to a birthday party or a sixteen-year-old whose boyfriend had dumped her for her best friend. He also told me that what goes around comes around. There's a time when you have to pay the piper."

"Your father liked clichés?"

She grinned. "Yes, as a matter of fact, he did. His theory was that if there wasn't truth to old adages, they wouldn't last long enough to become old adages." Then she became serious. "My point is someday Jason Trask *will* pay for what he's done. It may not be in a direct form, like going to prison, but somehow he *will* be punished. Maybe he'll lose his money or his prominence in this town. Maybe someone will break his heart, or maybe someone will kill him. Maybe it won't happen until he's dead and damned to hell. But it *will* happen, Travis."

He considered the conviction in her voice for a moment, then smiled faintly. "You're right. It's not much comfort . . . but it's better than none if you believe it."

"I believe it. That birthday party I didn't get invited to? It was a sleepover. Everyone came down with the measles. And the boyfriend who dumped me for my best friend? She got pregnant in our senior year, and they both dropped out to get married. Last I heard, he was pumping gas, she was a selfish bitch, and they had three snotty-nosed brats who were making a quick dash toward juvenile delinquency." She sighed complacently. "Justice."

Amused if not convinced, he pulled out of the parking space and followed her directions to the last cabin. A light shone through the open curtains at the front window, and a dark blue Mustang was parked out front. He'd seen the car before—last evening when he'd stopped Tucker Caldwell up near Ridge Crest. The Mustang had passed, then turned into the subdivision, but he'd paid it little notice. He had figured that someone had an out-of-town guest and then had turned his attention back to the more pressing issue of Caldwell and Kate.

So Colleen had gone up to Ridge Crest. To see the plaintiff in her personal injury suit? Not if it was the individual he had in mind. There was no way he could afford to live on the hill. But if he was right about the plaintiff, then the defendant *did* live there.

Her keys jingled as she pulled them from her purse. "Thanks for the ride, for dinner, and for the company."

His only response was a nod.

She hesitated, looking at her keys instead of him. "Would you . . . like to . . . come in?"

Such halting speech was clearly foreign to her. But then, he suspected, so was inviting a man she hardly knew into her room late in the evening. That knowledge and the suspicion of exactly what she was inviting him for made his voice husky when he asked, "For coffee?"

She smiled uneasily. "I don't drink coffee."

"For a drink?"

"I don't have anything in the room."

Which left . . .

He wanted to say yes, *really* wanted to. If she were any other woman, he would pull the Explorer around back out of sight, and he would spend the night, or at least most of it, and in the morning he would leave without regrets or entanglements. But she wasn't any other woman, and for the first time in years, he found himself thinking about, and maybe wanting, entanglements.

He touched her hair. It was soft, cold in the night air. "I think I'd better go on home."

Her gaze, shadowed with regret, met his, and she nodded once.

"I'll see you around noon tomorrow."

She nodded once more, then opened the door, slid to the ground, and hurried up the steps. He waited until she was inside, the door closed behind her, and waited a moment longer until she appeared in the front window. She smiled sweetly before pulling the curtains together.

There had been a time when he never would have turned down an invitation from a pretty woman. Sex for its own sake had always been worth a night of his time. He wasn't sure whether he'd grown up or simply grown stupid. As he drove away from Cabin 6 and the lovely woman inside, though, he was pretty sure the answer was stupid.

The sky was still dark, the street quiet, when Kate awakened the next morning. She looked at the clock on the bedside table, then sank onto her back again. It was six o'clock, a full hour before she had to get up and get ready for work. In her teaching days, she had anticipated spending the best part of her day with twenty-seven inquisitive six-year-olds. Now she had to make herself get out of bed.

So why didn't she quit?

Because the job and her home were the only things Jason hadn't managed to take away from her, and if she lost the job, she would also lose the house. Because quitting meant she was well and truly defeated, and she intended *never* to give Jason or anyone else that satisfaction.

Even if it meant living the rest of her life in misery.

She grimaced at that last thought. Two weeks ago she never would have said she was miserable. Unhappy, yes. Scared to death. Bitter. But she had found a certain pleasure in the fact that she wasn't quitting. She had been satisfied that her mere presence in the office annoyed the hell out of everybody else. She had been willing to spend every workday in the foreseeable future doing piddly little tasks, bored to tears and frustrated as hell, as long as it remained an act of defiance.

But this morning defiance wasn't enough. Annoying those arrogant, self-righteous bastards wasn't enough. For that, she could thank Tucker.

Maybe she would call in sick. No one would believe her, but no one would care. She had plenty of sick leave on the books, along with a few vacation days. They would be glad that she wasn't there, though no gladder than she would be.

Maybe she would take that vacation time. She could help Tucker on his house or drive down to Little Rock to visit Kerry. She could go shopping for new clothes, give the house a thorough cleaning, throw out her answering machine, and disconnect her phone. Or she could put some shape to her vague plan to kill Jason.

But it was too early in the morning for such grim thoughts. With a sigh, she rose from the bed, turning immediately to tuck the sheets and smooth the quilt across the top. After a long, hot shower, she went downstairs and set a pot of water on the stove for coffee. She drank it standing at the kitchen window, allowing herself to focus on nothing in particular, until precisely 7:52, when she called the office. Dr. Tyler prided himself on being punctual. He walked into the office every morning at 7:50.

He answered the phone as the first ring faded in Kate's

ear. "Dr. Marcus Tyler." Marcus Tyler, husband of Lou and father of Mark—Mark, best friend of Jason Trask. Mark was a doctor, too—a dentist, who probably got his kicks fondling female patients under anesthesia. He had testified in court that he had fondled *her*, that he'd had sex with her—back before there was a Mrs. Dr. Tyler, of course—and that she had wanted it rough. Like Jason and all other decent people, he had been appalled by her requests, had been too much the gentleman to slap and hit her, the way she had demanded.

The closest he'd *ever* gotten to touching her had been during his harassing phone calls.

His father repeated his name in an impatient tone, pulling her back from the memories. "Dr. Tyler, this is Kate Edwards. I'd like to take the rest of my vacation time starting today."

"You're supposed to give us two weeks' notice."

"I didn't have two weeks' notice. It doesn't present a problem, does it? I'm not so indispensable that you'll miss me if I'm gone for a few days, am I?"

Her sarcasm annoyed him, but he made no reference to it. "Very well. We'll expect you back when your time is up . . . unless, of course, you should decide not to come back."

"Not come back? To a wonderful job like this? You must be kidding, Dr. Tyler." Without waiting for a response, she hung up, then stood there, her hand on the phone.

She had to give the man credit. He was one among those who genuinely believed Jason's claims. Some people absolutely could not believe such evil existed in the Jason they knew. Add to that his only son, his namesake, swearing on a Bible that Kate had demanded from him what Jason had later given, and she could almost forgive him for being such a fool—provided she were a forgiving person, of course.

Moving away from the phone, she went upstairs, dressed quickly, then left the house. Her stomach was unsettled as she backed out of the driveway and headed not toward school, as was her routine, but for the east side of town. Too much coffee, she told herself, but it wasn't true. She'd had two cups, same as every morning. It was her destination that made her feel queasy.

There were only three streets in Ridge Crest. Oleander Circle passed through the big gate and circled through the neighborhood before returning to the street. It was intersected twice by one block of Wisteria Drive and two blocks of Magnolia Lane. Jason lived on Magnolia. She slowed as she passed his house.

It was a beautiful place . . . and the mere sight of it made her hands clammy and her lungs tighten until she could barely breathe.

Reaching the end of the fence, she pressed the gas pedal, taking it up to the speed limit and beyond. At the corner, she made a rolling stop onto Oleander and toward the gate. Toward escape. Just before she reached the gates, though, she turned back into the circle and drove around again. She had a job to do, but behavior like this virtually guaranteed failure. If simply seeing the place where she had been raped had such an effect on her, what would getting close to the man who had done it do? Face-to-face with him, would she be able to carry out her plan? Or would fear leave her helpless and vulnerable to him once again?

She drove down Magnolia Street once more. The house was just a house. It wasn't evil, though evil did reside there. The place itself, though, hadn't hurt her, couldn't hurt her. As soon as her plan was in place, as soon as she was strong enough to carry it out, neither could Jason.

Back in town, she went to the café two doors down from

the police station. There were curious looks as she walked in and an occasional smirk or whisper as she made her way to a table. Never fond of eating out alone, she hadn't been in a restaurant in town in months. She hadn't wanted to endure the looks, hadn't wanted to risk running into Tim Carter or Mark Tyler or anyone else. This morning, she didn't mind. She wanted the accusing looks. She needed the disparaging whispers.

The waitress was rude, at least until another diner joined Kate at the table. "Morning, Chief."

Travis responded with a nod, ordered coffee and toast, then fixed his gaze on Kate. "The old bat can't afford to be hateful to me. Half my department eats breakfast, lunch, and dinner here, plus they feed my prisoners. So . . . what are you doing here?"

"I believe it's called having breakfast."

"Why aren't you at work?"

"I took some vacation time."

"Why?"

"You're just full of questions this morning, aren't you?"

"I'm a cop. I'm always full of questions. Why did you decide to take time off now? Planning to go somewhere?"

She shook her head.

"Planning to do something?"

"Spring cleaning."

"Spring was six months ago."

"I was busy at the time." She shrugged and finally answered. "I'm going to Little Rock to see Kerry. I'm going to buy some new clothes, and I'm going to help Tucker on his house."

Predictably Travis's manner changed at the mention of Tucker's name. His smile transformed into a scowl, his eyes darkened, and he became much more the chief of police than her good friend. "You're still seeing him."

"Still? It was only a few days ago that you rousted him at my house. Yes, I'm still seeing him."

"Why?"

"Because I like him."

"What's to like?"

"What's not to like?"

"For starters, the fact that he murdered a man."

"It was an accident. Besides, Jeffrey Henderson was just another Jason Trask in the making. Tucker did the world a favor."

"Is that what you like about him? The fact that he killed a Trask?"

Feeling perverse, Kate leaned forward, smiled lasciviously, and softly answered. "What I like about him is that he looks damned good in his clothes . . . and out of them, too."

He leaned forward, too, so close they were almost touching. "Damn it, Kate!"

With a sigh, she sat back. "I like him because he's a decent person. He doesn't care what happened to me. He doesn't care what anyone thinks. He doesn't believe I was responsible for any of it."

"*I* don't believe—"

"You do, Travis. You think I should have known better, I should have listened to Mariana, I shouldn't have gotten myself into a situation where he could do what he did." Changing the subject before he could argue, she said, "Speaking of Mariana, did you know she's back in town?"

Travis sank back. "No, I hadn't heard."

"She claims she's got evidence against Jason. She's planning to take it to the DA. You might want to give her a call."

"I will. How'd you hear about it?"

She gave him a brief recounting of Mariana's visit. She didn't tell him what she thought of it. Travis knew Kate would never go back to court, not even with the promise of a conviction.

The waitress brought their meal, and Kate was cutting into her omelet when Travis spoke. "I met somebody a couple of night ago."

Raising one brow, she took a bite and chewed thoughtfully. "I thought you knew everyone in the county."

"I do. She's a lawyer from Little Rock."

"Here on business?"

"Yeah, but she's very close-mouthed about what the business is."

"As a lawyer should be." Jason's lawyers hadn't been discreet. They had slandered her as thoroughly and as publicly as his family and friends had. "What's she like?"

"She's nice."

"That's a change. *I* was the last nice woman you dated. Of course, that was before I turned kinky." The look he gave her made her feel ashamed, but she went on. "What's her name?"

"Colleen Robbins."

"Have you been out with her yet?"

"We had dinner together last night and the night before."

"Been to bed with her yet?"

"None of your business."

"Yes, it is. If you've had sex with her, then you're not really serious. If you haven't, then it may be the real thing."

She wondered how long it had taken Tucker to find his way to Nolie's bed. Considering where he'd spent the last half of his life, she would bet not long at all. What would he do the next time the urge struck? Make a trip to Little Rock or look someplace closer to home? She knew a number of local women close to his age who wouldn't deign to even speak to him in public, but what they would do with him in private was another story altogether. They would relish the wickedness of getting down and dirty with the resident ex-con, provided, of course, that no one ever found out about it.

The thought left her vaguely annoyed, and she wasn't even sure why. Was it offense on Tucker's behalf that any woman could so easily use and discard him? Or maybe a little feminine disappointment that wherever he turned for companionship, it wouldn't be to her? He knew too much about what Jason has done and how it still affected her. He had learned too quickly not to come too close, not to offer when she needed a hand. He would never think that he might be different, that his touch might not be as frightening.

She sat motionless, everything else forgotten. Was that true? Was it conceivable that she could not only endure physical contact with Tucker, but could come to enjoy it, to want and need it? Could he possibly erase from her memory the terror of intimacy Jason had beaten into her?

"What are you thinking about?"

She answered honestly, not thinking to censor herself. "Tucker."

"Oh, honey. If you could see your face . . ."

She didn't ask what he saw there. She wasn't sure she wanted to know. But his next words gave her a hint.

"You're not going to expect me to be friendly with him, are you?"

The idea of Tucker and Travis ever putting aside their mutual suspicion and distrust to be even remotely friendly was almost enough to make her smile. "I think that's asking a little too much, but maybe the next time you see him at my house, you could resist the urge to frisk and handcuff him."

"I didn't cuff him Saturday night."

"You came close," she pointed out, and he didn't bother to deny it.

"You don't belong with a man like him, Kate."

Pushing her plate away, she laid enough money in its place to cover the breakfast and a small tip, then met his gaze evenly. "You're wrong, Travis. Right now, Tucker Caldwell is exactly the sort of man I need."

Chapter Nine

Making decisions for himself had been the hardest adjustment Tucker had faced as a free man. Life in prison had been strictly regimented. He had gotten up when he was told to, had eaten the food he was offered at the times he was offered it, had worked, quit working, and gone to bed, all when the schedule demanded. Those first few weeks out hadn't been easy, with time on his hands and nothing to do except what he'd wanted to do. Sometimes he had found himself with so many options that he'd been unable to make a choice and had wound up doing nothing. Like today.

He had thought about working on the house, about driving into town for supplies. About visiting with old Ben or heading right on out of town and toward Little Rock. For two hours he'd thought about doing something and had done nothing. It was a vaguely satisfying feeling . . . and, at the same time, vaguely dissatisfying, because anything he might do would only serve as a temporary distraction from what he really wanted.

Kate.

He had wanted to accept her dinner invitation last night—to sit across from her at the glassed-in table and share a meal, to go into her pretty, cozy living room afterward, to sit and talk about things of no consequence. He had wanted to spend a lazy, leisurely evening with her, and when it was over, he had wanted to share a few lazy, leisurely kisses with her while contemplating all the other intimacies he would like to share with her.

And so, because he had wanted too much, he had instead returned home alone, regretting what he had turned down every mile of the way.

As he shifted his weight, he became aware of the sound of an approaching engine. His muscles tensing, he watched the corner of the house, waiting for the first glimpse of the car. After that first visit, she didn't park around front anymore but came around to the clearing in back, just as he did. Just as if she belonged.

Now that was a joke. No matter what had happened to her, no matter how low she had sunk in the town's estimation, she would never sink low enough to belong here. She could never sink low enough to deserve *him*.

Watching as she climbed from the car, he wondered why she was here in the middle of a workday. If her clothes were anything to judge by—faded jeans and a sweatshirt in fire-engine, look-at-me red—she'd taken the day off. The outfit should have looked simply comfortable and casual, and it did. It also looked sexy as hell—baggy sweatshirt hiding rounded breasts, delicate skin, and slender waist, tight jeans hiding nothing at all.

Sweet hell, he was in a sorry state this morning if wholesome, casual, and raggedy could make him feel so damned horny.

As she approached, she brushed her fingers over her hair, a purely feminine gesture. He wouldn't mind touching her hair, running his fingers through it, sampling its texture. Just the thought of such a simple touch was enough to make his erection harder, his desire stronger.

"Good morning," she greeted, and she looked as if it really were. Did a day off work please her so much, or had something happened? Maybe she'd gotten good news about her sister. Maybe lightning had flashed down from the heavens and struck Jason Trask dead. Or maybe she'd made some decision about her plan to kill him herself.

He shifted awkwardly, hoping like hell that she didn't notice his arousal, and forced his attention to an obvious subject. "Why aren't you shut up in your dreary little office?"

"I'm on vacation."

"They let you take vacation time on such short notice?"

"Usually, they require two weeks, but I *am* the most unimportant person in the system. They're happy enough to be rid of me that they don't care if it's a last-minute request." She came a few feet closer, stopping at last to sit on the worn-smooth stump of an old hickory. "Do you have plans for today?"

He shrugged. "I haven't decided on any. What are you planning to do with this vacation?"

She mimicked his shrug and parroted his answer. "I haven't decided. I'll probably go to Little Rock for a couple of days. Other than that, I may do nothing."

His gaze narrowed. "Why Little Rock?"

"Because that's where Kerry is."

"Any other reason?" Such as the fact that the city was probably her best bet for finding someone willing to kill a man for a price?

The look she gave him was genuinely innocent. If she had ulterior motives for planning a trip out of town, she was hiding them well. "I thought I'd do a little shopping—buy some clothes and a few things for the house." Her expression turned wistful. "I haven't bought anything pretty in a long time."

In a flash, desire overrode suspicion. It was that little bit of
longing in her voice, in her eyes, and the immediate image of
Kate in something pretty. A dress, maybe, in the same red as
her sweatshirt, the kind that flattered and drew attention to
the body she'd tried so long to hide. Better than seeing her in
such a dress, of course, would be helping her out of it . . . but
before he could allow that to happen, he would go to Little
Rock himself. Nolie, a hooker, a stranger in a bar . . . it
wouldn't matter who he used just as long as it wasn't Kate.
For her sake—hell, for his own sake—it couldn't be Kate.
She needed someone with qualities he didn't possess.

Feeling lower than he had in a long time—and, not coinci-
dentally, able at last to rise from the steps—he headed for the
truck. "I've got to get to work."

She twisted on the stump to watch him walk away. After
sixteen years in prison, where virtually every move he'd
made had been under someone's watchful gaze, he knew the
feeling.

He pulled a tape measure from the toolbox in the truck
bed, found a ragged notebook and a pencil in the glove box,
and took them inside the house. He was taking measurements when Kate's shadow fell across the floor. He knew
she was standing in the doorway, knew she was watching
him again. He didn't glance her way, but simply concen-
trated on doing a two-person job by himself.

He wasn't surprised when she came farther into the room,
when she caught hold of the clip on the end of the tape measure and held it in place while he extended the metal tape the
length of the wall. He *was* surprised when she finally spoke.

"Do you mind my coming out here?"

If he said yes, he minded like hell, she would help until
he'd finished the measurements, then get in her car and drive
away, and he would never see her here again. But if he said

no, she would believe him, and she would keep coming back. Which would be worse? Never seeing her, still wanting her, and knowing he'd hurt her, or seeing her often, still wanting her, and knowing he couldn't have her?

When he opened his mouth, he wasn't sure what answer he would give. The one short word surprised him and, at the same time, was exactly what he expected himself to say. "No."

The plain, simple answer was enough for her, but, perversely, not for him. For some damnable reason he felt compelled to say more, to be more honest than he'd been. "To tell the truth . . ." Wishing that he'd kept his mouth shut, he shrugged and grudgingly forced the words out. "I kind of like your company."

She smiled, an honest-to-God, cut-a-man-off-at-the-knees smile. "I like you, too." Almost immediately, the smile disappeared, though, and she asked, "Why?"

"Why what?"

"Why do you like me?"

Because he had too many answers and none of them the right ones, he scowled. "That's a stupid question."

"No, it's not. Travis likes me because I'm the younger sister he never had. My parents liked me because I was obedient, well-behaved—the perfect daughter. Jason liked me because I flattered him. I did what he wanted. When I didn't, he quit liking me."

He tugged on the tape measure, and she released her end. It retracted into its metal case with a snap. "In case you haven't noticed, there are a number of differences between Trask and me. He's got money. I don't. He's respectable. I'm not. He was sleeping with you. I'm—" The images that flashed into his mind made his breath catch and his throat tighten before he forced out the last regretful word. "Not."

"Would you like to?"

Her soft question summoned back the desire he'd so recently gotten under control, hotter and stronger than ever. Raising his gaze to the sky, he swore silently and viciously. Would he like to? God help him, would he like to find some bright pleasure in his life? Would he like to wake up every morning a free man? Would he like to continue breathing? Sweet Jesus, he would like to, more than she could possibly imagine, more than he could allow himself to admit.

Searching deep inside himself, he dredged up every bit of sarcasm he could find. "Well, let's see . . . I'm thirty-four years old. In my entire life, I've been with one woman and two teenage girls. I've spent sixteen years locked up in prison where I never even *saw* a real, live, breathing woman. You're pretty, you're available, and, hey, the word around town is that you're kinky. Would I like to sleep with you? Hell, yes, I would like to sleep with you."

The light faded from her eyes as they grew damp, and her lower lip trembled before she caught it between her teeth. She was so fragile, so damn easy to hurt. Cursing his own selfish need for protection, he turned away before she gave way to the tears that just might tear him apart.

When she finally spoke, her voice was soft, a little shaky, but not tearful. "You think I'm pretty?"

He looked over his shoulder in time to see her dab the corner of one eye. Slowly he turned to face her. She looked a little wary, a little wounded, but determined not to give in to it. His respect for her grew. So did his desire. "Of course I think you're pretty," he said gruffly.

"A couple of nights ago you said I was frumpy."

"I said your clothes were frumpy, not you." And in response she had found clothes that weren't—snug-fitting jeans, the green sweater, this red shirt. He had pointed out that playing down her looks wouldn't protect her from bastards like Trask, and she had started fixing her hair and wearing more makeup. This morning she even smelled faintly of perfume.

"So . . . Would you like to . . . ?" She finished with a shrug. "For real?"

For a time he simply looked at her, an odd little pain surrounded by bitterness settling in his chest and making his voice unsteady. "Is this some kind of game, Kate?"

"I don't know what you mean."

He moved toward her, one slow step at a time. She tried to stand her ground, but the closer he got, the harder it became. Suddenly she took a step back, followed by another and another until the unfinished wall was at her back, and still he didn't stop, not until he was directly in front of her, so close that he could see every bit of the fear in her eyes, could hear the uneven pace of her breathing, could feel the little shivers passing through her. He raised his hand, and she shrank back. He wanted to retreat, too, but he forced himself to touch her, to cup his palm to her cheek. He felt the muscles in her jaw tighten, felt the effort she was making to stand still and silent.

No man had been this close to her since Trask. No man had touched her like this. Certainly no man had kissed her.

He moved closer, bent forward, actually touched his mouth to hers, before a strangled protest escaped her and she escaped him, darting to safety at the opposite end of the room. Gripping the studs on either side of where she had stood with both hands, he leaned forward until his forehead touched the plywood. "You can't even let me touch you, Kate. What does it matter if I'd like to make love with you? What good is it, wanting what you can't give?"

The silence was heavy, broken only by the sound of his

ragged breathing. The room was so still for so long that he was beginning to wonder if she had slipped out the door when suddenly she appeared in his peripheral vision a half dozen feet away.

"Maybe that'll change." Her voice was steady. For all the emotion he was feeling, she sounded cool, distant, untouched.

Maybe what would change? Maybe he would quit wanting her? Maybe he would accept how futile it was and get over it? Maybe, like her friend the cop, he would come to view her as the little sister he'd never had and forget how much more he'd wanted from her?

"When you came to my house Saturday night, I was afraid to let you in. I hadn't been alone in the house with a man other than Travis in six months. Just a few nights later, I had dinner with you there." She paused, drew a deep breath. "I'm trying very hard, Tucker, to deal with my fears. I've discovered that I can talk to a man, even a stranger—even a stranger who just got out of prison. I can be miles from the nearest neighbor with you. I can go for a walk in the woods with you. Maybe . . ."

She broke off again, and this time he turned to look at her. Her back was to the wall, with one of the windows behind her. Her elbows rested on the roughed-in sill, and her hands were clasped together. She might sound cool and distant, but she didn't look it. She looked about as unsettled as he felt.

"Maybe I can learn to do other things. Maybe this is the right time to put Jason and everything behind me, to get on with my life, and maybe you're the right man."

He wanted to laugh at the notion, wanted to tell her that he had never been the right man for anything, that he sure as hell wasn't the right man for her. More than that, though, he wanted to believe her. He wanted to believe that she could trust him, that she could lose her fear of men—of living, of intimacy—in him. He wanted to believe that just once he could be what someone—no, what *she* needed. He wanted it so badly that it hurt.

For a long while they simply looked at each other. She was waiting for some response from him—acknowledgment, encouragement, some indication that he was willing to try. He gave it with a nervous nod and a sickly smile. "Yeah, maybe." Then he inhaled deeply of lumber and her faintly sweet, delicate fragrance. "I need to . . . uh, pick up some supplies in town. Want to go?"

Her responding smile was relief mixed with gratitude. "Yeah. I'd like that."

After securing a small diamond in each ear, Mariana studied her reflection. The suit—black, severely tailored—wasn't intended to flatter anyone, but it looked good on her. The stark ebony was becoming with her fair skin and hair, and the plain lines emphasized the shapelier lines of her body.

She was due in District Attorney Marquette's office in fifteen minutes. She would tell him everything and play the tapes for him, and he would make the decision to file further criminal charges against Jason. This time the bastard would be convicted. This time, with his own voice, his own words, to condemn him, there would be no way out. This time *she* would win.

She transferred everything from her everyday handbag to a black leather one, then went downstairs. Her mother was resting on the sofa, the television tuned to a rerun of *The Andy Griffith Show*. Growing up in Fall River had been almost as idyllic for Mariana as growing up in Mayberry had been for Opie. Life had been good, innocent, almost perfect. Then she'd turned twenty and married Jason and had discov-

ered that, yes, indeed, evil did live in Fall River. She hated
him almost as much for spoiling her illusions as she did for
the beatings and the manipulation.

"I'm going now, Mama."

Pat turned toward her, her expression a mix of pride and
fear. Not one hour had passed since Mariana's return that her
mother hadn't worried and fretted over her daughter's plans.
This morning's meeting with Mr. Marquette would ease her
fears. Once he heard those tapes, Pat could relax. They could
all relax . . . except Jason.

"I don't know about this, honey. Maybe you ought to can-
cel this appointment and give it some more thought. I'm not
sure—"

"I am sure," Mariana interrupted. "I've got to do this,
Mama. I won't be long, and when I come back, I'll bring
some lunch with me. Something from Miss Annabelle's,
maybe?" She pressed a kiss to her mother's forehead, then
headed out.

It was a short drive into the heart of Fall River, where she
found a parking space right in front of the courthouse. As
she fiddled with her hair and lipstick in the rearview mirror,
she avoided even a glimpse of the bank on the opposite corner, where Jason had an office. She was a woman with a purpose, she thought with a grim smile as she climbed out of the
car.

"Mariana."

That single utterance set a chill down her spine. Though
her brain gave the command to run, to escape, her feet refused to move. She stopped where she was, paralyzed by intense fear.

Jason came around to stand in front of her. He was still
handsome, still charming and polished. It was no surprise
people had trouble reconciling Kate's claims against him

with such classically perfect features. Evil had a face, most people believed, and Jason's wasn't it.

Most people were wrong.

"I told myself it couldn't possibly be true." Jason's voice was congenial, pleasant, almost friendly, and it made her shudder. It was the same voice he used before he'd hit her the hardest, before he'd forced himself on her the most brutally, exactly the same voice he'd used when he had threatened to kill her. "I'd heard that you were back in town, and I said no, it isn't possible. Why, Mariana and I had a deal. I gave her money, and she swore on her life that she would never come back to Fall River. She would never break that promise, not *on her life*." The friendliness disappeared, replaced by icy threat. "Why are you here?"

"This is my home," she replied, striving to keep her voice even and cool. "Where else would I be?"

"Don't think you can come home as if nothing happened. Don't think you can make a deal, take my money, then come back." He didn't move closer, but his words—his threat—made it seem as if he did.

"But that's exactly what I've done."

"I'll destroy you. I'll make you sorry you ever set foot in Fall River again. I'll—"

"You're wasting your breath, Jason." She clutched her purse a little tighter, able to feel the sharp corners of the tape cases through the leather, drawing some small bit of courage from them. "I'm not afraid of you anymore. You see, I took a few precautions before I left last time—during our negotiations. You remember our negotiations, don't you? When you threatened me? When you bribed me to leave town rather than testify?"

He stared at her with pure malevolence, no doubt remembering those conversations—how he had bragged, delivered threats and bribes, how he had gloated over what he had done and the fact that he was going to get away with it. In all their years together, he had never believed she was smart enough to put together anything more complicated than the proper ensemble for the proper occasion. He had never in his wildest dreams considered that she might be smart enough to outwit him, smart enough to trap him.

"So you've run out of money, and you've come to get more. How much do you think your 'precautions' are worth?"

Last spring it had been easy to summon a figure out of thin air, pack up, and go away to live a life of leisure—at least, in the beginning. Taking the money and going away had been the easy parts. Living with the knowledge of what she'd done and staying away, though—those had been impossible. She wasn't foolish enough to try again.

Still, she did name a figure. "Gee, I don't know. Maybe three to five?"

He laughed. "Three to five thousand dollars? Some 'precautions,' sweetheart."

"Three to five *years*," she corrected him, coolly disregarding his scorn. "In prison. Maybe more, maybe less. You know, I'm not up on this penal stuff. Now, if you'll excuse me, I have an appointment, and I don't want to be late."

He looked from her to the courthouse behind him, his gaze going automatically to the second floor, where the DA's office was located. When he looked at her again, her newfound courage shattered under the weight of his fury. "Remember who you're screwing with, Mariana. You cause trouble for me, and your life won't be worth living. I'll make you so damn sorry—"

Clutching her purse even tighter, she pushed past him. At the bottom of the broad stone steps, though, she looked back.

did, but I was afraid. For ten years *I* was his victim. *I* was he one he punched and raped and beat. I knew what he was capable of. When he said he would hurt me if I testified, I believed him. Jason Trask doesn't make idle threats. Kerry Edwards is proof of that." So what did that say about the threats he'd just made outside?

In the silence that followed, Marquette looked from Travis to her. "What is it you want from us, Ms. Trask?"

She chose the least noble of her goals. "I want you to make Jason pay. I want to see him punished. He admits to raping Kate Edwards. He threatens and bribes a witness to that rape. Those are crimes. They can't go unpunished."

"Chief McMaster and I will have to listen to the tapes in their entirety. We'll have to see exactly what's on there."

"And then?"

"If I believe the tapes warrant it, I have to get a ruling on whether a new trial would constitute double jeopardy. To do that, I have to convince the court that the evidence is substantive enough to have affected the outcome of the original trial, had it been presented then, and that it hadn't been discoverable before that trial through the usual diligence. The fact that you disappeared should help take care of that."

"You don't sound encouraged."

"Getting a retrial is never easy for the prosecution, Ms. Trask. With Jason Trask for a defendant and without the victim's cooperation, in this case, it may be impossible."

She looked at Travis. "Maybe you can convince her to cooperate." He and Kate had known each other all their lives. He had wanted vengeance almost as much as she had.

He shook his head grimly. "You've heard the old complaint about the way rape cases used to be handled—the way his case was handled. The victim gets raped once by the

"I've been sorry, Jason, every minute of every day. But no more. Now I'm going to set things right. You're going to pay, Jason. Finally, for all your sins, you're going to pay." Feeling the weight of his malice-filled stare on her back, she climbed the stairs and went inside. In the cool, shadowy privacy of the lobby, she sagged against a stone pillar and breathed heavily before heading for the stairs.

In the DA's office, David Marquette was standing behind his desk, and Travis McMaster was next to the window. The sight of him made Mariana's steps falter and intensified the shame she had lived with the last six months.

She hadn't really known Travis before the assault on Kate, though she had been aware of him. He was tall, handsome, and charming, and had been Fall River's star quarterback for three championship years. Every girl in town had been aware of him. Her first real contact with him, though, had come after Kate's run-in with Jason. He had come to see her at her mother's house, had asked questions about what she had witnessed the night before and also about her own experiences with Jason. He had been curious about why she had never sought help and regretful that he had never suspected what was going on. It had been the first time in years that a man had been genuinely concerned about her.

It wasn't his fault that he'd never noticed anything. Jason had been careful, and she had been skilled at putting on a good front. On the occasions that her injuries couldn't be concealed, she had simply stayed home until they had healed. No one had suspected a thing, not even her own mother.

She shook hands with Marquette, then Travis, then took a seat in front of the desk.

"You said on the phone that you had some evidence regarding last spring's case against Jason Trask."

She liked his direct tack—no chitchat, no idle pleasantries, just straight to the point—and responded in kind. Opening the flap of her bag, she removed the tapes, laying them on the desk.

Marquette leaned forward to pick up one. "What's on these tapes, Ms. Trask?"

"Conversations between my ex-husband and me. Confessions. Threats. Promises. Bribes."

Marquette pulled a tape recorder from his desk drawer, removed the tape it held, and placed hers inside. As the machine whirred slowly to the starting point, Travis came closer.

There was a moment or two of silence, then Jason's smug, arrogant voice. "I knew you would come. Have you talked to McMaster?"

"Yes."

"What did you tell him?"

"The truth."

"What truth?"

"That you raped Kate Edwards. That I saw it."

"You saw us playing a game—acting out a fantasy. That was all."

She recalled the scene she had walked in on that night and shuddered even now. Pots and pans had littered the floor where Kate had lain, her clothing torn, her face sickly white, her eyes rounded with terror. She had looked right at Mariana, had reached out one feeble hand and whimpered, "Help me . . ."

Help me. Mariana had been incapable of helping anyone. She had simply stood there, remembering all the times it had been *her* lying underneath Jason, all the times it had been *her* clothing that was torn, *her* blood on Jason's fists. She had stood there, horrified and helpless, and watched.

"Playing?" Her voice trembled on the tape. "It did like a game to me. If it was a game, why was she Why was she begging you to stop?" A pause for cour: was no game, Jason. You raped her. You threw he and raped her, and you loved every minute of it."

"So what if I did? That's our secret—yours, min Kate's. No one's ever going to know differently."

"She's talked to the police. *I've* talked to the police."

"But you won't be talking to them again, not if you what's good for you."

Silence. She had learned well what was "good" for h Jason's definition. His punishments, discipline, and deg tion had all been *good* for her, because she was stupid. She u been a bad wife. She had brought his displeasure on herself. Always it had been *her* fault, some failing within *her*, that had led to his violence.

"Kate likes rough sex. She gets off on pain. The more it hurts, the more she enjoys it. I was just giving her what she wanted that night."

"You know that's not true."

"No one cares about your version of the truth. By the ti this is over, no one will believe your truth or Kate's. C *my* truth will matter."

Marquette shut off the tape. "The other tapes are mo the same?"

She nodded.

"Did he pay you to leave town before the trial?" asked.

She nodded again. "It's on the last tape."

"Why are you bringing these to us now? If you' them to us before, we could have convicted him. H have gone to prison."

Mariana met Travis's gaze evenly. "I'm not prou   t!

man, the second time by the system. There's no way Kate's going to endure it a third time."

"If you wanted encouragement, Ms. Trask," Marquette said, "you should have brought these tapes to us months ago. You should have testified against your ex-husband when you were subpoenaed. Still, we'll see what we can do."

Mariana secured the snap on her purse and stood up. "I'll wait to hear from you."

"I'll walk out with you," Travis offered, moving to hold the door for her. "David, I'll be right back."

They were halfway down the stairs before she made an attempt at the apology she felt compelled to offer. "I couldn't have testified against Jason back then."

"I understand that. So does Marquette. It's just that your testimony and these tapes, combined with what we already had, would have made a hell of a case against him." They crossed the lobby to the double doors, and he went out first, once again holding the door for her. "Maybe we can still do something. You know the saying—better late than never."

Hadn't her mother reminded her? Still, she felt skeptical as she stopped at the top of the steps and looked up at him. "I also know the saying, 'Too little, too late.' I hope that's not the case here."

"Anything that helps bring Jason Trask under control can never be considered too little." Travis glanced across the street to the bank. "Does he know you're back?"

"He met me when I arrived this morning—with a friendly warning."

"What kind of warning?"

She repeated only the highlights of her conversation with Jason. When she mentioned the precautions she'd taken, his expression grew grimmer.

"So he knows you have some sort of evidence against him."

"I wouldn't be foolish enough to come back without something. Speaking of . . . those tapes are the originals. They're all I have."

"I'll have duplicates made and bring them by your house." He turned to go back inside but stopped after only a few steps. "If he contacts you again, let me know. If any of his friends contact you, let me know that, too." Pulling a business card from his pocket, he offered it to her. "Anytime."

She accepted the card, holding it tightly as if it might protect her. "Thanks. I appreciate it."

As she unpacked the grocery bag that was serving as a picnic basket, Colleen considered her day with satisfaction. It was only a few minutes past noon, and already she'd signed up two new clients. Randy Hawkins had called this morning with the news that Gary Pritchard and Carla Brownley were willing to join the lawsuit against the Trasks. Pritchard had suffered crippling injuries in a twenty-foot fall that never should have happened, and Carla's husband had been electrocuted in what was either the freakiest of accidents or pure, reckless disregard. He'd left her with three kids to support, more debts than her waitress's salary could cover, and a deep, unrelenting bitterness over losing the husband she'd intended to spend the rest of her life with.

Colleen was scheduled to meet with them this afternoon, but right now, she was putting business aside for pleasure. Lunch in a pretty park on a lovely fall day with Travis McMaster certainly was pleasurable.

He sat across from her, watching. If she'd been able to plan an ideal picnic, they would be on a quilt spread over grass near enough to the water to feel its occasional spray.

The paper bag would be a fragile basket, and the food would be sustenance for the soul—a loaf of bread, a chunk of cheese, a bottle of wine, a helping of sweet, juicy, perfectly ripened fruit, and, for dessert, a few pieces of sinfully rich gourmet chocolate. They would have hours to fritter away, to eat, drink, and talk, to explore and grow intimate.

Instead, they sat on cement benches flanking a cement table. The paper bag held foam containers from the deli at the Trasks' grocery store, their drinks consisted of a six-pack of cold pop, and they didn't have an afternoon. They had one hour, less if the pager on Travis's belt or the radio on the bench beside him commanded his attention.

But there was still tremendous potential for intimacy.

"So what do you think of our falls?"

She fished the plastic utensils from the bottom of the bag. "It's nice." The main fall dropped about fifty feet, sending splashes across the surface of the pool below, where the water collected before traveling through a dozen much smaller falls on its way downstream. "Anyone ever dive from the top into the pool?"

"Only once. The fall kills them. The pool's only about six feet at its deepest."

"So someone has tried."

"A few times. Not in the last twenty years."

"Accidents?" Travis had commented last night that this was a place for kids to go. To teenage boys, with too much to drink and the fearlessness of youth, such a dive might seem the perfect way to demonstrate their courage to lesser boys and impressionable girls. But he was shaking his head.

"Suicides. It's sad, but it happens."

She poked at the baked beans that filled one compartment of the foam tray. Such a hopelessly useless sentiment. She'd heard the words when her father had died and had wanted to argue that these things *didn't* happen, not to families like hers, not to good men like her father. She had wanted him to not be dead. Failing that, she had wanted to know *why*. Why had her father died when other less important, less loving men still lived? Why had Harry died when the people responsible for his death—the Trasks—still lived and prospered?

It had taken a long time to quit asking why. Why, she had finally realized, wasn't as important as putting things right. It wasn't as important as justice. As revenge.

"You look like you're a million miles away."

She looked up at Travis. "My father killed himself when I was twenty-two. I was just thinking . . ."

"I'm sorry."

"We were very close. He was my only real family. The first ten years I missed him so much that I thought I would die." Smiling faintly, she amended that. "I *still* miss him very much."

"Parents should die of old age with their grandchildren and great-grandchildren at their side."

Now *that* was a sentiment she could wholeheartedly embrace. "Are your parents still living?"

"In the same house I grew up in. My dad's parents live next door, and my mom's folks are less than half a mile away. My two older sisters still live here, but our brother Bobby has settled in Missouri."

"These days families tend to scatter across the country. It must be nice to have yours so close."

"Fall River is like that. Even people who leave tend to come back. Some people tend to stay around even when they would be better off elsewhere."

She studied him. His blue eyes were grim as he stabbed up

a forkful of barbecued pork. "Does that last statement apply to anyone in particular?"

He answered with a scowl. "Yeah. Kate."

Kate Edwards. Another in the long line of Jason Trask's victims. "Why would Kate be better off elsewhere? This is her home. Her family and friends are here."

"Family?" he repeated cynically. "Her father said the rape was her fault. She'd slept with Jason before, and he had every right to expect her to do it again. Her mother and Kristin wanted her to keep her mouth shut and pretend it never happened. After Kerry was raped, the family broke off contact with Kate. As far as friends, I'm the only one . . . at least, I was. Until recently."

"So she's made a new friend." Why was that cause for displeasure? He should be happy that Kate had someone else on her side . . . unless this new friend was male. Unless he was jealous. Unless Kate was more than the good friend he had claimed. She was starting to feel a little jealousy herself when he explained.

"Since the trial, Kate's been pretty much shunned by everyone. Most people believed Jason's lies that she's kinky and wanted him to hurt her. The people who do believe in her are too intimidated by the Trasks to say so. She lost her job. All of her family and most everyone else have turned their backs on her. She was even invited to find another church to attend. The people who support Trask are the most vocal, of course. They treat her with derision and scorn. They say she's perverted, sick, a slut. After six months of fighting, I think she's decided to accept their opinion of her. Why else would she be seeing this guy?"

"What guy?"

"An ex-con by the name of Caldwell. The bastard spent half his life in prison for murder. He just got out three months ago, moved here a month ago, and hooked up with Kate practically right away."

Colleen stared at him. Tucker Caldwell was here in Fall River. It had to be him. How many Caldwells serving time for murder had been released from the state penal system three months ago? She had wondered last weekend, after seeing mention of his parole, where he had gone and what he would do, but she had never dreamed that he might come here to Fall River. She had never suspected that he had any reason to do so.

Had he come for the same reason she had? Had he learned enough from fellow prisoners and life behind bars to realize that he'd gotten royally shafted at his trial? Had he come to suspect that his court-appointed lawyer had been on someone's payroll and it *wasn't* the taxpayers'? Had he come to make the Trasks pay for his sixteen years in prison?

Realizing abruptly that Travis was giving her an oddly curious look, she forced herself to look merely interested and ask, "Have you asked Kate why she's seeing him?"

That dark scowl again. "She says she likes him. He doesn't look at her the way everyone else in town does. He doesn't blame her for what Trask did."

Colleen wasn't surprised. For all his reputation, the Tucker Caldwell she remembered had been a frightened, naive, and trusting boy—genuinely sorrowful over Jeffrey Henderson's death, more troubled and believably remorseful than any client *she* had ever represented. Harry had filled him with false reassurances, had told him it was a simple enough case, that it had clearly been an accident, and Tucker had believed him. Harry had promised he would do his best, that he would get Tucker a verdict that was just and a sentence to match, and Tucker had believed that, too. Then Harry had sold his client's defense to the victim's family, and Tucker had shaken his hand when it was over. He had thanked Harry—*thanked* him—for the lousiest defense any accused had ever received.

Sometimes she thought that single act, more than any other, had driven her father to wash down those pills with a bottle of bourbon. If Tucker had been angry, if he had blamed Harry, the young girlfriend who had lied on the stand, the Hendersons, or anyone else, maybe it wouldn't have eaten at her father so relentlessly. But Tucker had blamed only himself. He had committed the crime—even if it had been accidental—and so the responsibility for the consequences had also fallen on him. It was only natural, then, that he would lay responsibility for Jason's actions on Jason himself and not on his victim.

"When people you've known all your life treat you with derision and scorn, when they believe lies about you, when they think nasty, horrible thoughts about you, I imagine meeting someone who doesn't is a tremendous relief," she said softly. "Kate doesn't have to defend herself to him. He doesn't blame her for being vulnerable and helpless, for being Jason's victim. She doesn't have to be ashamed with him."

Travis wasn't ready to agree. "People in town are already calling her trash. Taking up with Tucker Caldwell just proves them right."

"Is she supposed to care what people in town think? To give up a friend because mean-spirited, nasty-minded people don't approve? These are the same people who believe she's sick, the same people who support the man who raped her. She should give up her friendship with Tucker to make *them* happy?" She sat silently, waiting for his response. When it didn't come, she reached across the table to lay her hand over his. "Do *you* think she's trash?"

"Of course not!" The denial exploded from him, followed by a deep, calming breath. "I think she's too good for him. *He* is trash. He's been in trouble all his life. He's an ex-con, a murderer, for God's sake. Spending time with him in the long run will only hurt her. It will drag her down to his level."

"Or maybe it will heal her." Impatience crept into her voice. "Listen to what you've said, Travis. Her family blames her for being raped, for her sister being raped—her own *family*—but Tucker doesn't. Her friends shun her for being Jason's victim, but Tucker doesn't. She needs that kind of unconditional support, or she's never going to get over this. If Tucker Caldwell is willing to give it to her, then you should be damned grateful to him."

For a long time, Travis simply glowered at her, then gradually, grudgingly, the corners of his mouth lifted in a smile. "You present a good argument, counselor."

"But you're not convinced."

"I've had to try to help Kate put the pieces back together twice before. I don't want to do it again."

She began gathering the remnants of their lunch. "Maybe you won't have to. Maybe Tucker is exactly what Kate needs."

And maybe Kate was exactly what Tucker needed. Considering the way his life had turned out, a good woman was the least he deserved.

Chapter Ten

After spending a few hours working on the roof, Kate and Tucker finally made that trip into town. She wandered down the aisles of Mortenson's Lumber, idly glancing over the items on the shelves, occasionally looking toward the counter near the big side doors where Tucker was waiting to pay for his purchases. She had come here often as a child with her grandfather. There hadn't been a job around the house that Charles Edwards couldn't handle himself. Together they'd bought plumbing and electrical supplies, hardware and paint and sweet-smelling lumber—maybe, her grandfather had always suggested, from his own trees. She had been enchanted by the idea that the playhouse he'd built in his backyard had used lumber from trees that he had planted, nursed, harvested, and sold.

Her grandfather would have liked Tucker. Having worked with his hands all his life, Charles had thought that a man who needed others to build, fix, and repair things for him wasn't to be trusted. Jason needed help. Her own father needed help. But not Tucker. When it came to work, it seemed there was nothing he couldn't do.

Rounding a corner display, she joined Tucker at the counter. Lyle Mortenson was standing on the opposite side, wearing an unfriendly frown that eased only slightly when he looked at her. "Can I help you?"

"I'm with him," she said, and the antagonism returned full force.

He finished adding the figures on the pad, then announced the total. He might not like doing business with Tucker, but he certainly didn't mind taking his money. A man of principle would either refuse his business or treat him with the same courtesy as other customers. Then, remembering the waitress's differing attitudes toward her and Travis at breakfast this morning, she acknowledged that there were few people of principle in Fall River.

"I'll be outside," she murmured as Tucker handed over a stack of twenties. After he nodded, she headed for the front door and the porch where Mr. James sat. She sat down beside him and gazed across the street to the vacant lot on the other side.

After a moment, without shifting her gaze, she quietly asked, "Why did you send me to Tucker, Mr. James?"

"He seemed the best candidate for your job."

"Did you really think he would do it?"

Seconds ticked past in the gentle rustling of the breeze, the rumble of a truck on the street, and the sound of a siren several blocks over. Finally she turned to look at the old man and saw that he was looking at her. "I thought he would do what was right."

Right for whom? She didn't bother asking because he wouldn't answer. She suspected, though, that *right* for all three of them, in his opinion, was the same thing: nobody dying. When he'd told her that Tucker Caldwell was the man she should see, he had hoped that Tucker could talk her out of her plans, that killing Jeffrey Henderson had taught him a lesson she could learn from. Mr. James must have understood how deeply Henderson's death had troubled Tucker, how much difficulty he'd had in dealing with it, and the old man had hoped that Tucker could make her understand.

There were a few differences, though. Tucker had never intended to cause Henderson any harm. She *intended* to kill Jason Trask. It wasn't going to be a tragic accident, a fight between boys gone horribly wrong. The outcome wouldn't come as a shock. It wouldn't be anything to regret or suffer over for the rest of her life.

It would be justice.

"He did," she said in reference to Mr. James's last statement. "He turned me down. He said that it's easier to live with the knowledge that Jason's alive, a free man, than with the guilt of being responsible for his death. He said that living with his death would destroy me."

"Did you believe him?"

She smiled faintly. "I guess it was just a fantasy all along—a way of coping when I didn't have any other. I knew it wasn't going to happen, but it made me feel better thinking about it, wanting it. I didn't feel so helpless."

"And now?"

Once more she looked at him, her gaze steady and clear. "I'm not helpless. Jason has made me stronger than I ever thought I would be. I can deal with this. I can deal with anything." Even cold-blooded, premeditated murder. As soon as she got around to doing a little premeditating. Soon. She was going to start planning just as soon as she'd enjoyed a little freedom from her job and a little time with Tucker.

For a long moment, Ben studied her through thick-lensed glasses, then nodded with satisfaction. "Your grandfather would be proud of you, Kate."

She looked away to hide her doubts as the bell over the door announced Tucker's presence. Wiping her expression clean, she smiled at the old man as she rose from the rocker. "Would you like to have lunch with us, Mr. James, before we head back out to the house?"

He looked from her to Tucker, whose only response was a shrug. Although the invitation had been offered on impulse, she hoped the old gentleman would accept. His relationship with Tucker intrigued her—generations apart in age and worlds apart in experience, the most respected of Fall River's black community and the least respected of the entire community—and she would like an opportunity to observe them together.

But after a moment's consideration, Mr. James shook his head. "I appreciate the invitation, Miss Kate, but I believe I'll stay right here and enjoy this warm sun. You young people go on and have a good time."

"See you next time, old man," Tucker said as he waited at the top of the steps.

They were in the truck, the bed loaded with supplies and covered with an old tarp, and a block away from the lumberyard when Kate began to wonder. When Jason was dead, despite her hopefully well-constructed alibi, would the old man know that she was responsible? Would Tucker? Would it change the way they felt about her?

She would have to make certain that they didn't guess. If she could fool them, she could fool anyone. Even though some part of her really didn't want to be fooling Tucker. Instead, she wanted to explore the possibilities this morning's conversation had opened up, to discover where she'd gotten the courage to ask those questions. *Why do you like me? Do you think I'm pretty? Would you like to sleep with me?* Even now the audacity of that last question made her cheeks warm. She had no right asking such a question, especially when she wasn't likely to follow through. . . .

Was she? She had let him approach her, touch her, had almost let him kiss her. Right now the idea having sex with any man, even Tucker, seemed impossible, but a few weeks ago, the idea of spending time alone with any man had also seemed impossible. Who was to say that sometime in the future that sort of intimacy wouldn't be an everyday part of her life?

It was ludicrous. Unimaginable. Entirely possible. It was called healing.

"Were you just being polite with the old man or do you really want to have lunch in town?"

She glanced Tucker's way. They were sitting at the intersection, and he was watching her, his face expressionless, his eyes dark. What he was really asking was whether she wanted to go out in public with him. Didn't he understand by now that she was beyond caring what people thought?

"Of course I want to have lunch. We can go to Ozark Annie's over on the east side of town."

At the first break in traffic, he pulled into the street.

"How did you meet Mr. James?" she asked, as they drove past the schools and her office. It was overwhelming how good it felt to not be there.

"I don't remember. It must have been the first time I ever came to Fall River. My uncle used to come into town and drop us off while he went drinking or visited his women. We hung out wherever we didn't get chased away from. For me, that was with old Ben. As long as I was with him, people left me alone." He gave her another long, steady look. "Hard to imagine that your grandfather and I could be friends with the same man, isn't it?"

"Not at all. I was just thinking back there in the store that my granddad probably would have liked you. He thought you could judge a man by his work. You do good work."

He pulled into the nearly empty lot in front of the restaurant and shut off the engine. As he climbed from the truck, she gave the few cars around them a quick glance. An odd emptiness appeared deep inside as her gaze lingered over the last two, a sedan and a pickup, fifteen years old but in excellent condition. She had learned to drive a stick shift on that truck, had ridden more than a few miles in that car.

Across the cab, Tucker stood impatiently beside the open door. "Are you getting out?"

"Yeah. Sure." Opening her own door, she slid to the ground, then closed it harder than necessary. By the time she reached the restaurant entrance, he was already there, holding the door open for her. She paused for a moment in front of him. "Listen, when we get inside, you'll probably see a gray-haired woman with glasses and a tall man with graying blond hair. They won't be pleased to see us."

"Who are they?"

She tried to ignore that funny little emptiness. "My parents," she said flatly, then walked past him and into the foyer. She tried hard not to look when they entered the dining room, but since only three tables were occupied, it was impossible to miss them. They sat in a booth across the room, her mother on one side, her father and Kristin on the other.

Once she was seated, she looked at them, and they looked back with such hostility. It was that way every time she saw them—no words, no greetings, no accusations. Just harsh, unforgiving, judging looks.

"Do you see them often?"

"As seldom as they can manage. I'm sure they thought they were safe from me here. I've always hated going out to eat alone. Since Jason I've hated going out, period."

"Is that your other sister?"

"Can't you tell?" The Edwards girls all took after their father's side of the family—blond hair, blue eyes, naturally slender. Kerry was the prettiest of the three, the nicest and probably the smartest. Kristin was the most popular and definitely the most vain, and Kate was . . . What superlative could she lay claim to? The biggest idiot? The worst loser? The most pathetic?

The strongest. She was the strongest, the most determined, the toughest.

"You were close."

She focused her gaze on Tucker, deliberately ignoring her family as they were surely ignoring her. "We were the perfect family. My father worked, and my mother was a full-time housewife and mom. She baked cookies every day, was president of the PTA, and sewed costumes for Halloween and school pageants. We sat down to dinner together every night, we went to church together three times a week, and every Sunday we had dinner at my grandparents'. Ours was the most popular house in the neighborhood. Everyone loved my family. Everyone wanted to be part of it."

Now she was in the unenviable position of wanting what all her friends had once wanted. She wanted to be a part of such a loving family, but the family didn't want her. They didn't love her.

Annabelle brought menus and ice water, greeting Kate with a reserved nod, followed by a cautionary glance across the room. Without saying a word, she managed to be even less cordial to Tucker before leaving again. "We brightened her day, didn't we?"

Tucker was scowling. "People aren't usually too happy to have me around."

"Don't flatter yourself. It's me she doesn't want here. My parents are good customers. So are the Trasks. Jason and his buddies have dinner here every Tuesday night. He used to bring me every Friday night. His family and friends fill the private dining room every Sunday after church. And"—the most important of Annabelle's loyalties—"the Trasks own the property. If she lets me come in too often, they might not want to renew her lease next time it comes up."

"I don't understand why you stay here."

She glanced across the dining room. Kristin was already on her feet, and her mother was sliding from the bench while her father counted money for the bill. Their meal remained half-eaten on the table. Apparently she'd robbed them of their appetites—along with their peace, their dignity, and their younger, most dearly loved daughter.

Feeling more sorrowful than she had in weeks, she looked back at Tucker. Better that he see the tears filling her eyes than her family. "Sometimes neither do I."

Tucker had really meant his statement there in the restaurant. He brooded as he started work on the insulation the next morning. He knew Kate's reasons for remaining in Fall River, but he didn't understand them. So she'd lived here all her life. He'd spent eighteen years in Fayette, but he hadn't had even the slightest desire to return there, not when he knew that he would face the same bigotry he'd grown up with and worse. Fall River may have been Kate's home for twenty-some years, but it wasn't any longer. They didn't want her there. She didn't belong there.

But where *did* she belong? Someplace new, where the Trask name meant nothing, where no one would know about a rape trial in northwestern Arkansas. Someplace where she would be a stranger, would have no family, would have to make new friends. It would be frightening. It would be unfair as hell that she had to make a new start, when she hadn't done anything wrong. But she was completely on her own here, too, except for McMaster and old Ben.

And Tucker.

She didn't have much, but she thought it was better than nothing. He wasn't convinced. In a new town she could go back to the teaching job she loved. She could go back to church. She could make a place for herself, fall in love, get married. She could *belong*.

Scowling hard, he ripped the plastic from one round of insulation, pulled the first batt loose, and stuffed it into the space between two studs. Kate wasn't the only one who needed to move on. So did he. He needed to quit wasting money on this house that he wouldn't live in long and get out of Rutherford County. He didn't know where he would go, but anywhere had to be better for him than here.

But he had no place else. He had even less than Kate—a little money to get by, his uncle's place to live in, and this place to fill his time . . . and to keep her coming back. As long as she felt useful, she would continue to come, and that was why he kept working. That was why he kept spending money that would be better saved for the inevitable someday when he needed it to survive.

The sound of a car drew his attention to the window. Kate had said she would come out this morning and bring lunch with her. Today there would be no risk of running into people who still possessed the power to hurt her. When she had turned to him yesterday with tears in her eyes, he'd been angry as hell . . . and helpless to do anything about it. How could parents treat their own daughter that way? How could they look at her with such cold damnation, then walk away as if she weren't a very part of them?

Granted, his own mother hadn't stood by him when he was in trouble, but Noreen had never been much of a mother, and he and Jimmy had always been lousy kids. There'd been no father, no steady income, no respectability or church on Sundays or family dinners. There had been no rules, no teaching, no love or support. But Kate had had all those things. Her parents had provided her with the perfect place in a perfect family. She had been surrounded by love and support . . . until she had needed it most.

As the car came into sight, he realized that it wasn't Kate's. It was a '67 Mustang, the same one he'd seen up on the hill where Trask lived. His gaze narrowing, his muscles tensing, he watched as it parked a fair distance from his truck and a woman got out. She was pretty enough—slender, dark-haired, fair-skinned—but that wasn't his strongest impression of her. No, that was of competence. Confidence. Assurance. This woman would never lock herself inside the sanctuary of her own house. She would never tolerate obscene, threatening phone calls from arrogant bastards who got their kicks bullying a frightened, traumatized woman. If fate ever made her any man's victim, it would only be temporarily. She would fight back—like Kate—but, unlike Kate, she would win.

She was wearing a sweater, jeans, and loafers, but the clothes did nothing to diminish the aura of authority about her. Was she a cop, a lawyer, maybe an officer or investigator with the parole board? Was she someone with the ability to send him back to prison?

Spotting him in the open window, she started toward the house. She didn't go to the door, but stopped instead a few yards in front of the broad window. "You're Tucker Caldwell."

It was a simple statement of fact. She knew beyond a doubt that was his name, which put her at least one giant step ahead of him. "Who are you?"

"My name is Colleen Robbins."

That didn't exactly answer his question. She assuredly wasn't his parole officer, and it wasn't likely she was a cop, either. She was too slow in showing her credentials, and experience had taught him that cops—all cops—were hostile toward ex-cons, while this woman seemed almost pleased to see him.

"Who are you?" he repeated, scowling down at her as if fierceness could make her go away and leave him alone.

"I'm an attorney in Little Rock."

"I don't need an attorney. I'm not in trouble." But that was a joke. He'd been in trouble of one sort or another all his life, and Kate promised to be the biggest, most serious trouble of all.

"No, not with me, at least. We met a long time ago, Mr. Caldwell. You were on trial for murder. I was a first-year law student. My name was Baker then."

He gave her another hard look. Harry Baker had been Fayette's only lawyer, and he had volunteered to defend their hometown murderer. Despite his decision to practice in a town like Fayette, he'd had a reputation as a smart lawyer and a fair man. Tucker had been happy to have him.

He remembered the daughter vaguely. She had been around a lot in the beginning, eager to help, excited to be working on a murder case. Toward the end, though, things had gotten strained between father and daughter. Tucker had been too depressed to care about their troubles. He had been trying to accept that not only had the usual people lied, but so had his own best witness. Amy—his whole damned reason for the fight with Henderson—had sworn on the Bible to tell the truth and had lied. He had been trying to face the fact that he was going to prison for a long time, maybe the rest of his life.

"I remember you."

"I'd heard that you were granted parole. I had wondered where you might go."

"And so you drove all the way up here from Little Rock to find out?"

"No. I have business in Fall River. It was just luck that I heard you were here."

"Heard from who?"

"Travis McMaster."

He scowled. "The police chief."

"And Kate Edwards's friend."

His muscles went taut again. "You know Kate?"

"I haven't met her. But that's how you came up in the conversation. Travis is a little worried about her new friend."

Tucker moved to the door, jumped to the ground, then sat down in the opening. "Did he send you out here? Does he think the fact that your father defended me sixteen years ago gives you any influence over me?"

"No. My reason for coming here has nothing to do with Travis or Kate." Her expression tightened, turned bleak, then determined. "I came to offer an apology on my father's behalf."

Kate had come the other day to offer an apology. He was no better at accepting it now than he'd been then. "For what?"

"When you were arrested, my father requested your case. He knew that a Caldwell going up against the Hendersons in Fayette would need the best defense he could get. He believed he could offer that defense."

"Yeah, so?"

She looked around, shoved her hair back, then laced her fingers tightly together and answered abruptly, harshly. "He threw your case, Tucker. He wasn't trying to get you off.

The trial was a mockery. Your defense was a sham. Your attorney was bought and paid for by Jeffrey Henderson's family." She shook her head, and underneath the impatience, there was more than a little sorrow. "You never stood a chance."

A smart lawyer and a fair man. For sixteen years he'd believed that—had believed that his attorney had done his best. So the results hadn't been great. So a twenty-five-year sentence for an accidental death was less than just. Hell, who was he to expect justice? A Caldwell who had killed a Henderson. He'd been damned lucky his "justice" hadn't included a rope and that big old oak on the courthouse lawn.

Now this woman—this attorney, this attorney's daughter—was telling him that he'd never had a chance at anything better than what he'd gotten.

"If this apology is on your father's behalf, why isn't he here making it?"

"He's dead. He was a good man, Tucker. He'd always given his clients 110 percent, and he couldn't live with what he'd done. Three months after you went to prison, he killed himself."

So he had gone to prison for so long in part because of Harry Baker, and Harry Baker had died in part because of him. It wasn't a fair trade, Tucker thought regretfully. What did it matter that Baker had betrayed his trust, that he had helped the prosecution convict him rather than doing the job he had sworn to do? Betraying a loser like *him* wasn't worth dying for.

But maybe, to a good man, losing your self-respect was. Maybe losing your honor was. Tucker didn't know. He'd never been a good or honorable man, had never had any respect. He didn't know what it would cost to lose it.

"Why did he do it? Was it for money or for the Hendersons?"

"All I know is what he wrote in the note he left behind, which made reference to blackmail. As far as I could tell from his records, no money changed hands. Jason Trask must have found something in my father's past—"

"Trask?" he interrupted. "He was involved? The note said that?"

She reluctantly shook her head and explained. "In the beginning my father had every intention of giving you the best defense imaginable. He knew you weren't guilty of murder. He knew it was a horrible accident, nothing more. He was dedicated to helping you. Then one day Jason Trask went to see him at his office. When he left, Harry was a changed man. He'd lost all that determination, and from that day on he presented a defense shoddy and negligent enough to get himself disbarred."

Tucker had always known that the Henderson family had been a large part of the reason for his excessive prison sentence. Three to eight years—that was what he'd been told to expect. After all, it had been an accident, just incredible bad luck. He had known from the beginning that the Henderson name would add some time to that sentence, maybe even double it. But the family hadn't been content to rely on the power of their name. They had taken an active part in ensuring the harshest sentence possible. Jason Trask had played a major role in sending him to prison for nearly half his life.

His smile was bitter. All along he'd felt sorry for Kate for being one of Trask's victims, without ever suspecting that he was, too. Hell, Trask couldn't have been more than twenty or twenty-two at the time. He'd probably cut his teeth on Tucker before moving on to screw up other, better lives.

"I really am sorry, Tucker."

"It's no big deal."

"It *is*. He lied to you. He cheated you. He promised you—"

"He did what he felt he had to. It doesn't matter anymore."

"If I could change it . . ."

"I'm not sure it made a difference. You lived in Fayette. You know what people thought of the Hendersons." He almost smiled again. "You know what they thought of the Caldwells. The conviction was a sure thing. It was the sentence we weren't certain of, and I'm not convinced your father affected that in any way. The jury was determined to give me the harshest punishment they could. The Hendersons expected it of them, and in that town, everyone did what the Hendersons expected." Just as in Fall River, everyone did what the Trasks expected.

She remained silent for a long time, then a hesitant smile appeared. "You're more forgiving than I could ever be."

He shrugged. "What would holding a grudge accomplish? It wouldn't give back those sixteen years. It wouldn't bring Henderson or your father back to life." It wouldn't give them justice, because Jason Trask was still alive and well and making Kate's life hell. Tucker didn't much care what Trask had done to him, not at this late date, but what he'd done to Kate . . . She'd been right all along. The bastard needed to die.

The lawyer came closer, offering a business card. "If there's ever anything I can do for you . . ."

He took the card. If he ever found himself in trouble or in violation of his parole, he would be able to use a good attorney, especially one driven by her father's guilt.

"If you find yourself in Little Rock and in need of a job or a place to stay . . ." Once again her offer trailed off, interrupted this time by Kate's arrival. Tucker saw the puzzled look on Kate's face as she pulled into the space between the

Mustang and the truck, and he found himself wishing that she'd come ten minutes later so Colleen Robbins wouldn't necessitate an explanation.

Carrying a small cooler in both hands, Kate came to stand roughly equal distance from Tucker and Colleen. She seemed hesitant, uncertain, as if she might have interrupted something best left alone. "Good morning."

Finally Tucker rose from the doorway. "Kate Edwards, Colleen Robbins."

Relief swept across Kate's face, swiftly replaced by recognition. He wondered who she had thought the woman was. Nolie? "You're the attorney from Little Rock."

"Does everyone in Fall River know that?" Colleen asked drily as she approached, hand extended. Tucker felt a twinge of envy. Just yesterday morning Kate had implied that they could become lovers, and yet if he touched her, if he tried to take her hand the way Colleen had, she would shrink away, repulsed by the contact.

"Probably, but I don't hear much of the local gossip. We share a mutual friend," Kate replied.

"Travis McMaster," the other woman confirmed.

Kate gave Tucker a measuring look, as if wondering what connection he had to the lawyer, who decided to let him explain it on his own. "I appreciate your time, Tucker. Kate, it was a pleasure meeting you. I hope I see you again." With that, she made a quick retreat, leaving the two of them watching.

Long after she was gone, and the silence between them had grown, Kate finally spoke. "Who is she?"

He decided to tell her instead who the woman wasn't. "She's *not* Nolie."

Her blush confirmed that she had, indeed, wondered . . . and had been made jealous by the possibility. Good. He turned away, stepped up into the house, then stopped for one last comment. "She's a lawyer from Little Rock, Kate . . . and she's *not* my type."

Resting her gloved hands on her hips, Kate stood in the middle of the room and surveyed the last half hour's work. Installing insulation was an easy job. In little time at all, they had finished, and Tucker was gathering the wrappings and leftover bits of insulation while she pulled her gloves off and idly scratched one wrist.

"Don't do that." He brushed her hand away as he passed, a thoughtless gesture, so natural and automatic that, for a moment, he didn't even realize what he'd done. Kate realized. In the last six months the touch of warm, callused fingers against hers had become as foreign as a moment without guilt and fear. But right now she wasn't feeling guilty or afraid. She felt tingly. Curious. Needy.

At the door he stopped and looked back, aware at last that he had touched her. She stood still, her fingers curled together, and evenly met his gaze. "Don't scratch," he said, his voice odd and distant. "Shake out your jacket, then go inside and wash up." He remained where he was for a moment, still looking at her, then abruptly he went out.

She followed his directions, draping her jacket over a sawhorse on her way to his uncle's house, where she washed her hands quickly in the frigid water. After drying them with a faded yellow towel, she looked around. His bed was carelessly made, as if he'd climbed out this morning, pulled Nolie's quilt up over the rumpled sheets, and considered the job done. There was a depression in the center of the pillow on the right where his head had rested. There was no such indentation on the other pillow.

She sighed with relief and immediately felt guilty for it.

All right, so she had wondered if Colleen Robbins had spent the night here, if she hadn't driven out from town this morning but instead had come last night. After all, she was a pretty woman, and she wasn't sleeping with Travis, and Tucker was a handsome man who'd been alone far too long. But no one had shared the bed with him last night. The knowledge brought her satisfaction.

Behind her the door opened and Tucker came in. He gave her a curious look before turning to the sink.

"You don't have any hot water."

"I don't have a hot water heater. No electricity or gas, remember?"

"Doesn't the pump for the well require electricity?"

"We're downhill from the stream. Gravity brings it right into the pipes." When she offered him the towel, he took it from the dangling end, about as far from her hand as he could get.

Folding her arms across her chest, she tucked her chilled fingers into the crook of her elbows, then, surprising herself, she artlessly asked, "Are you involved with Colleen? She told Travis she was in town on business, but she wouldn't say what the business was. Is it you?"

He looked for a moment as if he didn't want to answer, then shrugged. "She's originally from Fayette. Her father was my lawyer."

It wasn't enough to satisfy her. Had there been some connection between Tucker and the lawyer, something personal, something to explain why she had come looking for him sixteen years later? "Is she in town because of you?"

"No."

"Then why was she here?"

His gaze settled on the rickety table between them. "She was in law school at the time of my trial. She helped her father with the case. When McMaster complained to her about you taking up with the resident ex-con, she recognized my name, got a little curious, and came out to see me." Finally he looked up, his gaze locking with hers. His expression was dark and just a little deceitful. "Are you jealous, Kate?"

She hesitated a moment, then bluntly admitted, "Yeah, I am."

"She doesn't mean anything to me. She's a stranger, and I have no desire to get to know her better."

"It would be only natural if you were attracted to her." Her smile was unsteady. "After all, she's everything I'm not."

"Which is?"

"Normal, for starters." There was no way a woman like Colleen Robbins would retreat from any man she found attractive. No way she would shrink back in fear from the simplest of touches.

"Some people might argue that with you. After all, she is a lawyer." His faint smile disappeared almost immediately as he moved a little closer to the table. "For a woman who's gone through everything you have, you *are* normal, Kate. If you *didn't* have these fears, I would worry."

"But they control my life."

"They have. But you're getting over it. Someday you'll be fine. The time will come when no one will ever look at you and see Jason Trask's victim. They'll just see an incredibly strong woman."

"I hope you're right."

"So do I. I'm counting on it."

"In what way?"

He glanced toward the door, as if he'd rather leave than answer her question, then looked back. "Someday, Kate, I'm going to ask you to forget Jason Trask and everything he ever did to you. I'm going to ask you to pretend that I'm the only man who's ever been a part of your life. I'm going to undress you and make love to you. I'm going to get lost inside you, and you're going to let me, Kate. You're even going to enjoy it." He stood there a little longer, giving her a look that dared her to contradict him. When she said nothing, he walked to the door and went out, closing it quietly behind him.

He sounded so sure of himself, so sure of her, that, when someday arrived, she would do what he wanted. Jason had been confident, too. That night in his kitchen he had told her to fight if she wanted, but in the end, he would get what *he* wanted. His words had frightened her, but Tucker's didn't. Jason's had been a threat. Tucker's were a promise. She hadn't believed Jason and had lived to regret it. She did believe Tucker and would never regret it.

I'm going to get lost inside you. That was an image she could get lost in. It made her feel warm—hell, damned near steaming. It made her want to get lost with him. More importantly, though, were the things it *didn't* make her feel: afraid. Threatened. Vulnerable. It didn't send panic rushing through her. It didn't fill her with sick dread or overwhelming anxiety.

Yesterday morning she had told Tucker that maybe he was the right man to help her put Jason behind her. This morning she believed it with all her heart. It was time to quit cowering in her sad little existence and start living, to strip Jason of his power over her and exercise a little power of her own.

A little power over Tucker. She liked the sound of that.

Feeling better than she had in months, she left the old house and went into the new one. Tucker had propped a sheet of drywall against the studs and was marking a line from edge to edge. "That was a hell of an exit."

He glanced up, doing his best to contain a grin. "I meant every word."

"Good. Because I believed every word."

He scored the line he'd marked, broke the sheet, then cut the paper backing. After setting aside the smaller piece, he positioned the large one, then gestured for her to hold one end. She waited until he had hammered the first dozen nails before she spoke. "Travis is really interested in Colleen Robbins."

He sank each of the next nails with only a few strikes. "Travis is overly suspicious."

"I mean interested as in I'm interested in you."

"Oh."

"He seems really serious. I'd hate to see him get hurt, falling for someone who's interested in someone else."

"I told you, I'm not involved with her. I didn't even know who she was until she told me. I hardly even remember her from before."

But Colleen remembered him. She remembered him well enough to find out where he was living, then drive all the way out here. Why? "Out-of-town lawyers make me nervous. Jason's attorneys were from some hotshot firm in Little Rock. They were good. They made him look like an angel sent down from heaven, while I was the bitter, warped, vengeful slut."

Tucker crouched in front of her to hammer in the last sets of nails, then looked up. "I've got news for you, honey. That's what lawyers do. They protect their clients at all costs, even if it means lying. The law says every defendant is entitled to a defense. It doesn't say anything about a truthful defense."

"What kind of defense did Colleen's father give you?"

His eyes turned a shade darker, and his mouth compressed a little tighter. Because she'd brought up the other woman again? Or because he was hiding something? "He gave me the best defense he could manage."

"It mustn't have been very good. You got twenty-five years."

"Can you imagine what the good people of Fall River would do to you if you killed Jason Trask?"

She released the now-secured drywall and turned away, gazing out the window to hide any guilt that might seep into her expression. "They would want me dead. About half of them think I should already be dead for the lies I told about him."

"Well, Jeffrey Henderson was Fayette's very own Jason Trask, and I was nowhere near as kindly regarded there as you are here." He came to stand beside her. "I stood there in the courtroom and listened to the judge sentence me to twenty-five years in prison—seven years longer than my entire life—and I was *grateful*. I was so damned grateful that they weren't going to execute me. Maybe my lawyer's defense wasn't the best, but at least I didn't get the death penalty."

Her protest was quiet and unsteady. "But it was an accident."

"Powerful people wanted me dead, Kate. I was lucky to get twenty-five years, and I was damned lucky to make parole after sixteen."

Shifting, she looked out the window again. When she killed Jason, if her plan failed, if her alibi was disproved, the Trasks would certainly demand the death penalty for her. Jason had raped and brutally beaten her, and his family would want her to die for it. It was a warped sort of justice that fitted this town and that family perfectly.

Dying was a tremendous price to pay for justice. Losing fifteen or twenty years of her life was bad enough, but actually being put to death—never seeing Kerry again, never seeing Tucker again . . . That was harsh.

Jason had already cost her too much. What little she had—a sweet sister who was traumatized beyond coping and a future, however uncertain, with Tucker—wasn't much, but it was hers, and it was much too precious to lose. Maybe she should rethink her plans for revenge. Maybe she should follow Tucker's advice and get some therapy. Maybe she should follow her own advice and find her vengeance in living well and happily ever after.

The corners of her mouth lifted in a cool little smile. Those were good ideas, but she had a better one. She would make her plans very, very carefully. She would avoid mistakes and suspicion. She would avoid getting caught. *Then* she might get some therapy. *Then* she would live well. *Then*, with Tucker's cooperation, she just might live happily ever after.

Chapter Eleven

The call Mariana had been waiting for came Friday. After the caller identified himself, she took the call in the privacy of the kitchen, one arm folded tightly across her stomach as if to contain the nervousness building inside her, the other hand clutching the receiver tightly. "All right, Mr. Marquette. I can talk."

She didn't, though. She simply listened, dread and disappointment combining to make her feel sick inside. He had listened to the tapes a number of times, and he agreed that they were damning, but the simple fact was they weren't enough. A phone call to Kate Edwards had confirmed that she wouldn't be cooperative in a retrial on the rape charges —assuming that he could convince a judge that grounds for a new trial existed. As for a charge of witness tampering, he'd already heard from Jason's lawyers down in Little Rock, promising a fight and endless appeals. The judge sure to hear the case was old Cyrus Hampton, the family friend who had helped make a mockery of Jason's first trial. The bottom line was simple, hard, and cold: there was no prosecutory merit to the case, not in Fall River. There would be no new charges filed against Jason. No new trial. No vengeance. No satisfaction.

And no protection. If the district attorney's office wasn't

interested in her tapes of Jason, then *he* wouldn't be interested, either. He wouldn't allow her to hide behind them. If she tried to blackmail him with them—her peace and safety in exchange for her silence—he would punish her. If she tried to go public with them, he would discredit her. The DA didn't consider them credible, he would brag, twisting the facts to suit his own purpose, so why should anyone else? Besides, his family owned the newspaper and the town's only radio station. He controlled the media, such as it was, in Fall River.

"Ms. Trask? Are you there?"

Shuddering again, she drew a deep breath. "I don't understand, Mr. Marquette. He bribed a witness. He admitted to raping Kate. Why can't you punish him for it? Why can't you see that justice is served?"

He answered with more honesty than she'd expected. "Because it's not about justice, Ms. Trask. It's about politics. It's about who owns this town, about power and wealth and the Trasks, who can do no wrong. You were a part of their family for ten years. Surely you, of all people, understand."

She understood. Jason had won again, and she had lost. He was going to make her life a living hell. Everything that had gone before—all the beatings, all her pain, all his anger—would pale in comparison to what faced her now. She had tried to hurt him, but she had failed, and now he would make her pay for it. "There must be *something* you can do."

"There isn't. I'm sorry."

" 'I'm sorry' isn't enough! You're the district attorney. You're supposed to protect the interests of the people, not Jason!"

He responded to her loss of temper with his own. "What

if I do charge him with witness tampering? Are you going to show up in court this time? Or are you going to take his money and disappear the way you did before?"

Her fingers tightened around the phone. "I ran because I was afraid, but it wouldn't happen again."

"So you've gotten over this fear of him."

"I know Jason. As long as he lives, I'll be afraid of him."

"So what's different? You promised you would testify last time, but you didn't because you were afraid. You're still afraid. Nothing's changed."

"Mr. Marquette, please. If you do nothing, don't you see the message you'll be sending Jason? That he's above the law, that he can do whatever he wants to whoever he wants, and nothing will happen. We have *tapes*—his own voice admitting to his crimes. Not even Judge Hampton can ignore that!"

"Judge Hampton is as crooked as these mountain roads," Marquette said flatly. "He can and will ignore the strongest, most compelling evidence imaginable if it's in Jason's best interests."

"So get him disqualified. Someone in this state has to have the authority to remove him from a case. *Someone* has to have the ability to make sure this is a fair trial."

"Frankly, Ms. Trask, this case isn't important enough. Jason has virtually unlimited resources to fight it. My office doesn't. We have other cases, better cases with more serious charges. If we pursued this, even if we won, it wouldn't be much of a victory. Jason might serve a little time, though I doubt it. He would probably pay a fine and be done with it. We would have expended a great deal of time, money, and effort, and would have very little to show for it."

"But you know he's guilty."

"Yes, and there's not a damned thing we can do about it.

That message you were talking about? It's the truth. In this town, in this county, Jason Trask *is* above the law." He sighed heavily. "I wish I had better news for you. I wish we could get a new trial on the rape charges based on your new evidence and send the bastard to prison, but it's not going to happen."

"Maybe you'll get another chance," she said numbly. "He's going to kill me for this." Before he could respond, she hung up.

It had been obvious Wednesday that Marquette was less than enthusiastic about her evidence, but she had been convinced that would change once he'd heard all the tapes. She had believed he would be impressed by Jason's boastful admissions of guilt, that he would immediately take Jason back into court. She had never imagined that he would decline to do anything at all.

Though it didn't make his decision any easier to accept, his reasons were sound. Without a fair and impartial judge and jury, his chances of winning a conviction were slim— and hadn't Kate's trial shown the impossibility of finding thirteen fair and impartial people in this county? The judge was crooked, one of Rupert's buddies from way back. Though the twelve jurors had been chosen from the population at large, every single one of them had had some connection to Jason's family. Instead of impartiality, they had been thinking about whose signature was on their paychecks and who held the mortgages on their houses.

This time would be no different. The same corrupt judge, another jury who owed their lives to the defendant's family, and a witness who had lost an enviable life of luxury after being rejected by the defendant.

Jason *was* above the law. He could do whatever his black

heart desired, and no one would punish him. No one had the courage to stand up and say, This has to stop.

He had to be stopped.

"Mariana? You off the phone yet, honey?"

Her mother's call made her straighten. She had to go into the living room and tell Pat that her grand plan had failed, that she hadn't made things right but had instead made them much, much worse. Jason would surely punish her for trying.

She opened her mouth to reply, but the ringing phone cut her off. "Just a minute, Mama." She picked up the phone, murmured a hello, and felt sick fear rush in a hundred times stronger than ever before.

"Hello, darlin'," Jason greeted her. "My lawyers just got a call from the district attorney's office. So much for your 'protection.' You tried your best, Mariana, and, as usual, you failed." The friendliness disappeared from his voice, and it turned deadly. "Now you're going to pay."

Frightened, she hung up, then took the receiver off the hook and laid it on the counter. She knew him. He would call back. When he couldn't reach her, he would start planning some other way to torment her. He would plan his most devious, most terrifying way to make her pay.

Shaking with the helpless panic she had lived with through most of her marriage, she clung to the counter for support. How was she going to stay safe now? God help her, what was she going to do?

It was nearly six o'clock, and Kate sat at the table in her kitchen, the newspaper and the day's mail pushed aside, a few sheets of paper in front of her, and a pot of stew bubbling on the stove. Tucker was due any minute, and she wanted to get a few last notes down before he arrived.

It had been a productive day. Though she had left in the middle of the afternoon to come home and start dinner, they had finished sheathing the roof, laid rolls of black roofing felt in place, and started on the shingles. They'd eaten lunch on Nolie's quilt, spread across a patch of yellowed grass where they could get a little needed warmth from the midday sun. Someday, she had decided, they would make love on that quilt, and she would make him forget the other woman even existed.

Her own smile mocked her. For a woman with all her fears, she sounded pretty damned sure of herself. But she *was* sure. She wasn't going to live the rest of her life the way she'd lived the last six months. She was going to deal with her fears, she was going to become lovers with Tucker, and one day she was going to realize the dream she'd given up on: love, marriage, sex, and kids.

Maybe kids with dark brown hair and intense dark eyes.

Her smile softened at the thought of a half dozen little Tuckers underfoot. It had been so long since she'd thought of herself as a normal woman with normal hopes and dreams. Deep down inside she had believed that she would never trust again, that she would never be intimate with a man again, that no man would ever want damaged goods like her. Now here she sat at her kitchen table daydreaming about babies and all that having them entailed.

Dreaming about sweet babies . . . and planning a man's death. Her smile faded. Before there could be any happily-ever-afters, she had to take care of Jason. When she'd gotten back into town this afternoon, she'd taken a little drive—past the bank downtown, the plant, Jason's house. Her route had taken her past the diner, where Mark Tyler's and Brent Hogan's cars were parked. No doubt the four of them had been in there for their afternoon coffee break, being their usual arrogant bastard selves, probably laughing about the filthy message Tim had left on her machine last night, maybe even arranging who would call tonight. Since she intended to turn off the machine and unplug the phones—at least while Tucker was here—they would be disappointed.

In her time with Jason she'd learned most of his habits. On the pages in front of her she had reconstructed his schedule, from the civic club luncheons on the first and third Mondays of every month to the Tuesday night dinners at Ozark Annie's to his Wednesday, Friday, and Saturday date nights. He was a man of routine, and his routine rarely varied. He hadn't let a little thing like kidnapping and raping a sweet, innocent girl interfere with his Monday evening with Mom and Dad or his Sunday evening get-togethers with friends to watch whatever was available on the satellite dish. No, he'd scheduled his attack on Kerry for a date night, just as he had raped Kate on a date night.

He could die on a Thursday evening home alone. Or any morning of the week when he made his regular visit to the plant, leaving the bank around ten and returning to town ninety minutes later. Or on Wednesday afternoon, when the bank closed early and he played golf in warm weather or swam in his heated pool when it was cold. He could be forced off the road when he returned home from a date or dinner with his pals or struck dead Sunday morning on his way to church. A hypocrite and sinner like him had no place in church, anyway, though they welcomed him—those same pious, godly people who had turned *her* away.

Feeling uncomfortably edgy, she put the pen down, then glanced at the clock. It was nearly five-thirty. Tucker had planned to finish a few more rows of shingles, clean up, and meet her here for dinner. She had suggested that he bring his clothes and shower here, had tried to entice him with the promise of all the hot water he could possibly need. He hadn't accepted, but he hadn't refused, either. After all, to a man used to bathing in icy cold water, a hot shower on a chilly October evening must sound inviting.

Besides, if they were going to have an affair, they would be sharing things far more intimate than the same bathroom.

The doorbell rang, and her pulse quickened. She neatly stacked the pages, slipped them inside the newspaper, then hurried down the hall. Through the peephole, Tucker looked cold in the frigid wind. She unlocked the door, pulled it open, and quickly closed it behind him. "Hi."

His response was a smile that disappeared quickly. He was wearing the same stained clothes he had worked in all day, and in one hand he carried a small gym bag. He shifted it to the other as he removed his leather jacket, which she hung on the doorknob of the coat closet. "I decided to take you up on your offer."

"I thought you would." She could send him upstairs alone or give him directions to the guest bath between the two spare bedrooms, but she didn't. She climbed the stairs in front of him, walked past the closed doors of the yellow bedroom and the extra bath, and turned into her own room. Stopping just inside the door, she gestured to the opposite side. "The bathroom's in there." It was warm, still a little steamy from her own bath, and smelled of jasmine from the plant in bloom on the counter. "There are towels on the table, and anything else you might need can be found in the drawers."

He remained where he stood, looking uncomfortable.

"I'll be downstairs in the kitchen." She closed the door behind her, then stood motionless. A moment later, she heard the click of the bathroom door as it closed.

Back downstairs, she stopped at the stove to check their

dinner. After her little tour this afternoon, she had gone to the grocery store and picked up the ingredients for stew, a loaf of bread, and a six-pack of beer. She had ignored the snide look the clerk had given her and brought the groceries home, chopping and cooking and all the while thinking about Jason and murder. The incongruity—little miss home-maker and cold-blooded killer in the same once-battered body—had bothered her, but not enough to make her put aside her plans for Jason.

She gave the stew a stir, then went to sit at the table. She wasn't living in a fantasy world. Jason's death wasn't the magic cure for what ailed her. It couldn't heal Kerry, re-store Kate's reputation, or bring back her family and friends. It couldn't possibly undo the damage of the last six months. But it would give her satisfaction. It would ease the burden of guilt she carried and the fear she had come to know intimately. It would make things better, and in her life, "better" was good enough. She could be satisfied with "better" . . . even if she was starting to want so much more.

Retrieving her notes, she turned to a clean page and began writing. She needed to see Kerry while she was on vacation, to see how her sister had settled in at the new hos-pital. Her parents spent weekends in the city, her mother visiting with Kerry while her father waited out of his daughter's sight and far out of her mind. They would be back home in time for church Sunday evening, which meant Kate was free to go on Monday. She could drive down to Little Rock, spend the afternoon with Kerry, do some shop-ping the next morning, and see Kerry again before returning home. She could stay at the same motel where she had stayed when her sister had first been transferred to Little Rock. The older couple who managed the place had come to know Kate well. They knew she came in before dusk and didn't go out again, not even to the Coke machine in the stairwell, until the next morning, and they would tell that to anyone who asked—Travis, the Trasks' lawyers—as if it were the gospel truth.

Before she checked into the motel, she would rent a car, something as different from her own car as possible, and have it waiting at the shopping center across the street from the motel. Then, after eating a takeout dinner alone in her room, as was her habit, she would slip out, pick up the rental, and drive back to Fall River in time to find Jason on his way home from Monday evening dinner at his parents' house.

And do what? Run him down as he walked to his car, giving Rupert and Eleanor the opportunity to recognize her? Force him off the road on his way home? Only the ravine just before the entrance to Ridge Crest offered much risk of death, and even that wasn't guaranteed.

She could be waiting at his house when he got there. He had no live-in help, so the house would be empty. The big fence around the yard was decorative rather than functional, and the gate across the driveway was rarely closed. Even if it was, she could easily slip between the posts. She could wait at the back of the house, slip inside the garage when he electronically opened the door, and be waiting when he stepped out of his car—waiting with her gun and the dead-on aim Travis had helped her perfect. She would wait until he turned and saw her—it was as important that he recognize her as that no one else did—and then she would pull the trigger. She would be back in the motel room in Little Rock hours before anyone discovered his body.

It wasn't a perfect plan, by any means. Could she even rent a car these days without showing her driver's license and a credit card? What if someone saw her leaving the motel? What is someone recognized her driving a strange car in Fall River? What if the distance between the houses that had effectively muffled her screams wasn't enough to muffle the sound of the gunshot? If Jason were killed with the same kind of gun Travis had picked out for her, wouldn't he naturally demand the gun for ballistics tests? She could buy another pistol in the city, but wouldn't that require identification and at least a few practice rounds?

She needed a better plan. Not the perfect murder. Just close would be good enough. She could do it. She would do it, and soon. Before her vacation ended, she would find peace.

She would kill Jason.

Tucker stepped out of the shower onto a thick white mat and reached for the top towel on the table. He rubbed it over his hair, then dried quickly, wrapping the towel around his middle as he approached the vanity. He opened the first drawer, seeking a comb, and found a brush with soft bristles, running it through his hair, slicking it straight back.

Curious, he opened the second drawer. A wicker basket filled with cosmetics shared space with a basket that held perfume bottles. The third drawer held more decidedly feminine items, but the contents of the medicine chest, for the most part, could have come from his own house: toothpaste, dental floss, aspirin, and antacid. The only thing that would never be found in his house—although he had a half-empty box of the men's equivalent in his nightstand—sat alone on the top shelf. Birth control pills.

The date on the prescription was March. She had been raped in April, probably the day the last pill had been taken. She had never suspected when she'd popped it from the package how drastically her life would change before the day was over. She had been infatuated with Trask, fantasizing that he was the right man, the man who would sweep her off her feet, the man she would live the rest of her life with.

Now she was entertaining fantasies that Tucker was the right man. He knew he wasn't, but, hell, at least he wasn't as wrong as Trask had been. At least *he* would never hurt her.

Returning the pills to their place, he got dressed, stuffed the dirty clothes inside the bag, and went into the bedroom.

It wasn't a frilly room, but Kate wasn't a frilly person. There were plenty of personal touches—a quilted wall hanging over the bed, a wreath of dried flowers on another wall, and a collection of glass bottles in front of a window. If the sun were allowed in, it would send a rainbow dancing across the room and up the wall, bright reflections in cobalt blue, ruby red, and deep amethyst. But the drapes were drawn so tightly that not even a single ray of light could penetrate.

He sat on the bed to pull his socks on. It wasn't a big bed—a double, like his, just big enough. He wondered as he tied his shoes how many nights Trask had spent there. How many times had the bastard seduced her, drawing her in, making her believe he cared for her, before shattering her life?

A scowl darkening his face, he left the room, leaving his bag beside the front door before continuing into the kitchen. The stew Kate had promised this afternoon was simmering on the stove, a loaf of bread sat on the counter, and she was sitting at the table, her chin propped in one hand, her gaze distant and troubled. She didn't notice him until he'd slid onto the bench across from her. Startled from her thoughts, she swiftly gathered up the papers on the table and carried them to the counter nearest the hall. Before she returned, she put the bread in the oven, then brought him a bottle of beer from the refrigerator.

"Thanks." He twisted the cap off and took a drink before asking, "What were you thinking just now?"

She gave a careless shrug meant to say, Nothing important, but the answer he got was clearer: Trask. "Dinner will be ready in a few minutes."

"You were thinking about him, weren't you?"

"Did I tell you I got a call from the district attorney this morning?"

She knew damned well she hadn't told him. It wasn't something she would casually toss into the conversation, then forget later.

"Mariana Trask is back in town. She came to see me a couple of nights ago. She said she had tapes of Jason admitting that he raped me, making threats against her, offering her a bribe to leave town. She was going to turn them over to the DA in the hope that they could be used to bring Jason to justice."

Tucker stared at her a long time, feeling a curious sensation deep in his stomach. It was hurt, because she hadn't thought to tell him about something as important as evidence that could exonerate her and get Trask the conviction he so richly deserved. "Why didn't you tell me?"

"Because it doesn't matter. The DA's not going to take any action, and Jason's not going to be punished." She shrugged again, then offered a purely womanly smile. "Because I've had other things on my mind when I've been with you the last couple of days."

That smile left no doubt exactly what she was referring to. Putting Trask behind her. Pretending, for a few hours at least, that he had never existed. Learning to trust again, to be intimate again. Making love again. And again. She believed she could do it. He hoped she could, or he just might die from the wanting.

Forcing his attention away from images of Kate naked underneath him and back to the conversation was one of the hardest things he'd done. The effort made his eyes narrow and his voice harden when he asked, "Is that what the DA called to tell you? That he wasn't going to do anything?"

She returned to the subject with obvious reluctance. "Travis had told him that I wouldn't cooperate in a retrial. Marquette wanted to confirm that."

"And?"

"Travis was right."

"But if they have proof—"

"I won't go through it again."

"You know Trask, Kate. You know he didn't say, 'Gee, I did it, but I'm awfully sorry.' He *bragged* about it. That could go a hell of a long way toward winning your case for you."

The timer she'd set for the bread went off, but she didn't respond to it. "They almost destroyed me the first time. This time they might succeed."

"Or maybe this time you'll win."

"No one wins against Jason." She drew a breath, then blew it out. "Prosecuting him cost me dearly. I lost almost everything. I don't have anything left to lose."

He hesitated, then laid his hand over hers. He didn't grip it, the way he wanted to, but simply covered it lightly so she could pull away. "You've still got Travis, and old Ben's still on your side." Then he softly added, "You've got me."

Her gaze was soft, teary, and more than a little defeated before she slowly looked down at their hands. He was barely breathing, waiting for her to pull free. When she did move, it wasn't to escape. She turned her hand over, her palm against his, and wrapped her fingers around his. "You're right. I have Travis, Mr. James, and you, and I won't jeopardize that by trying to stand up to Jason again." After giving his hand a squeeze, she withdrew, leaving the table to take the bread from the oven and ladle the stew into a serving bowl.

He wanted to argue with her, to insist that she *must* take Jason back to court, but he held his silence. He couldn't try to change her mind. It would give him great pleasure to see Trask in prison, but more than that pleasure, he wanted to see her safe. Going back to court, facing her tormentors, hearing their lies once more . . . She was right. It could destroy her, and damned if he would be a part of it.

"Did Mariana play these tapes for you?"

"No."

"Are you interested in hearing them?"

She dished up the stew before shaking her head. "I know what he did to me, and I can easily imagine what he had to say about it. I'm sure, in his mind, it was all my fault. I got only what I deserved."

"Maybe you should get a copy of them." She looked so puzzled that he didn't wait to explain. "A lot of people believe that you got what you deserved—that you got what you *asked* for. Hearing him admit it, hearing him brag about hurting you, could change their minds." It could make them see what they should have known all along, what they never should have doubted: that *she* was the victim, not Jason.

She sat for a long time, eating, refilling her glass with pop, before quietly asking. "Do *you* want to hear the tapes, Tucker? Does *your* mind need changing?"

He stared hard at her. "That's not fair, Kate. I knew you'd been raped before you ever told me. I believed you from the beginning. All these people who knew you, who loved you, who respected you—how many of them can say that?"

"Only Travis. Kerry used to believe me, but things like rape and violence don't exist in her world anymore." She pushed her dishes away, settled more comfortably on the bench, then sighed. "So . . . how long do you think it'll be before you can move into the new house?"

After studying her a moment, he let the change of subject stand. He answered her question as if he cared, talked about the roof, the Sheetrock, and the wood-burning stove he'd found over in Eureka Springs. They talked about nothing and everything . . . except Trask and the tapes and making the truth known.

By nine o'clock he was tired of talking, tired of listening, just plain tired. Since there was no way he was going to be invited to spend the night here—not doing what he wanted, at least—it was time to go home and to bed, where he might get lucky and sleep, where he would, more likely, pass a restless night dreaming about Kate. About avenging her. Protecting her. Taking care of her. Wanting her.

He rose from the sofa where he had settled after they'd left the kitchen in darkness. Kate stood up, too, walking to the door with him. "See you tomorrow." He said it as a statement of fact, though she answered with a nod. For a moment he simply looked at her, wishing that he could draw her close and kiss her, and, failing that, wishing that he didn't want to. He settled for a light touch, his hand brushing across hers, on his way out. "Thanks for the dinner."

It was a cold night, chilly enough to be better spent inside in front of a blazing fire, but Colleen had wanted a walk, and Travis had complied. He didn't mind the exercise or building the banked fire back to a blaze when they returned home. This entire evening he hadn't minded anything at all—not even seeing Jason Trask with one of Doc Roberts's girls—until he saw the old green truck pulling away from Kate's house.

At the sound of his muttered curse, Colleen looked up. "That's Tucker Caldwell's truck, isn't it? I assume that means Kate lives somewhere around here."

"Right there." He fixed a curious gaze on her. "How do you happen to know Caldwell's truck?"

Laughing, she slipped her hand into his. "Oh, it's even better than that, Chief. I know Tucker himself."

"How?"

"I told you the night we met that I was from a small town. Tucker's from the same town."

"You grew up with him?"

"Well, I'm a few years older than him, and we didn't exactly hang out with the same crowds. In fact, I was in law school before we actually met. I had just finished my first year when he got sent away." She pulled her hand free and tucked it inside her coat pocket. He missed the contact, but didn't reclaim it. "It never should have happened the way it did, Travis."

"He killed a man. He deserved to go to prison."

"Not for twenty-five years. Jeffrey Henderson's death was an accident. Everyone knew it. Everyone knew Tucker was a poor kid with lousy luck who'd never done anyone any harm—"

"Until the night he broke Henderson's neck," Travis interjected sarcastically.

"It was an accident," she repeated, her voice softer.

Travis shoved his hands into his own pockets. "So how

did you manage to live your entire life in the same town without meeting him until he went to prison? Did you have a thing for punks?"

"No. I had a father who was an attorney." For a moment she kept her gaze on the ground, her hair falling forward to obscure her face. Then she looked at him. "Want to hear the whole sordid story?"

"If you want to tell it."

They passed Kate's before Colleen began talking. He listened without interruption and even felt a moment's sympathy for Caldwell. A poor kid with lousy luck. The lousiest, Travis agreed, but he was still an ex-con. Accident or not, a man was still dead, and Kate still deserved better.

They were standing on his front porch by the time she finished. Holding his keys in one hand, he looked down at her. "Why didn't you tell me this that day at the falls?"

"I don't tell just anyone that my father betrayed an eighteen-year-old boy's trust."

He unlocked and opened the door before asking one more question. "So why tell me now?"

She walked past him, stepping into the darkened foyer, then gave him a solemn, steady look. "You're not just anyone." Then she walked away, moving through his house with ease, even though he'd left only one dim hall lamp burning. He stood where he was, watching as she followed the long hall into the den, shedding her coat, gloves, and scarf on the nearest chair, then moving out of sight. Slowly he closed the door, removed his own coat and gloves, and followed her.

She was sitting on the floor in front of the fireplace, her feet extended toward the warmth given off despite the closed doors. Opening them, he added more logs to the fire, then stretched out near her. "Is Caldwell the reason you came here?"

"No."

"Are the Trasks?"

Tilting her head to one side, she looked at him. "Why do you ask?"

"You said Jeffrey Henderson's family blackmailed your father into screwing up Caldwell's case. Jeffrey's mother is Rupert Trask's sister—or didn't you know that?"

Her smile was thin and not entirely pleasant. "I knew. They were in court every day of Tucker's trial, all the big shots, acting as if they owned the world. Unfortunately for Tucker, they owned enough of it to make his life hell."

"So are they your reason for being here?"

"No. Yes, in a way. It's a testament to how much the people in this town fear the Trasks that you haven't yet heard rumors about my business here. Because I can trust you to not go running to them, I'll tell you." She gazed into the fire, now burning brightly, for a moment or two before once more meeting his gaze. "I've been retained by three current or former Trask employees and the widow of a fourth to file a lawsuit against them."

"So I was right. The day after we met, I tried to figure out who your prospective client might be. Randy Hawkins was the only one I could come up with, but I couldn't imagine him hiring a big-city lawyer or finding the courage to take on the Trasks."

"He's got a family to support and no way to do it. Some people will do anything for their families."

He nodded agreement while considering the other possibilities. "The widow is obviously Carla Brownley. The other two . . . Gary Pritchard and Tommy Leonard."

"We have reason to believe that all four accidents were

the result of the Trasks' utter disregard for safety procedures. They like to save money wherever it doesn't hurt them. If it costs a few employees their ability to work or even their lives, well, that's the price of doing business."

"And you want to make the price of doing business a lot higher for them."

"I want to see these people get what they deserve."

He didn't ask which people she was referring to—Hawkins and the others, or the Trasks. However he interpreted the statement, he would be accurate. "When do you plan to make this lawsuit common knowledge?"

"I have an appointment with Jason Monday morning."

"He'll try to stop it. He'll threaten your clients. He might even threaten you. Unless they're all planning to cut their ties and move away from Fall River, there's a good chance he'll succeed at intimidating them into dropping the suit."

"I'm going to do my best to avoid that. I've already warned them. I intend to warn Jason." A hint of a smile touched her mouth. "It might help if I could tell my clients that the chief of police is on their side."

"Honey, they already know that I favor anyone who can bring down Jason Trask." He reached out to cup his hand to her face, to ensure that he had every bit of her attention. "Be careful. He's a dangerous man."

"He won't try anything with me."

"Pretty women who can't fight back are Jason's favorite victims."

"I do fight back. If Jason Trask ever laid a hand on me, I would kill him." The fierceness of her expression faded and transformed into a smile that was inviting, enticing, and tempting as hell. "On the other hand, I don't believe I would mind in the least if *you* wanted to touch me."

"You don't think so, huh?" He grinned, sliding his arms

around her, lowering his head until his mouth just barely brushed hers. "Well, darlin', let's find out for sure."

The phone awakened Colleen Saturday morning. Burrowing deeper into the pillows, she felt the bed shift, heard Travis swear, and smiled. Her night had been restless—a strange bed in a strange place, sleep interrupted by lovemaking—but she felt rested, energized, as if she could take on all the Jason Trasks of the world and annihilate them without even breaking a sweat. She felt *powerful*.

Beside her Travis was trying to act as if he hadn't been awakened by the call, as if he couldn't possibly have been still asleep at . . . She sneaked a look at the watch she'd forgotten to take off last night. It was exactly 8:01. Whoever was calling had probably sat, hand on phone, until eight, assuming it was the earliest hour he could reasonably call. On a weekday, Colleen would have agreed. On a Saturday, it seemed only fair to wait until nine.

"All right, all right," he was saying. "Do you want to come into the office to talk, or would you prefer that I come to your house?"

So much for anticipating a repeat of last night's pleasures. Colleen slid up to lean against the headboard, the covers tucked across her chest.

Travis completed the call, muttered another curse, then turned to face her. His smile when he saw her awake was slow, charming, and full of promise. "Good morning. Did you sleep well?"

"Very well." There was something comforting about sharing a bed with a man strong enough to protect her and gentle enough never to hurt her. It gave her a sense of being cared for that she was too independent to allow in her day-to-day life, but was certainly enjoying right now.

"I've got to go out and talk to someone."

"Anyone I know?"

"Mariana Trask, Jason's ex-wife. She witnessed his assault on Kate, but he threatened and, eventually, bribed her into leaving town before the trial. She came back last week with proof of his threats, hoping for a new trial—and a little atonement—but Kate won't cooperate, and, without her, the DA doesn't feel there's any merit in hauling Trask back into court."

"So Mariana doesn't get to redeem herself." Colleen's first impulse was to think that the woman got no more than she deserved. Rape was one crime rarely witnessed by anyone not involved. Her testimony in support of Kate Edwards's claims could have convicted Jason. Instead, she had taken his money and fled, leaving him free to persecute Kate and to attack Kate's sister. Redemption for those sins should be much harder to come by than simply turning over evidence to the prosecutor.

But there were always extenuating circumstances. Mariana had obviously been afraid of Jason. If he had raped and beaten Kate and her sister, chances were very good that he had also abused his wife.

"No redemption," Travis agreed, "but now she does get to endure his harassment. You don't try to send Jason Trask to prison and walk away unscathed. In less than twenty-four hours, she's gotten over a dozen phone calls from him and his friends, making threats."

"Do you think they'll make good on them?"

"I don't know. They've been doing the same thing to Kate for months. So far they haven't tried anything with her, but I worry. If they find such sick pleasure in tormenting her over the phone, how much more would they enjoy doing it in person?"

"Why doesn't Kate change her number or get a restraining order?"

"She's changed the number, but they kept getting the new one. For a restraining order, she would have to go to Judge Hampton, who heard the rape case, who told Jason with a wink and a smile that what he did was all right. He wouldn't issue one."

Colleen wanted to protest the injustice. There were laws to protect women like Kate Edwards and Mariana Trask, laws to keep animals like Jason under control. But she'd spent too much time in court and too many years in a small town to believe that justice was fairly applied to everyone. "You've got some sick people in your town."

Travis took a handful of clothes from the dresser drawers, added a pair of clean, pressed jeans from the closet, and started toward the bathroom. "I know. It makes my work a challenge."

While he was busy, she wrapped the bedspread around her and went downstairs, gathering their clothing where they'd scattered it last night. There was something clichéd about being seduced on a rug in front of a fireplace . . . and something tremendously satisfying about it, too. Something just the slightest bit scary.

She had been married once before, though she rarely thought about it. Fresh out of law school, she had thought she was in love. Looking back, she knew she had simply been looking for someone to fill the void created by her father's death. She had wanted someone there in the crowd at graduation, someone to share the thrill of winning her first case, to commiserate over the first loss. She had wanted her father but couldn't have him, and so she had settled for Steven Robbins.

The marriage had been bad, the divorce worse. She had

eventually come to terms with her father's death and had even come to like having no one to please but herself. Now she was thinking seriously about wanting to please Travis, about rebelling against all that solitude. Now she was acknowledging how easy it would be to fall for him.

It seemed impossibly foolish. His life was in Fall River. Hers was in Little Rock. He'd tried the city and didn't like it. She had come from a small town and preferred the city. He was a cop. She defended people arrested by cops.

But they had been drawn to each other from the beginning. The better she got to know him, the more she liked him, and the same seemed to be true of him. And their lovemaking last night . . . She smiled. She wasn't naive. Great sex of the curl-your-toes, make-you-giddy variety wasn't that easy to come by.

Maybe a relationship wasn't so impossible. Cops knew how to negotiate deals. Compromise was every lawyer's middle name. They could work something out . . . *if* he wanted to.

Back upstairs, she returned to the bedroom, dressed, and set about making the bed. She was just finishing when Travis came into the room, caught her around the waist, and drew her close. "You didn't have to do that. We'll just unmake it later."

"Later. But right now we're both going to work. I'll be on the computer back at my room. Why don't you come by when you're finished with Mariana?"

He agreed, then gave her a good-bye kiss that made her wish work could wait. Hers could, but his wouldn't. *Business before pleasure* had been her father's motto and was undoubtedly Travis's, too. But when the pleasure was oh, so pleasurable, it was worth the wait.

She didn't wait to be shown out, but got her jacket and

purse and left. Traffic was light as she drove across town, singing along with her favorite CD. She punched the volume down as she followed the gravel drive to her cottage, then shut the music off completely when she saw the car parked out front.

She parked beside it and got out. The slam of the door drew Trask's attention her way. Upon seeing her, he put away his pen and the note he'd been writing and turned to face her.

It was easy to see why Kate had been attracted to him. He was even more handsome than he'd been at twenty. Blond hair, blue eyes, strong, and muscular, and he could undoubtedly charm the rattles off a snake. A snake always recognized its own kind, though, while Kate hadn't had the vaguest idea what she was dealing with. He had sucked her in, convincing her that he was exactly what she wanted him to be, hiding his true nature from her the way he'd hidden it from the entire town.

"Is there something I can do for you?" she asked coolly as she climbed the steps, room key in hand.

"I didn't realize when we met that we have a few mutual acquaintances."

"So we do. Travis McMaster. Kate Edwards."

The glint in his eyes wasn't pretty. "And Randy Hawkins. Gary Pritchard. Carla Brownley. Tom Leonard. You haven't been in town long to make so many friends."

So he knew. She had asked each of her clients not to tell anyone about the lawsuit until she had informed Trask, but obviously someone had talked anyway. Maybe one of them had boasted that he was taking on the all-powerful Trasks or, more likely, had warned some family member of what was about to happen. "I'm a friendly person," she said in response to his last remark.

"Not to me. You went looking for all these other people, but *I* have come to you."

"I have an appointment with you Monday."

"I didn't want to wait. There are a few things we need to discuss, Ms. Robbins. Can we go inside?"

"I don't discuss business in my motel room. However, I will see you in your office Monday." She started to move past him, intending to lock herself inside her room until Travis arrived, but Jason moved, blocking her way without touching her.

"Don't make things difficult for yourself, Colleen. You're new around here. You don't understand how we do business."

"I think I do. You say, 'Jump,' and I'm supposed to ask, 'How high?' You say, 'Drop this lawsuit,' and I'm supposed to say, 'Yes, sir, Mr. Trask.' " She smiled icily. "That's *not* how I do business. I'll see you in your office Monday." She stepped around him, inserted her key in the lock, and opened the door before facing him again. "You know, prowlers and intruders are such a frightening thing to a woman alone. Please don't come around here again. I'd have to call the police if you did."

For just an instant fury flared in his eyes. He looked as if he wanted to do something, anything that would hurt her. His jaw worked, and his right hand clenched into a fist before he regained control. He took a few deep breaths, along with a few steps back, then managed a phony smile. "Enjoy your stay here in Fall River, Colleen. And be careful. As you pointed out, you're a woman alone. Things could happen."

She watched him walk away, get in his car without slamming the door, and drive off without spinning his tires. *Be careful.* Coming from Travis last night, it had been a concerned warning. From Trask this morning, it was a carefully worded threat. He could save his breath. She had no intention of ending up like Kate Edwards or her sister. She sure as hell had no intention of winding up like her father. She would be *very* careful indeed.

Chapter Twelve

Saturday had been a good day, Tucker thought as he and Kate finished the dinner dishes that evening. The morning chill had disappeared, the sun had shone brightly, and the sky had been a clear, deep blue. They had finished the job of shingling the roof, then had driven to Eureka Springs to pick up the stove he'd bought weeks ago. They'd spent most of the afternoon there, window-shopping but buying nothing. It had been nice, being in a town where neither of them knew a soul, where no one looked at them as anything but a man and a woman, where no one knew that he'd spent half his life in prison or the intimate details of the worst ordeal of her life. It had been *normal*. They had both needed to be normal for a time.

Beside him, she finished rinsing the sink, then dried her hands. "Want some coffee?"

He shook his head.

"Want to watch television? Listen to music? Talk? Go somewhere?"

He glanced toward the window, where the closed curtains couldn't disguise that it was dark outside. Starting tomorrow, nighttime darkness would be arriving even earlier when daylight saving time gave way to standard time. By the middle of winter, it would be dark around five. She would become even more of a prisoner than she already was unless she somehow dealt with her fears. Unless she dealt with Jason Trask.

Forcing his mind away from such an unpleasant subject, he asked, "Where would you like to go?"

"Little Rock. Tulsa. Memphis. New Orleans." She shrugged. "Anyplace away from here."

He wished he had unlimited freedom and money. He would take her to all those places and more. He would accompany her to every city and town in the entire country, until she found one where she could live, where she could make a new life for herself. Where *they* could make a new life for themselves.

That last thought made him stiffen. Of course, he was planning to leave Fall River himself, but not until he had no other choice. Not with Kate. That wasn't even a possibility . . . or was it? "Are we running away, or do we have to come back?"

She gave his question a moment's thought. For more than six months, she had sworn that she would never leave Fall River, that she wouldn't let Trask have that last victory. Why couldn't she see that staying here let Jason win? It kept her in the role of victim. Leaving would take courage that no one believed she had. It wouldn't mean giving in but taking control.

Distracting himself from the unanswerable question, he made a choice from her offerings. "Since you don't have an answer for that and I can't leave the state without my parole officer's permission, maybe we should just watch TV tonight."

With a distant smile, she nodded and started toward the living room. He followed. They had just walked through the wide doorway when the phone rang. Kate automatically stopped in her tracks and stiffened. Tucker looked at her, but she was staring at the answering machine with dread.

"Hey, Katie, I went by your house on my way home and saw your lights on. I saw that old pickup in the driveway, too. You entertaining tonight?"

"That's Tim Carter," she said flatly. "He's Jason's best friend. He coaches his son's Little League team, sings in the church choir every Sunday, and calls me every other night."

"There are rumors around town that you've taken up with that ex-con. Trash with trash. Seems suitable to me. Has he heard all about you, Katie? Does he know what a sick bitch you are? What you did to Jason, what you made happen to your own sweet, innocent, little sister? By the way, how is Kerry? Is she ever going to get out of the loony bin? If she does, Katie, we just might take turns with her, but you'll be first. We're all going to have our turn with you, so you'd better enjoy your ex-con while you can. What do you do with him, Katie? Did you fuck him the very first time, like you did with Jason? Do you like getting nasty with him? Do you get on your knees and—"

Kate moved toward the phone, but Tucker reached it first, yanking it up, gripping it so hard that his fingers ached. "Hey, Timmy. You want to talk to somebody, why don't you talk to me?"

There was a brief, stunned silence, then the line went dead. Tucker hung up, then watched the phone, expecting it to ring again immediately. When it remained silent, he turned to Kate. She was rigid, so pale and tense that her entire body was shaking. "Kate—"

As if she hadn't heard him, she walked to the table and disconnected the answering machine. She pulled first one cassette, then the second, from the recorder, and stripped the tapes into a long, curly pile on the floor. Next she picked up the machine itself, broke off the lid that covered the tapes, then lifted the entire machine and slammed it against the table.

"*Kate.*"

She smashed it again and again, doing more damage to the table than to the equipment, denting the wood, sending slivers into the air along with bits of plastic. Reacting instinctively, Tucker forced the machine from her hands and pulled her into his arms. He didn't think about her fears, about her aversion to being touched. All he thought about was holding her, calming her, somehow, some way, damn it, protecting her. "Kate, it's all right. They just want to scare you. They want to make you feel vulnerable and at their mercy. Don't give them that satisfaction, Kate. Don't give them that power."

"I *am* vulnerable! I *am* at their mercy! They can do whatever they want, and I can't stop them! As long as Jason's alive, *I can't stop them!*"

As long as Jason's alive . . . He closed his eyes and stroked her hair. Maybe she'd been right all along. Maybe killing Trask was the only solution. As long as she lived in Fall River, as long as he continued to live at all, she would never find peace. Maybe killing him was the only way out. Immediately, though, he denied it. Murder was no solution. If she killed Trask, she would find that the last six months had been nothing compared to the hell she would live in the rest of her life, provided in part by these same bastards who tormented her now but mostly by her own conscience, her own grief and guilt.

Getting her out of Fall River was the only real solution. Somehow he had to convince her to leave. He had to make her see that living well—living a normal, healthy, happy life—was the best revenge. He had to make her recognize the value of starting over, to see the rewards a new town and a new life would bring. Even if her new life had no place for him, he had to convince her.

"They're not going to hurt you, Kate. I won't let them. I'll take care of you, I swear."

After a moment the trembling calmed. A moment later she brought her hands to his waist, then gradually slid her arms around him and leaned against him for support. For days he had been wanting this—fantasizing about it, barely sleeping at night for dreaming about it. She was so soft, so slender and delicate, and so damned easy to hurt. He was afraid to move, afraid to make her realize exactly how close they were, afraid of bringing to life the fear that had controlled her for so long, and so he satisfied himself with simply holding her.

Until she moved.

It was simple—just a shift of her body against him, the rub of her breasts across his chest, the brush of her hips against his—but it made his breath catch in his throat, made his blood a little hotter and his desire a little stronger. He hoped like hell that she didn't notice the beginning swell of his erection, hoped that if she did notice, it wouldn't scare her away. This was such a big step for her—hell, for both of them—and he would hate to see it brought to an end by a resurgence of that damnable fear.

"Tucker?" Her voice was little more than a whisper. "You're holding me."

"Do you want me to stop?" His own voice was barely a whisper, all he could manage with the tightness in his chest and his own fear in his throat.

She gave a soft sigh. "No. I want . . . I want you . . ."

He raised one hand and gently tilted her head back. The stress caused by the phone call was gone from her face, but there was tension of an entirely different source there now. Her eyes were hazy, soft, and shadowy. Her lips were slightly parted, and her cheeks were tinged the faintest shade of pink. It didn't take experience to recognize desire, and the recognition sent his own arousal flaring out of control.

He was tempted to talk, to ask if the time was right, if she wanted to test her theories, if she was ready for kisses and more. But he'd never been very good with words, and a kiss seemed much more appealing than cautionary conversation. He cradled her face in both hands and touched his mouth to hers. She didn't stiffen, didn't panic and pull away. Instead, she opened to him, welcoming his tongue.

The first kiss was tentative—sweet and gentle, like nothing he had ever experienced, not as a kid, certainly not with Nolie. It was as innocent as a kiss could be, and yet it promised more. It made him hot and hard, made his desire incredibly strong, and at the same time made him feel incredibly weak. Such power in a simple little kiss.

The second kiss was still sweet, but far from innocent. She caught his lip in a sensuous bite, then suckled his tongue, drawing so hard that he felt the pull all the way down to his groin. Her arms tightened around his waist at the same time he slid his hands lower, over the long curve of her neck to her shoulders, along her arms, settling one hand at her waist while the other glided down to her bottom. He held her closer, hard and tight against his erection, while he fed on her mouth, stroking, probing, tasting. She was drawing the very breath from his lungs, the very need from his soul, leaving him desperate and greedy for more—more hunger, more passion, more need. He wanted to undress her, to lay her down, look at her, touch her, caress her. He wanted to learn her body intimately, to know what made her tremble, what made her burn. He wanted to arouse her until she lost control, until she writhed and whimpered, until she begged for release, and he wanted to give her that release. He wanted to crawl inside her, to feel her body hot and tight around his and know that she wanted him, that she welcomed him, that she just might die without him.

He wanted to make her forget her name.

Desperate for air, he drew back. Still holding her so tightly that even the clothing between them couldn't protect him from her heat or her from his greed, he gazed down at her. Eyes closed, lips apart, she looked like a woman thoroughly aroused. Her smile came first—sweet, seductive—then she looked at him. "Come upstairs with me."

He thought of her bedroom up there, soft green and white, comfortable and inviting, and the bathroom and the unused birth control pills in the medicine chest there, and he began a halting, apologetic, damning-himself refusal. "I don't have anything . . ."

Her smile deepened, sending another jolt of heat through him, making his erection swell a little harder, making the raw need in his belly a little more intense. "Did you use a condom with Nolie?"

He nodded.

"Every time?"

Another nod. It had been her one and only rule. No pregnancies, no sexually transmitted diseases, no risks for Nolie.

"And she was the only one since Amy?"

He nodded again.

"Then we don't need one. I want you, just you." She pulled free, took his hand, and led the way upstairs.

The bedroom was dark, lit only by the hall light that spilled through the open door. Tucker hesitated inside the door, bringing Kate to a stop, turning her to face him. "Are you sure?"

She nodded solemnly.

"I don't want to hurt you."

"You won't. You couldn't. You're too honorable a man."

Honorable. Not once in his entire thirty-four years had anyone considered him honorable, but Kate did. Feeling a surge of all new desire, he pulled her to him and kissed her hard, thrusting his tongue inside her mouth, while his hands fumbled with the buttons on her shirt. Maneuvering blindly to the bed was easy, as was working open the metal button and the zipper on her jeans. At that point, though, he forced himself to break the kiss, to take a deep breath and find some shred of control. He couldn't push her any faster than she was prepared to go, or he could ruin things between them. As eager as he was, as fragile as she was, he couldn't afford a mistake.

His hands trembling, he slid the shirt off her shoulders, pulled the chambray free of her arms, and wrapped his hands in it. The shirt was old, worn soft, and smelled tantalizingly of her. Knotting his fists, he pulled the fabric taut between them, then slowly let it fall to the floor, a pale shadow on darker carpet. For a moment he simply looked at her, standing silently, trustingly, wearing faded jeans and a plain white bra, its only decorative touch a bit of lace between her breasts. Then he allowed himself the luxury of touching that lace, of drawing his fingertips across it before gliding them lightly along the swell of her breasts, making her tremble.

"You're a beautiful woman, Kate." His voice was rough, harsh. In contrast, hers was as soft as a whisper.

"From frumpy to pretty and now beautiful." She managed a breathless little laugh. "You certainly do change your mind."

He responded with half a smile as he unfastened the hooks, then coaxed the flimsy garment away. He hadn't changed his mind. He had realized she was beautiful from the beginning, but had let himself overlook it because he had known she was other things, too. Dangerous. A threat to his peace of mind. A risk he hadn't yet been ready to take.

The dim light revealed her breasts, soft, beckoning to his touch, inviting his kisses. Sliding his arm around her waist in an embrace so loose she could easily break free, he cupped one breast in his palm and ducked his head to nuzzle it, to suck the nipple into his mouth, to make her shudder so sweetly. He treated her other breast to the same attention before turning to the task once more of undressing her.

Her jeans came off easily, the silky panties she wore gliding along with them. She kicked off her loafers, then stepped out of the last pieces of clothing and stood naked before him. His breathing was labored, his touches tentative. He felt sixteen again and facing that pretty little girl down in New Orleans. With the arrogance of a dumb kid, he had thought he'd known all he needed to know about sex, but she had taught him how wrong he was. This time he knew he didn't know nearly enough, not about women like Kate, not about making love. He didn't know anything at all about being in love . . . except that he thought he was.

After a moment of his scrutiny and gentle caresses, Kate lifted his hand to her mouth, pressing a kiss to his palm. "Let me undress you."

He nodded, and she traded his hand for a handful of his shirt. It was red, soft cotton, and tucked snugly inside his jeans. She pulled it free, then tugged it over his head. She had seen him without a shirt before, all hard muscles and sun-browned skin, and had been favorably impressed. Tonight she was even more so. She laid her hand flat on his chest and felt the uneven beat of his heart against her palm. He was solid, strong enough to hurt her but too honorable.

She believed that with all her heart. He could never be like Jason. He could never find pleasure in anyone else's pain.

As she slid her hands to his waist, he sucked in his breath. After unbuckling his belt, she turned her attention to the metal buttons that secured his jeans, working each one free. It wasn't an easy task, hampered by her unsteady fingers and the solid length of his arousal that pulled the denim taut. By the time she finished, his muscles were quivering, and a sheen of sweat dampened his skin. "Jesus, Kate, you're killing me."

She smiled and, despite her nakedness, managed to sit primly on the bed. "Then you finish."

He kicked his shoes off, then began undressing. His gaze was on her—she could feel its heat—but she was watching his jeans slide away, revealing smooth skin and an erection hard enough to make her damp, powerful enough to make her tremble.

He stood naked in front of her. "You don't have to go through with this."

In response she lay back on the bed, then gently stroked his groin. Her fingers grazed over soft skin, coarse curls, and the rigid, heated penis that surged against her palm. Dropping her hand to her side, she offered a faint smile of invitation. "I want to," she said, then simply added, "I want you."

He joined her on the bed, momentarily blocking the light from the hall, looming over her, strong and powerful . . . but not menacing.

Supporting himself on his arms, he leaned over her, leaving a trail of damp kisses along her jaw, down her throat, and across her breast to her nipple. The sucking and tugging sent quivery, heated sensations curling through her belly and made her breath catch in her chest. They made her wriggle underneath him, made her grasp his waist and pull him lower, closer, until his hips were intimately cradled against hers, until his arousal was rubbing enticingly against her.

"Come inside me, Tucker. I need you . . ."

For a moment he chose instead to continue his tormenting little kisses. Then he raised his head, his gaze locking with hers, and moved slowly, probing, seeking, filling her with his flesh. When she held him tightly, all of him, he swallowed hard and drew a shaky breath. "Oh, Kate."

She slid her palms along his damp skin, over muscle and bone and small, hard nipples. As her fingertips brushed his mouth, he caught one between his teeth, sending a dozen tiny shocks down her arm. Closing her eyes, she took a moment to savor his kiss, the ragged tenor of his breathing, the heat radiating from him, the tautness of his muscles, the solid strength of his body pressing hers down, the joining of their bodies together, the unsettled, sharp-edged need spreading through her. All these things she had thought she would never feel again, had thought she could never want again, but she had been wrong, oh, so wrong.

With a strained groan, he finally moved, withdrawing, filling her again, pulling back once more. His rhythm was slow, feeding a need that already threatened to consume her, adding to heat that was already intense. When she lifted her legs higher, he sank deeper inside her, so deep that the muscles in her belly quivered, so deep that she could feel the size and strength and force of him in her chest.

"Oh, please," she whispered without words as her release grew, threatened, demanded. She moved against him, meeting his hips, each long, strong thrust of his aroused flesh rubbing satisfyingly hard over her own. She pleaded, trembled, moaned helplessly, and then with a great rush it came. *She* came, her body growing rigid, her breath impossible to catch, as pleasure so pure it was painful washed over her, claiming her, overwhelming her.

Tucker was beyond stopping, beyond giving her the time she needed to recover. He slid his hands underneath her and lifted her as he continued to ride her, long, hard, fast, leaving her nothing to do but hold him and gasp at the tingly aftershocks that made her entire body tremble. With a great groan, his body stilled, then jerked as he emptied into her, hot, wet proof of his need, of his satisfaction.

He sank against her, his breathing harsh, his muscles trembling, his body still hard, still straining, and he gave her the sweetest, gentlest kiss she had ever known. Closing her eyes on the tears gathering, she held him tightly until finally he pulled free and shifted to lie next to her, facing her. His arm was heavy underneath her breasts, and so was his leg where it rested between hers, his knee pressing where he had so recently filled her, but she didn't feel trapped. She didn't feel the urge to push him away. She felt safe. Protected.

She rested her head on his shoulder, clasped his arm over her chest with both hands, and fixed her gaze on the ceiling. "Thank you, Tucker."

"For what?" His mouth was close to her ear, his breath tickling.

"Making me feel normal again."

He raised his head to look at her. "You *are* normal. Kate. You always have been."

"These last few months . . ."

"You've been afraid. Any woman in your position would have been afraid."

"Thank you anyway. For being a man I could trust. A man I could want more than I could want to be left alone. A man I could . . ." She broke off, leaving the sentence unfinished except in her head. *A man I could need. Rely on. Have faith in. Love.*

He gave her another of those tender little kisses, then settled beside her. In no time at all, his breathing deepened, then leveled off into the slow rhythm of a sound sleep. Kate lay there listening, feeling the soft, warm puffs of air on her shoulder, still clinging to the muscled arm across her chest, and smiled a silly, goofy smile of triumph.

She hadn't been kidding herself. Life really could go on. She really could put Jason and the rape behind her. Making love with Tucker wasn't a slight possibility in the distant future. She had actually done it. A normal life with normal expectations wasn't an unreachable dream. It was going to happen. She was going to recover.

Healing would come, Kerry had assured her after the trial. It might be painful, and it might take time, but one day, she would be all right. Kate hadn't believed her. She would survive, but, deep in her heart, she had believed she would never get over what Jason, his friends, his lawyers, her family, and this town had done to her.

And then she'd met Tucker.

She turned onto her side and watched him in the dim light. When she had asked Mr. James to help her hire a man who would kill for a price, she had never dreamed that *this* was the man she would find. He was everything she wanted, everything she needed . . . and he was surely going to break her heart. Before that happened, though, he was going to accomplish—had already accomplished—a tremendous amount of healing, and that, plus the pleasure of his lovemaking, could make the heartache bearable.

Then she touched his mouth. Automatically, even in sleep, he pressed a kiss to her hand, and she rephrased that last thought. The healing could make the heartache *almost* bearable.

In all of Tucker's life, only a short portion of it—those two months with Jimmy—had been spent in a place with a telephone, so when the phone beside the bed rang, it startled him awake. He needed only a moment to realize where he was, to remember that the warm, soft body snuggled against him was Kate's, only a moment to remember the lovemaking they'd shared and the damnable call that had led to it.

The phone rang again. She was sleeping so deeply that her breathing didn't shift at all when he untangled his arms and legs from hers, when he left her to slide across the cool sheets to the opposite side of the bed and pick up the receiver after the third peal. He glanced at the clock, yawned, then murmured hello.

"Sounds like I woke you."

He'd never heard the voice before, but he knew who it was. Who else could sound so genial, smooth, and menacing all at once? Who else would call here at 11:45 at night and not be surprised to hear a man answer? Who else could make him feel, with no more than five simple words, so damned edgy? "No, I wasn't asleep. I assume your pal Timmy called you when he hung up on me."

"I had a message from him when I got home. I was out on a date. She wasn't as much fun as Kate, but for my needs tonight, she was good enough."

Tucker glanced over his shoulder at Kate, still asleep, and lowered his voice anyway. "What do you want, Trask?"

"To talk."

"About what?"

"Kate." His chuckle was low, mocking. "You know, she was pretty well used by half the men in this town long before you ever got out of prison, but *our* relationship was special. I'm sure she's told you about it. The bitch has caused me no end of trouble, but she and her sister were worth it." Another chuckle. "You owe me, Caldwell. If I hadn't raped Kate, she never would have given you a second look. She sure as hell never would have fucked you."

Feeling sick deep inside, Tucker had to struggle to speak. "So you're not denying it tonight."

"Why lie when you know the truth? Yeah, I raped the bitch. I fucked her for all she was worth, struggling and screaming and fighting all the while. I made her plead, Caldwell. I made her beg me not to hurt her, and then I hurt her anyway. It was powerful, man—lying on top of her, inside her, listening to her cry, 'Please, Jason, don't hurt me, I'll do whatever you want.' " On those last words he mimicked Kate's higher-pitched voice, then dropped back to his normal register, heavy with scorn and hatred. "Damn right she did whatever I wanted. The first thing she did was stop the whining after I broke her damned jaw. Oh, but she cried. You should have heard her. Every time I hit her, every time I rammed my cock inside her, she cried like a baby. And you know what, Caldwell? I liked it. It made me hotter. It made my dick harder. It made me come like a gusher."

Rigid with fury, Tucker forced his jaw to unclench. "You're a sick bastard, Trask."

"That's funny, coming from trash like you." Without a pause, he went on. "Are you a praying man?"

"Aren't we all?"

"Then you'd better pray that I don't decide to nail Kate again. This time I won't be so gentle. This time she might not survive."

"Listen up, Trask," Tucker said, making his voice as hard, as threatening, as dangerously cold, as he could. "If you or your buddies ever call here again, if you ever speak to Kate again, if you ever even look at her again, I'll kill you."

"Like you killed my cousin?"

"No. He died quickly. I'll make you suffer. I'll make you hurt so bad you'll wish to God you'd never been born." Tucker hung up, went into the bathroom, and closed the door behind him. He made his way to the sink, turned on the cold water, and listened to it run while he waited for the sickness in his stomach to settle.

He had to get Kate out of this town, had to get her away from that son of a bitch before long-distance threats lost their thrill and he came after her again. If he couldn't convince her to leave, then he would have to rethink her original request. Hell, he was already rethinking it. Jason Trask deserved to die. Someone as sick as he was couldn't be helped. The only safe thing was to kill him. Knowing that he was dead, that he could never hurt Kate again, would be worth going back to prison. Knowing that she was safe would be worth dying himself.

But he would much rather live with her, someplace far away, where Trask's evil couldn't touch her.

Deciding that he wasn't going to throw up, after all, he took a cup from the dispenser next to the sink and filled it with water, drinking it down in one gulp. Then he returned to the bed, sliding in behind Kate, who immediately scooted back against him. No one would ever hurt her again. Not as long as he could stop them. Until the day she no longer wanted him in her life, he was going to make sure of that.

After a while, he dozed off, but it was a fitful rest. Every noise—a car passing on the street, a branch tapping against the window, the settling of the old house—awakened him. Soon after seven, he gave up, pulled on his jeans, and went downstairs to make a pot of coffee. He hadn't had even the first taste when the doorbell rang.

Feeling the same trepidation Kate must feel over the phone calls, he checked the peephole, only to discover that the trepidation was called for. McMaster stood on the other side, and, judging by his expression, he wasn't too happy.

He opened the locks, then the door. He and McMaster faced each other in hostile silence for one long moment, before the other man finally spoke. "I was told I might find you here."

Told by Jason Trask. The perverted son of a bitch called here, said the things he did, then went whining to the police chief because of what Tucker had said in response.

"Where is Kate?"

"She's asleep. I don't plan to wake her."

McMaster nodded grimly. "Can I come in?"

Stepping back, Tucker allowed him entry, then closed the door. "The coffee's about done, and we'll be less likely to wake Kate in the kitchen."

McMaster waited until they were seated at the breakfast table with their coffee before he got to the point. "Did you threaten to kill Jason Trask last night?"

"Yes, I did."

The cop grimaced, either at the taste of the coffee or what he perceived as Tucker's stupidity. "You spent sixteen years in prison. Didn't you learn anything? You don't go around making threats against a man like Trask."

"They weren't threats. They were promises. If he comes near Kate or bothers her in any way, I *will* kill him."

"How did you happen to talk to him in the first place?"

"He called."

"To harass Kate?"

"No. He wanted to tell me how much fun he had raping her. He wanted me to know how she begged him not to hurt her and he did it anyway and got off on it." Tucker drew a deep breath, and his voice lost the disdain and the sharp edge. "He said he might do it again, only this time she might not survive."

"And you said you would kill him." McMaster shook his head. "I can't fault you for that. I'd like to kill the bastard myself. Where was Kate during this conversation?"

"She was asleep. She doesn't know, and I don't intend to tell her."

Reaching across to the window, the cop pushed back the curtains and let the sun in. "Trask has told everyone he knows about your threat. If anything happens to him, you'd better have a damned good alibi, because you're the first one they'll go after."

"So he and his buddies are free to call here and threaten Kate, but I can't respond in kind."

"You want to stop them from harassing Kate? Get her the hell out of Fall River. Persuade her that there's nothing left for her here. Tell her whatever it takes to get her to leave, and then go, both of you."

"And if she refuses?"

McMaster's expression turned grim. "Stay close to her . . . and get her to buy you a gun. You may need it."

A gun. Other than a hunting rifle, he had never handled a gun before, and he had little desire to start now. He had less desire to violate his parole. But if it was best for Kate . . .

The shuffle of footsteps down the hall interrupted his thoughts and turned his gaze toward the door. She came in yawning, her hair mussed, her robe belted at the waist. She saw him and smiled, but the smile faded when she realized that he wasn't alone, that McMaster was sitting across from him. "Good morning."

Tucker met her in the middle of the room. He wanted to pull her into his arms, to kiss away the sleepiness that softened her eyes, to bring back the arousal that would turn her cheeks pink. He wanted to hold her, long and tight, and never let go—but not in front of McMaster. Instead, he gave her hand a light squeeze as he passed. "Sit down. I'll get you some coffee."

She took his seat on the bench, then scooted over to the wall and looked out the window. "Jeez, I've got a ton of leaves in the backyard," she commented before finally greeting her friend with less than friendliness. "What are you doing here?"

"Having a cup of coffee."

"Right. You woke up at this ungodly hour on a weekend and decided that, of all the places you could go to have coffee, you would come here, and of all the people you could have it with, you would choose Tucker."

"Well, what do *you* think? That I was driving by and saw his truck in the driveway, that I decided to find out what the hell he was doing here at this ungodly hour on a weekend, and so I invited myself in?"

"That sounds more like you."

Tucker sat down beside Kate and slid a mug across to her. She thanked him with the flash of a smile. "He's doing his job, Kate."

"Harassing you is written into his job description?"

"He wasn't harassing me. We were just talking."

"About what?"

"About Tim Carter and what it'll take to make him and the others leave you alone." It wasn't the entire truth, but neither was it a lie.

She held his gaze for a moment, serious and concerned as she remembered last night's call. Then, abruptly, she looked away.

"You want my best advice, Kate?" McMaster waited a long moment before answering. "Move away."

In the heavy silence that followed, she looked from him to Tucker, then out the window at the yard. "This is my home. I grew up in this town. I played in this yard. I spent as much of the first eighteen years of my life in this house as I did in my parents' house. I have a right to live here."

McMaster started to reach across the table, but reflexively he stopped. "You can live wherever you want. But tell me one thing: are you happy here? Do you love your job? Could you miss your family any more than you already do? Is there any part of your life in this town that wouldn't be better someplace else?"

Shyly, she looked at Tucker, who shook his head. "Don't stay on my account, Kate, because I'm leaving someday, too." He didn't go on, didn't offer the invitation that was struggling to get out. He didn't ask her—beg her—to please go with him. That could wait until they were alone.

"Do you know how much satisfaction it would give them to see me leave town because of them?"

It was McMaster who answered. "Not as much as they get calling here every damn night, talking dirty to your machine. Not as much as they get knowing that, even if you don't answer, you're in here listening. Not nearly as much as they get seeing you around town and knowing that they've destroyed your nice, comfortable life."

"Kate, they're not going to quit." Tucker slid his fingers between hers, holding tightly. "You're too easy a target. They're too sick. If they get bored with the phone calls, they'll just start harassing you in person. Remember what that son of a bitch said last night? That one of these days they're all going to take turns with you, and when they're done, they're going after Kerry. Do you think they won't do it? Do you think it was just talk?"

"Yes. You don't know these guys, Tucker. They talk big, but they don't carry through. They're cowards."

"A man like that may be a coward on his own, but you put him together with other cowards, with someone like Trask to lead them, and you've got a dangerous bunch. Maybe Carter doesn't have the balls to come after you himself, but with the others egging him on, with Trask telling him how good it was, what fun it was to make you beg, he'll find the courage."

She stared out the window a moment longer before flatly asking, "Where would I go?"

"You could go to Little Rock and be close to Kerry. You could go to Tulsa, Memphis, New Orleans—anyplace away from here." Deliberately he chose her own words from last night and saw that she recognized them.

"Run away. That's what you're saying. You both want me to run away."

McMaster looked down, leaving Tucker to respond to her disappointed statement. "No. We want you to move on." And he wanted to move on with her. He was ready to see someplace else, to make a stab at living a normal life, to make a real effort at respectability. He was ready to see Kate happy.

She scowled at them both, then gave the only answer she could face at the moment. It wasn't what he wanted to hear, but, for the time being, it was enough. "I'll think about it."

"What are your plans for the day?"

Looking up from her breakfast, Colleen smiled at Travis. The last two days had been one of the most pleasurable weekends she'd spent in years. Everything came with a price, though, and she was about to pay it. "I've got a meeting in fifteen minutes with Jason Trask."

Travis scowled at the mere mention of the man's name, and why not? He'd spent a good portion of his Saturday dealing with Trask's ex-wife and then had been roused from bed early Sunday morning by Trask himself, ranting and raving about Tucker Caldwell. He'd wanted the son of a bitch locked up at that very moment, but simply threatening someone wasn't necessarily a crime. If it were, Trask and his friends would have been in jail long ago. Still, once Travis had gotten off the phone, he'd had to go over to Kate's house. The whole incident had disrupted Colleen's plans for a lazy, leisurely morning in bed, and those plans *hadn't* included sleeping.

"I wish you didn't have to deal with him."

"It's hard to sue a man without having at least some contact with him." In truth, she wasn't eager to see Jason again, not after Saturday morning. He was so damned arrogant, so utterly convinced of his God-given superiority over the rest of the world. He honestly didn't think that the law applied to him the same as to others. With any luck—and with a lot of courage on the part of her clients—he would soon find out how wrong he was.

With a glance at her watch, she picked up her briefcase. "I've got to go. Can't be late and let Jason think he's scared me out of town."

"I'll walk with you." Travis accompanied her to the cash register. Outside on the street, they turned together toward the bank, walking in silence until they stood on the corner. "You could give me a kiss," he suggested.

"Right here on the street? What would people think?"

"That their chief of police is the luckiest man in the county."

"Unless one of those people is Jason Trask. He might get the idea that this whole lawsuit was set up by you to get back at him for Kate. He might think it's purely personal and not take it seriously."

"Isn't it?" Travis shrugged at her look. "If he had done to my father what he did to yours, I'd want to make him pay."

"You're right, it is personal. But if that's all it was, Travis, I wouldn't be here. These people have a legitimate claim against the Trasks. They've suffered through no fault of their own, because the Trasks wanted to save money. They need help, and I can provide them with that help. The fact that I'll be working against Jason simply makes a good case better."

"Well, I hope you win *so* much that every person the Trasks have ever harmed decides to sue."

"I appreciate your support," she said with a laugh. "I'll see you later." As soon as the light turned green, she crossed the street. A glance back from the bank doors showed Travis still standing where she'd left him.

Inside, a receptionist directed her to the elevator. She stepped inside and pressed the second-floor button, then closed her eyes, breathed deeply, and conjured up images of the toughest sons of bitches she'd ever beaten in court. By the time the elevator doors opened, she was prepared mentally as well as physically to meet with Jason Trask.

But she wasn't prepared for the scene that greeted her. The door to Jason's office was open, and he was standing there, smiling, engaging in an awkward handshake with another man—awkward because the man's right hand was gone.

Colleen's feet moved automatically, carrying her toward the two men. Jason had noticed her the instant the doors had opened, but he didn't acknowledge her until she was less than ten feet away.

"Talk about coincidence. Tommy was just saying that he would get in touch with you, and here you are. Do you want to tell her the news yourself, Tommy, or do you want me to?"

Tommy Leonard was a slender man with washed-out blue eyes and heavy scarring on his arm where the mixer that had chewed off his hand had tried to take more. In her meetings with him, he had been quiet, brought about by equal measures of depression, despair, and fear. He was quiet this morning, too, but this time it was shame. He wouldn't raise his head, couldn't bring himself to look at her even when she spoke to him.

"Good morning, Mr. Leonard. Is there something you wanted to tell me?"

He was staring down at his remaining hand, and she looked down to see the easily identifiable form of a check clutched in his fingers. So Trask had bought him off.

She laid her hand on his arm. "It's all right, Mr. Leonard. I hope whatever he gave you was worth it." Then, losing the softness, she directed a cold gaze to Jason. "Are you ready for our meeting?"

"See you later, Tommy," he said, sounding so friendly, so damned phony. "The next time you think you have a little problem, come and see me first, you understand?" After the man's mumbled response, Jason turned to her. "Now, Colleen, step into my office. We'll talk."

She walked in, went straight to a chair near the desk, and made herself comfortable. Once Jason had done the same, she asked, "How much did it cost you?"

"Tommy? Small change. Not enough to concern myself with."

Probably five thousand, maybe even ten. It must have sounded like a lot to a man like Tommy, who had no income, who was behind on his bills and in danger of losing everything. No doubt he figured that a little cash in hand was worth a lot more right now than a settlement that might not ever happen. If she were in his place, she might have made the same decision.

"So, it seems you're down to only two clients."

She had begun to open her briefcase. Startled, she jerked back and stared at him. "Only two?"

"I went by Gary Pritchard's house on my way in this morning and explained to him that we don't like strangers coming in and stirring things up. It causes problems. People get hurt. Business gets disrupted. Workers get laid off. If a person doesn't have a job to go to, there's no paycheck coming in, and without a paycheck, how is he going to pay those bank loans on his house and car?"

She wondered exactly to whom among the people important to Gary Pritchard Jason was referring. If the Pritchards were like most families in town, probably half their relatives worked for the Trasks. Probably all of them owed them money. "And did you pay him, too?"

"Of course." He smiled, reminding her of the lowest of snakes. "We take care of our own, Colleen. We don't want someone like you coming in and trying to profit from the misfortunes that have befallen our neighbors."

"Misfortunes. Is that what you call them? Misfortunes? Accidents? A little rough love play?"

His gaze narrowed and turned cold. "Tell me, Colleen, did you know Kate Edwards before you came here?"

"No. I'd never met anyone from Fall River before."

He looked as if he didn't believe her but let it slide. "You would be well advised to pack up your briefcase and go back to Little Rock. This lawsuit isn't going anywhere. You've already lost two clients, and it's only a matter of time before you lose the other two. You're wasting your time, sweetheart. These people aren't going to take me to court. They know better. They know what I'll do."

"And what is that? Will you run them out of town, like your ex-wife? See to it that they lose their jobs, like Kate Edwards? Or will you put their innocent young daughters in a mental hospital, like Kerry Edwards?"

His smile was the coldest she'd ever seen. It sent shivers down her spine and unsettled her stomach. "I'll do whatever it takes to protect myself. *Whatever it takes*."

She got to her feet, clasping her attaché case in both hands to hide the trembling she couldn't quite control. "Then understand this: *I* will do whatever it takes to protect my clients." She waited a moment for that to sink in, then smiled icily. "Good day, Mr. Trask."

Chapter Thirteen

So much for grand plans.

Kate stared out the car window, watching the dark shadows of trees flit past, and thought about the plans she'd made last week. A trip to Little Rock, a car rental, a gun purchase, a furtive drive back to kill Jason, and all her problems would be solved. Well, she had made the trip to Little Rock, accompanied by Tucker, but the rest of it . . . Silly plans. Fantasies that she no longer needed. She wasn't going to kill anyone. She wasn't throwing away her future to avenge her past.

"How was Kerry?"

She glanced at Tucker, his face dimly illuminated by the dashboard lights, then smiled faintly. "Beautiful. She was wearing a yellow dress, and her hair was braided the way she likes it, and she looked so pretty and sweet. She looked so normal that, for a moment, I thought the Kerry we all loved was back. But it was an illusion. She walks, she talks, but when you look into her eyes, no one's home." She drew a deep, unsteady breath. "How was your brother?"

"Still lazy. Still keeping Dawn busy." Then he grinned. "Actually, he's got a job. He's good at it, according to Dawn, and he seems to like it."

"Did you get to spend some time with him?"

"Only for an hour or so. That was all he could spare."

"Then what did you do all afternoon?"

He glanced at her. "Would it be easier if I tell you right up front that I didn't see Nolie and didn't want to?"

"Actually, it would be easier if you had seen her, and she left you absolutely cold."

"I told you, Kate, I don't believe in sleeping around. As long as you and I are together, there won't be anyone else."

How long would that be? she wanted to ask, but she didn't. There were too many answers he could give, and she wasn't ready to hear some of them.

Tilting her head back, she let the silence join them again. She had enjoyed being in the city today and was dreading the return home. The closer they got to Fall River, the bleaker her mood grew. She loved her home, but even when life was relatively peaceful, there was a tension that came from being there. She had been free of it Saturday when she and Tucker had gone to Eureka Springs and again today, but now it was coming back. She didn't want to go home. She didn't want to be in her pretty house in that picturesque town. She wanted to be free.

For weeks she had thought freedom would come from killing Jason, but Tucker and Travis were convinced that it could only come from leaving Fall River and starting over. Starting new. Nice words, full of possibilities, especially if Tucker could be persuaded to start anew with her. It wouldn't be so hard giving up the home she loved if she made a new home with someone she loved more. But what were the chances? Sunday morning he had talked about her leaving and about his own eventual departure, but he hadn't mentioned the two of them going away together.

So *she* could mention it. She could offer him a deal: *Go with me, and I'll leave today.* Did he care enough to accept?

Would he go with her, get her settled someplace, then leave, or would he refuse to go at all?

It was hell not knowing.

Before she realized where the miles had gone, Tucker was turning into her driveway. The lights were on, but the place looked deserted. It wasn't much of a home anymore, but a place she would soon be saying good-bye to.

Tucker opened the trunk and picked up an armload of shopping bags. Buying something pretty had been her goal today—pretty dresses, sweaters, and shoes, pretty pillows for the sofa, pretty curtains for her bedroom windows. All of it had cost a good portion of the raise with which the school board had bribed her, but what finer way to spend their money than to make herself look good and feel better?

"Do you want to go out to dinner or fix something here?"

Inside, he set down the bags he carried, then drew her into his arms. "I'm not really hungry."

A moment ago she had been, but his simple act had chased the thought of food right out of her mind. Sliding her arms around his waist, she looked up at him. "Thanks for going with me today. I enjoyed it."

"Even wondering about Nolie?"

"You don't want Nolie."

"No, I don't. I want you."

For how long? A night, a week, a month, a year, a lifetime? The obvious answer, based on the heat and strength of his arousal pressing against her, was *right now,* and for now, that was enough. For the next few hours, it would be all she needed.

He had just bent his head to kiss her when the phone rang. She flinched. He stiffened, then started to draw away, but she refused to release him. "I'll answer it, Kate. It could be important."

"I don't get important calls."

"It could be Travis."

She shook her head.

"It could be the hospital calling about Kerry."

She wavered, then shook her head again. "It's one of them, Tucker. You know it is."

"So let me talk to him." When she still refused, he sighed. "Then let me unplug the phones."

Kate hesitated, then released him. "I'll get the one in the living room. You get the kitchen." That would leave only the phone in the bedroom, where they would be going soon.

In the living room she disconnected the plug at the wall. The phone went blessedly silent, although the more distant rings from the other phones could still be heard, until they both stopped at once. Had the caller hung up, or had Tucker decided to disregard her wishes and answered anyway?

The murmur of a voice from the kitchen answered the question for her. Scowling, she left the bag with the sofa pillows, picked up the rest, and started upstairs. If he wanted to listen to an obscene call, fine, but *she* had better things to do.

In her room, she set the bags down, kicked off her shoes, and began unbraiding her hair. That done, she peeled off her hose, then slipped out of the tapestry vest. Her blouse and skirt would be easily dealt with once Tucker came upstairs, which, if she was lucky, would be soon. The caller would hang up on him, just as Tim had Saturday night, and she wouldn't have time to unpack her new purchases.

Lifting the first bag to the bed, she removed its contents. The red dress wrapped in tissue paper wasn't casual enough for the office or modest enough for church, should she ever decide to go again, but she had bought it anyway because she had liked the look in Tucker's eyes when he'd seen her in it. She had liked the look in her own eyes, had liked seeing herself in something that fitted snugly, that revealed the swell of her breasts, the narrowness of her waist, and the curve of her hips.

Laying the dress aside, she unfolded sweaters in vivid colors and patterns, pleated navy trousers, and a simpler dress in emerald green. From another bag she took a box containing a pair of strappy black heels. She was about to open it when she heard Tucker's footsteps on the stairs. Smiling, she slipped the lid back into place. Putting the clothes away could wait until later. She needed the bed for better things now.

He came through the door, his expression troubled. "I told you not to answer," she said quietly. When he didn't respond, she laid the shoe box aside and began picking up the clothing from the bed. She was putting everything on the dresser when he finally spoke.

"I need to ask you something, Kate."

In the mirror she caught a glimpse of his face, so serious, so concerned, before she turned to face him.

"Did you buy a gun today?"

She frowned. "Tucker, you were with me. You saw everything I bought."

"I wasn't with you after lunch. You dropped me off at Jimmy's."

"And I went to the hospital to see Kerry."

"Maybe you stopped somewhere along the way."

Briefly at a loss for words, she shook her head. "I didn't. I went straight to the hospital and straight back. Besides, I have a gun, Tucker. Why would I buy . . ." The muscles in her stomach clenching, she let the question trail off. Three nights ago she had sat at the kitchen table and made notes for the killing of Jason Trask, notes that had included buying another gun in Little Rock. Notes that she left together with the mail on the kitchen counter—the end of the counter closest to the phone he'd just been using.

"Did you?"

Folding her arms across her chest to contain the chill shivering through her, she nodded toward the shopping bags. "There are my bags. Do you want to check?" He looked at them as if he really wanted to but couldn't quite bring himself to do it. "I left one bag and my purse downstairs, plus there's the car. I could have hidden it in there. Searching might be a waste of time, though. After all, I could have hidden it anywhere in the house while you were on the phone."

"You were planning to kill him tonight, weren't you?"

She wanted to deny it, to lie, but when she opened her mouth, the truth slipped out.

"I considered it." She had never gotten so far as concrete plans, because she'd made love with Tucker and suddenly killing Jason had no longer seemed so important.

"Did you buy another gun?"

"No."

"Did you decide to use your own gun?"

"No. I decided to take your advice. I decided to let him live until someone else kills him. Until old age catches up with him. Until God has mercy on those of us who have to deal with him."

He came closer, moving carefully, as if sudden movement might be too jarring. "Do you know what they would do to you, Kate? They would *destroy* you."

"I thought they already had . . . until Saturday night." Hesitantly she reached out, and he took her hand, holding so tightly that she couldn't possibly escape. She didn't feel the slightest desire to try. "There's no reason why you should believe me, Tucker—I've lied about it often enough—but I've got better things ahead of me than a life in prison.

Killing Jason is no longer part of my future." She stated it
with the simplicity of absolute truth. All her talk about taking
back control, about not letting Jason run her life, and now
she'd done it. He was no longer important to her. He wasn't
worth all the fear, trauma, and heartache he'd caused her. He
wasn't worth her freedom or her life. He certainly wasn't
worth losing Tucker.

For a long time he simply looked at her, studying, searching, then finally accepting. He pulled her into his arms, gave
her a long, leisurely kiss that stole the breath from her lungs,
then solemnly asked, "Is there room in that future for me?"

Her smiled started tiny, then expanded to completely fill
her, all the way through to her soul. "Absolutely."

He kissed her again, with less patience and more need,
creating a matching need inside her. It was so easy for him.
He merely looked at her, and her blood grew hot. Touched
her, and her desire flared fierce and greedy. Kissed her, and
her body ached with the emptiness that he would soon fill.
No other man had affected her like this, not even those she'd
been infatuated with, not even the few she had imagined herself in love with.

But there was no imagining with Tucker. She did love
him.

His tongue was in her mouth, his erection swelling against
her belly, his hands sliding her skirt up, tugging her panties
down. He was as eager as she was, unwilling to wait one second longer, groaning as she fumbled with his zipper. When
she finally freed him from his jeans, he lifted her onto the
dresser and filled her at the same time.

Finally ending the kiss, he rested his forehead against hers,
then sought a deep breath. "Do you want to wait until we get
undressed and in bed?"

She wrapped her legs around his hips and pulled him

closer, a little deeper, a little tighter. "It's a little late to ask, isn't it?"

"I can stop," he offered, but he didn't sound too sure, and the twitch his body gave deep where it was sheltered within hers wasn't a vote of confidence.

Kate nibbled his lower lip, then slipped her tongue inside his mouth, tasting his need and her own desperation, making every muscle in his body tighten, increasing the tension and edginess in her own body. "I don't want you to stop," she whispered, her voice too breathy for substance, as he began moving inside her, deep thrusts that rubbed his flesh against hers, that made her body twitch and tremble, that made his erection harder and hotter and powerful enough to send sweetly painful need rocketing through her. "I want it fast and hard. I want you to come inside me, and then I want to strip down and do it again, long and slow, all night long, until you can't do it again, until I can't take you again, until . . ."

She caught her breath in a gasp as he brought his hand between them, between her thighs, and stroked her with tormenting caresses that matched the rhythm of his hips. Another helpless little gasp escaped when he became still for one timeless moment before, with a savage groan, he came, leaving her on the edge, filling her. "Oh, please," she whimpered, and he gave her what she needed, sliding trembling fingers inside her, moistening her swollen, hot flesh with his seed, bringing her in seconds to a shattering climax.

For a time they remained exactly as they were, then Tucker gently drew back. Without leaving her body, he unbuttoned her shirt, slid it off, and cast it aside. When her bra was gone, too, he sucked her nipple into his mouth, sending tremors through her, making her body convulse around his. He kissed and teased the other nipple, too, then began opening her skirt. When she was naked, he lifted and carried her the few feet to the bed, where finally, to her regret, he withdrew from her completely.

But not for long. He undressed hastily, knelt between her thighs, and filled her with one long, sure stroke, then kissed her. Was there room in her future for him? he had asked, so serious that even now her heart ached. In her future, in her life, and in her heart. As long as he wanted to be there. Always.

"You've got to do something."

Travis raised one hand to rub the back of his neck. It wasn't even ten o'clock on an overcast Tuesday morning, and his day felt as if it had already lasted at least twelve hours. Two of his officers had called in sick, and the vandals had been out in force the night before, leaving him with a town full of angry citizens. And how here was Mariana Trask, looking as if she'd spent a restless night curled up with a bottle of bourbon. "Mariana, I wish I could help—"

"You could arrest the sons of bitches! *That* would help!"

"Arrest them for what? Driving down a public street? Making phone calls?"

"They're threatening me. They're harassing me. They don't have the right to do this to me."

"No, they don't. If you want to go to court and try to get a restraining order—"

She broke in with an unamused snort. "Yeah, right, from that old fart Hampton? You think he's going to issue a restraining order against the sons of his nearest and dearest friends? You think he's going to do anything that might help you put those bastards in jail where they belong?"

"No." Sometimes Travis thought he'd accepted politics as the price of being police chief in a small town. Other times he thought he would never accept it. He would never get used to watching people like Trask break the law and know that he couldn't do anything about it.

"What am I supposed to do?" Mariana demanded. "They call my mama's house at all hours of the day and night, or they're driving by out front real slow. Brent Hogan followed me to the grocery store yesterday. Jason was watching me from his office just now when I was coming in here, watching and smiling that big arrogant smile of his. He's not going to stop. He's not going to give me any peace. We can't live like this, Travis. Something has to be done!"

"You want the advice I've been giving people who've made enemies of the Trasks?" So far, only two people—Kate and Tucker Caldwell. Mariana would make three . . . and Colleen would be four. He grimaced at the unsettled feeling in his stomach stirred by the idea of telling Colleen to leave and not come back. He liked having her here. He had even been considering asking her to stay, before he'd witnessed the impotent rage her meeting yesterday with Trask had caused.

"And what would that be?"

"Get out of Fall River. Pack up, move away, and never come back."

She stared at him, her helplessly angry expression reminding him of Kate. "But this is my *home*. I grew up here. My mother lives here."

"Take her with you. Living someplace other than Fall River would probably do Pat a world of good."

"She won't leave. I tried to get her to move to Tulsa with me, but she refused. She's lived all her life here, and she intends to live the rest of it here." Clenching her fingers into a fist, she hit the metal desk with enough force to make it clang. "Damn it, why should I have to leave just to live in peace?"

"Because that's the way Jason wants it." He rubbed his neck again, wishing the ache that had settled there would go away. "I know it's not fair, Mariana, but this is Jason's territory. He does what he wants, and what he wants right now is to make your life miserable. You can stick it out like Kate has. You can hope that he gets bored and turns his attention to someone else. Or you can leave. There aren't any other options."

She sighed heavily. "This is wrong, Travis. It's *wrong*."

"Yes, it is."

For another moment, she sat there, her hand still tightly fisted. Then, abruptly, with sudden determination, she moved to the door, where she looked back. "Thanks for the advice."

But she wasn't going to take it. Just as Kate wasn't going to, just as Colleen wouldn't. Damn Jason Trask to hell! Everyone's life would be easier if Eleanor and Rupert had drowned him at birth. He wouldn't have destroyed so many lives. He wouldn't be actively trying to destroy a few more.

What could he do? Talk to Jason? He'd tried that when the calls to Kate had first started. Trask had known that talk was *all* Travis could do, and he'd been amused by it. He had reminded Travis that he could do what he wanted with Kate—hadn't that been the jury's message with their not guilty verdict?—and there was nothing anyone could do to stop him. Any attempt to talk to him now would only make matters worse, because the situation hadn't changed. Jason could still do whatever he wanted, and Travis still couldn't stop him.

But Tucker Caldwell could. Travis had little doubt that if Jason or one of his buddies tried anything with Kate, Caldwell would kill him. It was an odd thing to respect in a man, but Travis did. It gave him some peace of mind knowing that

Caldwell would protect Kate with his life, just as *he* would protect Colleen with his.

He was about to return to the work schedule on his desk when the phone rang. His tone was curt when he answered, but it softened as soon as he recognized Colleen's voice. Almost immediately some of the tension eased from his neck. "If you're calling to invite me to lunch, I'm available. If you want to skip lunch, take me home, and take me to bed, well, I'm up for that, too."

There was the faint hint of a smile in her voice. "I bet you are, but that's not why I'm calling. I wanted to let you know that I've got to go in to the office today. Something's come up on one of the cases that I turned over to an associate, and they need me there. I don't know how long it will take. I'll definitely be back tonight, although it may be late."

How was he going to advise her to return to Little Rock permanently when he very much disliked the idea of her going back only for an afternoon meeting? He had plenty of reasons for protest—it was a long drive, it was getting dark earlier these days, she would be on those narrow, twisting roads at night, he would rather spend the evening with her than worrying about her, and very simply, very basically, he didn't want her that far away. But he didn't protest. He didn't ask if her business could be conducted over the phone. He swallowed a put-upon sigh and said, "All right. At the rate things are going, I might be working this evening anyway."

"Bad day?"

"So far . . . and with you leaving town, it doesn't look like it'll be getting better."

Her soft laugh sparked desire deep in his belly. "Well, when I get back, we'll make it better, all right?"

"All right." There was a brief pause, then he quietly said, "Be careful."

She was quiet for a moment, too. Her answer, when it finally came, was little more than a whisper. "I will."

Travis hung up, leaving his hand on the receiver for a moment as if he might snatch it up again, call the lodge, and ask her not to go. He didn't, though. Like Mariana, Kate, and Tucker, the best place for Colleen was away from Fall River and Jason Trask—and not just for a day but for good.

He was beginning to wonder if maybe it was best for him, too.

Tucker slowly opened his eyes and looked at the ceiling. He was lying on his back in the middle of the bed, and Kate was beside him. Yawning, he rubbed his face with his free hand, then stretched the other, easing the stiffness before letting it fall back to rest on Kate—on her breast. He moved his palm from side to side, rubbing her nipple, feeling it harden, feeling a corresponding stirring deep in his belly. He would have sworn when he'd fallen asleep that he couldn't possibly get hard again for a while. He had come so many times in the last sixteen hours that he felt tender and achy. But there was that edgy little throbbing starting all over again. He was exhausted, but his body didn't care. He wanted rest. It wanted Kate. Sweet, sensual, damned-if-she-wasn't-going-to-be-the-death-of-him Kate.

Moaning, she arched her back, pushing her breast against his hand, then slowly worked her way through the layers of sleep to wakefulness. She twisted, remaining in the circle of his arm, looking incredibly soft and delicate. "Good morning."

"Hmm."

"It is morning, isn't it?"

"Can't tell with the curtains closed."

She raised up to see the clock on the night table, then sank back down. "It's lunchtime. How about barbecue?"

He was hungry. Neither of them had eaten since this time yesterday, and they had certainly expended a lot of energy last night—all through the night, just as Kate had wanted. "Let me shower and shave—"

"We can shower later." She rubbed her hand over the stubble of beard that covered his jaw. "I like the unshaven look. It makes you look—"

"Disreputable?"

"Sexy. Dangerous." She grinned. "And disreputable." With a surge of energy, she threw back the covers, left the bed, and disappeared into the closet, coming out with an armful of clothes. She lent him a toothbrush and a comb and shared the bathroom sink with him, then they left the house.

The restaurant wasn't yet busy with the lunch crowd when they arrived, so they had their pick of seats and got their meal quickly. They were almost finished eating and the restaurant was filling up when a familiar face came through the door. "There's your cop friend."

Kate, with her back to the rest of the diners, didn't turn around to look. Instead she carefully wiped barbecue sauce from her fingers, then gave him a chastising look. "It wouldn't hurt to call him by his name, you know. It's easy enough: Travis."

He gave her a mocking smile. "I've never been on a first-name basis with any cop, and I don't see any reason to start now."

"You two have a lot in common. You're both good men. You both dislike Jason and people like him." She smiled. "You're both inordinately fond of me."

He surely was. He'd never been so fond of anyone in his life. Of course, he'd never loved anyone in his life.

With a scowl, he glanced around. "It's getting kind of crowded."

"Does that make you uneasy?"

It did. He knew how people in town felt about him, and he'd seen how most of them felt about Kate. Being seen together in a busy restaurant just seemed to invite their scorn. He didn't care for himself, but he would rather spare her.

Without further argument, she slid out of the booth and started toward the door. He stood up, drew his wallet from his hip pocket, left enough money to cover the tab and a tip, and went after her. She was halfway across the room, weaving between tables, doing a better job than he was of ignoring the looks they were getting from the other customers. He forgot the customers, though, forgot everything the instant he saw a man catch Kate's arm as she passed his table. She stopped short, the color draining from her face, but she didn't try to free herself. She simply stared at the guy with such icy intensity that Tucker knew immediately who it was.

"Hey, Kate." Trask greeted her as if she were an old friend. "I haven't seen you out in a while—and by yourself, no less. You're getting brave, aren't you?"

Tucker was dimly aware of two men rising from separate tables nearby. One was Kate's father, the other McMaster. The old man sank back down in his chair, but the cop headed toward her. Tucker reached her first, stopping beside her, clamping his hand over Trask's. "Let go of her, or I'll break every bone in your wrist."

Startled blue eyes met his. The bastard really had thought Kate was alone. He might have spoken to her if he'd known Tucker was only a few feet away, but he damn sure wouldn't have touched her. He wouldn't have wanted to provoke Tucker.

After that brief, unguarded moment, Trask masked the fear with a look of smug superiority. "Let go of me, or I'll have you arrested for assault."

Tucker didn't say anything. He simply tightened his grip, making Trask grimace, then squirm in his chair, trying to relieve the pressure. Finally the bastard dropped Kate's hand, then wrenched his own free. As Tucker moved her around behind him, Trask started to rise from his seat, but the cop pushed him back down.

Trask put on a blustery front, his voice loud and booming. "You saw it, McMaster. This ex-con trash assaulted me. I want him arrested."

"Yeah, I saw it." McMaster leaned close so no one away from the table could hear. "Remember Saturday's phone call, Jason? The threats you claimed were made? This is the man who made them, the man who promised to kill you if you even looked at her again. And what do you do? You grab her in a public place in front of him. How damn stupid can you be?"

The blood drained from Trask's face. "Now listen to me, McMaster—"

Tucker interrupted, and he didn't lower his voice. He didn't care who heard. "*You* listen, Trask. I wasn't kidding. I *will* kill you. Leave her alone, or you're a dead man." Without waiting for a response, he ushered Kate through the gawking crowd and out of the restaurant. He didn't let go until they reached her car around back, and not even then when he realized that his hands were trembling.

Kate was quiet, pale. She was probably angry that he hadn't told her about Trask's call that night, that he and McMaster had lied to her about the purpose of his visit the next morning, that he had created a scene in the restaurant. He was wondering how to apologize when the only thing he regretted was leaving the restaurant with Trask's face intact when she turned to him. "Thank you."

Of all the things she could have said, he wasn't prepared for that. He didn't have anything to say in response, and so he said the obvious. "You're welcome." Then . . . "You're not upset?"

"Upset? Because you stood up to Jason in front of his pals? Because you made him back down? Because you protected me?" With a gentle smile, she shook her head. "No, Tucker, I'm not upset."

"Because he touched you. He grabbed you."

"I knew you were there. You wouldn't let him hurt me. Besides, once the pain in his hand goes away, he'll think twice before he does it again."

He touched her chin, wanting her to look at him, wanting her to understand the absolute truth of what he was about to say. "If he does it again, Kate . . ." His gaze locked with hers, and he made them both a promise. "He'll be dead."

Colleen sat in the Mustang, tapping her gloved fingers restlessly on the steering wheel. It was nine o'clock, time for Ozark Annie's to close. In the last half hour from her place in the shadows across the street, she had watched all the customers leave except the four in the private dining room. They were talking and drinking, but the mood didn't seem quite as carefree as before. Jason seemed withdrawn and downright testy. Had something happened while she was out of town today? For once in his life, did Mr. High-and-Mighty Trask not get what he wanted?

Yesterday's meeting with him should have prepared her for today's. She had known he would try the same tactics on her two remaining clients. She had even met with Randy Hawkins and Carla Brownley yesterday to warn them, to strongly advise them against even speaking to Jason or any of his representatives. They had both promised her that they would make themselves unavailable to anyone.

In a town like this, she supposed that was impossible. Someone had gotten to them. There was no more lawsuit, no more business for her in Fall River. She had tried, like others before her, to bring down Jason Trask, and she had failed. She had failed herself, and she had failed her father. Jason had laughed at her, and, worst of all, he had laughed at her father.

He had hired some flunky to do a background check on her, he had announced when he'd shown up at her motel room this morning to inform her that her last remaining clients had dropped the suit. He had learned her maiden name and made the connection to her father. He remembered Tucker's trial, his lawyer, remembered well his one and only meeting with Harry Baker. It had been his first real exercise of the family clout, his first real experience at threatening someone, and he had *enjoyed* it. It had made him feel powerful.

And the best part? he had bragged. The evidence he had used to blackmail her father had been manufactured. The Trasks and the Hendersons had known it, and Harry, of course, had known it, but it had been effective all the same. They had built so tight a frame around him that he never would have been able to prove his innocence. Her father had thrown a case to protect himself from lies. He had died because of lies bought and paid for by the Trasks.

And Jason had found it amusing. Even the news of Harry's suicide had failed to elicit the faintest hint of regret.

That was the price Harry paid for getting in the Trasks' way. His death was of no consequence.

Jason Trask was the coldest, most callous, uncaring bastard she had ever met. She had never met anyone whom she believed with all her heart needed to die, but *he* did. For all those excess years Tucker had spent in prison. For Harry's death. For Mariana's misery. For Kate. For Kerry. For Travis, Randy, Carla, Tommy, and Gary. For everyone he'd ever harmed and everyone he might harm in the future. But most especially for Harry.

Tonight he would pay for Harry.

The lights in the restaurant's main dining room went off. A moment later, the front door opened, and the four men came out, getting into their cars and heading off in the same direction, all to the same exclusive neighborhood up above the town. She started the engine, but didn't pull out after them. She knew where to find Jason. She would go there, do what had to be done, and then she would go home—not to her empty condo in Little Rock, not to the impersonal comfort of the motel, but *home*. To Travis.

She wished she hadn't found it necessary to lie to him this morning, but she couldn't tell him the truth—that she was returning to Little Rock to get a gun that couldn't be traced back to her. That she'd tried and failed to avenge her father's death in a legal manner, and so now she was determined to do it illegally. That she wanted—*needed*—to see Jason Trask pay for his sins. That she needed to kill him.

She was familiar with guns. Defending the sort of people she defended, she had thought it a necessary skill. She had an expensive pistol locked in her office at home, but she hadn't wanted to use it. She had wanted something inexpensive and common, something that could never be tied to her, and she had known exactly where to go to get it. Over the years she had kept Arlen Roberts out of prison on a few wrongful arrests, as well as a couple of legitimate ones. He had been only too happy to provide her with a virtually untraceable .22, no questions asked.

She had the motive. She had the means. Now all she needed was the opportunity. All she had to do was drive up the hill to Ridge Crest, to the brick house she had identified as Jason's on her first day in town, and . . . She forced herself to form the words in her mind. *Kill him.*

She switched on the headlights and pulled onto the street. It was a quiet night. She didn't pass a single car in the few miles to Jason's house. The gate was open, and she pulled in, following the drive to a small parking area for guests. A broad walk led to the house's main entrance, where bright lights were shining, but it was the dimmer lights around on the side that interested Colleen. Dramatic arched windows were uncurtained and allowed a clear view of the room and its occupant. There was a small brick patio outside the room, suggesting that the tall middle window was a door. An easy way in and out, complete with shrubs to hide her actions inside from a nosy neighbor's view.

She patted her pocket to make certain the gun was in place, then climbed out, leaving the car door slightly ajar. She'd dressed in dark clothes from head to toe and blended well with the shadows, except for her face, which was undoubtedly empty of color. But that was good. Fear, apprehension, reluctance—she wanted to feel those things. She would worry if she was capable of taking a life, even one as miserable as Jason Trask's, without feeling them.

The shadows had sheltered her as far as they could. Squaring her shoulders, she tucked her hands in her pockets and strolled across the lawn, right up the steps to the French door, where she rapped twice on the glass. Jason, sprawled in the chair behind his desk, looked startled. Putting his drink down, he got easily to his feet and came to the door, twisting the lock, pushing it open. "What do you want?" he demanded sourly. "Your lawsuit is history and your pathetic excuse for a father is dead and rotted in the ground. Why are you still hanging around?"

"May I come in?"

He made a grand, sweeping gesture. Once she was inside, he closed the door, then returned to his desk. She glanced around at the walls of built-in bookcases, the inlaid mahogany desk, the delicate crystal decanters behind the desk. Everything fairly shouted *money,* money used to control and destroy good, innocent people, money used to destroy the only family she'd ever known.

"What do you want?"

"A drink would be nice, for starters. I like scotch."

He moved behind the desk, choosing a decanter and glass from the shelf there. When he turned to his desk to pour, he was facing her gun. He looked from her to the pistol, then back again. "What is this?"

"Nothing less than you deserve. Harry Baker was a good, honorable man. You weren't fit to even be in the same room with him, and yet he died because of you, because of your lies and your manipulations. The best man I've ever known is dead, but a sick, perverted bastard like you lives on to bring misery into other people's lives. It's not fair."

"So what do you want? An apology?" He shrugged. "I'm sorry the old man killed himself. Satisfied?"

"No. I won't be satisfied until *you're* dead and rotted in the ground."

The first flicker of fear entered his eyes, then almost as quickly disappeared. "So you're here to kill me. Is that it?" He came around the desk again, careless, disinterested. "Do you really think you can do it, darlin'? The daughter of the best man you've ever known? What would ol' Harry have to say about that?"

"He would say it was wrong. He would say don't do it." She smiled tightly. "But he's not here to stop me because you killed him."

"The old man was weak. He was a fool. We tried to reason with him, tried to pay him, but he wouldn't listen. So we gave him no choice."

"Weak? A fool? That was *honor*. You couldn't buy him off because he had honor. Of course, that's something you know nothing about. All you know is taking advantage of vulnerable people and terrorizing helpless women. For what you did to all the others, you deserve to die. For what you did to Harry, you *have* to die."

"What about McMaster? You think he's going to look the other way on a murder just because it's his little whore doing the killing?"

She hadn't allowed herself to give much thought to Travis, largely because if anyone could change her mind, it was him. He knew about Harry. Wouldn't that make him suspect her? If he did, it would ruin their relationship. He wouldn't ignore a capital crime just because she was the one who committed it. Even if he didn't arrest her, he would never look at her the same again. He would never be able to forgive her.

But she would have won, and Jason would have lost. Wasn't that what mattered—*all* that mattered?

Doing the right thing mattered. Making her father proud of her had always mattered. Travis and her future mattered.

Jason hadn't won a complete victory. Her lawsuit had cost him plenty. Her clients were better off now than they'd been last week. They had money to pay their debts. Their futures weren't quite as bleak, thanks to her.

Curiously she looked down at the gun. She could kill

Jason. She could pull the trigger and walk away, leaving him dead on the floor . . . if she didn't mind also walking away from Travis, the best man she'd known since her father. If she didn't mind sacrificing her self-respect. If she didn't mind dishonoring her father's memory.

He caught her off guard, lunging forward, twisting the gun out of her hand. From his triumphant grin, it was clear he felt he'd won a major victory. She didn't diminish it by demanding the gun back or struggling to reclaim it. She gave a faint sigh, relieved that it was no longer in her possession, and started toward the door. "Forget it, Jason. You're just not worth it."

"You're a loser, Colleen, just like your old man," he taunted. "You can't even handle a simple problem. Go on, get out of here, and you'd better pray to God that I don't tell McMaster everything and have your ass thrown in jail. Go on, you stupid bitch, you—"

She closed the glass door behind her, muting his words, and walked across the grass. For the first time in sixteen years she felt free—of sorrow, of hatred, of Jason. It was time to go home to Travis. Time to start planning for the future.

It was time to make a visit to her father's grave, to show him that she was finally a daughter to make a man proud.

Chapter Fourteen

Jason slapped the gun down on the desk, finished his drink, then tossed down another. He raised his hand to drag it through his hair and saw that it was still shaking. The damned bitch had scared him. Jeez, he had thought she really was going to shoot him. She'd turned out as weak as her father, though. She hadn't had the nerve.

He *would* tell McMaster. Tomorrow morning he would call the police chief to his office and tell him exactly what his slut had tried here tonight. He would threaten to go to the district attorney and promise a complaint to the bar association, and the chief—being the sort of man he was—would probably try to protect the bitch.

Jason's smile was wide. Colleen might have done him a big favor. He might come out of this with the chief of police in his pocket.

A knock at the door made him glance in that direction. It was probably her again, come to ask him not to tell McMaster. Maybe she would be willing to deal. He wouldn't mind having her in his bed for a few hours . . . and then he would still talk to the chief in the morning.

It wasn't until he opened the door that he realized his guest wasn't Colleen Robbins. Scowling fiercely, he returned to his desk, sat down, and poured himself one more drink.

"What do *you* want?" he asked, not bothering to hide the disgust he felt.

"We have some unfinished business."

"We've got *nothing*. Get out of my house and off my property."

"Your house, your property. Everything is yours, isn't it? It must be nice to be so damned special, to have your very own town full of people to torment and terrorize, to know that no matter what you do to those people, the law can't touch you." His visitor sat down in front of the desk. "They say that power corrupts. Is that what went wrong with you—the Trask power? Would you be just as evil and malicious if you weren't the great Jason Trask? I think you would be. I think you're a sick, depraved, sorry bastard who just happens to have the money to make the most of it."

"You think," Jason spit out. "Like anyone gives a damn what you think. You're stupid, worthless trash. You don't deserve to live in my town, and I sure as hell won't have garbage like you in my house." He reached for the phone on the desk and pressed the speaker button. A dial tone filled the air. "I'm giving you five seconds to get the hell out, and then I'm calling the police. You'll go to jail, and I'll see to it that you never get out."

The seconds ticked by. Five passed, then ten. Muttering a curse, he dialed the prefix for the police department, stopping only when the person opposite him stood up. Weak people, he thought, disgusted. He was tired of dealing with weak people. Everyone around him was so damned easy to manipulate. No one put up a fight anymore. No one offered a challenge.

After a moment he realized that, contrary to his expectations, his visitor wasn't leaving. Instead, giving him a look of utter hatred, the person calmly picked up Colleen Robbins's gun where he'd left it on the desk and pointed it at him.

"Put that down and get the hell out of my house," he commanded, starting to rise from the chair.

The first shot hit him in the shoulder, knocking him back, burning like fiery hell. He slumped in the chair, absolutely shocked, unable to believe that this worthless piece of shit had just shot him, but the proof was in the bitter odor of gunpowder in the air, in the hot agony streaking through his shoulder.

"Are you crazy? What the hell are you—" The second shot hit a few inches lower, a few inches to the center. It robbed the air from his lungs and sent terror pumping through his veins. He tried to speak but couldn't form the words, tried to move but couldn't command his legs. Then he *was* moving, against his will, sliding from the chair to the floor, landing in a limp heap on the antique rug.

Through the rushing in his ears he heard footsteps as his attacker moved around the desk, then stopped only inches away. He tried to move, tried to focus on saving himself, but all he could see was the gun as it steadied and fired again. Dear God, he was going to die, right here on the floor. It wasn't fair! He was Jason Trask. He *owned* this county. No one had the right to touch him. No one had the right . . .

He felt his body jerk when the fourth bullet entered it, and again with the fifth, but he couldn't tell where. He felt no new pain, no stinging, nothing. He was a Trask . . . but that wasn't going to save him now. There was so much pain, so much blood. He couldn't breathe, couldn't focus his eyes, couldn't even lift his hand for mercy. He was dying. He was dying, and it was all Kate's fault . . .

Karl Edwards sat in his pickup, parked on the street outside the Trask home. All the miles he'd driven around Rutherford County this evening had brought him here, to the shadow of a massive old maple only twenty feet from Jason's gate. He didn't know why he'd come. It wasn't likely he was going to confront Jason about the scene at the restaurant today. He didn't have the courage to stand up to a Trask and never had.

He hadn't returned to work this afternoon. Instead, he'd driven for hours, brooding over the changes in his family. A man couldn't have asked for a more contented family than he'd had a year ago. Kristin and her husband had been talking about having a baby, Kate had been working at a job she loved and dating a nice man, and Kerry had been enjoying her senior year in school. His family had been happy, and Karl had been happy.

Then Kate had begun dating Jason Trask. Karl had been pleased at the time. It was a fact of life in Fall River that the Edwardses weren't on the same social level as the Trasks, and it gave them a bit of a boost for his daughter to be dating the Trask son. There had been other, less selfish reasons for his approval. The Trasks had money, and Jason had this fancy house up here on the hill. He could provide for Kate, could give her a life of comfort and luxury, if the relationship ever got that serious.

Then the call from Bernard McMaster's boy had come in the middle of a Saturday night. Kate had been raped, and Jason Trask had done it. *Raped*. Any decent father would have gotten a gun and killed the bastard. But not Karl. No, he had been afraid to stand up to the Trasks, and so he had blamed the whole mess on his own daughter. He had accepted Jason's lies about her, had let the son of a bitch live to spread those lies, and to do the same thing to Kerry. Maybe Kate had been courting trouble by sleeping with Jason, but Kerry had been innocent. She hadn't deserved one second of the terror and horror Jason had put her through.

Rubbing his weary eyes, he cursed himself. Kate hadn't deserved what Jason had done, either—hadn't deserved the shame or ridicule or the treatment she'd received in court—and she sure as hell hadn't deserved the abandonment by her family. Family was supposed to stick together. When something bad happened to one, the others were supposed to close ranks and take care of them. Only Kerry had stood by Kate, and after Trask got hold of her, Kate had stood alone.

Except for today. Jed Caldwell's nephew had stood up for her. A white-trash ex-con—that was what Kate had sunk to. No decent man in town would have her, and so she'd turned to the least decent of them all. Jason had done irreparable harm to her reputation, and she had finished destroying it by taking up with Caldwell.

But at least Caldwell had been there looking out for her today. That made him a better man than Karl.

He was reaching down to start the truck when, out of the blue, a car came tearing out of the Trask driveway, squealing in a tight turn to the right, racing to the stop sign, then making another turn. Karl stared in shock, the muscles in his stomach growing tight. The nearest streetlamp was fifty feet behind him, but it gave off enough light to show that the car was a little red compact, just like Kate's. It showed that the driver was a woman, and he wasn't sure, but—*Jesus, please don't let it be*—he thought it was Kate.

His hands trembling, he started the engine and turned into the driveway. In the parking area, he climbed out and simply listened. The night was quiet. The houses were too far apart for one neighbor to disturb another with loud music, television, or a fight. Not even the screams of a woman being beaten and raped could carry next door.

He started down the sidewalk to the front door, but before going more than a few feet, he noticed the brightly lit office on the side. The glass door stood open, swinging slightly, as if it had been shoved back with enough force to make it bounce on its hinges. Reluctantly, apprehensively, Karl turned in that direction, crossing the grass and the patio, stopping at the door. "Jason?"

The room appeared empty. Lights were blazing, and two decanters of liquor, along with two glasses, sat on the desk. Maybe he'd been entertaining. Maybe he'd simply left the room without realizing that the door was open. Or maybe . . .

Karl went inside, moving one slow step at a time into the center of the room. He saw the gun first, a pistol so small and compact that it looked like a toy, lying discarded on the rug. Then he saw Jason.

He should check Jason, should use that phone on the desk to call for an ambulance, but the sick feeling in his gut told him it was too late. Jason was dead. The man who had destroyed Karl's family, who had shattered their future for his own selfish pleasure, who had ruined life for them all, was dead.

Bending, he picked up the gun and wiped it vigorously on his jacket before cradling it in one palm. "Oh, my God, Kate," he whispered, bowing his head over the discarded pistol. "What have you done?"

The annoying bells and whistles of a late-night commercial awakened Tucker from a restless sleep, stiff and unaccountably edgy. He had fallen asleep on the floor, Kate in his arms and one of her new sofa pillows under his head. The pillow was still there, but Kate was gone. Maybe that explained his edginess.

The opening and closing of the front door brought him swiftly to his feet. He reached the hallway in time to see Kate slip out of a jacket and hang it on the doorknob. When she heard him, she turned and smiled. "I didn't mean to wake you."

"Where have you been?"

"I went out to the car. When we got the groceries out of the trunk this afternoon, the cinnamon must have fallen out of the bag. I went to find it." She held up the small plastic can and grinned. "Want some cinnamon toast?"

"You went outside at—" He stepped back far enough into the living room to see the mantel clock. "Twelve-forty-five at night for cinnamon? Why didn't you wake me?"

"Because I could get it, and I wasn't even scared . . . well, only a little. But I've *always* been a little scared out alone late at night." Still holding the spice, she wrapped her arms around his waist.

"What if something had happened? What if Trask or one of his buddies had been out there?"

"If *anyone* had been out there, I would have screamed bloody murder."

"I was asleep. I might not have heard you."

"Darlin', the *dead* would have heard me. Now, do you want some toast or do you just want to frown at me while I eat?"

He let her drag him into the kitchen and talk him into two slices of toast. When it came out of the oven, he ate four. When they were finished, she pushed the table to one side of the booth, slid onto his lap, and snuggled close. She smelled of cinnamon and real butter, of faded perfume and fresh air, and her skin was still cool. He had the impression that she wanted to talk, but when she did finally speak, it was with a rather wistful request. "Make love to me, Tucker."

Ignoring his body's immediate tightening, he rested his cheek against her hair. "Does the word 'insatiable' have any particular meaning for you?"

"Yeah. I figured it was what came after bold, brash, and easy when you described Nolie," she retorted teasingly. "If you don't want to, that's fine. I just thought . . . well, you've got a lot of lost time to make up for."

"Do you think that's what this is—making up for all those years I went without?" He resettled her on his lap in a position where she couldn't help but notice the erection her simple request had induced. "It isn't. Even if I'd gotten laid every single day of my life since I was sixteen, I would still want you." But maybe making up for lost time was what *she* was doing. She'd had a relatively normal, active sex life before Trask. Maybe *she* was playing catch-up.

"If you don't want to fool around, can we at least go to bed so I can lie in your arms?"

He chuckled. "I didn't say I didn't want to. We can go upstairs or . . ." He lifted her so she was straddling his legs, so her groin was pressed indecently hard against his. "Get those jeans off and we can do it right here."

Tentatively she rubbed against him, testing the logistics, then wrapped her arms around his neck. "This has potential, but I think I'd rather—"

The doorbell interrupted her, and he felt her muscles tense. He lifted her to the floor, then started down the hall, aware that she was right behind him. Through the peephole the porch light showed McMaster, flanked by two officers. "It's Travis," he murmured to Kate as he undid the locks, then opened the door.

The cops looked grim, especially McMaster. He looked from Tucker to Kate, then back again, before asking, "Can we come in?"

"It's a little late, isn't it?" Kate asked.

"Yeah, but sometimes things happen a little late."

Even though they weren't touching, Tucker felt her tension increasing. "What happened?" she asked quickly, no doubt thinking about her parents and her sister, showing more concern for them than they deserved.

"It's not your family, Kate," McMaster said. "It's Jason Trask. He's dead. Somebody killed him."

From his position by the fireplace, Tucker wished he could say that he'd *known* from the instant he'd heard the news that Kate wasn't responsible. He wished he didn't have these damnable doubts, wished he didn't keep wondering whether she had lied to him again when she'd told him last night that killing Jason was no longer her goal. He wished he didn't wonder whether she really had simply gone out to her car to find the missing cinnamon or if she had only used that as an excuse to cover a late-night trip across town.

"He was shot six times with what appears to be a small-caliber weapon," Travis was saying. "I'm going to need your gun, Kate, for ballistics tests."

"Do you think I killed him, Travis?"

"I didn't say—"

"Tucker and I have been here since two-thirty this afternoon. We had dinner and watched TV. We fell asleep in front of the fireplace." She glanced at the floor where two pillows and a knitted throw still lay before facing her friend again.

"I just need to see the gun, Kate," he repeated, his voice strained.

She went to get her purse, leaving Tucker with the three silent cops. He didn't look at them. His thoughts—doubts— kept him too preoccupied. She had been quick to offer their whereabouts. Because she needed an alibi? Because, if he was asked privately about their evening, she'd wanted him to say exactly the same thing?

When Kate returned from the hall with her purse, she removed the pistol and handed it to the nearest officer. He sniffed the barrel. "Doesn't smell as if it's been fired recently."

"Of course it hasn't." She sat down in the armchair. "I'm not stupid. Do you really think that if I were going to shoot Jason, I would do it with my own gun? I would have gotten another one, one that the chief of police didn't pick out for me, one that no one else would ever know I had."

One that she would have bought in Little Rock. One that she'd sworn last night she *hadn't* bought.

"Frankly, Kate," McMaster said, "I don't think you shot Jason at all. But then, you weren't the one who threatened to kill him in front of a restaurant full of people."

Tucker felt a shudder of panic as everyone turned to look at him. Sure, he'd threatened Trask, and he had meant it, but he *hadn't* carried it out. But who was likely to believe him? If anything happened to Trask, McMaster had advised, he'd better have a damned good alibi because, after his threats, he would be the prime suspect. And now that something *had* happened, what was his alibi? He'd been here asleep, beside the woman who might—just might—have committed the crime herself.

He was about to open his mouth to deny any involvement when Kate spoke up. "Don't be ridiculous, Travis. Jason provoked him, and Tucker responded. It didn't mean anything. He couldn't have killed him."

"He's killed before."

"And that's precisely why he wouldn't do it again. He couldn't."

"I haven't been out of the house since this afternoon," Tucker said. "I haven't fired a gun. You can test my hands for gunpowder residue."

"We assume whoever shot Jason wore gloves," Travis said. He came forward and offered a business card. "You want to call Colleen?"

The card was McMaster's, with his home number written across the face. For a moment he resisted. Calling a lawyer seemed like something a guilty person would do . . . but that was naive. Under the circumstances, calling a lawyer was something an *intelligent* person would do.

He went to the phone and punched in the numbers. It was answered on the second ring. "Colleen, this is Tucker Caldwell. Remember the offer you made the other day—if there was ever anything you could do for me?" He glanced at Kate, staring mutinously at McMaster, who looked pretty damned grim, then at the other two cops, who looked as if they'd like nothing better than to slap the handcuffs on him and haul him off. "It seems I'm in need of your services. Could you come over to Kate's?"

Hours passed before Travis and his officers, and later the lawyer, finally left. Kate locked the door behind Colleen, then leaned against it for a moment. She had been naive in her confidence a few weeks ago that she could handle an interrogation by Travis, that she could kill Jason and then calmly, believably, convince everyone that she hadn't done it. There was no way she could have pulled it off.

She had to give Colleen credit. The woman might be sleeping with Travis, but that hadn't affected her dealings on Tucker's behalf tonight. She hadn't cut Travis one bit of slack in his interview. Kate was sure she couldn't set aside their personal relationship so easily if she and Tucker suddenly wound up on opposite sides of an issue.

They were at odds now. He doubted her. From the very moment Travis had announced Jason's death, she'd seen the uncertainty creep into Tucker's eyes. He thought she might have lied to him yet again, that she might have sneaked out while he slept and carried out her plan. He thought she might have murdered Jason.

She went down the hall to the kitchen, where he still sat in the booth, a cup of coffee in front of him. She gathered the dirty cups and set them in the sink before joining him. "The DA won't bring charges against you. They have no evidence."

Travis had told them so privately, and Colleen had repeated it before she'd left. Tucker looked no more convinced now. "I'm an ex-con, Kate. I'm out on parole. I killed Jason's cousin sixteen years ago, and I threatened to kill him today in front of thirty witnesses. Do you really think they *need* evidence?"

She reached out to touch his hand, but he clumsily drew back, taking a sip of the cold, bitter coffee as an excuse for avoiding her. Hurt, she clasped her hands together in her lap. "I didn't do it, Tucker."

He couldn't bring himself to look at her. "You were gone when I woke up."

"For less than five minutes. I put on a jacket, went out to the car with a flashlight, found the cinnamon, and came back in. It was *less* than five minutes."

At last he did look at her. "I don't know that. However, I do know that you planned to go to Little Rock, buy a gun, come back, and kill Trask at his house. I know that you *went* to Little Rock yesterday, you came back, and tonight Trask is dead."

"Tucker, I'm not stupid. After the scene at the restaurant today, if anything happened to Jason, you would be the prime suspect. Do you think I would leave you without an alibi while I killed him?" Tears dampened her eyes. "I could never do that to you. I *love* you."

For an instant, the look in his eyes was one of surprise, pleasure, and sweet longing. Then it faded to grim concern. Sounding weary all the way through his soul, he said, "They'll want to talk to me again tomorrow. What do you want me to tell them?"

"The truth."

He gave her a faintly mocking look. "The truth might get you locked up alongside me, darlin'."

"I didn't do anything wrong," she said stubbornly. "Neither did you."

"I thought you learned from Trask's trial. Whether you've done anything wrong doesn't matter when you're dealing with them. So what truth do you want me to tell?"

"That you were asleep. That when you woke up, I was coming in from outside."

"You tell them that we were both asleep. That neither of us set foot outside that door all evening." He slid out from the bench and started toward the hall. Her words stopped him halfway.

"You're going to lie. You want me to lie."

Slowly he turned back to face her. His expression was as defeated and sorrowful as she'd ever seen. "You've been lying to me all along, Kate. For your own safety, don't stop now."

He went upstairs. A moment later she heard water running in the bathroom, then silence. He'd gone to bed, but she didn't go up to join him. Instead she drew her feet onto the bench and stared at the curtains. This was a turn of events she hadn't expected. Jason was dead, Tucker was Travis's number one suspect, and *she* was Tucker's prime suspect.

Jason was dead. She should be happy, dancing for joy. Instead she just felt emptiness . . . and the fear that Tucker might never believe that she didn't do it. That he might never forgive her, might never trust her or want her again.

A future without Tucker was too bleak to contemplate. She would gladly restore life to Jason if it were in her power, if doing so meant that Tucker would stop looking at her like a man betrayed. She would let Jason live a long, depraved life if only she could have the Tucker she had come to love in her life.

Wearily, she rested her head on the table and blanked all thought from her mind. She was too worn-out to think any longer tonight. In spite of the awkward position and the ache in her heart, she managed to doze off, awaking only at the dreaded sound of the doorbell. For one blessedly blank moment, she wondered why she had fallen asleep, fully clothed, at the kitchen table. Then, with another peal of the bell, she remembered everything. She stood up, stretched out the kinks, them combed her fingers through her hair as she headed for the door. As she undid the locks and opened the door, she heard Tucker's steps on the stairs behind her, but she didn't risk a look at him.

Travis didn't give her a chance to invite him and Colleen in. "Jason's neighbor saw a man leaving the grounds last night at the approximate time of death. He drove away in an old pickup."

"It wasn't Tucker," Kate insisted when he said nothing himself.

"They have a search warrant for your house, Tucker," Colleen said. "I think you and I should accompany them."

Without a word Tucker took his jacket from the closet and pulled it on. Wanting something—a look, a touch, anything—Kate reached out, but he ignored her, walked outside, and followed Colleen to her car. Kate watched Travis drive away in his Explorer, followed by the Mustang, then closed the door. As she did, she whispered a desperate prayer for Tucker . . . and herself.

She busied herself around the house, then went upstairs, finding the bed in near pristine condition except for a few wrinkles on Tucker's side, as if he had lain down fully dressed atop the covers. She took a shower, dressed to face another day, then returned to the living room to wait.

How long could a search possibly take? Tucker's places were both only one room each, and the new one wasn't even completed. There were few hiding places, and other than the rickety furniture, the only possessions he owned were his clothes, a few dishes, and Nolie's quilt. There was nothing to connect him to Jason, nothing to indicate that he might have ever even considered killing the other man.

Though she'd been waiting minute after slow minute for the doorbell to ring, when it finally did, it startled her. She rose quickly from her chair and hurried to the door, throwing it open without looking, expecting to find Tucker waiting there. But it wasn't him. It was Colleen Robbins, and she looked as grim as Tucker had when they'd left. "Can I come in?"

Kate stepped back, then closed the door behind her. "Where is Tucker?"

"They found a gun of the caliber used to kill Trask hidden between the mattress and springs of the bed in Tucker's house. They've arrested him, Kate."

Colleen sat on the sofa, listening to the sounds of Kate in the kitchen making coffee. Ever since the news of Jason's death had reached Travis last night, she'd been sick with fear. He had most likely been killed with *her* gun. Could she be positive that her fingerprints were nowhere on it? What if it somehow got traced back to Little Rock, if whoever it led them to gave up enough information to allow them to work their way back to her? Arlen Roberts was fond of her, but not fond enough to get involved in a murder investigation without giving her up. And what would Travis think? He would know that she had planned and very nearly executed a murder. He would know that she'd been aware of some important evidence in his case and had kept quiet to protect herself. How much respect would he have for her then?

Deliberately she forced her worries out of her mind as Kate returned with two mugs of coffee. "They'll have a bond hearing for Tucker this afternoon. If by chance the judge will set bail, can you help pay it?"

"I have ten thousand dollars in savings, and I could probably borrow against the house, but not locally. There's no way the Trasks' bank will give me a loan to help Tucker."

"We'll worry about that when the times comes." Colleen didn't expect bail. In a capital crime, the judge was allowed that option, and Tucker seemed the perfect flight risk. Colleen wasn't sure she would trust him not to take off. But she would worry about that when it became necessary. Right now she had a case to prepare. "Do you believe he's guilty, Kate?"

"No."

"What makes you so sure?"

"He didn't leave the house last night, not even for a minute. Besides, that boy's death sixteen years ago was an accident, but he *still* feels guilty. He still lives with that on his conscience. He could never kill anyone unless his life or someone else's was in danger."

"So you believe he could kill to protect someone he loves. He could kill to protect *you*."

She shook her head. "I wasn't in danger from Jason."

"He confronted you in the restaurant yesterday. For months his friends have been harassing you by phone. Just a few nights ago Jason himself made threats against you to Tucker. Maybe he thought you were in danger."

Again Kate shook her head. "He told me to get a restraining order or to cooperate with the DA in reopening the rape case. He advised me to quit my job, sell the house, and move away. But he didn't consider killing Jason a reasonable response."

"Yet he threatened to do just that, both on the phone Saturday night and in the restaurant yesterday."

"He was upset. He was just trying to frighten Jason into leaving me alone."

"Would you lie to protect him, Kate?"

The other woman met her gaze. Her blue eyes were weary, as if she hadn't slept. "Absolutely, if it was necessary. But it's not. *He didn't kill Jason.*"

"Did you?"

Disappointment crept into Kate's eyes. "Is that what he told you?"

"No. He's not saying much at all beyond the fact that you were both here. Would he lie to protect you?" The thought had entered her mind last night and again this morning that Kate might have committed the murder. She hadn't wanted to believe it. She had sympathy for everything Kate had gone through and respected the strength with which she had borne it. Still, if she was the guilty one, she wouldn't be the first woman abused by a man and denied justice in the courtroom who had sought her own justice outside the courts.

Could the same strength that had helped her survive also help her face the consequences of what she had done? Or would she sit back quietly and allow Tucker to take the blame for her actions? For his sake, Colleen hoped not.

Kate combed her fingers through her hair, then sighed. "Yes, he would lie for me."

"Why would he feel that was necessary?"

She weighed the consequences of her answer. Was she afraid that it might hurt her or that it would somehow make things worse for Tucker? After a moment, she slowly replied. "Tucker and I met when I offered him ten thousand dollars to kill Jason."

Immediately Colleen raised one hand. "Let me stop you now, Kate, and explain that I'm Tucker's lawyer. If you say anything to me that I can use to clear him, I will . . . even if it means casting suspicion on you instead. Even if it means getting you arrested."

Kate didn't hesitate. "I wanted Tucker to kill Jason for me, but he refused. He advised me to get help, to get on with my life, and then he stuck around to make sure that I did. But he thinks . . ." Her voice wavered. "He thinks that I might have killed Jason. I didn't. But he'll lie, even to his own disadvantage, to keep anyone else from thinking it."

Colleen knew Kate was telling the truth about not killing Jason. If she were guilty, she wouldn't have that teary little wobble in her voice because Tucker believed she might be. She wouldn't have that wounded look in her eyes because he didn't trust her as wholeheartedly as she trusted him.

"So he did lie about your whereabouts last night. You weren't both here all evening."

"We *were*. I just went outside to get something from the car. He was asleep, but woke up as I was coming in. He doesn't know whether I was gone a few minutes or long enough to go to Jason's house, kill him, plant the gun at *his* house, and then come home. He doesn't trust me enough to believe it was just a few minutes. He doesn't trust that I would never do that to him."

"But the witness saw a man leaving Jason's house."

Kate sniffled, then pulled a tissue from the box on the end table and crumpled it without using it. "Maybe he thinks I hired someone. Maybe I was outside paying the guy off when he woke up."

"And maybe he's not thinking at all. Maybe he's just so damned afraid that he can't think." Colleen leaned toward her. "I'll be honest with you, Kate. Things don't look good. As long as he has any doubts about you, Tucker's not going to cooperate with me. He's afraid that anything he says might get you in trouble, and he's not willing to do that, not even to save himself."

"Should I go to the jail and talk to him?"

Colleen hesitated, wishing she didn't have to say this, knowing she did. "I asked him if he would see you, and he said no. I think he's ashamed for you to see him there. I'll talk to him for you. I'll tell him that I don't believe you killed Jason. I'll do what I can, Kate." And she would pray that it would be enough.

Tucker lay sprawled on his back, his gaze fixed on the barred window set high in the outside wall. As cells went, he'd been in better and he'd been in worse. At least here he had the window and a little privacy, but damned if he wouldn't sell his soul to be someplace else.

Damned if he wouldn't deliver it to the devil in person to know that Kate had told the truth this morning. Damned if he wouldn't just give it up and die a satisfied man if he could believe what she'd so naturally tossed into the middle of her denial. *I love you.* No one had ever said that to him—*no one.* He hadn't thought he would ever hear the words, hadn't known they could sound so sweet or hurt so bad. He wanted to believe she meant them, wanted to believe so much that he couldn't bear it, but how could he? After the sheriff's deputy had pulled the pistol from the bed, from the place where he kept his money, where Kate had *known* he stashed his cash, only a fool would believe anything she had to say.

"Mind if I come in?"

He twisted to see Travis McMaster and the jailer standing on the opposite side of the bars. "It's your jail," he said flatly, sitting up, letting his feet hit the bare floor.

McMaster handed his gun to the jailer, who unlocked the door, then closed and locked it again behind him. Once he was out of sight, McMaster sat down on the opposite bunk. "Sorry about the hearing."

Tucker shrugged. Colleen had warned him not to expect reasonable bail at the bond hearing, but he'd known better. He hadn't expected *any* bail, and he'd been right. The judge had deemed him too dangerous to be released. He had called Tucker a flight risk, had decreed that anyone crazy enough to post bail for him would lose it. He'd been right, too. If they'd made the mistake of letting him out, he would have packed his belongings and taken the first road out of town. He wouldn't even have taken the time to say good-bye to Kate.

Kate, who might have committed the murder that had landed him here. Kate, who had made love with him so sweetly, so intensely, only two nights ago. Kate, who had said she loved him.

"I don't believe you killed Jason."

"Then why am I here?" It wasn't a fair question. McMaster had wanted to wait until test firings from the gun had been compared to the slugs recovered from Trask's body, but the sheriff had insisted on taking Tucker into custody. Just as with the bail, it had been a wise move. There was little doubt the bullets would match. Someone had set him up for Trask's murder.

"You're here because someone wants you here. Any idea who?"

Tucker offered no response. Who could he name? Kate? He'd rather go back to prison than say anything that might get her in trouble. Hadn't Trask already cost her enough? Hadn't the son of a bitch made her suffer enough while he was living? There was no way she was going to keep paying now that he was dead.

"Jason's body was discovered by one of my officers last night after we got a call from a neighbor. She'd seen a man drive away from the house in an old pickup that didn't look as if it belonged in the neighborhood."

"It wasn't me."

"I don't think it was. The gun we found at your house matched, though. It was the one used to kill Jason. No fingerprints on it, of course. It had been wiped clean—even the shell casings inside. I think you're smarter than that, though. You had to learn something in prison. You had to at least learn to get rid of the weapon someplace other than your own house."

"So what's your theory?"

"I think someone knew about your threats against Jason. I think this person killed him, then decided to lay the blame on the most likely suspect—you. It was easy. Everyone knows about you and Kate. All he had to do was drive by Kate's house, make sure you were there, go out to your place to hide the gun, then sit back and wait for us to find it."

Although he figured the chief's theory was pretty accurate, Tucker's tone was cynical. "You have any way of proving this?"

McMaster shook his head. "I suppose we could start looking at everybody who had a reason to want Jason dead."

"That could be a long list."

"Then we could compare it to everybody who drives or has access to an old pickup. That's probably 80 percent of the county."

"And by the time you do all that, I'll be tried, convicted, and back in prison." Back in prison. God help him, he'd sworn he would never go back. He had thought he would rather die than go back . . . but that was before he'd met Kate.

As if his thoughts of her had brought her to the cop's attention, McMaster changed the subject. "I understand you don't want any visitors. Does that include Kate?"

"It includes everyone."

"Why? Besides Ben James, Kate's the only person in this county who ever gave you a chance. She's the only one who ever thought there might be someone worth knowing behind the reputation. Why won't you see her?"

"Think about it, Chief," he said sarcastically. "Would you want Colleen Robbins coming to visit you in a place like this? You want her to see you in a jail uniform, behind bars or manacled and shackled like some dangerous animal?"

"No, I wouldn't. Maybe I can arrange something—"

"Don't bother." If Kate was responsible for his arrest, he didn't want to see her. If she wasn't responsible, chances were good she wouldn't want to see him, not after he'd proven how little he trusted her. The stupid thing was he didn't *care* whether she'd killed Trask. He cared that she might have lied to him, might have used him, might have set him up to take the blame for her crime. If she had killed the bastard, he would have willingly taken the blame if she had just given him the chance. His first goal would have been to protect both of them, but if that were impossible, he would have made sure that she was safe. He would have gotten the details from her, and he would have confessed.

And if she hadn't killed Trask? What if someone else had killed him, then set up Tucker for it? What if he had wrongly accused her?

Rising from the cot, McMaster walked over to the door and called the jailer's name, then looked back at Tucker again. "I wish you'd taken the advice I gave you Sunday to take Kate and get out of town."

"So do I." Tucker's smile was mocking. "So do I."

Chapter Fifteen

For the first time since destroying the answering machine, Kate regretted it. All day the phone had rung, and she had answered every time, hopeful that it would be Travis, Colleen, or maybe even Tucker, fearful that it would be Tim Carter or one of the others. Tucker had warned that they would blame her if anything happened to Jason, and they did. They wanted her to pay. They wanted her to suffer.

When the doorbell rang that evening, she considered not answering. She was too frazzled, too on edge, to deal with anyone. She wanted to talk to Tucker or no one, and she knew it wasn't Tucker out there.

Whoever it was, he was persistent, standing out there in the chilly rain and ringing the bell a second time, then a third. Of course, it was hard to hide the fact that she was home, with the lights blazing and her car and Tucker's truck parked outside. Muttering a curse, she checked the peephole to see whether she should open the door, wait out the person on the other side, or call the police.

Numbly she opened the door and, feeling suddenly stiff and uncomfortable, silently faced her caller. Her father. The first thing she noticed was that the look was gone—the shamed, unforgiving, sorry-that-she-was-his-daughter look that he'd subjected her to for six months and counting. There was still shame there, but it wasn't directed at her. There was also sorrow and a heavy-hearted, troubled look.

He waited for an invitation, and she gave it with a gesture. He didn't go into the living room or the kitchen, as he would have six months ago. He simply stood in the hallway, his jacket dripping rain on the faded rug. When minute after minute passed without his speaking, she finally did. "It's been a long time since you've come here." Sarcasm darkened her voice. "I thought you'd forgotten where I lived."

"I don't blame you for being angry, Kate. I haven't been a good father to you."

She hadn't ever really been angry. At first her parents' position against her had stunned her. Later she'd been too hurt to feel anger. This evening she just didn't care. All she cared about now was Tucker. He was the important one in her life.

"I wanted to tell you that I'm sorry—sorry I couldn't face what had happened to you, sorry I couldn't deal with what happened to Kerry—and I wanted you to know that you don't have to worry."

"Worry about what?"

"Last night. I took care of it."

"I don't understand. You took care of—" Suddenly Travis's announcement when he and Colleen had come to pick up Tucker this morning echoed through her mind. *Jason's neighbor saw a man leaving the grounds last night at the approximate time of death. He drove away in an old pickup.* Her father drove an old pickup, the one she'd learned to drive in. "Oh, God? *You? You* were the man seen leaving Jason's house? *You* killed him?"

His eyes took on a confused look. "No, of course I didn't. I just meant— Oh, I see. You don't have to pretend with me, Kate. I'm not going to tell anyone."

"What are you talking about?"

Smiling shakily, he reached out and patted her arm. "It's okay, honey. I was there, parked outside the gate, when . . . when you . . . I know I haven't done right by you in the past, but I'm going to protect you now, the way a father should. I'll never tell anyone I saw you leaving his house. I'll never tell anyone about the gun. When they find it—"

"They've already found it. You put it there, didn't you? You hid it at Tucker's house. *Why?*"

"You've suffered enough, Kate. After everything Trask put you through, no rational person could blame you for killing him. Of course, there aren't many rational people around here, not when it comes to them. People look up to them or are indebted to them or are afraid of them." His expression turned sorrowful again. "*I* was afraid of them. I stood by and did nothing while that bastard destroyed my family. I should have supported you. I should have protected you. Hell, if someone had to kill the bastard, it should have been me, not you."

Kate rubbed her hands across her face and heaved a sigh before looking at him again. "I didn't kill Jason."

"Kate, I *saw* you," he insisted even as she shook her head. "I was parked under that maple out by the street. I saw you come flying out of his driveway like a bat out of hell."

"You didn't see *me*. Daddy, I *wasn't* there. I was home all last evening. I haven't been anywhere since yesterday afternoon."

He started to protest, but the words wouldn't come.

"What exactly did you see?"

"A car. *Your* car—or one like it. There was a woman driving who looked like—There wasn't much light, but—I thought it was you."

"It wasn't. So you went to the house to see what had happened and . . . ?"

"The door to Jason's office was open. He was dead, and the gun was on the floor."

And, believing *she* had killed him, he had picked it up, wiped it clean of prints, and taken it to Tucker's house—getting seen, in the process, by Jason's neighbor. He had framed Tucker, had tampered with evidence, and had possibly destroyed fingerprints that would have identified Jason's killer and cleared Tucker. "Oh, Daddy, what have you done?"

He was bewildered by her response. He had come expecting gratitude so great that she would forgive and forget his abandonment. He hadn't been prepared for anything else. "Kate, I thought—I thought I was helping you. I thought I was protecting you."

"By getting Tucker arrested for something he didn't do? You know they'll convict him. They'll send him back to prison."

"It's no great loss. Kate, you can do better than that. With Jason gone, people will eventually forget. Your friends will come back. The decent men in town will come back."

"You mean I'll be good enough for them again now that Jason's dead? They'll forget my sordid past and make me respectable again?" She shook her head in dismay. "Daddy, Tucker is the most decent man I've ever known. I won't stand by and let him pay for a crime he didn't commit. Come on." She took a jacket from the closet and her keys from the hall table.

"Where are we going?"

"You're going to tell Travis everything you just told me." She opened the door and waited, but Karl held back.

"No."

"Daddy—"

He caught her arm. "What do you think they're going to

do when I tell them I saw the person who killed Jason and I thought it was my own daughter?"

They were going to suspect Kate. The DA couldn't ask for a better eyewitness identification than a father pointing a reluctant finger at his daughter.

"I'm not going with you, Kate. I'm not telling them anything. I'm not going to give them reason to arrest you."

She stared out into the dark night. The rain was puddling in the yard, running in miniature streams down the sides of the street. It reminded her of the rainy day at Tucker's house, when he'd reneged on their deal and returned her money. He'd taken it from underneath the mattress, the same place the gun had been found this morning. He probably believed she had put it there. How would he feel to learn that she *was* responsible, that her father had put it there to protect her?

"Daddy, I love Tucker, but he thinks I might have killed Jason and framed him for it. For my sake, you've got to tell the truth. If you don't, you'll be destroying any chance I might have of ever being happy again. Please . . ."

He came to stand beside her. "And if they arrest you?"

"I know a good lawyer. Maybe she can help me."

"What if she can't?"

The entire time she'd been planning Jason's death, she had believed that she was prepared to go to prison. She had convinced herself that being locked up for twenty years was a small price to pay for ridding the world of evil like Jason. She had been wrong. She wasn't prepared to live out her life behind bars. She wasn't prepared to give up the freedom she had so recently gained. She wasn't prepared to live without Tucker. But all those things were preferable to letting him go to trial. She was innocent, but he was even more so. He had never intended to kill anyone. He wasn't guilty of anything but trying to change her mind.

"Then I'll adapt. I'll survive. You, Mama, Jason, this town—you've all made me very good at surviving." She offered him a smile. "Let's go, Daddy."

The house was quiet, the phones unplugged. Kate was at the window seat, lying on her side on the thick cushions, surrounded by pillows. Tucker watched her from the couch, but he couldn't see her face.

Funny how quickly things changed. Last night a suspect in a murder, today a prisoner in jail, and tonight he was a free man. Tonight Kate was the suspect, identified by her own father at her insistence. Even though she'd known it would make her the DA's prime suspect, even though she'd understood that it might result in spending the rest of her life in prison, she'd made the old man tell anyway, and she'd done it for Tucker. She was willing to go to jail for him . . . or maybe she was willing to go because she was guilty. Damned if he knew.

And damned if he cared. All he cared about was keeping her from having to pay anymore.

"Kate?" He watched her shift. "Let's get out of here. Let's pack our stuff and go someplace far away, where they'll never find us."

Finally she turned to face him. "I can't leave town, remember?"

"If we leave now, no one will know until it's too late."

"I'm not running."

"If you stick around, they'll send you to prison, Kate. I've been there, remember? It's not a place you want to go."

"I didn't kill him, Tucker."

"The result will be the same either way: they'll lock you away for a long time. You don't belong in prison, Kate." He left the couch and crouched in front of the window seat.

"Let's go. Grab whatever you can't bear to leave behind, and let's get the hell out of here."

"You're willing to run away with me, to spend the rest of our lives running, but you're not willing to trust me." She smiled sadly. "You've believed me from the beginning, but not now. Not when it's most important."

"Did you kill him, Kate?"

"No."

"All right. Now let's go." He pulled her into an upright position, but that was as far as she cooperated. Tugging free, she drew her feet onto the seat, then rested her chin on her knees.

"Where would we go?"

"Florida? California? How about Alaska?"

She allowed a small smile. "And what would we do in Alaska?"

"Build a cabin a hundred miles from nowhere, fish and hunt and make love."

"Two fugitives living in the wilderness." The smile faded. "Sounds like fun . . . but I don't want to be raising little fugitives in the wilderness."

Babies. He had given more than a few thoughts to building a new life for themselves, but he'd never considered babies. Of course she would want one or two. To his surprise, he had just discovered that he did, too. Just a casual mention stirred urges he'd never thought he might have, paternal urges in a man who'd never had a father, who knew nothing about how to be a father. But he could learn. Kate could teach him.

He gave her a little shake. "Honey, you sure as hell don't want to be raising babies in prison," he said, his voice harsh enough to dim the light in her eyes. "Come away with me. Don't risk your future—don't risk *our* future—on the slight chance that you might actually get a fair trial in this place."

"Tucker, I haven't even been charged yet."

"You will be. Unless they find some other woman who hated Jason and drives a car like yours, unless her conscience gets the best of her and she's driven to confess, they're going to haul you into court, and, darlin', your fate will be sealed. Trust me. I've been through this with the Trasks before. You won't stand a chance."

She sat silent for a long moment. When she finally spoke, it wasn't about leaving. "Do we *have* a future, Tucker? The two of us? Together?"

Not if the Trasks had their way. They were determined to make one of them pay for Jason's death, and there was no way in hell it could be Kate. He didn't point that out, though. He simply gave the answer she wanted, the answer he wanted to believe with all his soul. "Absolutely. You, me, babies—the whole thing."

She hugged him tightly, desperately, then got to her feet. "It's been a long day. Let's go to bed. Get the lights, will you?"

He watched from the living room as she climbed the stairs, then began shutting off lights. He double-checked the doors, too, and the alarm before he headed up. Not many people knew he was out of jail. Someone, expecting Kate to be here alone, might think tonight was a good night to move beyond crosstown threats to something more personal, more satisfying, more menacing. But the locks were secure, the doors sturdy. Anyone who wanted to come in would make a lot of noise doing it, and he didn't intend to sleep soundly enough to miss it.

She was undressed and in bed by the time he got upstairs. He shut off the lights, went around to the other side of the bed, and sat down to remove his shoes and socks. His shirt came off next, then he sat there, almost too tired to finish undressing.

"I'm sorry for the problems my father caused you." Her voice was soft in the dark room, sweet and purely feminine. In spite of the grimness that colored her words, the mere sound was enough to put him in mind of things heated and erotic. It was enough to make him forget his weariness, almost enough to make him forget their problems.

"He was trying to protect you. I can't blame him for that. How do you feel about his change of heart?"

The sheets rustled with her shrug. "It comes a little late. He's made so much trouble. The fingerprints on that gun could have cleared both of us."

"If there were any prints to start with. Maybe the killer wore gloves. Still, your father thought he was helping you. He broke the law to protect you. That's got to count for something."

"I guess. But nothing changes the fact that he wasn't there when I needed him most, that he believed the awful, horrible things people were saying about me, that he blamed me."

Tucker stood up, stripped off the rest of his clothes, and slid under the covers beside her. She automatically moved closer. He automatically shifted to accommodate her, to hold her. "But he realizes he was wrong. He regrets it now."

"Yeah." Her sigh was feathery soft against his chest. "I guess that counts for something."

A few minutes before ten Thursday morning, Travis pulled his jacket on and headed for the door. "If you need anything, Wally, I'll be on the radio."

The dispatcher glanced up. "Where're you going?"

"Out."

"What should I say if anyone calls?"

"Tell them I'm out." Ordinarily Wally didn't ask for any information his boss didn't offer, but this wasn't an ordinary day. Ordinary days didn't include frequent phone calls and visits from Eleanor and Rupert Trask, demanding justice for their poor dead son, or require dealing with the friends and high-powered legal representatives of the deceased.

Travis had known from the moment he'd eavesdropped on Colleen's phone call this morning exactly where he would be at ten, but he'd chosen not to tell her. This trip was more than a little improper. He was, after all, being paid to build a case against Jason Trask's murderer, but damned if he was going to let it be Kate.

Although he wasn't persuaded that she was guilty, he wasn't convinced that she was innocent, either. He knew better than anyone but Tucker how traumatic the last six months had been for her. A person could only bear so much, could only be pushed so far before he or she pushed back. Maybe that incident in the restaurant had been Kate's breaking point. Maybe she had decided it was time to push back.

At least she had an alibi. The jury wouldn't find Tucker the most trustworthy witness in town, but he would be unshakable. Of course, Caldwell would lie to God Himself to protect Kate, but he might even convince Him.

Travis pulled to a stop at the side of the street. Kate's and Colleen's cars were in her driveway, and Tucker's truck was parked ahead of the Explorer. They weren't expecting him and very well might not want him there, but rather than spend one second of his time trying to prove Kate guilty, he was going to help prove her innocent.

Even if she wasn't.

Tucker answered the door, his expression wary. "I haven't come to arrest anyone," Travis said. "I'm here to help."

With a shrug, Caldwell moved back and Travis stepped inside. The women were sitting at the kitchen table, both watching him with the same wariness as he came down the hall. Raising both hands to show they were empty, he said, "Look—no handcuffs, no warrant. I just came to talk."

"We're a little busy here," Colleen said. "Unless you have a confession from someone else, maybe you could come back later."

"No news, no confession, just an offer of assistance."

"This isn't appropriate." It was still Colleen protesting. "You're a cop—"

"I've been Kate's friend a hell of a lot longer than I've been a cop. I figure, under the circumstances, she could use—*you* could use all the help you can get."

"Frankly," Kate said, "I think you could help most by finding out who really killed Jason—and you're not going to learn that here."

He waited until he was seated at the end of the table to respond. "It shouldn't be too hard. We'll just make up a list of every woman who had reason to dislike Jason Trask, then I'll run them, their family, and friends through DMV to see if they drive or have access to a car like yours. Then we'll find out where everyone was and what they were doing at the time of Jason's death."

"I guess I automatically come at the top of the list." Kate's smile was unsteady.

"I don't drive a red car, but I'm a woman, and I certainly disliked Jason," Colleen added.

"I imagine my mother, Mariana, and her mother all disliked him."

"As well as every woman whose husband, son, or brother has been injured, killed, or otherwise harmed by the Trasks and their reckless pursuit of profit." Colleen's gaze came to rest on Travis. "If you had to guess off the top of your head who killed Jason Trask, who would you pick?"

Five minutes ago, Travis's immediate response, without thinking, without censoring, would have been Kate. But in the last minute, another name had begun nudging hers aside—another woman who had good reason to want Jason dead. He didn't offer her for discussion, though, not just yet. "What about you, Kate? You know everyone in this town as well as I do. Who would you choose?"

"I would pick me. Most people who hated Jason were smart enough to keep it to themselves. I made sure everyone in town knew. Who would you choose?"

"She would have to be a certain type, wouldn't she?" He paused, then added, "Jason's type."

For a moment Kate remained still. Then, surprise widening her eyes, she faced him. "Oh, Travis . . ."

"What?" Colleen asked. "What is Jason's 'type'?"

Kate's answer came reluctantly. "When I first started dating Jason, there was talk that blue-eyed blondes must be his type. As soon as he'd divorced one, he had started dating another."

"Mariana Trask?" Colleen asked. "Jason's ex-wife?"

"She doesn't drive a red compact," Kate protested. "She has a Mercedes."

"That was Jason's Mercedes. He didn't let her keep it after the divorce. I don't know what she's driving now."

"But she was afraid of him, Travis—so afraid that she didn't utter a sound while he raped me. How could she ever find the courage to kill him?"

"She came back to town wanting justice," Tucker said, "but she wasn't able to get it. The DA wasn't willing to bring new charges against him, and you wouldn't help get a new trial on the old charges. She had planned to save the day,

Kate. Everyone would have admired her courage. They would have been impressed that the great powerful Jason Trask had been brought to his knees by a nobody from the wrong side of town. But she failed. It must have been a hell of a disappointment."

"And it brought Jason's attention back to her." Travis spoke quietly. "He wasn't pleased to find out that his ex-wife had tried to hurt him. She called me Saturday to tell me that the harassment had started. She was in my office Tuesday, damn near begging me to find some way to stop him. I told her she could either stick it out and hope he lost interest, or she could leave. Those were her only options."

"So maybe she found another option," Colleen murmured.

Maybe she had. Maybe she had gone to Jason's house to plead with him to leave her alone. Jason would have made her grovel, and then, after she had sacrificed her pride and dignity and humbled herself to him, he would have laughed and ordered her out. Humiliation, failure, and the utter sense of helplessness Jason inspired in his victims might have been enough to persuade her to kill him.

"No matter who did it, the son of a bitch brought it on himself," Tucker said. "It's too bad anyone has to be held responsible for it."

"But since someone does, better the guilty one than Kate." Travis walked to the phone and started to dial before noticing that it was unplugged. He reconnected the wires, then dialed the nonemergency number that would ring at the dispatcher's console. "Wally, do me a favor and check with DMV both here and in Oklahoma. See if you can find out what make and color of car Mariana Trask drives. I'll hold on."

Three pairs of eyes watched while he waited for a response. When it came, he hung up and looked at them.

"Same model, same color. Just a few years newer." Crossing the room, he picked up his jacket where he'd left it.

"Where are you going?" Kate asked.

His expression was grim to match his voice when he answered from the doorway. "To see if I can get a confession from a killer."

Kate paced the length of the living room, then retraced her path. It was the middle of the afternoon, and there had been no word from Travis. District Attorney Marquette had called, though. He was under a lot of pressure from the Trasks to arrest their best suspect. Though their evidence was shaky, it was enough to satisfy Jason's parents and Judge Hampton. It was enough, in Rutherford County, to take Kate into custody.

Colleen had argued with him. Kate wasn't the only woman who had hated Jason. She had an alibi. Her father's identification wasn't a positive ID. She couldn't be tied to the weapon. Her fingerprints hadn't been found in the office. There was hardly enough there to qualify her as a suspect, and certainly nothing to justify an arrest.

Poor Colleen. She was playing the game by the rules, when, here in Rutherford County, there were no rules but one: whatever the Trasks wanted, they got. If Eleanor and Rupert were satisfied that she was their son's murderer, that made it so. If they wanted her arrested based on no more than her father's identification and her well-known hatred of Jason, then she would soon find herself in a cell.

She hoped Travis found something to connect Mariana to the murder. She hated to think of the other woman in prison, but she certainly wasn't willing to go for her. She had other plans for her life, like settling someplace new with Tucker and starting a family. *You, me, babies—the whole thing.*

When she passed Tucker, he pulled her down on the sofa beside him. "I owe you an apology," he said, his voice quiet so Colleen, reading a newspaper at the window seat, wouldn't hear.

"For what?"

"Not believing you from the start."

"I had lied to you. It was only natural that you should wonder."

"I should have known. I should have trusted you. I'm sorry, Kate."

With a weary smile, she sank back against him, resting her head on his shoulder. "You were right. We should have left last night. We should have just disappeared."

"Maybe it's not too late."

"I'll bet you somewhere down the street, there's a cop watching the house."

"Travis doesn't expect you to run."

"So now it's Travis." She gave him a teasing grin before turning serious again. "No, he doesn't. But he would want to be prepared in case someone comes over with the intention of causing trouble." She slipped her hand inside his. "I'm scared, Tucker."

His fingers tightened around hers. "So am I, sweetheart. But it'll work out. Trust me, you're not going to trial."

"Do you know something I don't?"

"Maybe."

She stared at him, her gaze searching his face. The ringing of the doorbell barely registered, and Colleen's and Travis's voices in the hall were unintelligible murmurs. What did he mean by *maybe*? What was he thinking?

When Travis came into the room, she forced her attention to him. His expression was stony and controlled. "Mariana swears she was home all night, and her mother backs up her story."

"Do you believe her?" Colleen asked.

"No. But I can't shake her."

"Let Kate try." The suggestion came from Tucker. "Mariana felt guilty about not testifying at the trial. She came back here against Trask's wishes to set things right and make it up to Kate. If she killed him, she must feel even guiltier now about letting Kate take the blame."

Travis looked at Colleen, who shrugged, then Kate. "Do you want to talk to her?"

"I guess."

"Get your coat. I'll take you over."

"I can take my own car—"

"No." The disagreement came from all three of them in varying degrees of intensity. Travis continued. "There are some angry people out there. You're not leaving this house without me."

She gave Tucker a kiss, then followed Travis out, climbed into the truck, and fastened the seat belt. "All these months I wanted Jason dead. Then, when I finally decided he could live to be a hundred for all I care, someone killed him, and I get blamed. It isn't fair."

"No, it isn't. But that's life in Fall River." He made a U-turn and headed downtown.

"I'm going to get out. Provided they don't send me to prison, Tucker and I are leaving. You should go, too."

"I'm thinking about it. I've still got a lot of friends on the Little Rock PD. I could go back there."

"And you could continue seeing Colleen. Are you going to be getting married again soon?"

"Don't know. What about you?"

"If the ceremony doesn't have to take place in a prison chapel," she said drily.

They reached Mariana's house too quickly. Travis parked out front, then shut off the engine. "I'll wait here."

"What should I say?"

"Anything that will make her feel guilty."

Kate left the truck and climbed the steps to the porch, where she rang the doorbell. There was a call from inside, the words indistinguishable, then Mariana opened the door. She wasn't happy to see Kate. "What do you want?"

"To talk."

Mariana pulled her cardigan tighter, stepped outside, and closed the door. She scowled at the Explorer. "I already told your friend that he's wrong. I didn't kill Jason. I wasn't anywhere near his house Tuesday night."

"Neither was I, but that's not going to stop them from charging me. It's not going to stop them from sending me to prison."

"I'm sorry about that, but I can't help you."

Kate shoved her hands into her coat pockets as she studied the other woman. Was she a little paler than usual? Were her movements a little more jittery? "Mariana, I know I treated you badly when you tried to warn me about Jason. You tried to help me then, and I brushed you off. I'm sorry about that. But I need your help now."

Mariana walked to the opposite end of the porch, where a wooden swing hung. She wrapped her fingers around the chain that supported one end and made it twist and sway. "I tried to help you when I came back. I had proof against Jason that might have gotten him sent to jail, but you didn't want any part of it. You didn't want to try again. If you had, maybe this wouldn't have happened. Maybe he wouldn't be dead and you wouldn't be facing jail."

"Are you saying this is my fault? If you had testified at his trial, if you had come forward with your proof then, maybe he would have already been in jail."

"I can't help you," Mariana repeated, her arms folded across her chest in a defensive posture. "I wasn't there."

"My father saw a blond woman in a red car leaving Jason's house right after he was killed. You have a red car." It was parked in the driveway behind Kate.

"So do you."

"But I didn't kill Jason. I had no reason to."

"Oh, right. How about the fact that he raped you? That he put your sister in a mental hospital, turned your own family against you, and cost you your job and your friends? They sound like damned good reasons to me."

Kate shook her head. "I have Tucker now. I didn't care about Jason anymore."

"I didn't kill him," Mariana said once more, her voice stiff and unyielding. "No one can prove that I did. I have to go back in before my mother starts to worry."

When she reached the door, Kate spoke. "Don't do this, Mariana, please. You think taking a bribe from Jason to not testify at his trial bothered your conscience? That was nothing compared to the guilt you'll have to live with if I go to prison for your crime. Please . . ."

"I didn't commit a crime," Mariana said, enunciating each word with chilly finality. After a moment's pause for emphasis, she went inside and closed the door behind her.

With a hopeless sigh, Kate returned to the truck. "She's a little on the stubborn side, isn't she?" Travis asked as she settled in the seat.

"Why should she confess? So far, it's the perfect crime. You can't prove she did it, but you won't have any trouble at all convincing twelve jurors of my guilt."

"Kate . . . I got a call from Marquette while you were up there. He said I have to bring you in. I tried to talk him out of it. I told him we had other leads, but . . ."

No one cared about leads. No one cared about justice.

"I called Colleen. She's going to meet us at the jail."

Kate sat numbly, only vaguely aware of Travis pulling away from the curb. She saw scenery go past, but couldn't focus on it, saw people but couldn't recognize them. *I'm scared,* she had told Tucker a short while ago. Terrified would be more appropriate.

It wasn't *fair*. Six months ago Jason had committed a crime, and she had been punished for it. Now he had antagonized Mariana into killing him, and Kate was going to jail for it. Even though he was dead, he was still defeating her, still making her pay for daring one time to tell him no.

She smiled thinly at her reflection in the window. Such was justice, Trask-style.

Chapter Sixteen

Tucker climbed the steps to the porch at Mortenson's Lumber and took a seat in the empty rocker there. The old man glanced at him, but didn't speak right away. He continued rocking, his gloved hands resting on the chair's arms, his gaze on things distant. After a time, he broke his silence. "You're dressed up. You going to court or something?"

"Yeah, at eleven."

"That girl didn't kill anyone. She's capable, but she didn't do it."

"I don't suppose you saw who did."

"This old man is asleep by nine o'clock most nights," he said with a grin that quickly faded. "You know, most people who get themselves killed, it seems, are killed by someone close to them—a brother, a cousin, maybe even a father or a son."

"Or an ex-wife."

"Sometimes things get so bad that people just can't see any other way out. Sometimes the people making things so bad don't leave any other way out."

That was true of Trask. He'd been so damned arrogant, so convinced that everyone in this town was his to do whatever the hell he wanted with. He had made people suffer until the only solution they could find to save themselves involved destroying him. He had deserved to die. "They're arraigning Kate this morning. The judge is going to refuse bail, and they're going to keep her locked up until the trial starts. It's not right, Ben."

"No, it sure isn't."

"Do you know Mariana Trask?"

Ben shook his head. "I used to see her daddy around before he drank himself into the grave. Marvin Wilson was a worthless man. That wife of his, Pat, had her hands full trying to take care of him and the little girl and work, too. Made her life easier when he drove off the road into a gully and smashed up his car and himself. That was years ago—fifteen, maybe sixteen."

"How can Mariana stand knowing that someone else is going to pay for what she did?"

"Some people can stand anything. Some people aren't overly troubled by conscience." Ben rocked for a moment, the weathered wood squeaking from time to time. "Have you talked to her?"

"No. I was thinking I might."

"Can't hurt anything, can it?" He tilted his head back and closed his eyes. As Tucker rose from his chair, he spoke once more. "Tell Miss Kate I've been praying for her."

Tucker nodded, even though the old man wasn't looking. He returned to his truck and drove to the nearest pay phone. Even though Marvin Wilson had been dead for years, the phone was still listed in his name, the address a short distance away. He parked on the street, then gave the red car in the driveway a long look as he made his way to the porch.

The woman who answered the door was probably a few years younger than he was, but this morning she looked as if she were aging rapidly. Her blond hair was carelessly combed, and her blue eyes were bloodshot. Even though she held a tall glass half-emptied of some liquor, he didn't think it was responsible for the red eyes. "Can I help you?"

"Mariana? My name is Tucker Caldwell. I'd like to talk to you."

"About Kate?" She scowled. "Everyone wants to talk about Kate—even my own mama."

"Can I come in?"

She looked behind her, then reluctantly stepped back. "You'll have to be quick and quiet. My mother is resting. It has *not* been a peaceful week around here." After he stepped inside, she gestured toward another door on the left. "We'll go in there."

The room had probably once been a study, but now it was serving as storage, filled with things not needed but too important to throw out. There were a few pieces of furniture, but most of the room was filled with boxes haphazardly stacked. He walked as far as the stacks would allow, then turned to face her, where she was leaning against the closed door, sipping her drink.

"So you're Kate's Tucker. I remember you. My daddy and your uncle were drinking buddies." Her gaze narrowed. "If you came to ask me to confess to killing Jason, I'm not going to do it."

"No, that's not why I came." Noticing a picture frame upside down on the nearest box, he picked it up and studied the photograph. It was a portrait of Mariana in an elaborate white gown, with Jason in a tuxedo at her side. She looked dazzlingly happy. "You loved him, didn't you?"

"More than I'd thought I was capable of." Her smile was tremulous. "When we began dating, nobody thought he would ever marry me. He was a Trask, for God's sake, and I was just Mariana Wilson."

A nobody from the wrong side of town. Sort of like him, compared to Kate.

"That day was a dream come true for me. I thought we would have the perfect marriage, the perfect children, the perfect life . . . and then he hit me for the first time." She took another drink, draining half the liquid in the glass. "I lived the last half of our marriage in fear for my life. I was convinced that he was going to kill me."

"But instead you killed him."

For a moment she didn't react to his softly spoken words, then she snatched the frame away and slapped it facedown on another box. "Why didn't Kate cooperate? Why didn't she work with me when I came back?"

"She'd given up hope that anybody could stop the Trasks. The trial was bad for her. She couldn't go through another one."

She studied him for a moment, then asked, "Are you in love with her?"

"Yeah."

"What are you going to do if she goes to prison?"

"I'm not going to let that happen."

"How do you plan to stop it?"

He'd lain awake most of last night, looking for a way out for Kate. Short of Mariana's confessing, he could think of only one. "I know you killed Jason. I don't blame you for denying it. Having spent sixteen years in prison, I sure as hell don't blame you for not wanting to go there. I didn't come here to ask you to tell the truth."

"Then what *do* you want?"

"I want you to back me up."

She looked puzzled. "On what?"

He glanced around the room again. It wasn't much bigger than the cell where he had spent those sixteen years, hating every minute. He'd sworn he would never go back. A lot of first-timers swore that, but they came back anyway. Most found life outside too hard. Tucker found his option— watching the woman he loved go to prison for no crime beyond being some sick bastard's victim—too hard. He was better suited to prison than she was. He knew he could handle it.

"The only evidence they have against Kate is that her father saw a blond woman in a red car leaving Trask's house right after he was killed. I want you to tell the DA it was you."

"Are you crazy? *I'm* the woman the Trasks hate most in this county, next to Kate. You want me to admit to them that *I* killed him?"

"No, I just want you to tell them that it was you Kate's father saw. That'll clear Kate. It'll get her out of this mess."

"And who will clear me?"

"I will. Tell them that you went to talk to Trask, to ask him to leave you alone. When you got there, you saw the side door was open. You went in, found his body, panicked, and ran. That'll put me back at the top of their list of suspects, and I'll confess. That will clear you."

For a long uncomfortable moment, she simply looked at him. Then she murmured, "You *are* crazy, aren't you? Crazy about Kate." She finished the last of her drink and set the glass aside. "You're willing to go to prison for her? You love her that much?"

"Yes."

"She's a lucky woman."

Tucker doubted Kate felt lucky after spending the night in jail and before facing an antagonistic judge and a hostile courtroom for her arraignment.

"All right." Mariana looked almost as relieved as Tucker felt. "I'll do it."

After showing her visitor out, Mariana returned to the storeroom, looking at all the boxes stacked there. Her wedding dress was in the tall one at the back, wrapped in tissue and hanging from a padded hanger. A few dried flowers from her bouquet were in another box. Old clothes, a few mementos, a souvenir or two . . . All that was left of her marriage was in this room.

She'd thought her life was a fairy tale when she'd married Jason all those years ago. But her prince hadn't been so charming. She should have left before it had all turned to poison. Maybe if she had, things wouldn't have come to this.

Kate Edwards *was* a lucky woman. After everything she'd been through, she'd come out of it with the best prize of all: a man who loved her enough to sacrifice anything for her. Even in their best times, Jason wouldn't have given up much for her. But Tucker Caldwell was willing to spend the rest of his life in prison for Kate—willing, even, to risk execution—and, in the process, he was going to save Mariana from her own folly.

She picked up the wedding picture again, touching it gently. How sad that her love had come to this, for in the end she had hated Jason far more passionately than she had ever loved him. He had destroyed her fairy tale, and he had tried to destroy her life. He had deserved to die.

Putting the picture down, she left the room. Her mother was still in her room. Pat hadn't had much to say in the last few days. She had verified Mariana's claim to Travis McMaster that she hadn't left the house Tuesday night, and she had never asked her daughter whether she had, in fact, gone out after Pat had gone to bed. She had never asked if Mariana had killed Jason.

Maybe she was afraid of the answer.

At the bottom of the steps, Mariana hesitated. If she had any sense, she would throw her clothes into her bags, toss the bags into the car, and get as far away from Fall River as she could. But she had run away before, and it hadn't solved any problems. Besides, Tucker hadn't asked for so much. All she had to do was tell the DA a story, half-true, half-not, and make it impossible not to believe. Kate would be cleared, and she would be cleared.

And Tucker Caldwell would be left to take the blame.

Forcing herself, she climbed the stairs to her bedroom. Inside the bright, sunny room she dressed in the same suit she'd worn to Marquette's office on her previous visit. Its stark color was fitting for today's purpose.

A glance at her watch showed that it was 10:40. Kate's hearing was scheduled for eleven. Mariana should be able to catch the district attorney before he left his office for the courtroom. There was just one thing she had to do first.

Downstairs at the back of the house, she tapped lightly on her mother's bedroom door, then pushed it open. Pat was sitting in the old armchair beside the window that looked on the backyard. She looked even wearier, even more vulnerable, than she had when Mariana had arrived home last week. Smiling weakly, she pulled the knitted throw closer over her legs, propped on a needlepoint hassock. "You look pretty, darlin'. Where are you headed? Out to lunch with friends?"

"No, Mama." Mariana crossed the room to sit on the edge of the hassock. "You've been awfully quiet these last few days. I know you've been worrying about me and Jason and what was going on."

"Honey, I'm not going to ask anything. Jason Trask got exactly what he deserved. That's all that matters."

Mariana smiled gently. Her mother had never harbored bad feelings for anyone, not even Marv, who had run around, drunk away her hard-earned money, never given her an easy day, and then died on her. Her sentiments toward the Trasks in general and Jason in particular came as close to hatred as Pat was capable of feeling. "Well, don't waste your energy worrying about it, Mama. Everything's going to be all right. Everything will work out just fine." She hugged her mother, then stood up. "I'd better get going."

Quickly, before she could change her mind, she left the house. She made the drive downtown in record time, but there wasn't a parking space to be had anywhere near the courthouse. Painfully aware of the seconds ticking closer to eleven, she parked in the space reserved for Travis McMaster at the police station, then hurried to the courthouse.

"Mr. Marquette's got to appear in court," his secretary told her when she reached his office. "You'll have to come back later."

"This is in regard to the Trask case," she said, forcing deep breaths to steady her voice. "I'm sure he would want to hear what I have to say before he goes into court and arraigns an innocent person on murder charges. Tell him that, will you?"

The secretary left her desk and disappeared into the inner office. Only a moment later, she reappeared in the doorway, beckoning Mariana to follow her.

Marquette was standing behind his desk, pulling his suit coat on. He adjusted his shirt collar, then his tie, before facing her. "What is it you have to say about the killing of Jason Trask, Ms. Trask?"

Mariana took another deep breath, seeking courage, then

rushed out the words before her cowardice returned in force. "Plenty, Mr. Marquette." She tried to smile, but it wasn't steady. "Starting with the fact that you've arrested the wrong person."

The conference room across the hall from Judge Hampton's courtroom was small, more than half its space taken up by a battered table and chairs. There were no windows, no pictures on the wall, nothing to distract a person. Kate felt as if she'd been waiting forever, yet she was no more prepared to walk into the courtroom than she'd been months ago when Jason's trial had begun. That time she had expected justice. This time she didn't.

Colleen sat on her right, looking every bit the cool professional from the big city. Her expression was serene, but Kate suspected it was covering a case of nerves almost as bad as her own.

On her left, at the end of the table, sat Tucker. When Travis and his officers had shown the women in, Tucker had been waiting, looking ridiculously handsome in pressed jeans and a pale blue cotton shirt. He hadn't kissed Kate or spoken, but had taken her into his arms. She had forgotten how good simply being held felt. She could have stayed there forever, but after too few minutes he had released her and pulled out the chair for her. They had talked but hadn't said anything important. She hadn't told him how much she loved him or how scared she was. She hadn't admitted that the only thing that had saved her from all-night-long hysterics in that tiny cell had been the knowledge that she would see him today.

What would save her when she was in prison? When it wasn't one night, but night after dreadfully long night, hundreds, thousands of them?

She wrapped her cold fingers around his and smiled. "My hands are clammy." Her heart was racing, her knees were weak, and her stomach was churning. If Travis's officers didn't have to drag her kicking and screaming into the courtroom, she would be surprised.

"It'll be all right."

She wished she could believe him. She wanted it with all her heart.

With a sigh, Kate checked the time. They should have started nearly ten minutes ago. She wondered what the delay was. She wasn't anxious to go into the courtroom, but this waiting was driving her crazy. Better to get it over with now, so she could return to her cramped cell and start getting used to the confinement.

When the door opened, she started to rise from the chair, but Tucker pulled her back. Travis and the district attorney came into the room, circling the table to sit on the opposite side. Travis refused to meet her gaze, and Marquette directed his attention to Tucker, not her. "I understand you're on parole."

He nodded.

"Ask your attorney what effect making a false statement to the police would have on your parole."

Surprise replaced serenity on Colleen's face. "It would be grounds for revoking it. You would have to serve day for day the rest of your sentence. Why? What false statement did he make?"

It was the DA who answered. Tucker simply lowered his gaze to the table. "He hasn't made it yet. He was planning to, though. It seems he made a deal with Mariana Trask this morning. If she lied to us and cleared Kate, he would confess to killing Jason. Seems he couldn't bear the idea of Kate going to prison for something she didn't do."

Kate stared at Tucker. So that was what he'd meant when he'd told her yesterday that she wasn't going to trial, when he'd said just a few minutes ago that everything would be all right. He had intended to save her by sacrificing himself. "Tucker?" she whispered, squeezing his hand so tightly that he needed his other hand to ease the pressure.

"If they're going to send the wrong person to prison, it might as well be me," he said with a defensive shrug. "I've been there. I can handle it."

She continued to stare at him, furious that he had even considered such a deal. She *knew* how much he had hated prison, knew how desperately he'd wanted to avoid it. At the same time, she was touched more deeply than words could express, because he'd been willing to go back there to save her. A woman couldn't ask for better proof of a man's love than that.

Still holding her hand in both of his, Tucker looked from Kate to the DA. "I guess Mariana didn't keep her end of the deal."

"Not exactly." Marquette turned to Travis and gestured for him to elaborate.

"She talked to the DA as you asked, but she didn't lie. She confessed to killing Jason. She went to his house to beg him to leave her alone. He ordered her off his property, threatened to have her arrested, even picked up the phone to call the police, and she picked up the gun that was on his desk. She shot him six times, dropped the gun, and ran. That was when Karl Edwards saw her."

Poor Mariana. She had never stood up to Jason in her life. Now that she had finally managed, she was going to pay almost as dearly as he had. Then, abruptly, Kate realized the ramifications of the other woman's confession and looked up. "That means . . ."

Marquette was smiling. "That means you can go. Both of you. I apologize for the inconvenience, and I hope I never see either of you in here again." Rising from his seat, he left the room. In the moment the door was open, Kate heard the clamor of voices, grumbling over the delay of the hearing. Rupert Trask's overshadowed them all. Once the door closed again, she stood up, accepted a hug from Colleen, then turned toward Tucker. He stood up, but he didn't look at her. With his gaze lowered and the thin set of his mouth, he looked as if he fully expected anger. Maybe later he would get it—*much* later—but not now.

She moved in close enough to feel his heat and hear his uneven breathing and wrapped her arms tightly around his neck. Rising onto her toes, she gave him the sweetest, best kiss she could manage. When she ended it, she looked up into his eyes, so dark and serious, and softly whispered, "Thank you, Tucker. I love you, too."

"When are you expected back in Little Rock?"

Colleen gazed into the fire, feeling lazy and dreamy and incredibly *whole*. It had been quite a day, with the charges against Kate being dropped. The four of them had celebrated over lunch, then Travis had taken the rest of the afternoon off and brought Colleen to his house for a few hours of lazy loving. No doubt Kate and Tucker had indulged in the same pastime on the next street over . . . unless they were packing to get out of town as soon as possible. She couldn't blame them for going. Anyplace in the country would be better for them than this place that had brought them together.

With a sigh, she pressed a warm, wet kiss to Travis's chest. "Monday."

"Only a couple of days." He sounded disappointed. Good.

"They expect me Monday . . . but they're not going to see me."

"You taking some time off?"

"No. I'm quitting."

He was still for a moment, barely breathing. Then, his voice unnaturally cautious, he asked, "To do what?"

"Well, I know a battered woman whose ex-husband continued to abuse and threaten her long after the divorce. Even though she admits to killing him, I'm not convinced that she's responsible for her actions. I think she needs a good lawyer."

"This is still the Trasks' town. You may not be able to do any more for Mariana than you could for Kate or Tucker."

"Hey, the charges were dropped against both of them. Maybe I'm on a roll." She stroked his face, then cupped her palm to his cheek. "Rupert Trask is an old man. He can't live forever. When he dies, there will be a lot of power up for grabs. This county won't know what to do with itself. Maybe, with a good police chief and a good lawyer working together, things will work out more equitably for the average citizen."

"This police chief was thinking about going back to Little Rock."

She shook her head. "They need you here, Travis. Your family is here, your friends, your work . . . and me. *I'll* be here."

"A good police chief and a good lawyer," he repeated thoughtfully. "Working together, living together . . . You know, in a town like Fall River, that means married."

"Married." She softly echoed the word. "After the divorce, I thought I would never marry again."

"But . . . ?"

"Well, seeing that I love you more than I ever loved anyone, I think I've changed my mind."

"You mean, I've changed your mind," he teased with sweet, thoroughly lovable arrogance.

After another moment in his arms, she reluctantly pulled away and sat up, searching for something to put on. Sliding her arms into the sleeves of his uniform shirt and wrapping the excess fabric around her middle, she turned to face him. "There's one thing I have to tell you first, Travis. It might change your mind."

He stretched, then pillowed his head on his arms, unselfconscious of his nakedness. "You don't want children."

"I do."

"You don't want to be married to a cop."

"Why would you think that when I'm in love with a cop?"

"Then what is it?"

She wished she could say, "Nothing," shuck the shirt, and seduce him again. It *was* her turn, wasn't it? But she'd started, and her conscience wouldn't let her stop. "It's about the gun."

"What gun?"

"The gun Mariana used to kill Jason." It had seemed logical for Tucker or Kate to have bought the gun for the express purpose of killing Jason, taking it to his house with them. But Mariana had insisted that she'd found it on Jason's desk. While Jason had had a number of weapons in the house, they'd all been rifles. There hadn't been an unregistered, serial-number-etched-off handgun in the bunch. His friends were insisting that it couldn't possibly have been his, that if he'd wanted a pistol, he would have bought a top-of-the-line model, not a cheap piece of work like the .22. They insisted that Mariana must have brought the gun with her, which would make Jason's murder premeditated rather than what it really was—a crime of passion.

"Karl Edwards did a real good job of cleaning it. They didn't find a single fingerprint anywhere."

"One of the sets of fingerprints they didn't find . . ." She looked away, swallowed hard, then forced herself to meet his gaze. "The gun was mine, Travis. I got it in Little Rock that afternoon. Jason had come to see me that morning, to tell me that my last two clients had dropped the lawsuit and that he knew about my father. He bragged about how they had blackmailed him, how they had manufactured evidence to use against him. He laughed about my father's death. After he left, I went to the city and got the gun from someone I know. When I came back, I waited for Jason to leave Ozark Annie's, then I went to his house. I intended to kill him."

The surprise that flickered through his expression was the only change. There was no anger, judgment, or moral disappointment. "What happened?" he asked, his voice as even as if they were talking about something totally inconsequential.

"I was telling him why he had to die—because my father had been a good, honorable man, because he had been the best man I'd ever known—and I realized that killing Jason would cost me more than I could lose. It would dishonor my father's memory. It would destroy my self-respect, and it would destroy you and me. Giving up this need for revenge that I'd nurtured for the last sixteen years seemed well worth what I would get in return: peace. A future. You."

"So you put the gun down and walked away."

"He took it from me, but I let him. I was relieved to walk away."

"And when Mariana showed up soon after, he provoked her, and she found the other option she'd been looking for."

Looking serious, he sat up and faced her. "Anything else you want to tell me?"

She shook her head.

"All right. So . . . will you marry me?" She must have looked incredulous—she certainly felt it—because he went on. "If Mariana wanted to kill Jason, she would have accomplished it with or without your gun. As far as *you* wanting to kill him, under the circumstances, who could blame you? The important thing is you didn't. When you walked out of his house, he was alive and unharmed. It isn't your fault that someone else changed that. So . . . since I do love you, and you've already said you love me, will you marry me?"

Her smile seemed to form somewhere deep inside and grow until she was damned near bursting with it. "Yes," she said, moving into his welcoming embrace. "Yes, I'll marry you."

Kate was standing in front of the fireplace, staring at the empty mantel, when Tucker came in from loading the last box in the back of his truck. He wrapped his arms around her from behind and pressed a kiss to her neck. "You're not having second thoughts, are you?"

"About leaving?"

"About leaving, about me, about us."

"Not about us. Never about us." She leaned back against him. "I'm a little sad, I guess, about leaving the house. It holds a lot of good memories."

"We'll make new good memories."

She considered it a moment, then nodded. "We will. Are you ready?"

"Whenever you are."

Moving from his embrace, she picked up the last item they were taking with them, the string quilt that had covered his bed the last few months. It was funny how perceptions changed, he thought. He'd shared that quilt with Nolie a number of times, but he'd had no sentimental attachment to it. It had just been a cover to keep warm, no more special than a blanket he could pick up for five bucks at the store. No longer, though. After last night, he would never again look at that quilt without remembering what had undoubtedly been the best, most incredible, most passionate night of his entire life. Even just thinking about it made him wonder if they could delay leaving just a little longer.

But Kate was already heading for the door, and he followed her with only a moment's regret. They would be together tonight and the next million nights that followed. They would be together forever.

As soon as he stepped outside, she locked the door, then rested her palm for a moment against it. Just as Tucker stared to reach for her, she turned to him. Her eyes were damp, but her smile was bright and steady. "One more stop, and we'll be gone."

He knew what she meant. They'd made all their arrangements yesterday afternoon—giving notice on Kate's job, listing the house for sale, disconnecting the utilities, closing bank accounts, packing—and had said most of their goodbyes last night. Colleen had given them the key to her condo in Little Rock, where they would stay until they found a place of their own, and she had also given Tucker a referral to a client who ran the biggest construction company in the city and was expecting a call from him Monday. There was only one thing left to do now.

In spite of the morning's chill, old Ben was sitting in his usual place, rocking, humming softly. A wide smile split his face when he saw them. It saddened when he saw the truck, loaded with their belongings. "I wish you didn't have to go, but I understand why you do."

Kate gave him a gentle hug. "You're a good man, Mr. James. You've been a good friend."

"I was just looking out for Mr. Charles's granddaughter. Where are you going?"

"Little Rock," Tucker replied. It was an easy choice. Kerry was there, it was close enough to Fall River to come back and visit, and Jimmy lived there. His brother wasn't a bad guy, not really, and he would make a hell of a doting uncle.

Old Ben's expression turned dreamy. "Little Rock's a big city. Plenty of room for two people starting over. Plenty of room to forget things that need forgetting and to concentrate on the important things."

Like being happy. Being married. Being in love. If not for Ben, Tucker would know no more about those things now than he had two months ago. He owed his friend a lot.

"We'll be back next weekend to get married," Kate said. "We would be honored if you'd come."

"I'll be there," he promised delightedly. "When you make it back to town to visit, you come and see me. And when you have that first baby, you bring him back, too."

Kate moved, leaving Tucker to say his good-byes over the lump forming in his throat. "I'm going to miss you, old man."

"You know where to find me if you need me." Using the cane for leverage, Ben got to his feet and laid a bony hand on Tucker's arm. "You take care of that girl. Tell her every day and show her in every way how much you love her."

"I will." After a moment's hesitation, he wrapped his arms around Ben's frail body and hugged him. "I love you, too, old man," he whispered, too low, he thought, to be heard, but Ben patted his back.

"I know, son," he murmured. After a moment, he stepped back. "Go on now. You've got a new life waiting for you. Get on out there and meet it."

Tucker took Kate's hand at the top of the steps, and they started toward the truck. Halfway there, old Ben called out, "And you didn't trust a crazy old coot like me to set you up with a woman." His laughter followed them as they climbed into the truck.

They drove through town in silence that extended as the road began climbing out of the valley. Before they'd gone five miles, Tucker pulled off at a wide spot that served as a lookout and turned in the seat to look at Kate. "I love you."

"I love you, too." Then, as his gaze grew more intense, she grew self-conscious. When he reached for her with a glint in his eyes, she asked through laughter, "What are you doing?"

"Taking the advice of a wise old man." He pulled her across the seat and bent his head to kiss her as gently, as sweetly, as tenderly, as he knew how.

Tell her every day and show her in every way how much you love her.

Forever and always.

Please Turn the Page
for a Bonus Excerpt
from Marilyn Pappano's
December 1997 release:
Season for Miracles,
a new romance
coming from
Warner Books

Chapter 1

Bethlehem, 5 miles.

If she hadn't been so close to crying, the legend on the highway sign would have made Emilie Dalton laugh. She'd known she had made a mistake when she exited the interstate a couple hours back for gas and there wasn't an access ramp back onto the freeway. She'd known she was taking a chance on getting lost when she'd decided to forge ahead on unfamiliar state routes until one of them eventually led back to I-90. She had known that with the snow falling the way it was and the kids tired the way they were, it would be best if they stopped right where they were, checked into the motel across the street, and waited for morning.

But where they were had been too close to where they were fleeing. The snow, which had been falling sporadically throughout the day, hadn't looked as if it had any intention of stopping, and, according to the map, she'd needed to go only about fifteen miles on the twisting highways to reach the interstate again, and so she had pushed on. Her second mistake.

Bethlehem, 5 miles.

385

She'd never heard of Bethlehem, New York, but she wasn't familiar with this part of the country, except for Boston, where she'd lived the past twelve months. She was a Southerner, Atlanta born and bred, who, until last year, had never traveled farther north than Asheville, North Carolina. And now here she was with three exhausted, hungry, frightened kids, lost in western New York, driving through a snowstorm toward a little town called Bethlehem.

A strangled sound, part hysterical laugh, part despairing cry, escaped before she clamped her mouth shut, but it was enough to rouse nine-year-old Alanna in the seat beside her. The girl straightened and looked around. "Where are we, Aunt Emilie?"

"A couple of miles from Bethlehem."

"Bethlehem . . . Pennsylvania?"

"No, honey, New York." At least she hoped so. As far as she could recall from last year's drive up from Atlanta, Bethlehem, Pennsylvania, was in the eastern part of the state and a long, long way from where she needed to be. She prayed she hadn't gotten so turned around that she'd messed up that badly.

Not that it would be the first time she'd done something incredibly stupid. Moving to Boston hadn't been her brightest decision. Helping Berry hadn't been too brilliant. Running away from Boston was pretty darn stupid—to say nothing of criminal. Oh, yeah, she was great at making messes.

Emilie looked around, searching for something that indicated a town nearby, but the only thing around them was forest and hills. There was no other traffic, no houses, no turns leading off the highway. Just wilderness, loneliness, snow. And them.

"Are we lost, Aunt Emilie?"

She opened her mouth to deny it, then sighed heavily. "Yés. But only for tonight. We're going to rent a room in Bethlehem and get some dinner. Tomorrow morning, I'll get directions to the interstate and we'll be on our way home. We'll be fine. I promise."

"Home," Alanna echoed in a whisper, as if she were testing the word. Nine years old, and she'd never had a real home. From the time she was a baby, Berry had dragged her—and later Josie and Brendan—from city to city, state to state, house to apartment to shelter. There had always been a man involved, of course. Berry needed a man in her life the way most people needed food, and she always picked the wrong men, the ones who cultivated her own weaknesses for the easy fix, the easy oblivion, until she was no longer capable of caring for herself, much less her kids.

Emilie understood, forgave, and forgot a lot about her sister, but that was one thing she would never understand: how Berry could care more about the men who were temporary parts of her life than she did about the three innocent children she'd brought into the world. It was the one thing Emilie couldn't forgive, especially now that her sister was locked up in a court-ordered substance-abuse program and Emilie's own life was on hold while she took responsibility for those kids.

A year had passed since her sister's frantic call for help. Emilie had tried to talk her into moving back to Atlanta, where she could better help them, where she had a home, a job, and a good salary. With the great lack of wisdom that colored most of her decisions, Berry had refused. The great love of her life was in Boston— the man who had been preceded by two dozen other great loves, the man who had just thrown her and the kids out on the street—and she had been convinced that, with just a little help, she could get straightened out and win him back. She'd had no place to live, no money for food, and a job that paid minimum wage— on the days she was able to work—but all she needed to make things right was Emilie, just for a while.

In her heart, Emilie had known Berry wasn't going to change. She could devote herself twenty-four hours a day to the task and even achieve some degree of success, but it wouldn't last. It never did. Before long, there would be another man, another bottle of booze, another dealer of drugs, and another frantic phone call.

But she had heeded Berry's call anyway. After all, if she hadn't, what would have happened to the kids? She had quit her job with no more than a day's notice, had sold her furniture, closed out her bank accounts, and gone to Boston. She'd done it for the children. They were the only family she had, and she would do anything for them—give up her job, leave her home, move across country.

Defy a court order.

Gripping the steering wheel tighter, she turned away from that line of thought. She hoped Bethlehem was around the next curve, hoped it was big enough to have a motel and a restaurant that would be open tonight. She hoped the motel was clean and cheap—really cheap, since she had only seventy-six dollars to get them back to Georgia. She hoped the people in town weren't nosy about strangers and that whatever law enforcement they had was home for the night, where all people of good sense should be on a snowy Thanksgiving eve—

As they rounded the next curve, she stared in amazement at the sight ahead. One second there was no hint that they were within a hundred miles of civilization, and the next an entire town was spread out in the valley below. It looked like a scene from a glass paperweight, bright, welcoming, and oh, so charming. But that was from a distance. When the road descended into the valley and they saw the town close up, it would be exactly like every other small town they'd passed through today—shabby, worn, showing the effects of tough times.

Like her.

"Pretty. It looks like Bedford Falls in that movie you like so much—the one with the angel named Clarence."

Emilie's smile was thin. Alanna was right. With the lights and the snow, Bethlehem did remind her of the town in *It's a Wonderful Life*. But Bedford Falls existed only on the television screen, and she had learned all too well in the last six months that angels didn't exist at all. Neither did miracles, not even in the holiday season. In the last few months, she'd even begun to doubt the power of prayer.

The road snaked down at such a gentle descent that by the time they reached the valley floor, they had circled halfway around it. From a distance, Bethlehem appeared a place of fantasy. Close up, it was even better—Norman Rockwell come to life. It was decorated for Christmas with wreaths and big bows on every street lamp. Holly with bright red berries hung in shop windows, and clusters of mistletoe were suspended over the doors. Six-foot-tall nutcracker soldiers painted in bright blues, reds, and greens and wearing black-plumed caps stood guard over each block, and evergreens up and down the street were decked out with velvet bows, silver bells, and glittery gold ribbons.

It *was* a fantasy, Emilie thought as she drove slowly along the wide thoroughfare appropriately named Main Street. A lovely, charming fantasy. Tomorrow morning, though, when the sun shone and the snow melted, all the shabbiness would be revealed. The decorations would have been defaced and vandalized by the young punks who roamed the streets at night, and the quaint little storefronts would show signs of peeling paint, dirty windows, and economic depression.

But tonight, in the glow of soft lights, it was lovely.

The businesses they passed were closed for the holiday, and there was no sign of a restaurant that might be open, no sign of a motel, cheap or otherwise, where they might find a place to sleep. Emilie was about to give up hope and accept that she would be driving miles more in the snow when suddenly Alanna spoke. "Look, Aunt Emilie, that place is open."

Sure enough, lights were on in the diner in the middle of the block, and a half dozen customers were visible through the plate-glass windows. She parked in front and immediately felt a little stress drain away. She'd been driving for hours in weather that was best enjoyed from a snugly warm house, and she felt it in every muscle.

But they didn't have a house. They'd spent the last seven nights in a shelter. Only a year ago she had berated Berry for allowing things to degenerate to the point that she'd been forced to take her children to a shelter for the homeless, and yet with her own expert management, that was exactly where *she* had landed them, right back in the same shelter.

In her entire adult life, she had never needed help from anyone. She had worked since she was eighteen, paid her bills and her taxes, built up a tidy sum in savings, and still had money left over to give to those less fortunate. She had been a responsible member of society. How in the world had she gone from that to standing in the cold asking a stranger to please give the kids a place to sleep and something to eat?

It had been humiliating.

And it wouldn't happen again. She would get them safely home to Georgia, find a new job and a new place to live. They would have to be satisfied with cramped quarters and lots of spaghetti and other cheap food, at least until she got back on her feet, but it wouldn't take long. Atlanta was her hometown. There was nothing she couldn't accomplish there with hard work and determination. Unlike Boston, where hard work and determination had gotten her nothing but trouble.

And that was very definitely spelled with a capital T, she thought as a police car pulled into the space beside her.

Sitting very still, she watched as the officer got out. For a moment, he simply stood beside the car, fat snowflakes shading his brown hair white. How long would it take the authorities in Boston to discover that she and the kids were missing? When the social worker had arranged for her to retain custody over the Thanksgiving holiday, she had counted on four days of freedom, to get home, get settled, and get started on keeping the promises she'd made.

But what if Social Services had decided that putting the kids into foster homes was better than leaving them in a women's shelter with her? What if they'd gone to the shelter to pick them up, only to find that they'd disappeared before the turkey dinner? What if they'd turned over her name, description, and the license number of her car to the police? What if the police officer standing only a few feet away and looking in her direction had seen such a bulletin?

After a moment, he shook off the snow, clamped his hat on his head, and went inside the diner. She watched him slide onto a stool and pick up the coffee cup the waitress had waiting before she blew out her breath in relief.

"Josie, Brendan, wake up." She leaned over the seat to shake first one child, then the other. "Come on, guys, it's time to eat."

Six-year-old Josie sat up from the pillow she'd been sharing with her brother, yawned, and asked, "Are we there yet?"

"No, sweetie, but hopefully this is as far as we'll have to go tonight. Brendan, are you awake, baby?"

Three-year-old Brendan sat up, yawned, then took a look around. Emilie wondered what he thought of all the lights and decorations. She wondered if he was still tired, if he was hungry or needed to go to the bathroom. She wondered if he missed his mother or if he understood that for now Emilie would be doing all the motherly things for him. She wondered, but didn't ask. It wasn't that he couldn't talk. He could, and on the occasions that he did, he did it quite well. He just seemed to have a preference for nonverbal communication.

It was one of the many consequences of his mother's lifestyle. Emilie had no doubt that Berry loved her little boy, but cuddling, loving, and teaching were tough to do when you were drunk or stoned as often as Berry had been during his short life. It was just one more thing for Emilie to deal with once they got home.

"Listen, guys, we're going to go into the restaurant and have dinner, and we're going to be on our best behavior. No fussing, no fighting, no crying. And no talking to strangers—*any* strangers." Especially cops.

"But the waitress is a stranger. How can I tell her I want a hot dog and a sundae if I can't talk to her?"

That was from Josie. Like Alanna, she'd been forced to grow up far too soon. Unlike her sister, she could still be perfectly childlike at times. Emilie hoped that was a quality Alanna would regain once they got settled in a stable environment.

"Don't be difficult, Josie." Alanna sounded a hundred and nine instead of just nine and so much like her mother. Don't be difficult, Berry had pleaded when she'd called to ask her sister to move to Boston. Don't be difficult, she'd told the kids whenever they had behaved like kids as well as whenever they hadn't. Don't be difficult, she had begged of Emilie before telling her that she'd been arrested on drug charges.

Don't be difficult. Berry was always making the request—or demand or plea—of someone, when, in reality, *she* was the one who was difficult. *She* was the one who made everyone else's lives hard.

"Josie's not being difficult, Alanna," Emilie said gently. "It's a very good question." From the sheltering hood of a hand-me-down coat that was much too big for her, Josie stuck her tongue out at her sister. With a faint smile, Emilie opened the door to a blast of icy air. "Let's get inside, kids, before we freeze."

Nathan Bishop was starting his second cup of coffee when the restaurant door opened, lowering the temper-

393

ature a few degrees before it swung shut again. He knew without looking that the new arrivals were the woman in the wagon and her kids. He wondered what was so important that they would travel in weather like this. It was bound to get worse before it got better, and that car of hers didn't look particularly reliable.

But as long as they weren't doing anything wrong, they weren't his responsibility. If they did do something wrong, he could probably muster the energy to call Sadie Simpson, who was dispatching for both the town and the county tonight, but that was about the extent of his willingness to act. He'd put in a full fourteen hours today, and he was tired. He was the only one in the department without family in the area, and so he had volunteered to work what had come close to a double shift. He worked all the family holidays—Thanksgiving and Christmas, Easter and Father's Day and the Fourth of July.

Although the hours could be long, he didn't mind the job. Law enforcement in Bethlehem was a snooze in a hammock compared to big-city police work. Today his first call hadn't come until after dinner, and it had been no big deal—a minor fender-bender in front of the nursing home. After that, he'd made a routine patrol, taken a report about a nuisance dog, and chased a few kids from the roof of the carousel house.

A typical day in Bethlehem, which was exactly what he'd moved here for.

Shrugging out of his jacket, he draped it over the stool beside him, then gazed around the dining room. With the exception of the woman and kids, he knew everyone. There was Harry Winslow, owner of the restaurant, who opened the place every day whether he was likely to have customers or not. He said he did it because any town that was fit to call itself a town had to have a place to eat every day. Nathan thought it was because, with his wife dead and his kids moved to bigger and more distant places, home was too lonely a place to stay.

Nathan knew loneliness. He recognized it when he saw it, and he saw it on just about every face in the place.

Dean Elliott sat at Harry's table. He was one of the few people in town who had come to Bethlehem from someplace else. He was an artist whose sculptures had bought him fifty acres halfway up the mountain and a home too elegant for the description suggested by its log-cabin construction. But his art and the comfortable living it afforded hadn't brought him happiness. He worked alone, lived alone, and acted as if he expected to die alone.

Over by the door was Sebastian Knight. He lived outside town, too, just down the road from Elliott on the farm his family had settled over a hundred years ago. Although he hadn't carried on the tradition of farming, Sebastian still worked with his hands. He was a carpenter, and a damned fine one. He'd been married, but one day his wife had packed up her clothes and walked away, leaving him and their little girl to fend for themselves. Chrissy must be at his parents' place, where the rest of the family had gathered. Why wasn't Sebastian with them, instead of over here looking morose and ignoring everyone around him?

Nathan gave the rest of the diners—Holly McBride, old Jeremiah Dent, and Colleen Watson—a brief glance before his gaze settled on the strangers in a distant booth. He could see the two smaller kids now, too. They looked even more tired than he felt, especially the littlest one. He leaned against the middle kid—a boy or girl, Nathan couldn't tell. The face was perfectly average, too young and unformed to lean toward masculinity or femininity, and the blond hair, cut in a careless, shaggy unisex style, offered no clue.

The older child was definitely a girl, about ten, pretty, delicate, and solemn. Their mother was also pretty, delicate, and solemn. Other than the color of her hair, she bore little resemblance to any of the kids. As far as that went, beyond the hair, the kids didn't look much like each other, except in that unfinished way that all kids looked alike.

Wherever they were headed, the woman should have planned better. This wasn't a good night for driving, and, except for Holly's inn, there wasn't a motel for miles. Judging from their clothing and the condition of the car outside, they probably couldn't afford Holly's place, not with rooms starting at ninety bucks a night.

"Are you sure I can't get you anything?"

He looked from the strangers to the waitress in front of him. Maeve was old enough to be his mother, widowed, and more than a little sweet on Harry. She thought she hid it pretty well, but Nathan was used to watching people, learning what he could from the way they looked, moved, and acted. For example, the mother in the corner was weary—not just tired from hours of travel, but weary from the inside out. Soul weary.

"Some turkey and dressing?" Maeve coaxed. "A sandwich? A piece of pie?"

"No, thanks. I'm heading home to bed."

"Not after drinking two cups of Harry's coffee, you're not. It's got a kick, it's so strong."

"Yeah, but I've been working since six this morning. I don't think I'll have any trouble sleeping." Sliding from the stool, he pulled his jacket on.

"You have tomorrow off, Nathan?"

"I've got the whole weekend off. Want to run away with me?"

She laughed. "If I thought you meant it, I'd take you up on it."

"If I thought you'd take me up on it, I would mean it." He started toward the door. "See you next time, Maeve."

"Have a good weekend . . . and happy Thanksgiving."

Nathan returned Harry's and Elliott's farewells as he passed their table, acknowledged Holly's wave with a nod, then stepped outside. The temperature felt like it had dropped another ten degrees while he'd lingered over the coffee, and the wind had kicked in, too. The valley would be snowed in before morning. Until the state got the highway cleared—or until the sun did the job for them—no one would be coming into or leaving Bethlehem for a while, which suited him fine. With three days off and no way in or out of town, he could hibernate. By Monday morning, when he had to return to work, the holiday would be completely past, and he wouldn't have to face another one—the worst one—until Christmas rolled around.

His boots crunched on the snow as he ducked his head against the wind and started toward the four-wheel-drive Blazer. Back in the city, he'd hated nights like this. People didn't have enough sense to stay home, traffic was god-awful, and the simple act of getting to a call was nearly impossible. Nothing ever went right on nights like this in the city. But he was in Bethlehem now, where nothing ever went wrong.

After starting the engine and turning the heater to high, for a moment he simply sat there, shivering inside his jacket. Directly in front of him inside the café, the mother and her kids were talking to the waitress. How had he failed to notice that Harry had hired a new waitress? This woman, like her customers, was a stranger. Young, slender, with pale brown hair that had a silvery tinge under the fluorescent lights, she looked too fragile to hold on to such a job for long. Harry's was a busy place, and waiting tables was tough work.

Not that she was working hard tonight. She had served the family their drinks and was now chatting. Something she said made the older kids laugh and coaxed a smile from their mother that, somehow, made her look sad. After patting her arm, the waitress left the table, and the mother turned to stare out the window. Her gaze met Nathan's for only an instant, then she immediately turned her attention to the kids. Immediately. Almost guiltily.

Pushing the clutch in, he shifted into reverse. When he began second-guessing the behavior of tired mothers traveling with three kids on a nasty winter evening, he'd been working too long. He needed to go home, get out of his uniform and into bed. He *needed* this three-day weekend.

Home was on Fourth Street on the east side of town. The neighborhood was one of Bethlehem's best—although, in all fairness, the town had no bad neighborhoods. People in Bethlehem took pride in their town and in their homes. The properties were well maintained, clean, and in good repair. Even the shabbiest house in town was one he wouldn't mind calling home.

He lived where he did only because the two elderly sisters who owned the house had taken him in. Miss Agatha and Miss Corinna lived across the street and over one house in the Winchester family home, a rambling Victorian, and rented its toy-sized duplicate to him for a fraction of its value. It was big enough for a family, but he lived there alone.

Alone and lonely.

He let himself in the back door, flipping light switches until the darkness was banished from the first floor. The light showed the way upstairs, where he traded his uniform for sweatpants and a T-shirt and put his gun belt on the top shelf in the closet. Back downstairs, he stopped for a moment in the front entry. Such quiet. At one time Miss Corinna and her husband had raised four kids here. They had raced down the halls, slid down the banister, and swung on the front porch swing. They'd had camp-outs out back, sleep-overs upstairs, and first kisses on the porch. They'd left echoes of themselves in the very structure of the house. Echoes of laughter, of arguments, of life.

Nathan had lived too many years with echoes of another kind.

When he had first moved in, the stillness had taken some getting used to. He'd passed many midnight hours on the porch, seeking distraction, but his neighbors were quiet people. In six years he hadn't heard one shouting match, hadn't seen one neighbor come home drunk, hadn't had even one mildly irritating experience with any of them. They were home early and in bed early. Their dogs didn't bark, their cats didn't stray, and their kids were unfailingly polite.

On the street where he'd lived in the city, something had always been going on. It'd been as busy at three in the morning as it was at three in the afternoon. Loud music, blaring TVs, domestic disturbances, squealing tires, sirens—those had been his music to sleep by. He had been comfortable with his environment . . . at least, until the last year he was there. Sleep had been a problem then. Misery had been a problem. The noise, the crowds, and the hustle of the city had begun to grate. He had been unable to deal with it any longer, unable to become a part of it.

And so he had come to Bethlehem looking for quiet, which he'd found, and peace, which he hadn't. He had accepted that life was never going to be good again, but at least here, it was better. It was livable. It was bearable.

Most of the time.

And the rest of the time? He survived. It wasn't easy, but he did it. He'd been doing it for seven years.

He would be doing it for a long time to come.

A table full of dirty dishes in front of her, Emilie stared out the window at the snow that had turned the car into a long, featureless lump and felt its chill all the way through. When they'd arrived forty-five minutes ago, she had been able to see clearly all the way to the far side of the square. Now, if she squinted, she could just barely make out the tall, round structure in the middle of the block. They needed to find a place to spend the night, before conditions got any worse.

"Can I get you anything else?"

She glanced up at the waitress and tried to smile. "Just the bill."

Noelle, as she had introduced herself with a million-watt smile, pulled a pad from her apron pocket, tore off the top page, and did some quick figuring before laying it on the table. "I'll take that for you when you're ready. Just let me clear these dishes first."

Emilie checked the total. Eleven dollars and forty-seven cents. The amount made her wince and wonder where they could have saved a little. Maybe by ordering water or skipping dessert. But the kids needed milk, and their child-sized sundaes had cost so little. Besides, they had missed Thanksgiving dinner. They'd deserved a little splurge. Tomorrow was soon enough to start scrimping.

She counted out the money, then added a small tip for the waitress. When the woman returned, Emilie asked, "Can you direct me to the nearest motel?"

Noelle paused, balancing a coffee cup atop three sundae glasses. "That would be in Howland."

"Where is that?"

"About forty-five miles west of here. There's an inn here in town—Holly McBride's place—but it's usually booked over the holidays. She may have something available if you want to go by, but I doubt she has any vacancies and . . ." She tried not to be obvious in her appraisal of their worn and ill-fitting clothes, but Emilie felt the assessment all the way down to her toes. "The inn is awfully expensive. It'll run you over a hundred dollars a night. It's a beautiful old farmhouse that's just meant for lots of guests. When it's all decorated for Christmas, it's absolutely breathtaking. Next to the Pierce house, it's the most beautiful house in town."

Emilie felt numb. Forty-five miles to the nearest motel. Under good conditions it would take her nearly an hour to get there, and conditions tonight were about as far from good as they could get. She had to find another way—*had* to find a place to stay. But where?

The inn was out of the question. She didn't have a hundred dollars, and her only credit card had been cancelled after she'd missed the last three payments. The only place likely to be open all night in a town like this was the police station—certainly the last place *she* wanted to be when the state of Massachusetts might have issued a warrant for her arrest. But where *could* she go?

Through her despair, she realized that the waitress was still talking. To keep the panic at bay, she forced herself, just for a moment, to listen.

"It's a wonderful old Victorian," Noelle was saying. "It's stood empty for about seven years. Mrs. Pierce left it to her niece, but the woman has never come to even see it. She lives somewhere in Massachusetts, but no one in town has met her. A trust pays the taxes and provides for routine maintenance, but the house needs a family, someone to take care of it and give it life." She paused, then her eyes brightened. "You know, you really should see it before you leave. It's at 311 Fourth Street. You go straight down Main, then left on Fourth. It's only a block or two over. Even though it's nighttime, it really is worth seeing."

Emilie returned to the original subject. "I don't think we could make it to Howland in this weather. Are you sure there's no place here in town, besides the inn, where we could get a room for the night?"

The light in the waitress's expression dimmed. "I'm sorry."

"Maybe . . . maybe we could stay with you?" Emilie's voice quavered with pleading and barely disguised desperation. "I would pay. I don't have a lot, but I could give you something . . ." Her voice trailed away as Noelle shook her head. There was genuine distress in the woman's eyes, but she was still turning them down.

"I'm sorry." Noelle scooped the money from the table, counted it, and returned the dollar tip. After sliding the rest into her apron pocket, she laid her hand on Emilie's arm, her fingers curving in a tight squeeze. "Go see the Pierce house. Please. You won't be sorry."

The insistence in her voice lingered after she walked away. Why should she care if Emilie took the time to see someone else's house when she desperately needed a place of their own for tonight? Unless . . . Could she possibly have been hinting that the Pierce house might be that place? Was she suggesting that they stay in a place that didn't belong to them, that the house's emptiness and their need made it all right?

More likely, Emilie thought, her own desperation was reading something into the words and gestures not intended by Noelle. Besides, borrowing someone else's house, even just for one night, wasn't all right. It was breaking and entering, and the last thing she needed now was more trouble with the law. She had enough already.

"Aunt Emilie, what are we going to do?" Alanna's voice was pitched low to avoid frightening the kids, but the softness didn't disguise her own fear.

"I'll think of something. Don't worry. We'll be okay." She took a look around the room and saw no sign of

Noelle. The other customers were getting ready to leave, and the older waitress and a gray-haired man were turning chairs upside down on the empty tables in preparation for closing.

"Put on your coats, kids." She gave Josie and Brendan her best smile. "It's time to head back out. Enjoy the snow while you can. Once we get back to Georgia, you'll see it only once in a blue moon."

"What's a blue moon?" Josie asked as she struggled into Alanna's hand-me-down.

"It's just a saying." Emilie went to the opposite side of the booth to help Brendan with his coat. Chocolate was smeared around his mouth, and his blue eyes were glazed over. The poor kid was asleep on his feet. She didn't ask him to walk, but lifted him into her arms. He immediately snuggled close, turned his face into her neck, and went limp.

They were almost at the door when the gray-haired man spoke. "You folks have far to go?"

She looked at Josie and Alanna, felt Brendan's weight in her arms, and knew what she had to do. No matter that she didn't want to, no matter that it was going to break her heart. The kids were her first priority.

"No," she replied quietly, the word very small. "Not far at all."

She hustled the kids to the car, settling them in the back seat so they could snuggle. After starting the engine so the heater could warm, she began clearing snow from the windows. The storm was bad and getting worse. There was no way she could go on.

By the time she joined the kids in the car, she was shivering and her ungloved hands were numb. She backed out of the parking space, the tires bumping over the hard-packed ruts, and headed at a crawl down Main Street. To go to Howland, they had to drive east, until the road slowly curled its way back up and around the mountain.

But they weren't going to Howland. They weren't leaving Bethlehem.

She should have asked for directions to the police station, but it couldn't be too hard to find. Still, when she left the business district and headed into a neighborhood of neatly kept houses, she didn't turn around. She was delaying, looking for the courage to turn herself in and the kids over to total strangers who could provide for them better than their own family could.

What failures she and Berry were.

Realizing that she'd reached the edge of town, she turned, drove a few blocks, then turned again. Her intent was only to delay the inevitable, but she succeeded in getting herself lost. Three times she thought she made the proper turns to take her back to Main Street, and three times she was wrong. Street signs were of no help. The snow had turned them into white-frosted ornaments atop tall poles. Tears of frustration choking her throat, at last she pulled to the side of the street, bent over the steering wheel, and fought the sobs. Only when she was sure they were under control did she look around.

They were parked in front of a house, with brick columns supporting a wrought iron fence. Recessed into one column was a plaque painted with birds and an address: 314 Fourth Street. According to Noelle's directions, they were only a block or two from Main, and the wonderful Pierce house must be . . .

Without seeing the numbers on the fence, she easily picked it out—across the street and one house down, the only house on the block that didn't have welcoming lights in the windows. It *was* a beautiful place—three stories with towers and turrets, fish-scale shingles, rambling verandas, and yards of ornate gingerbread—but it looked abandoned. Forlorn. Definitely empty.

For a moment Emilie envied the woman who owned it so deeply that it hurt. How full this stranger's life must be that she could own a house such as this and not even want to see it . . . and how empty her own life felt in comparison. Right now she had nothing, *nothing* but her sister's beat-up old car, sixty-four dollars and change, and three frightened kids.

She glanced over her shoulder at them. They were all asleep, an old quilt tucked around them. The car was warm. Spending the night in it would surely kill them—there was no way they could keep warm with the few clothes they had—but for only five minutes, they would be fine. They probably wouldn't even awaken, and she could delay losing them by that much.

With the driveway blocked with drifts, she pulled to the curb in front, shut off the engine, and quickly, quietly, closed the door behind her. Forging through mid-calf-deep snow, she followed the driveway to its end. The snow in the backyard was undisturbed except for a three-foot-tall hump that snaked along the back fence. It was a woodpile, an immense supply of firewood that could heat even this big old house through multiple hard winters. If it had been there since the old lady's death, it was undoubtedly as dry as paper and would need no more than a match to set it ablaze.

Now all she needed was a fireplace, a match, and four walls to contain the heat. Then she wouldn't have to worry about the kids freezing to death. Then she wouldn't have to turn them over to the police. Then she wouldn't have to break the promises she'd made them.

Go see the Pierce house. Please. You won't be sorry.

Noelle's insistent voice echoed in Emilie's mind and brought her slowly around to face the house once more. Would it be so wrong if, just for one night it was used for the task for which it had been built, if it provided shelter to a family who desperately needed it? If she paid for its use, if she tossed in a few bucks extra for the wood they burned?

Yes, it was *wrong,* she insisted as she made her way across the yard to the side steps and over increasingly higher mounds of snow collected there to the partially protected veranda. Even if everyone would understand how desperate she was to take care of the kids. Even if she apologized, made restitution, and asked God to forgive her.

Even if it just might be her last chance to keep her family together. If she lost the kids now, she would never get them back. The state would put them in separate homes, always promising them that when their mother was better, they could be together again. But *she* knew a few things the state didn't. She knew how it felt to be forcibly separated from the only family you have. She knew how it felt to live with strangers, to always be apart, to never belong, no matter how many weeks or months you lived with them. She knew how it felt to always come last, to always be the outsider.

And she knew that Berry was never going to get better. Her sister had spent most of her life desperately seeking some bond, some tie that would stop people from always leaving her. It had been with her since she was seven years old, and it would be with her forever.

This house might be Emilie's last chance to save Alanna and Josie from their mother's fate.

She came to a stop at the front door. Staying here, even for one night, *would* be terribly wrong, but she was desperate. And once she made it safely to Georgia, she would make it right. The owner would forgive her. The children would forgive her. And because she truly was sorry, God would forgive her, too.

Reaching out, she wrapped her fingers around the doorknob. If only it would swing right open, she could take it as a sign from above that what she was considering was excusable. But the icy metal didn't turn. It simply froze her fingers.

She was turning away, her heart even heavier, her spirits lower, when a breeze blew across the veranda. It wasn't a hard wind, not even enough to make her shiver. It came with a sprinkle of snow and a whoosh of sound, passing from one end of the long porch to the other before disappearing.

Emilie stopped where she was. Her breaths grew slow, shallow, and for one moment she forgot the cold and the hopelessness. For one moment she believed that the kids would be all right, after all. *She* would be all right. Heavens, maybe even Berry would be all right.

If the door were unlocked, she had thought only seconds earlier, she could accept it as a sign from God that it was all right for her to claim shelter in this house for the night. The door hadn't been unlocked. The sign hadn't appeared.

Or maybe it had. Because that slight little breeze that had blown along the veranda had left a gift for her. With no more strength than a child's puff—than an angel's puff—it had uncovered a key on the window sill buried in snow, and *that,* she wanted to believe, did believe, was a sign.

She wrapped her fingers around the old-fashioned brass key, then inserted it into the lock. It turned easily, the door swung inward, and her heart grew about a million pounds lighter. She stood motionless a moment, her eyes squeezed shut, then started away with an energy she hadn't felt in weeks. At the top of the steps, though, she paused to direct her gaze to the snow-obscured heavens and whisper a heartfelt prayer.

"Thank you."